BROWSING COLLECTION
14-DAY CHECKOUT
No Holds • No Renewals

Las Madres

Las Madres

A NOVEL

Esmeralda Santiago

ALFRED A. KNOPF · NEW YORK · 2023

THIS IS A BORZOI BOOK PUBLISHED BY ALFRED A. KNOPF

www.aaknopf.com

Knopf, Borzoi Books, and the colophon are registered trademarks of Penguin Random House LLC.

LIBRARY OF CONGRESS CATALOGING-IN-PUBLICATION DATA
Names: Santiago, Esmeralda, author.
Title: Las madres : a novel / Esmeralda Santiago.
Description: First United States edition. | New York : Alfred A.
    Knopf, 2023.
Identifiers: LCCN 2022043051 (print) | LCCN 2022043052 (ebook) |
    ISBN 9780307962614 (hardcover) | ISBN 9780345803894 (paperback) |
    ISBN 9780307962621 (ebook)
Subjects: LCGFT: Novels.
Classification: LCC PS3569.A5452 M33 2023 (print) |
    LCC PS3569.A5452 (ebook) | DDC 813/.54—dc23/eng/20220926
LC record available at https://lccn.loc.gov/2022043051
LC ebook record available at https://lccn.loc.gov/2022043052

Jacket painting: *Once, 2022* by Catherine Repko. Courtesy of Huxley-Parlour, London, UK.
Jacket design by Jennifer Carrow

Manufactured in the United States of America

First United States Edition

1st Printing

for the Puerto Rican people

Contents

Contents

Protagonists, Characters, and Others

LAS MADRES

Shirley Templeton Vélez
Ada Gil Méndez
Luz Peña Fuentes

LAS NENAS

Graciela Gil Templeton
Marysol Ríos Peña

THE ANCESTORS

Alonso Peña Rivera (**Abuelo**)
his son, Federico Peña Ortíz (**Luz's father**)
Concepción de Los Angeles Santa Virgen María Argoso
    Torregrosa de Fuentes (**Güela**)
her daughter, Salvadora Fuentes Argoso y Peña (**Luz's mother**)
Winslow Templeton (**Shirley's father**)
Cordelia Vélez Jiménez (**Shirley's mother**)

SECONDARY CHARACTERS

Josué Gil Echevarría (**Ada's first cousin and Luz, Graciela,
    and Marysol's godfather**)
Oliver Gil Figueroa (**Ada's first cousin**)
Miriam López de Gil (**Oliver's wife**)
Lucho Colón Arenas (**Miriam's nephew**)

Loreta Frías Hernández (**Alonso's housekeeper**)
Warren MacKenna Collazo (**Marysol's boyfriend**)
Minaxi Otero Polanco (**Luz's friend**)
Claudio (El Vikingo) Worthy Villalobos (**Ada's distant cousin**)
Kelvin Cabrera Pou (**Luz's friend**)
Miss Rita (**Luz's dance teacher**)
Kyryl Kyryl (**guest dance teacher**)

OTHERS

The conquest of our hemisphere meant the erasure of our clan and familial names. In this novel, I endeavor to name even minor characters to honor the historically nameless.

Las Madres

Luz

After Luz Peña Fuentes settled in the United States, the accent mark over the *n* in *Peña* was left out in English. In Spanish her full name means "Light Rock Fountains" but without the tilde, Pena Fuentes means "Sorrow Fountains" or "Penalty Fountains" or "Pity Fountains" or "Shame Fountains."

"Crossing an ocean made me sadder," she tells her daughter, Marysol Ríos Peña, whose first name in English means "Sea-and-Sun." "I'd rather be rock than sorrow."

"You are who you believe you are, Mom. Your name and your identity are different things."

"Sí, eso es verdad. That's a good way to look at it." Luz makes note of Marysol's words in her journal.

At a clinic, Luz is annoyed when a nurse calls for Mrs. Pena. "Am I Señora Pitiful?"

"No, Mom. Far from it. You have a good life and you're loved. Nothing to pity there."

Luz doesn't have to add that to the page. At fifty-seven years old, and in spite of some old injuries and age-related creaks and aches, she's physically fit, has satisfying work, and lives comfortably.

On weekdays, Marysol walks Luz to Mi Casa Adult Daycare,

around the corner from their home. There, Luz feeds clients, wheels them from one table to another when they want to play cards or dominoes, keeps them company in the garden behind the building, and three times a week, leads them in chair-bound exercises.

She often interrupts her tasks to add entries in her journal. When the pages are full, she shelves the journal next to those already arranged in her living room, the spines labeled by day, month, and year so she can later consult what she did when, with whom, and where. She reads her memory books with the same excitement and engagement she does beloved novels, finding new details with each reading. Sketches, drawings, cartoons, tickets from visits to a museum, the theater, the zoo, or the Botanical Gardens interrupt her looping handwriting. She lingers on the text or on the details that evoke a memory, a curiosity, a revelation.

This is my life, she'll tell herself, and just as often, *Is this my life?* The statement does not invalidate the question.

After work and dinner, Luz enters her studio, formerly Marysol's childhood bedroom. On the wall, Luz has lettered PEÑA on a granite slab her friends brought from the abandoned quarry near their house in Maine. Now Luz prepares the materials for her next art project.

Soon after she met Danilo, the man who became her husband, Luz drew his portrait on a stone she picked up in Van Cortlandt Park. He liked it so much, she gave him a self-portrait for their first wedding anniversary. A year later, she painted Marysol's image and for every birthday after that. Marysol now displays them in her apartment across the hall in their two-family house.

The portraits began as a hobby, but friends and neighbors begged Luz to paint their children or their favorite singers or movie stars. Soon, she had commissions from strangers. This week, she's working on a series for a family who sent photographs and stones from their Vermont property.

Luz has laid out the stones on her table, has cleaned and prepared their surfaces, but before she turns the lights off in her studio, another one catches her eye. It's green slate, one inch thick, ten inches long by three and a half inches wide, too big and distinctive for the family group. Its boundaries are like the map of Puerto Rico on her wall, the landmass wider on the left, shaped like a dog's snout, and narrower toward what would be the canine's tail. Inspired, she writes a reminder to create a portrait of the island with its rivers, lakes, and mountain ranges as a Christmas gift for Marysol. She scrolls through stock images of Puerto Rico on her computer, and is overcome.

It's her last Navidades in Puerto Rico. She's fifteen, a ballet dancer poised for her cue, the first notes of a sparkling Tchaikovsky suite imminent, her muscles vibrating. She's about to perform solo on a shimmering stage meant to simulate fog, her tutu speckled with rhinestones, her satin pointe shoes secured by ribbons. She tries to hold on to the moment but it dissipates as quickly as it appeared.

Eighteen months after that performance, Luz was whisked from San Juan, a sixteen-year-old healing from physical and emotional trauma, mired in grief and loss, her memories diffused and disjointed. As the plane lifted into the sky toward New York, Luz left behind what happened that fateful summer of fireworks, Bicentennial celebrations, and perfect 10s in the Olympic Games.

Luz has forgotten so much, she's sure she's invented most of her life so she can say she's Luz Peña Fuentes. On July 4, 2017, she vaguely remembers that dancing girl in Puerto Rico, strong as a rock, who in the United States is sorrowful, penalized, shamed, and pitiful.

That Saturday was to be a day littered with exclamation points and tiny hearts punctuating the ends of sentences in her diary. Luz was so excited, she packed her dance bag as if she'd be spending a week at Miss Rita's Toes and Taps dance academy instead of a three-hour master class with a guest teacher, Kyryl Kyryl, who, trained at the Bolshoi, had been a principal dancer in ballet companies in Iceland, Belgium, and Finland.

When she came down for breakfast, her mother was in the kitchen, still in her filmy negligee, her hair in rollers.

"Buenos días, baby." Salvadora put a small bowl on the table. "Two soft-boiled eggs today. Come con calma. Tu as le temps."

"I'll need the energy," Luz said, liberally sprinkling salt, pepper, and paprika on her eggs. "Ce sera un grand jour."

Luz and her scientist parents, Federico and Salvadora, were quadrilingual in English, Spanish, French, and German. Their conversations en famille were inscrutable to friends and neighbors when they switched from one language to another as if they were all one.

Salvadora buttered a square of toast and cut it into triangles. "¿Estás nerviosa?"

"Un peu. Miss Rita said he'll challenge us."

"Personne n'est plus exigeante de toi que toi."

Luz grinned. "C'est vrai."

Salvadora peeked into a paper bag. "Te empaqué dos guineos, and a double portion of gorp con extra pepitas." She folded the top and clipped it with a hairpin from her curlers. "Why do you have to be there so early?"

"Miss Rita wants to make sure no one is late. He's coming an hour later. Ella nos dio un discurso entero about what we should and should not say or do. Apparently he'll challenge us."

"Bist du bereit, mein Lieber?" Federico came down carrying his lab coat on a hanger inside a plastic bag. "Llámame if you need anything. I can stop at the store on the way."

"Gracias, mon cher," Salvadora said.

"I'll be at the lab until it's time to pick her up." He kissed his wife's lips.

"Y yo aquí, pelando plátanos." She glanced at the ripe plantains. "I'm making three trays of piononos."

"They always want you to bring them because you make the best, Liebchen," he said. "Alors, nena. Miss Rita will have an infarto if you're late."

Luz threw her dance bag in the back seat and unlocked the driveway gate as Federico backed out to the street. He seemed happiest inside his 1971 Impala, bought from a used-car dealer near the pharmaceutical company where he and Salvadora worked. Luz would have preferred another vehicle as the family car. The four-door Impala was too much like the públicos that were stuffed with sweaty passengers and their bundles. Because it reminded her of a whale, she'd named it La Ballena.

In a week, she'd turn sixteen and could get her learner's permit and go to driving school. Federico wouldn't let her drive his car, so Salvadora agreed to let Luz practice on hers. After she had her full license, he'd buy a cacharro she could ding and dent until she had more experience.

"Bist du nervös?" He cranked open his window to the fresh morning and Luz did the same. He tuned the radio to rock and roll, not so loud they couldn't talk.

"Maybe a little nervous," she said. "Pero no se lo digas a Mami. She was more upset than I was when Mr. Kyryl canceled before."

"Je ne lui dirai pas. It was kind of el maestro to change his schedule."

Kyryl Kyryl had been expected two weeks earlier, but his flight was canceled in advance of Hurricane Eloise. The storm had uprooted trees, caused floods, and eroded the slopes that spilled into the valley from the highlands, where Luz and her parents lived. With so many trees downed, it was now possible to see over the roofs and towers of Ovestran, where Federico, a chemist, and Salvadora, a pharmacologist, headed teams researching, developing, and testing female birth-control drugs.

Federico finessed La Ballena down the narrow road and around the hairpin turns, as Luz gazed over the buildings and parking spaces below.

"The view from up here always reminds me of my father's stories about what it was like to grow up down there"—Federico pointed to the valley—"in what was left of a famous sugar hacienda. Er sagt es ist deprimierend, es jetzt zu sehen. Nothing left but rusting hulks of machinery among weeds, surrounded by arrabales and collapsing fences."

"Does it make you as sad as Abuelo?"

"Sometimes, pero el progreso deja consecuencias, aunque it usually leaves traces of what had been there. C'est pour que nous n'oubliions jamais."

Signs at the entrances of tightly packed housing developments and strip malls recalled the hacienda's heyday. As Federico took the last curve downhill before the straightaway into Guares, Luz caught a glimpse of the roof of Miss Rita's Toes and Taps dance academy occupying its own building in Los Gemelos shopping center. By the time they pulled up to the curb, four students were already waiting for Miss Rita to unlock the doors. A poster of Kyryl Kyryl mid-leap hung over vases bursting with flowers and surrounded by welcome messages Miss Rita had insisted the students prepare in advance of his visit.

"This is it," Luz said.

"Einen Moment, meine Prinzessin." Luz's father came around

to open the passenger door and helped her out. He grabbed her dance bag from the back seat.

"Mierda." He embraced her.

"Oui." She hugged him back and ran inside.

༄

Miss Rita organized the dancers into a circle.

"As with other master classes, your teachers will observe, but Mr. Kyryl is in charge."

"Did he escape from Russia?" The ballet boys were in thrall of Mikhail Baryshnikov.

"I suppose, but don't be impertinent. It might be a touchy subject for him." She adjusted a hairpin on her topknot. "I expect discipline and respect from you. Take his corrections seriously. We should leave him with a positive image of Puerto Rican dancers, able to perform as brilliantly in ballet as in bomba y plena." The students snickered but Miss Rita was serious. She waited until they realized it. "If Mr. Kyryl is impressed, he might recommend you to a top ballet company school."

Luz flushed when Miss Rita looked at her. She was the most accomplished dancer in the academy, but she was also the tallest girl and the only Black one. She'd been ridiculed and scorned by students and their parents, who could only envision female ballet dancers as petite, light-skinned, delicate swans, even in racially diverse Puerto Rico.

Although Miss Rita was a dance snob, she believed in Luz. She had encouraged Federico and Salvadora to take her to the ballet in New York. The first trip, when Luz was eleven, had been discouraging. Luz and her parents despaired that there wasn't a single brown face and body like hers on the stages.

When Salvadora told Miss Rita, she said, "We'll have to do something about that," as if she alone could change dance culture.

The next summer, Miss Rita arranged for Luz to study at the

Dance Theatre of Harlem School, where she was neither the darkest nor the tallest. Her dorm mate was Tere, another Puerto Rican girl, who lived in Chicago. Like Luz, she was delivered to their dorm by her parents, who exchanged phone numbers with Federico and Salvadora. The girls were expected to have dinner with Tere's great-aunt in Queens at least once a week and were to call their parents every other day. Even when they found time before or after classes, workshops, and rehearsals, Luz and Tere weren't rebellious enough to seek adventures. Equally determined to perform on world stages, they protected their future by having less fun than their classmates. When she returned to Toes and Taps, Luz was inspired and encouraged, but soon realized her new confidence was interpreted as arrogance.

"You know your potential." Miss Rita held Luz's face in her hands. "Erase the opinions of ignorantes from your mind. Save your emotions for the stage, not for them or for envidiosos."

Miss Rita meant well, but she couldn't protect her students when she wasn't present, and those being bullied, Luz among them, didn't complain, because snitching made things worse. Instead, Luz kept to herself and pretended not to be bothered by every snicker, comment, racist remark, or disdainful gaze. They pained her, but she swore not to let it get in her way, agreeing with her mother: No one should demand more from her than she demanded from herself.

◦—

Kyryl Kyryl was no Baryshnikov. He was a round little man whose shiny pate ended where a mass of graying curls started. He reminded Luz of Benjamin Franklin, but when he moved, a lithe dancer was released from his portly body. His English was heavily accented and when he couldn't come up with a word in that language, he resorted to what could have been Russian. No one knew.

Luz was thrilled Mr. Kyryl noticed her right away.

"Extend." He pinched her middle finger. "Relax wrist, reach. Arrêtez!" He slapped her hand. "Not flatten. Hand not is paddle." She was shocked, but maintained an imperturbable expression. Miss Rita and the other teachers didn't correct through physical punishment, but maybe things were done differently at the Bolshoi.

Mr. Kyryl sauntered down the line of dancers, lifting chins, tapping hunched shoulders, flicking fingers at rib cages, then returning to Luz's spot at the barre. He tickled the back of her knees.

"Soften, amazone." Luz corrected, and he studied other dancers, only to return to her each time. As he grew more excitable and his critique venomous, she wished he'd focus on someone else.

"Relevés plus hauts!" He prodded her arch with his toes. "You have floppy feet, amazone."

Luz was aware she could always be a better dancer, but no one had ever called her an Amazon or complained she had floppy feet. On the contrary, she was proud of her strength and balance en pointe. She'd spent hours watching herself in the mirror, adjusting and altering her posture and positions, seeking perfection. Part of a dancer's training was physical vigilance and constant evaluation of every inch of the body. Luz arched her feet, lifted from her ankles, softened her knees, lengthened her hamstrings and quads, turned out from the hip joints, sucked in her belly button, imagined she was being pulled by a string, keeping her semi-suspended above the floor.

She followed Mr. Kyryl's instructions, but there was one thing she wouldn't be able to change, no matter what. She was five feet nine in bare feet, towering over every dancer in the studio, including Mr. Kyryl. He circled the floor, adjusting postures with little slaps, pinches, and knocks and crimping his facial features into disappointed or contemptuous expressions. He stalked the dancers at the barre, always returning to Luz. "Longer neck, ama-zone. Up, up, up. Drop shoulders, lift head, chin parallel au sol. Soften!" He slapped her shoulder and turned his back from her. "Hopeless . . ."

Correction from her teachers meant they had faith in her talent and ability to take direction. Luz endured Mr. Kyryl's derision, aware professional ballet was a competitive, often abusive world. As he berated her, other dancers adjusted their bodies according to his complaints about hers. They were jealous of the attention he paid her, even if he was offensive, and they sought opportuni-ties to show off their own techniques. Luz was unnerved, but the harsher he was, the harder she worked, determined to prove her-self. Her efforts seemed to challenge him and make him meaner.

"Come, amazone. Fly!" Mr. Kyryl barked when they moved into the center. "Light as cloud, not clomp like hippo on énormes feet."

Some of the dancers snickered. Someone shushed them, but Luz put every effort into maintaining her composure, although she was humiliated. Mr. Kyryl's comments were like punctures, impossible to ignore, piercing through her confidence, wreck-ing her concentration until even her muscle memory fled. Kyryl called out combinations that confused her, but she was deter-mined, and did her best to keep up. She kept making mistakes, moving left when the other dancers went right, forward when they went back, stumbling a couple of times, once falling on her rear.

Mr. Kyryl sneered and pointed to the door. "Va-t'en. I can do nothing with you."

Luz had never felt so alone. She hoped Miss Rita would inter-vene, but the teacher avoided her gaze, as if she agreed with everything Kyryl had said about her.

"Go, amazone," he repeated, dramatically pointing at the door.

Luz couldn't move. Miss Rita left her spot and led her to the door. "It's better for you," she said softly but firmly.

Luz ran from the studio. A part of her expected Miss Rita or another teacher to follow her, but none did. In the dressing room, surrounded by gaping dance bags haphazardly stuffed with street clothes, leg warmers, tape, powder, and wads of cotton, she untied the fraying ribbons around her ankles as she suppressed her tears. She refused to cry where anyone could see her, and left the studio before the room filled with excited girls who would pretend to comfort her while mocking her.

She was relieved her father was at the curb and they could leave before everyone else came out.

"How did it go, Lieber?" Federico's cheerful air didn't allow for anything but enthusiasm.

"Fine," Luz said. He never pressed her. He was used to her moods, often commenting on her "artistic temperament," as if he'd invented the phrase. They returned home in silence.

Salvadora was assembling the last tray of piononos for the pot-luck supper in honor of Mr. Kyryl.

"Smells great." Federico scooped a spoonful of meat filling left over from the ripe plantain cups. "And tastes even better."

"Stop picking." Salvadora pushed his hand playfully. "Your salad está en la nevera," she said to Luz. "I'll warm up your chicken . . ."

"Un baño primero." Luz kept going toward her bedroom but heard her mother ask how things went.

"She said it was fine."

Luz sprinkled Epsom salts under the tub's spout and cried heaving sobs, muffled by the running water. She was ashamed of letting Mr. Kyryl get to her and was hurt by Miss Rita, who didn't interfere when it was clear he was picking on her. On the other hand, Miss Rita had warned them he'd be tough. Maybe she'd praised Luz too much and he'd expected a prodigy.

Luz had been dancing since she was four years old, and her accomplishments were the result of dogged, hard work. She'd pushed her joints beyond their natural stretch to improve her turnout and extensions. She was lean and muscular but not as flexible as she'd like, especially in her cambré derrières. Her fouettés could use more precision. As she grew taller than the other girls in the studio and the boys made faces when assigned to partner her, she'd considered quitting ballet, but her parents had invested so much in her already, she wanted to be absolutely certain before talking to them about it. Federico and Salvadora had devoted every hope and resource to what an expert had today determined were her enormous, floppy feet. If she quit dance, she'd fail them, and her mother would grouse about years of wasted time, money, and effort.

Salvadora knocked on her bathroom door. "Get dressed— we're leaving in twenty minutes."

"Je n'y vais pas."

Her mother came inside. "It's like a sauna in here. What do you mean you're not going?"

"I've got cramps."

"That's a lame excuse." She had a way of looking at Luz as if she were studying a specimen under a microscope.

"You go."

"¿Qué pasó?" Salvadora sat on the edge of the tub. "You've been crying."

"I told you, it hurts."

"Take the Midol and get dressed. Josué and Gina agreed to host the party to impress Mr. Kyryl, on your behalf. How would it look if you weren't there?"

"He hates me. He was mean," Luz whined. "Pas de compliments, sólo quejas."

Salvadora arched her brows and just as quickly switched to a neutral expression. "The more critiques from the teachers, the more potential they see. Tú lo sabes."

"Me insultó."

"You're used to compliments. Puede ser que you were overconfident y no hiciste your best effort."

"I worked my butt off!"

"Not enough to impress him, évidemment!" Salvadora grabbed a towel from the rack and helped Luz climb from the tub. "Puede ser que you were not at your best y que él estaba irritated or bothered by a personal issue, nothing to do with you. Les hommes ont leurs règles aussi."

Luz smiled feebly at the idea that men got their periods, too. Salvadora held the terry robe for her to slip into. "Stop feeling sorry for yourself, ma chérie. Mr. Kyryl will be gone tomorrow, but you have to live with yourself el resto de tu vida. Don't give him more importance than he deserves." She riffled through Luz's closet. "Porte cette robe rose. Pink looks good on you, and these sandals con las margaritas." She fluffed the skirt on the dress and laid it across Luz's bed.

She held Luz close. "We'll go to the party and you'll be polite and let everyone see you can take a critique. The teachers, the students, and their parents know you're the best dancer, and the only person who can change their minds is you and your attitude. After Mr. Kyryl leaves, everyone else will still be here, expecting the best from you. In a few years, you'll be starring in *Giselle* in New York and he'll be boasting he was one of your teachers. His dancing days are behind him, mi amor, but your brilliant future is still before you."

Pastor Josué was Luz's godfather. He, Salvadora, and Federico had been college classmates at the University of Michigan, although in different departments. Josué had started as an economics and business major but, inspired by the success of José Ferrer, rebelled against his family's expectations and switched to dramatic arts. After graduation, he moved to New York City and later to Los Angeles, hoping his Puerto Rican accent in English wouldn't interfere with a career in the movies. But casting directors only called Josué for roles as a drug dealer or addict, as the aggressor in domestic disputes, as a gang banger, or conversely, as a priest whose saintly character allowed for no depth. He returned to Puerto Rico, where he became a popular television presenter in a daytime show. His pale skin, butter-blond hair, azure eyes, and full lips inspired lustful letters to the station, some covered with red lipstick kisses, others reeking of perfume. Gossip columnists followed Josué's every move, but inevitably, reported lurid stories about his drug addiction, orgies, subsequent divorce, estrangement from his children, and DUI citations. He spent time in rehab in Tennessee, where he was saved by Jesus. Upon his return, he became more famous as a preacher than he'd ever been as an actor or TV personality.

Federico and Salvadora had remained friends with Josué over those troublesome years. After his divorce, he leaned on them as he re-created himself as an anti-drug crusader and preacher. He married his second wife, Gina, and shepherded a growing flock of disciples. Most of the time, they lived in San Juan, but spent time in their vacation home, steps from the Caribbean Sea in a secluded inlet known as Consuelo's Cove. There, he could relax from his obligations in San Juan and New York, where he also ministered.

A frazzled Gina met them at the door. "¡Ay, querida! Josué's been in the Bronx since Tuesday and his flight was delayed. He'll be here as soon as possible."

Salvadora, Federico, and Luz carried in the piononos on rectangular casserole pans.

"These need to go in the oven for fifteen minutes." Salvadora handed hers to one of the employees organizing the food.

As she dropped off her dish, Luz noticed Miss Rita and Mr. Kyryl on the terrace overlooking the water. They stood close, her hand lightly on his shoulder as he chatted with one of the guests. Rita moved her head slightly, aware someone was looking at her, and for a moment seemed startled to see Luz. She dropped her hand from Kyryl's shoulder. Luz turned her back on her.

"Introduce us to el maestro," Federico said.

"We'll introduce ourselves." Salvadora took his hand. She winked at Luz. "I'm sure you'd rather be with your friends."

She didn't. She wanted to be alone, actually, to stew in her misery. A couple of girls came over to say they'd told their parents about Mr. Kyryl's hateful behavior. Luz brushed it off.

"I've had worse critiques in New York," she lied, but she knew her friends saw through it.

"Oh, look! Los muchachos put up the volleyball net."

Luz joined the group cheering for the players. At some point, she looked up at the terrace, where her mother was talking to Miss Rita, who kept shaking her head as if she didn't agree with what Salvadora was saying. In another corner, Federico and a couple of men from the pharmaceutical company laughed and looked around to make sure no one had heard what Luz guessed was a naughty joke. Mothers and some of the dads fluttered around Mr. Kyryl, a few pushing their children toward him as if this were a market and he the only buyer.

In her sulky mood, Luz studied the adults with the same intensity the scientists among them displayed in their white-tiled laboratories, surrounded by the stainless-steel and glass implements of their work. Outside of their natural element, they were like puppets, their gestures stilted. Luz knew most of the parents on the terrace. They'd been guests at her house, the men in their starched, light-colored, button-down shirts or guayaberas, the women in halter-neck mini or maxi dresses in bright prints. This house was, by far, bigger, fancier, and flashier than any of theirs and maybe that was why the adults seemed to be so mannered, their gestures as contrived as those of the performers in silent movies.

Gina announced the buffet was open and led Mr. Kyryl to the beginning of the line. Assuming he wasn't familiar with Puerto Rican cuisine, she explained what each dish was and made sure he had at least a small portion of everything before seating him at one of the tables in the shady part of the terrace.

Luz stayed as far as possible from him, even when her parents introduced themselves to him and seemed to be speaking respectfully. She had no idea whether Salvadora had told Federico about what had happened at the master class. In the back of her mind she'd hoped they'd say something to Mr. Kyryl, but, like Miss Rita, they behaved as if it were no big deal. Their deference felt like a betrayal.

Although the party was in the home of the most famous antidrug activist on the island, liquor was plentiful. A few guests walked down to the beach to see the sunset over the Caribbean, returning to the deck and gardens with stupid grins on their faces. Luz followed a couple of her friends to the rear of the garage, out of sight of their parents. She was grumpy, and her defenses were lower. The beer, the weed, her inexperience with both, fifteen-year-old hormones, unstable emotions, and the sight of her teachers, her friends, and her parents paying court to Kyryl Kyryl erased years of admonitions that her body was her temple and she shouldn't pollute it with recreational drugs or alcohol.

After everyone had consumed and lavishly complimented her piononos, Salvadora came to the side yard and saw Luz with a beer in one hand, puffing on the weed someone had passed her. Her friends scattered, laughing, while Luz stood paralyzed before her mother, who seemed to be hurling lightning bolts from her eyes.

"¿Y eso, qué es?" Salvadora slapped the beer from Luz's right hand and the weed from her left, grabbed her wrist, and pulled her behind her in full sight of the guests, stopping only long enough to snarl at Federico.

"Nos vamos. ¡Ahora!"

As he backed out the door, he excused himself to the hostess and followed his wife and daughter to their car.

"¿Pero qué pasó? Qu'est-ce qu'elle a fait? Was hat Sie getan?" he asked Salvadora, and when she didn't answer, he turned to Luz. "What did you do?"

Inside La Ballena, Luz's head floated above her torso while her legs and feet kept her land-bound. The unfamiliar sensations were pleasant, and she giggled for no reason. Salvadora sucked her teeth and frowned in her direction.

"¡Basta!"

"What?"

"Deja esa jodienda," Salvadora said, barely moving her lips.

Luz and Federico exchanged a glance in the rearview mirror. They knew that when Salvadora was angry she'd get very quiet, but when she spoke, she used Spanish. She didn't want to hear excuses or explanations while she stewed. She searched for a station on the radio so that Federico and Luz wouldn't talk to her.

Luz closed her eyes. It made her dizzy. She opened them again. They were on the familiar road from the Guares Valley to the San Bernabé highlands. The landscape looked different at night. Through what was left of the vegetation, she glimpsed yellow lights on dim porches and strobing televisions in otherwise dark rooms. She craned her neck to see whether the full moon was following them.

The tension inside the car reminded Luz of the fruit in a Jell-O mold, seemingly floating but actually contained. Federico curved in and out of sharp turns and up and down steep hills without his usual flair. The headlights caught shards of broken glass, and the orange reflectors, supposed to mark the edges of the road, dangling uselessly toward the ground. The metal barriers meant to keep cars from driving off the steeper slopes had bent into themselves and in some cases barely clung to what was left of solid ground. Federico had written to the mayor about the dangerous conditions of these roads, but his complaints had gone unanswered.

Radio reception improved in the hills, and Salvadora stopped searching when Pastor Josué's voice broke through the speakers.

While neither Federico nor Salvadora was in his congregation, Josué often called for their opinion about his preaching. Luz had overheard her parents on the phone, elaborating on or rebutting Josué's most recent radio or television sermon, usually a rant about drugs followed by assurances of the unconditional love provided by Jesus.

"Can you please turn it off?" Luz asked.

Salvadora reached for the knob and turned up the volume.

"Come on, mi amor," Federico said. "You don't need to do that."

Luz shouted, "You're not even religious."

Salvadora harrumphed, gazed out the passenger window, checking out from further interaction with Federico or Luz.

The back seat didn't get enough air-conditioning. Luz used the hem of her dress to dry her forehead and neck. If she could lie down, sleep, and awaken tomorrow refreshed and clear, she'd explain what had happened in the studio. They'd understand her frustration and remorse. She'd apologize for sneaking into the backyard with a bunch of boys and girls while the adults fluttered around Mr. Kyryl.

". . . and when we doubt the power of redemption, hallelujah"—Pastor Josué's voice had risen to a falsetto—"we invite the devil into our lives . . ."

Luz's ears hurt. "Please turn it down, Mami," she yelled.

Salvadora reached for the knob again and turned it to a deafening volume. In the rearview mirror, Federico's eyes warned Luz to avoid further communication with her mother until they reached home. He shook his head slightly. *Leave it,* he was saying. *You know what she's like when she's this angry.*

Luz understood the warning, but she wasn't herself and didn't know how to curb her new sensations. She was dizzy, hot, nauseated, and knew not to vomit inside Federico's beloved leviathan Impala.

"I have to throw up."

"Hold on, mamita. There's no place to pull over—"

She lowered the window and, half-in, half-out, retched over the side while Salvadora and Federico howled that she should get back inside. Salvadora leaned over her seat to keep Luz from falling out headfirst, as Federico sought a safe place to stop on the narrow road.

Salvadora grabbed Luz's dress. The fabric ripped, and, unable to get a solid hold, she clambered over the front seat in an attempt to drag Luz inside the car. As she did, her knee knocked the gear shift into Park. La Ballena lurched and slid into the left lane. Salvadora lost her grip on Luz, who couldn't hold on to the window frame. A panicked Federico switched the car to Drive and swerved right, but instead of braking before the downslope, footed the accelerator.

The last Luz heard from her parents were screams as she flew through the open window. The car clattered down the embankment, crunching metal and branches as it slid, flipping before it stopped at the bottom of the ravine, where Pastor Josué's voice still urged the faithful to be humble and beg forgiveness for their sins, hallelujah.

GLAMS

JULY 5, 2017

Graciela Gil Templeton doesn't know her godmother, Luz, named her father's doomed car La Ballena. But her mother Ada calls her Subaru Pan Am, its color similar to the defunct airline's logo. Her other mother, Shirley, honors her Scandinavian ancestors by referring to her Volvo as Fisk, meaning "Fish." When

Graciela got her SUV, she named it Beyoncé. Graciela wonders whether naming inanimate objects is a Puerto Rican thing, or a family thing.

At the end of June 2017, she attends a convention for professional website designers in New York City. She drives down from Maine, leaves Beyoncé in Luz and Marysol's driveway, and spends the week in a hotel in Manhattan, learning and networking with los nerdos, as Marysol calls them. She returns to the Bronx for a Fourth of July barbecue in Luz and Marysol's backyard. When the sun goes down, the whizzing and booming explosions begin in earnest.

"Drop the shades," Marysol tells Luz and Graciela as she locks the doors. "And stay away from the windows."

"¡Ay, bendito!" Graciela tsks. "As Mami would say, it would be el colmo for another Puerto Rican to be killed by stray bullets in celebration of United States independence."

"That's a good one!" Marysol laughs as she enters her apartment across from Luz's.

Early the next morning, Graciela merges Beyoncé onto the northbound Hutch. The drive between New York and mid-coast Maine, a sixteen-hour round trip, feels shorter when she listens to audiobooks, catches up on multi-episode podcasts, and learns languages. In the last five years, she's practiced enough French to understand Luz when she switches tongues.

Graciela's mothers raised her to speak Spanish to Mami Ada and English to Mommy Shirley until she was fluent in both. When she's with them and with Luz and Marysol, the languages coalesce and Graciela can utter and understand sentences like "Mañana I'll call la flower shop a confirmar que los carnations estén ready para la fiesta en el community center."

In the Bronx, such linguistic acrobatics are common, and Graciela loves the freedom to speak either language, as she does with her mothers in Maine. The state isn't as homogenous as it was when she was growing up, but especially after the 2016 election, some people are offended when they hear other tongues in public spaces. Graciela has been silenced by strangers snarling, "Speak English!" or, "This is America," when she's not talking to or about them. Unlike them, she knows America is a hemisphere, not a country, where several hundred languages are spoken.

She's been with Spanish-speaking friends at restaurants where servers shrug off requests for menus or take their time delivering the food. Diners mutter insults, hoping to get a reaction that will confirm their xenophobic views. Graciela is light-skinned and has been picked on for associating with people of darker hues, as if she were devaluing what racists hold most dear. More than once, she and her friends have left establishments whose staff make it clear it's best for them to leave rather than face bigots in open-carry states.

Graciela has been verbally assaulted while browsing at malls, carnival midways, and agricultural fairs. As a child she was hurt and scared by such comments. As an adolescent, she was embarrassed to be scolded by strangers. As an adult, her hackles go up but she isn't mentally agile enough for a comeback and knows better than to engage with insecure monolinguals itching for violence. She's not like Marysol, who is quick-witted and can drop a linebacker with a well-placed poke to the throat or a kick to the solar plexus. Marysol knows how to defend herself if she's threatened, but Graciela has never seen her resort to one of the martial-arts techniques she still practices. She carries her Afro-Caribbean features and history with pride, while Graciela is defensive about her Caucasian appearance, which, to some people, at least, aligns her with rapacious, colonizing, enslaving white supremacists.

"Your liberal upbringing in a conservative community has given you an inferiority complex," Marysol concluded.

When Marysol was a teenager, Graciela was scared of her. She seemed so unafraid, so willing to take on any challenge, as if she thought herself invincible or was suicidal. She grew up too tall too fast to be a gymnast and switched to kung fu until the time commitment became impossible on top of her responsibilities to her mother. As she matured, Marysol embodied self-assurance and poise. Graciela, nearly five years older, eventually realized Marysol was all attitude and confidence on the outside, but a marshmallow inside. She admires and simultaneously worries about how much effort it must take for Marysol to protect her vulnerabilities so well and so consistently.

Unlike Marysol, Graciela doesn't pretend she isn't soft inside and out. Raised by and surrounded by strong women, Graciela feels puny around them. She leans on Ada, Shirley, Luz, and Marysol for advice, love, and comfort, safe in their embraces. Like her mothers, who name inanimate objects, Graciela has a penchant for naming things, categorizing people and their roles in her life. Her tag for their group of five women is GLAMS, for the first letter of their first names: Graciela, Luz, Ada, Marysol, Shirley.

Marysol snickered when Graciela first added #GLAMS to their electronic communications. "We're a lot of things, but glamorous isn't one of them. Or do you mean it aspirationally?"

Graciela didn't change it. She uses acronyms, emojis, and hashtags as shorthand and uses them liberally. Marysol has teased her that, when Graciela speaks, everyone can see hashtags floating above her head.

She's #fortyyearsold, #amicablydivorced, living in a sturdy house facing a #pebblybeach in #Maine. She considers herself #spiritual, her beliefs shaped and informed by Internet searches, YouTube videos, Great Books lectures, and #meditation apps. After her most recent birthday, she's felt more #contented than she has in years.

There are three men in her life who occasionally bring her #pleasure. Two she met online, the third is her ex-husband, Ted, now married to someone else. She chooses among them depending on her sexual appetites, their ability to fulfill them, and schedules.

In just over two decades she's moved from her childhood

home in Eventide, to a college dormitory in Brunswick, to an off-campus apartment in Topsham, to Ted's apartment in Bath, to their marital home in Westbrook, to her divorcée apartment in Portland, back to Brunswick, then finally settling in her grandfather's cottage, half a mile from where she grew up.

Like his father, brothers, uncles, and their predecessors, her grandfather fished in the Gulf of Maine his entire life. His only trip out of state was when, on a lark, he crewed on a commercial vessel delivering lumber from Searsport to Puerto Rico. There Winslow Templeton met twenty-year-old Cordelia Vélez Jiménez, who'd been recently widowed. Winslow spoke zero Spanish and Cordelia's English was limited to a handful of nouns. House. Dog. Tree. Ship (pronounced "sheep"). Ocean ("oh chan"). She was supposed to wait another six months before she could ease her obligatory mourning period. Her dresses had been dyed black, her reddish-brown hair pulled into a knot at the nape of her neck.

But Cordelia and Winslow eloped two weeks after they met, scandalizing locals in Puerto Rico, and, when they arrived in Eventide, puzzling the residents, who had no experience having such an exotic foreigner in their village, unaware that, as a Puerto Rican, she was an American citizen. Cordelia spent the rest of her life in the timber-and-clapboard house overlooking the #rockycoast on the southeastern shore of Eventide. She never returned to Puerto Rico, but their daughter, Shirley, does, and considers the island her homeland, even though she was born in Maine.

During the months before he died, Winslow told Graciela about his and Cordelia's unlikely romance, several times mentioning the auburn hair below his beloved's knot, and how the pins often slid from their places.

"How did you communicate?"

"She was smart and learned English fast," Winslow said, "but she always had a heavy accent. She was embarrassed by it, so she hid behind her cameras. That's why we don't have more pictures of her."

Graciela was a toddler when Cordelia died and knows her grandmother only from images in the albums Shirley saved. Taught by her father, Cordelia had been an avid photographer from childhood. She also loved home movies, and she documented family, friends, neighbors, and the landscape as Eventide changed over the thirty-six years she lived there. She co-founded the #EventideHistoricalSociety and, upon her death, Winslow donated her photographs and films featuring the peninsula and its residents to its archives, which Graciela now manages.

Graciela's favorite photo of Cordelia was taken by Cordelia's father on her eighteenth birthday, two years before she left Puerto Rico. Other than a few clothes, it was the only thing she brought from her life there. Winslow hung the framed portrait in the front hallway and, upon entering the house, the first thing a visitor saw was Cordelia's face behind curved glass in an oval frame with flaking gilding. Her father had tinted her cheeks and lips, and had emphasized the red in her mahogany hair. Her light-brown eyes tipped up at the outer corners. The background behind her hair was unfocused, creating a halo effect, but he captured a charming expression, a wry smile and mischievous gaze. Graciela wishes her own features recalled Cordelia's, but Shirley isn't her biological mother. According to her mothers, Graciela takes after Ada and her father, a nameless one-night stand from the summer of 1976 who disappeared from the scene as mysteriously as he had arrived. Ada doesn't even remember his name.

"What can I say, nena? It was the seventies."

Graciela has accepted Ada's explanation for her conception and doesn't judge her mother. Still, in the past month she's been creating a website for a genealogist and has been fascinated by familial historical research. She wonders whether DNA testing might shed some light on her parentage. Could there be siblings who will lead her to her father? It's a tantalizing possibility she hasn't discussed with her mothers. She doesn't want them to worry whether they're not enough for her. They are—they've always been.

"Hello, house," Graciela calls as she unlocks the door. "Hola, Cordelia," she says at the first sight of her grandmother's portrait in the same place it's been for decades. Graciela inherited the house upon Winslow's death and, while she's renovated most of the interior, Cordelia's place has stayed the same. Graciela now opens the windows, and as she unpacks, she's grateful for this refuge, a place where she's comfortable—and everything in it makes her happy.

During her adolescence, the only thing keeping her from total despair was her grandfather Winslow's delight at her accomplishments, his stories, his unconditional love unmarred by reservations about his daughter's sexual orientation. He was polite but distant toward Ada, and referred to her and Shirley as roommates long after everyone else in the family understood they were more than that. Shirley's three siblings and their families split into factions, with the conservative members shunning her and Ada while the more open-minded ones treated them like other couples. A few townspeople sided with the siblings on either side, but most abided by live-and-let-live.

Her mothers' decision to live openly might have made it easier for them, but it didn't relieve the teasing and bullying Graciela endured among her cohorts. She ran away from home, rebelling against Shirley, Ada, their unconventional relationship within their conservative community, and their strict rules, which seemed at odds with their liberal views.

Confused and annoyed, she'd stuff her backpack with a couple of days' worth of clothes, her Swiss Army knife, and Chapstick. She'd trudge the half mile in rain, snow, or blazing sun to Winslow's house, where he always had soft, sliced white bread instead of gritty whole grain and soda, pork chops, hamburgers, hot dogs, Oreos, and sugared breakfast cereals with regular, not skim, milk. Graciela believed she was punishing her mothers by consuming food not allowed at home. The ringing phone in Winslow's kitchen a couple of hours after she had slammed their door should have hinted at why they were so nonchalant, never asking for explanations when she returned.

Clueless! Graciela has never felt smart. Her school grades were good enough for graduation, but not to distinguish her from classmates. She competed in sports, hoping they'd help her shed what her mothers called baby fat, which strained her waistbands long after she could be considered a baby. In adolescence, her body morphed into an hourglass figure that continues to defy the media-created ideal of scrawny, big-headed, pouty women who always look #hangry.

She earned a degree in computer science and is adept enough to dazzle technophobes but not to impress technology companies around New England, let alone those farther afield. She married Ted when she was twenty and he twenty-two, neither mature enough to navigate the arguments and irritations that always felt personal when they weren't. After her divorce, she lived alone in a dismal apartment above a hardware store, two doors from a local bar. She woke up one morning with a hangover and a stranger beside her. That day she decamped, so remorseful she took only what she could stuff inside her car.

She returned to Eventide, worked with Winslow on his lobster boat (*Cordelia*), attended AA meetings, took up #yoga, and hustled for work as a tech consultant, graphic designer, and social-media coordinator in a village in coastal Maine whose year-round population is fifteen hundred residents but boasts excellent Internet access.

Ted had accused her of being selfish and self-centered, so she worked on herself and concluded he was wrong. What she was was too empathetic and sensitive. For protection, she distances herself from those who might upset her, including Ted, except when she needs his particular sexual dexterity.

Some of her friends have taken ayahuasca, seeking insights into their current lives. A few others have done past-life regressions.

Graciela has tried neither. When she wants to revisit her younger self, she leafs through the thick albums Shirley and Ada assembled of her babyhood, childhood, and adolescence. She still has the album as a record of who she and Ted were on that promising June day. She giggles at the cover photo of them, entwined inside a heart surrounded by plastic pearls, wearing garments that children might choose for dress-up games.

She can laugh now, but she was hurt by Marysol's appalled expression when she saw Graciela's stark-white, long-sleeved, lace-ruffled, sweetheart-necklined, corseted dress with a bustle, a long train, and enough tulle to outfit every swan in the ballet. Graciela and her bridesmaids were high when she chose it at a bridal shop in Augusta. The gown vaguely resembled Princess Diana's wedding dress without improving on it. The six bridesmaids chose different variations of green dresses with vertical ruffles to the floor. Again, they were all high when they were ordered. Their ensembles are among her few regrets.

She's just finished driving for eight hours and now, barefoot, she enters her yoga and meditation room, a sacred space facing the rising sun. A year after she inherited the house, she had the yellow pine floors refinished throughout, and on a rare visit, Luz, Marysol, and Marysol's longtime boyfriend, Warren, helped Graciela paint every room in blues and grays, recalling the ever-changing hues of the sea. As a housewarming gift, they brought colorful cotton blankets from a Mexican market in the Bronx.

Graciela now unrolls her mat, places a blanket, blocks, and belts within reach, and moves through a slow flow of asanas, breathing rhythmically, reviewing stretches of the highway, the shifting shape of the horizon, the congestion as I-495 merged into I-95, the welcome curves of the Piscataqua River Bridge, marking the boundary between New Hampshire and Maine.

As she stretches and contracts, she releases the kinks and cramps from her spine and legs, opening her hips, loosening her shoulders and neck, greeting every part of her body, breathing into the aches and pains that started surfacing after her fortieth birthday. Toward the end of her practice, she sits in lotus posture, envisioning her chakras pulsing with color. But she soon finds it difficult to transition from one chakra to another. The luminous sacral chakra bleeds into the red, the yellow, the green, the turquoise, the blue, the purple, obliterating them, as orange swirls lick the air around her and above her head.

The orange incandescence reflects #desire. Graciela has a cache of vibrators and sex toys, but hasn't had sex in weeks, unable to coordinate her schedule with Ted, or the two men she met online, Hassan and Luis. She has sex only with men she's thoroughly checked out online, and meets them in motels at least an hour from her home, unwilling to contaminate her house with their testosterone energy, upturned toilet seats, and emotional demands. She's had female lovers but has confirmed she's heterosexual. Having lived in a community with a large contingent of religious fundamentalists terrified by homosexuality, and been raised by lesbians, Graciela can prove neither is catching.

After savasana and unable to still her racing thoughts enough to feel relaxed, Graciela returns downstairs to her office, a small room off the kitchen facing the shore. Like Marysol, she keeps a shelf dedicated to rocks Luz has painted. Her favorites are the three portraits of Graciela, five of Ada, and five of Shirley, each woman at different ages. There are two group portraits, with Marysol and Graciela in front. Behind them, Shirley and Ada flank Luz. It's striking that each woman looks like herself at the stage Luz painted them. Luz's expression is mysterious, allowing the viewer to imagine what she's thinking. Sometimes she seems puzzled, quizzical, interested. Other times she's distracted and seems unhappy to be the artist's subject.

Mostly, Luz paints from photographs, but her best renditions are from her sketches, captured in charcoal or pastel pencils. Watching her sketch is like watching a performer on her best day, in a fugue state, every movement precise yet seemingly unrehearsed or practiced. She seems to leave her self behind, as if only this moment matters, when the act is both, the artist and the performance, timeless yet fleeting.

Graciela, Ada, Shirley, and Marysol have talked about, argued over, studied, and discussed what's going on in Luz's mind, coming up with guesses and theories but few conclusions. She's sequestered within, unable to profit from or share her intelligence with others but, thankfully, able to express herself. They all agree Luz is a true artist, unselfconscious precisely because her memories are mislaid in the convoluted whorls inside her brain.

To make sure Luz doesn't forget them, Graciela and her mothers call Luz several times a week, travel to the Bronx for holidays, and take short vacations with her. They share memories and tell stories of their times together. Meanwhile, Graciela searches the Internet for more insight into Luz's condition. Luz is an important part of their lives, and they want to make sure she's aware they are in hers. But neither Shirley, Ada, Graciela, nor Marysol will ever know the specifics of how Luz became Luz.

Doña Tamarindo

OCTOBER–NOVEMBER 1975

Luz sought the moisture in the air but something was pressing down her tongue. She tried to scream but could manage only a low grunt. A monster was wheezing next to her, but her head was boxed in and she couldn't move it. She couldn't lift her arms or legs, as if she were buried under sand below the neck.

"Mamá? Papá? What's happening? Where am I?"
Darkness.

❦

The monster sighed. Its breathing was rhythmic, interrupted by eerie beeps and blips. Luz blinked and she was in a small room with a window to her left. The sky was dark purple. Dawn? Twilight? No moon. No stars.

Muffled distant horns, a siren, voices. The *thunk-thunk-thunk* of something wheeling past, coming and going. Faint music. Luz sniffed. Lysol and urine. She slid her gaze right and her head throbbed, as if the movement had sparked internal fireworks.

Darkness.

❦

The next time Luz opened her eyes, she was facing a hallway. She blinked. Someone walked by, didn't notice her. She grunted. A woman wearing a stiff white cap heard her and gasped. Next, Luz was surrounded by nurses, doctors, equipment rolling in and out, bleeps, clicks, buzzing. She closed her eyes again.

❦

A cold cloth was pressed against her lips, and Luz thirstily lapped up the moisture. She was no longer gagged and could move her head side to side but her limbs were immobilized. She tugged on the restraints but was unable to free herself. Her head hurt deep inside, made worse when she moved. Why was she being tortured? Why a wet cloth when she wanted a mouthful of cool water?

Darkness.

❦

Needles pricking her eyeballs. She shut her lids hard. Moans. A voice that wasn't hers but came from her. "Agua, por favor."

Las Madres

"Here, baby." Fingers slid an ice chip between her lips that didn't quench her thirst. Unfamiliar voices.

"Close the blinds."

"Don't fight me, mamita—we're trying to help you."

"Hold her legs down."

She was besieged by unknown hands, male and female voices.

"Mami! Papi! They're killing me!"

Darkness.

⁓

Luz died at least once during the four weeks she was in the coma. By the time she arrived at the Guares Hospital Center following the car wreck, she was unresponsive. She had four broken ribs and numerous sprains, bruises, scrapes, and cuts, but the most serious injury was a concussion, causing brain swelling and a stroke. She was kept alive by drugs and connected to lifesaving machines.

It took days for her to emerge, wired to devices that blipped and hissed, like creatures chasing her. Later, she learned they helped her breathe and monitored her organ functions. She could only grunt and moan because of the plastic tubes down her throat. When they were removed, it hurt to swallow or speak. At first, when she spoke, she was aphasic; what she tried to say made no sense to others. When they spoke, it sounded like gibberish to her.

She was in and out of consciousness, in a tangle of lines delivering medications, fluids, and nutrition. She was strapped to the bed so she wouldn't fall or injure the nurses during those times when, still semiconscious, she fought anyone who touched her or when she had seizures. She didn't know her name, what day it was, where she was, or why she was there. She babbled, stuttered, repeated questions she'd forget as soon as they were answered.

X-rays revealed bruised vertebrae to be treated with physiotherapy and a back brace. Her wrists, hips, and ankles had been severely sprained but, miraculously, hadn't fractured.

"You're one lucky young lady," a doctor said.

To Luz, it sounded like "Gbldguk herngonz gbldguk."

She had no memory of the accident or her life before it. The doctors expected the retrograde amnesia to be resolved with therapy and counseling. Over time, they assured her, she'd create new, post-injury memories. Of more immediate concern was her short-term memory. Without recall of her life before the brain injuries and with short-term lapses, Luz was in an incessant present, devoid of historical markers. With no context, she had no identity.

Someone told her that Federico had died before the ambulance reached them, Salvadora en route to the hospital. Luz didn't remember who relayed this news or how she responded or who Federico and Salvadora were. She was sedated at the time, and her grief was masked by a stupefying numbness.

The first time she tried to stand, her legs wouldn't support her. She'd lost muscle mass during the bedridden weeks and couldn't lift her arms or point her feet. She had to relearn how to balance, how to stand, walk, lift a spoon to her mouth, and other tasks she'd learned as a toddler. Her physical progress was excellent, though, and nurses and therapists credited her discipline and knowledge of her body.

"It helps you were a dancer."

"Www . . . ?"

"I mean, you are," the therapist said.

⌒

There was a woman. Not a nurse. They wore white uniforms and white caps, but this one wore a brown sack. Her long hair was in a braid to her knees.

"I'm your grandmother," she said. "You call me Güela. We spent every other Sunday together."

"Bbb . . . Bbnn . . . bbnndd . . . bbb . . . ndddsssnnn."

"Que Dios te bendiga."

She leaned close to Luz. Cloves?

⌒

Another time Luz came to with a voice close to her ear.

"I'm Güela, your grandmother. We spent Sundays together in my parcela."

Herngonz. Gbldguk. She couldn't understand who this person was and why she was there. Luz turned her head away. When she did, the woman disappeared but her voice was insistent, a near whisper.

"Let us pray," Güela said. "Pater noster qui es in coelis . . ."

". . . sanctif . . ."

"You remember! . . . sanctificetur nomen tuum . . ."

"Www. Whh. Wha . . . what . . . sss . . . sssays?"

"It's Our Father," Güela said. "I taught you your prayers, in Latin, like God intended. Let's continue . . ."

She could pray.

"—ora pro nobis."

There was the old woman who smelled like cloves.

"I have to go before dark," she said.

She rolled the side table so Luz could reach the . . . the . . .

"You have many get-well cards."

The get-well cards.

"I'll pinch the dead leaves and wilting flowers from the bouquets," she continued.

Leaves. Flowers. Bouquets.

"I'm going now."

"Bbb . . . bendición."

"May the Virgin protect and bless you."

She didn't look back. Her braid slapped the hem of her long sack. Luz's heart hurt. Alone.

Another woman. "I'm Nurse Gloria. Your abuelita is extraordinary."

Abuelita. Extra.

"Every Puerto Rican town has its . . . how do I put it . . . su personaje. She's ours."

"Ppp . . ."

"A personaje, someone like no one else. She lives like it's the olden times. She grows vegetables and herbs she sells in her parcela, you know, her little farm."

Herngonz. She understood only half of what she heard. The rest was a scramble of sounds with no meaning.

Luz closed her eyes. Everyone disappeared, but she had ears. She had a mouth. She had hands. Arms. Legs. Feet. Her nose smelled cloves but her tongue was a stone inside her mouth. She had a body that did not work. It had a brain that was broken. She had a mind trapped inside her broken brain.

Gbldguk.

There was a woman. She had a name.

~

As she took vital signs and checked on Luz, Nurse Gloria talked to her and to the patient in the other bed in the same room. Gloria was trained to speak to her patients as if they understood her. It was part of their therapy. She was not to get upset if they forgot her name or what she told them. Those who could picked up words and concepts. Nurse Gloria had noticed that Luz could already tell the difference between the nursing staff and visitors.

Brain injuries were fascinating to Nurse Gloria. If every patient in the neurology ward had the same injury at the same time, the prognosis and outcome would be different for each. Some might never wake from comas and would wither in a long-term facility, often over the course of years. Others might return to what had been normal for them before the damage, or might develop disabling aftereffects for the rest of their lives. They might suffer from seizures, permanent paralysis, migraines, psychotic breaks, issues with impulse control, flashbacks: a dictionary-full of diagnoses and medical concerns difficult to predict and hard to treat.

It didn't bother Gloria that Luz had closed her eyes. She could tell the girl was listening.

"Your abuelita lives in an area not considered rural," Nurse Gloria said. "Her parcela is circled by cement houses, tiny yards, and few trees. But in her small finca she grows a lot of fruits and vegetables. She raises chickens and other animals she sells at a farm stand. She's a Franciscan. They're good with animals. Many won't eat meat. I've heard your abuelita is fulfilling a promesa. That's why she dresses and lives the way she does. Like San Francisco, she has taken a vow to be poor."

The other patient in the room was also a teenager who'd had a stroke, but hers had been caused by a reaction to birth-control pills. Her mother came to see her every day, and, like Nurse Gloria, talked to her daughter even if she didn't respond.

"I know the girl's grandmother," she said to Nurse Gloria. "I've seen her around town since I was a kid. She's hard to miss. We call her doña Tamarindo."

"Don't call her that, doña Cuca," Nurse Gloria said. "That sounds like an insult."

"It's not. It's a nickname because she's so tall and skinny, and her skin and sackcloth are the same color as a tamarindo shell."

"Well, I don't think she answers to doña Tamarindo. Her name is doña Concepción. And Luz here called her Güela."

"She was a beauty," doña Cuca said. "Maybe she was too proud. Beauty doesn't save you from tragedy. Look at my poor Jenny." She brushed hair from her daughter's cheek.

Nurse Gloria was called away. When she came back, doña Cuca was still talking.

"So, according to the story . . ." She was hovering over Jenny, but spoke loud enough for Luz to hear. "Doña Tamarindo got pregnant but each baby was born dead or died minutes after birth.

A jealous person had put a curse on her. That's why she went to a bruja."

"I wish you wouldn't tell those stories, doña Cuca. It scares Luz."

"I'm not talking to her, I'm talking to my daughter," doña Cuca said. "Anyway, I've heard the doctors say the poor girl's mind is like a running tap. She can't hold on to what anyone says. It's forgotten in seconds."

"We don't know that for sure," Gloria said, squeezing Luz's hand. "And even if true, it's wrong to take advantage of her impairment."

Luz heard them bickering but soon forgot them. It was work trying to understand what people said, and it took even more effort to respond. Much of the time, doña Cuca's voice faded into the background like the beeps, blips, sirens, and other noises in the hospital.

Doña Cuca felt sorry for Luz. She'd noticed that doña Tamarindo didn't talk much to her grandchild. Most visitors to the neurology department brought flowers and homemade food for those who could eat, or balloons, or stuffed animals, anything to bring a smile to their loved ones' faces. But doña Tamarindo did little but pray by Luz's bed. She didn't buy the girl pretty nighties to wear instead of the hospital gown. Didn't pat Luz's forehead with a dry cloth, didn't massage her arms, hands, legs, and feet like doña Cuca did for her Jenny two or three times a day. No, it wasn't right. Doña Cuca decided she had two daughters to care for now, and kept chattering at them as if her own life depended on it.

"It's the family's duty and responsibility," she said to Nurse Gloria, "to help that poor child recollect her lost memories."

"Her grandparents do that."

"All she does with her is pray, and he hardly ever comes."

"He lives in San Juan."

"That's less than two hours away, not across an ocean."

Doña Cuca felt compelled to help the neglected, orphaned child. She didn't know the family, but she'd read the horrific reports of the accident, and she'd seen the grandmother around for years. Luz's mind was empty, and doña Cuca would fill it with stories about doña Tamarindo.

What she knew about Luz's grandmother was what she'd heard here and there, cacareando over the fence with her neighbors, or with patients' relatives smoking in the courtyard or waiting for the outcomes of surgeries while sipping a cafecito from one of the chinchorros in front of the hospital. To add color, doña Cuca added a few details from her own experience.

"Like I was saying, Lucecita," she said, "doña Tamarindo went to a bruja, who said, 'My remedies will help you grow a healthy baby in your womb, but only God can keep it alive.' The woman might have been a bruja, but she was a good Catholic. She advised doña Tamarindo to appeal to the Holy Virgin to intercede for her with Papá Dios."

Luz seemed to be dozing, like Jenny, but doña Cuca kept talking. That very morning, she'd overheard one neighbor chatting to another: "Puerto Ricans love to talk but doña Cuca es una exageración. She talks even through her elbows." She didn't care what others said about her. She had a mission: to fill Luz and Jenny with stories.

"Well, Lucecita, you know, it was more complicated than doña Tamarindo expected. She knelt by her bed every night and begged Papá Dios. She crossed herself and bowed her head and said a prayer at each Angelus. She went to church daily and observed the holy days like the rest of us good Catholics. The thing is, she got pregnant, but the babies were born dead or died soon after. It had to be a curse, and the bruja said it was a powerful one. She gave her herbs and told her to boil them in plenty of water and while it was still warm, to pour the whole tiringanga over herself. She should fast for three days after that, and go to confession. Once her body was clean and her conscience clear and she'd done her penance, she should take a tonic the bruja gave her, and as she drank it, she should pray one Ave María after each sip and ask Papá Dios to grace her life. She had to do all that and in that order."

Nurse Gloria came back while doña Cuca was jabbering as if someone had turned her on and didn't know how to turn her off.

"And how do you know all this, doña Cuca? I hope you're not making it all up just to entertain Luz and Jenny."

"Well, I wasn't there, of course, but this was how things were done in those days. Today if you have a problem like doña Tamarindo had, you go to a doctor and they photograph your insides with their machines to make sure you have all the parts where they belong, and if so, they give you drugs to help things along, nothing having to do with prayer or hocus-pocus. But in those days, pshaw!" Doña Cuca scoffed, dismissing centuries of traditional medicine. "Doña Tamarindo had no choice but to follow the bruja's advice. She did what she was told, but still her pregnancies ended in dead infants. Remember, Nurse Gloria, those brujas were powerful, and once you went to one, you couldn't exchange her for another. You did what she said or there would be consequences."

"Like what?"

"Stronger curses, hexes, that sort of thing. No, you didn't mess with those women, Nurse Gloria! Never! You did what they told you." She poked her left palm with her right index finger. "And to the letter. Don't forget, doña Tamarindo wasn't getting any younger, either. So, she went back to the bruja, who asked, 'What have you given God to make you worthy of His generosity?'"

"Obviously, dead babies weren't enough," said Nurse Gloria.

"That's right. She knew she was fertile. The bruja said she had to prove her humility and devotion by walking on her knees around the town plaza seven times, up the stone church steps, down the nave, to the altar, praying her rosary, begging Jesús, María, José, and San Francisco to bless her with a child born alive who would thrive."

"That bruja sounds very demanding."

"And how!" Doña Cuca didn't catch Nurse Gloria's sarcastic tone. "I'm telling you, those women had a lot of power. They don't exist anymore."

"Maybe in el campo?"

"Possible. Those jíbaros in the mountains still live like in the olden times, before electricity and running water. They don't care it's almost 1976. But here in a big town? No. What happened to doña Tamarindo can't happen here."

"Good thing she got her wish eventually."

"It wasn't easy, I tell you." Doña Cuca found her way back to her story. "Doña Tamarindo did as she was told, but her monthlies came again. So back to the bruja, who said everything she'd done was still not enough. What Jesús, María, José, San Francisco, and Papá Dios expected was for her to give up something precious in their holy names. Those days were not like today, when we have the very poor and those who are poor but not starving. No. In our modern Puerto Rico we have the lower middle class, the middle class, and the upper middle class in their gated urbanizaciones, with paved roads, sidewalks, electricity, and running water. Above them you have the fulanos y menganas living in air-conditioned mansions, who eat meat every day, even on Fridays. Yes, it's true. Puerto Rico is a paradise now compared to those days, when either you had nothing or you had a little. Now we have many steps between poor and rich."

"So, what did doña Concepción give up if she was so poor?" Nurse Gloria was almost at the end of her shift and eager to get home. She also knew something doña Cuca didn't. Luz was shortly to be moved to the Doña Ana Rehabilitation Hospital in Guares. Despite her initial reservations, Nurse Gloria wanted the rest of the story. The only way to get it was to let doña Cuca finish.

"Ay, mija, imagine! The bruja told her she should make a vow if the Santos Seres fulfilled her request. Back to fasting and herbal baths and confessing and drinking a concoction, followed by more prayers, but this time she must swear to live by the Bible, renouncing the seven deadly sins, and, in case you don't know"—doña Cuca counted on her fingers—"they are pride, avarice, envy, wrath, lust, gluttony, and sloth. Part of her promesa was to wear the Franciscan habit—that brown sack she wears with the rope."

"I'd heard something about that."

"Everyone knows, but there was one problem," doña Cuca said in a near-whisper, as if she didn't want the in-and-out-of-consciousness Luz and comatose Jenny to hear. "Maybe the bruja didn't tell her, or doña Tamarindo didn't know. When she vowed to wear the Franciscan habit, doña Tamarindo didn't set an end date to that promesa. Usually you'd say you'd wear it for three months, or a year, or whatever the priests said was appropriate. But once her daughter was born and survived beyond her baptism, doña Tamarindo put on her habit, and that was it. She's worn it for at least forty years, or however many years Salvadora was alive."

Flags

JULY 2017

In the summer of 2017, Marysol Ríos Peña sees Puerto Rican flags everywhere. This is the Bronx, but still. La bandera waves from fire escapes, eaves, and store awnings. It flutters from windowsills.

Las Madres

It decorates bodega walls, mirrors in barber and beauty shops. It's a cake. It's plastered on murals, light posts, and the columns holding up the train tracks. T-shirts, leggings, swimsuits, and Daisy Duke short-shorts sport the monostar. It's a beach towel on the sands of Orchard Beach. It's stitched into cushions, pasted on coffee mugs, and etched onto fried plantain pressers. Girls push their hair from their faces with headbands stamped with the flag, or it's sewn into scrunchies to hold ponytails tight against scalps. Forgoing giant hoops, some wear the rectangular flag as earrings or dangling from gold chains around their necks. Others feature it as fingernail art. The most ardent have tattoos.

The first time Marysol was naked with Warren MacKenna Collazo, she was surprised by the red, white, red, white, red stripes and five-pointed white star on a blue triangle over his left nipple. "You must be very patriotic."

"I am, but it's also a political statement," he said.

"Isn't displaying a national flag always political?" She licked her finger and traced the design.

"I think what you're asking is why I'd choose the Puerto Rican flag as a tattoo."

"Yeah." She lay on her back. "Also . . . why is there another one over your bed?"

He studied it, as if weighing whether sexual intimacies were easier to share than political ideology. "Because when I wake up, it's the first thing I see that tells me who I really am, before the rest of the world shares their opinion."

It was a surprisingly thoughtful response, but she had no deeper comment than "Hmmm."

"Do you know why Puerto Ricans are so proud of our flag?"

"You're about to tell me, aren't you?" She placed her head on his chest again to listen to his heart and snuggled even closer, melting into him. They'd known each other a few months then, had spent hours talking before they found their bodies as compatible as their intellects.

"Because it took decades of struggle, blood, and tears to win the right to fly our own flag over our own homeland."

Warren was born in Vieques and raised in Brooklyn but spent his school vacations on his paternal grandparents' finca. "Our people were imprisoned and fined for having a Puerto Rican flag, even when they kept it where no one else could see it."

"My godmother Ada told me my dad talked about that," she said. "He said a revolution needs a symbol. No flag, nothing visible to fight for."

"It's true even when it sounds simplistic . . ."

"He wasn't a scholar. He was a bodeguero—"

"Don't get defensive, cariño," he said. "I wasn't criticizing him—or you."

Marysol is sensitive to mentions of her father, who died when she was five years old. Each time she thinks about him, pressure builds in her chest and she forces herself to breathe, hoping to lighten the grief that never, ever lifts.

She's read dozens of books, has had years of therapy, has spent hours watching Phil Donahue, Sally Jessy Raphaël, and Oprah Winfrey, and knows her love for Warren is inextricably linked to her lost father. Like Warren, her father was raised in the United States but spent childhood summers in Puerto Rico with grandparents, a platoon of tías, tíos, primos, and primas. The two men's rosy-brown skin tones are similar, but Warren's is darker and redder. He's the seventh Puerto Rican Warren MacKenna in his family, descended from a shipwrecked captain, or so goes the legend. When Warren has had too much to drink, he tells stories about Warren MacKenna One through Six, sprinkling some of his own adventures into the sancocho of his intrepid ancestors. Marysol has vague memories of her father's stories about his less colorful but numerous forebears. His family was split between those who never left Puerto Rico and those who settled in the United States, mostly in Brooklyn, Chicago, and Florida.

Marysol has been to Disney World and was stunned by how many Puerto Ricans lived in the Orlando area, proudly displaying the flag. But here she is, in the Bronx, in July 2017, noticing another flag swinging from the front mirror of the taxi delivering her to her new patient, Carmen Luisa Sánchez Polo. When she reaches the apartment door, there's a flag sticker above the peephole.

Inside, she's introduced to a seventy-eight-year-old woman whose bed faces the biggest Puerto Rican flag Marysol has ever seen indoors.

"It reminds her of home," her daughter says. A plaintive jíbaro song plays nearby. On a shelf, a ceramic army of coquí frogs marches between papier-mâché vejigante masks.

"Buenos días, doña Carmen Luisa." Marysol touches her hand.

"Everyone calls her Cuca," Juanita explains.

"Doña Cuca, yo soy Marysol, la norsa."

Cuca babbles, squints to better study her features. Her eyes brighten and she smiles toothlessly.

"She was a chatterbox in her day. Always telling stories . . . Now it's mostly nonsense."

"It's good she tries to communicate." Marysol presses Cuca's palm. "You've done a good job with her room, Juanita. So bright and colorful."

On the sunniest spot under a window, a luxurious, three-foot-tall avocado tree grows in a terra-cotta planter with a flag stuck into the dirt. The air is sharp with the competing scents of antiseptic, earth, VapoRub, and Agua de Florida. An image of the Virgen de la Providencia is pasted on a tall candle guttering inside a glass jar. On the wall above it, the thorny heart of Jesus bleeds between portraits of President Obama and First Lady Michelle, she in a yellow gown. Beneath them, on top of a closed Bible, is another Puerto Rican flag on a plastic stand.

Juanita leaves Marysol alone so she can bathe and dress her

mother. Cuca's chatter is mostly unintelligible, but as the hours pass, Marysol recognizes some words and a name. While Cuca dozes, she seeks Juanita in the living room.

"She's calling for my sister Jenny," she explains. "She was in a coma for over twenty years and Mami talked her to death." She gasps and covers her mouth. "Oh, my God, that's not what I meant . . ."

"Don't worry—I got it. The doctors told her to keep talking to your sister and doña Cuca expected Jenny to wake up any moment."

"After we buried her, Mami volunteered at the facility to talk to other unconscious patients. My dad said it was because none of them could talk back." She smiles sadly, a family joke no longer funny. "Some of their relatives complained, and they told her not to return."

"That must have been hard for her."

"It was. Mami never quite recovered from my sister's death. That's who she's calling for. Never me, or my other sister, or my dad. Jenny. My whole childhood . . . it was like we didn't exist because Jenny needed her." Juanita flicks moisture from her cheeks. "She probably expects me to talk to her like she did to Jenny, but . . ." She swallows the rest of the sentence.

"She knows you love her."

"I don't think she does. It's a terrible thing to say but I don't know if I do. She wasn't a good mother, at least to me." She crosses herself. "God forgive me."

"You're under a lot of pressure. It's hard to care for a parent who needs so much, but I'm here to help, okay?"

"You're so kind."

"I know what you're living through."

Juanita goes down the hall, but her muffled sobs come through a closed door.

Marysol's patients' children and spouses carry so much guilt, she often feels they, too, need her care. She listens to their regrets or, like Juanita, their mourning over what they didn't get from a mother, father, wife, husband. In the years she's been a nurse and an in-home caregiver, she's noticed adult children with dying parents grieve what they didn't get from them but express more remorse about their own regrets than about their parents' neglect. It's different for parents caring for a dying child. They express lavish love while adjusting expectations of the future.

Marysol's time with her patients is limited, but nevertheless, the hours or days she spends with them affects her more than their families imagine. She mourns them when they vanish into the ground or into smoke, remembered by a few but ignored by the masses in the roaring city they share. Her patients are mostly Spanish speakers like her, poor or middle class like her, brown or Black like her, invisible to almost everyone in New York City, like her. But her patients are suffering, lonely, frightened human beings, often unloved and easily forgotten.

She asks for selfies with them. Those coherent enough to talk, she asks for stories she then records on her phone.

"Nobody has time for an old woman's stories," her Peruvian patient Doris said.

"I do," Marysol said. "You honor me by telling them."

She swore an oath to respect her patients' secrets even after death. She never shares the media she captures. They're an inventory of her work, a way to prove her patients existed, laughed, cried, ate, danced, had joys and sadness, loved and were loved. She hated that their stories might disappear when they did.

Her patient don Jorge couldn't believe anyone would be interested in his experiences.

"It helps me understand my mother," Marysol answered.

"She doesn't tell you?"

"She can't. Mom has amnesia."

"How sad. Memories are the only things we truly own."

Comments like that keep Marysol listening to her patients. Their concerns and worries help her understand what their relatives are going through. Nobody wants to watch the suffering of a family member ravaged by illness. They want to remember their parent or spouse or child at their most vibrant moments, not when they're feeble, gasping for breath, groaning in pain, wrinkled, shrunk with age and disease. They prefer to remember them before they fell into infirmity.

Years ago, Marysol read that most people are forgotten by the third generation that follows them, and she mourns the silenced stories, the knowledge and wisdom that vanish when her patients die. The images and recordings of their testimonies are meant to rescue them for posterity. Poor people, too, have a history, but they're footnotes to the exploits of the great men and women who leave monuments and written accounts. Marysol appreciates technology that makes it easy to chronicle individuals without relying on a single observer's interpretation, often from loftier heights and through foreign eyes.

Walking home after her shift with Cuca, Marysol again notices the Puerto Rican flags like beacons. When she was with them during the Fourth of July weekend, Graciela asked her and Luz to mark their calendars for a group vacation. Her mother Shirley wants to celebrate her seventieth birthday in Puerto Rico, and Graciela is planning what sounds like an extravaganza of eating, dancing, family visits, and treks through historical sites.

Luz and Marysol don't often travel far from their house, due to Luz's condition. Seven years ago, they spent three weeks in Maine, helping Graciela settle into her house. Before that, nearly twenty-three years ago, Luz, Graciela, and her mothers, Shirley and Ada, took Marysol to Orlando for her thirteenth birthday. They stayed in adjacent rooms in a hotel inside the park, living in luxury and in fantasyland for four days. Marysol had worried she was too old for Disney World but Ada and Shirley convinced her she'd enjoy it, and they were right. They had a great time. Las madres didn't bug them when she and Graciela wanted to go on the scarier rides or when they flirted with boys glancing in their direction. But she's not thirteen anymore and not so easily distracted.

There's a flag on the side of a moving van. She lives in a great metropolis, but Marysol barely registers its greatness. She's always lived within a three-mile radius of where she was born, with rare forays beyond its confines. It embarrasses her to be so provincial. She's awed by her patients, who have left their countries, their families, their cultures to settle in a foreign land that doesn't always welcome them. She admires their courage but worries about the strain of being here, creating a new life, when their most valuable memories reside in faraway lands.

Marysol is a Puerto Rican in the Bronx who's never been to Puerto Rico but yearns for a place she's never seen. Would being there alter her sense of herself?

She'll set aside the two weeks and will travel with her mother, Graciela, Shirley, and Ada to what they all consider their homeland. She'll have a good time because she always has fun with them, sometimes in spite of herself. All these Puerto Rican flags are guiding her toward something she's been missing, toward, hopefully, stories as compelling and memorable as the ones she collects from her patients. Except these will be hers. It's not enough to collect others' memories. She, too, has a right to experience life so she can claim her own story.

Orphan

NOVEMBER 1975–JANUARY 1976

Luz moved to the Doña Ana Rehabilitation Hospital, where she had a private room. Nurse Braulio explained the images on the wall.

"This is your father's father, don Alonso. He and doña Felipa, who used to clean your house, spent hours doing this." There were photographs, recital programs, diplomas, clippings from newspapers and magazines.

"That's you." The nurse pointed to a photo of a girl balancing on her toes, with the other leg behind her in a full split. "You're a ballerina, mi amor." He jiggled a pair of pointe shoes dangling from the ceiling. "Those are yours."

Another day, Nurse Patricia helped Luz stand before the wall. "I don't know who all the people are, but I recognize your grandfather don Alonso here and here. Oh, and here he is again. I think the man next to him is Dr. Federico Peña Ortíz, your dad—they look so much alike. And this pretty lady with the flowered dress is your mom. You take after her, I think."

Those people were her parents. Her father was Federico. He was a doctor chemist. What was a chemist?

"This is one of his diplomas," Nurse Patricia read aloud. "University of Michigan."

Luz wanted to ask but her lips wouldn't form words. She made them move with her mind inside her broken brain. She stammered. Nurse Patricia waited. Waited. Waited some more. "Michigan?"

"It's afuera," she said.

She was in a hospital. There was also afuera.

"In this picture, your dad, Dr. Peña Ortíz, is giving a speech. See? He's on a stage."

Luz stuttered but Nurse Patricia waited. Her nose was crooked and there was a scar over her upper lip.

"Numbers? Letters? Together?"

"Very good! Yes, it's a chemical formula. Your dad is so cute! Look at his tie. You can make out the same symbols on the formula behind him."

Formula. Her father, Dr. Peña Ortíz. He wore a suit the same color as his skin. Chocolate like pudding. Blue shirt. He was cute.

She was in front of the wall. Next to her was Nurse Braulio. He was round and his fingers looked boneless. He pointed to a picture.

"This is your mother, la doctora Salvadora Fuentes Argoso y Peña."

Salvadora. A white mound. "What is?"

"Snow. In El Norte there is snow," Nurse Braulio says. "I love her one-piece puffy suit with those heavy boots like the ones astronauts wear."

Luz stammered. He waited. His neck was thick but his shoulders were narrow and sloped as if his arms were too heavy.

"Astro . . . ?"

He explained but she heard "Herngonz."

~

The wall had many pictures. There was Salvadora. Her eyes were almost closed. She was laughing and Luz could see her teeth, square and white. Salvadora was in another picture, her face partly hidden behind a scarf with stripes. Two of the stripes were yellow like corn, two as black as when Luz closed her eyes.

"That pom-pom on her hat is as big as her head," Nurse Patricia giggled. "Enchanting!"

Salvadora wore a big pom-pom on a hat. It made Nurse Patricia laugh. The hat was yellow, the pom-pom black. Like the scarf in the other picture, where Salvadora is laughing in the snow. She was enchanting.

~

Nurse Patricia waited outside the bathroom. Luz appraised the face in the mirror over the sink. That was her, brown like Federico and Salvadora, with big eyes and short lashes. Her lips were rosy in the middle. She had a scar over an eyebrow. Left? Right? She touched it. That side. She whispered, "I am Luz. My father is . . . was Federico. His father is Abuelo. My mother was Salvadora. Her mother is Güela. So many names!"

Now Luz was inside the shower stall. Water dripped on the floor.

"Do you need help, Luz?" Nurse Patricia peeked through the crack in the door.

She slid the curtain open and walked into clouds. Someone was there. No. It was a reflection.

"Am I Luz?"

She was who they said she was, a shadow behind the mist on the surface of a mirror.

⸺

It took her days to understand who Federico and Salvadora were, and months to finally accept they were no longer in her present, nor would they be in her future. Their deaths disconnected her childhood from the rest of her life. Once she grasped the tragedy and began to feel the grief, she was unmoored, adrift from a past she'd forgotten and with no clear path to the future. Between physical and occupational therapies and dreamless, drugged sleep, she lay in bed trying to remember but failing to conjure more than elusive flashes of Salvadora, Federico, and their family life, as static as the snapshots on the wall, which captured one blinking moment and were gone.

Güela came to see Luz daily. She didn't smile or chat with the nurses. She didn't tell Luz about the people in the pictures on the wall. She was not in any of them. Luz sensed Güela expected something from her she couldn't recognize or fulfill, but the nurses were awed by her.

"Did they tell you what she did when you were in your coma at the other hospital?" Nurse Braulio asked.

Luz shook her head.

"Your abuelita was there, sitting by your bedside for hours, praying to God to heal you."

"She was?"

"They called her the ward angel. Other people asked her to pray for their relatives and, like you, they improved."

Luz accepted what people told her because she had no idea otherwise. Her history, and so her identity, belonged to others. They dispensed bits and pieces she tried to understand and save, but her mind didn't keep them for more than a few breaths.

As the days passed, she began to identify the nurses and some of the therapists by name. She couldn't keep track of the doctors, who shone lights into her eyes, asked her to follow their index fingers up, down, right, left. They asked her to squeeze their hands, to push them back, to push them down, to resist their force. They tapped her knee with a little rubber mallet. They said she was improving and used words she didn't understand. She was still somewhat aphasic, they said, but it was resolving. Gbldgk.

"Your speech therapist reports you can read," one doctor said. Luz nodded. If they said she could read, she believed it. Actually, the words fled as soon as she read them aloud, with little idea what they meant.

She now recognized Güela, but because her grandfather Alonso didn't come daily, he had to introduce himself each time. He told her stories, but her brain couldn't save them for her mind to think about later. Alonso, Güela, her doctors, and the nursing staff spoke only Spanish and she had no idea she spoke other languages.

Doña Felipa, her parents' house cleaner and Luz's companion when Salvadora and Federico had traveled together for work, came to see her. Noticing Luz's hair tufted into tangled clumps, doña Felipa brought wide-toothed and rattail combs the next time she came. She washed Luz's hair, massaged oil into her scalp, and cornrowed her hair. She, too, told stories that were fascinating, but once she was out of sight, her name and her stories dissipated into vapor.

She dreaded her grandmother's shuffling steps toward her bed every afternoon in her penitent's habit, her aura of piety that made Luz feel wicked and culpable of unspecified sins.

"Bendición."

"Que Dios te bendiga, nena." As she bent to kiss her, Luz caught a whiff of the cloves Güela kept in her mouth to alleviate the ache in her teeth.

Before Güela asked Luz how she was doing, or what progress she'd made with her therapies, she spoke to the head nurse or the doctors, distrustful Luz could give her accurate information. Once she'd heard the reports from the medical staff, Güela told Luz what they'd said.

"You walked down the hall on your own."

"The nurse was next to me."

"That was in case you fell, but you didn't need the walker or to hold on to her."

"Only a few steps."

Whenever Güela was with her, Luz felt not only inadequate, but untrustworthy. She sensed she wasn't enough, that Güela wanted something Luz could never provide.

After listing what Luz had accomplished that day according to the medical staff, Güela prayed a couple of courses of her rosary, expecting Luz to accompany her.

"Pater noster qui es in coelis, sanctificetur nomen tuum . . ."

After that, a string of Ave Marias, Glory Be, Our Father again. Luz complied. It surprised her that she could follow the prayers in Latin Güela had taught her before she could even pronounce "dah" or "buh." The prayers were imprinted, and with every syllable she resented how much space they took up in her brain when so much of her memory had fled. ". . . ora pro nobis . . ."

Other than praying alongside Güela, Luz didn't have much to say to her grandmother, who seemed incapable of idle chat.

Las Madres

"I have to get home before dark."

Güela made sure the side table was close enough for Luz to reach her water pitcher and plastic cup.

"Bendición." Luz watched Güela dodder away, never once looking back, her braid grazing the frayed hem of her sackcloth. With each step her grandmother took, sentimientos compressed Luz's chest, threatening to overcome her. She felt more alone when Güela walked away, but she didn't look forward to seeing her again. She heard nurses talking about her.

"Her religiosity is extreme and weird," one said.

"It is!" The other giggled. "I mean, is it right to make deals with God, saints, and virgins to get what you want?"

"Right! It's like showing off how much she's sacrificed so everyone else can feel guilty."

"I know what you mean."

It embarrassed Luz that everyone had an opinion about Güela, and it mortified her they knew doña Tamarindo was her grandmother.

⟜

While in rehab, Luz was overwhelmed by kindness and affection from people who'd known her most of her life. She didn't recognize them at first, but stitched together a network of men, women, and children who knew more about her than she knew about herself. When they thought she was asleep, she heard two people talking about her as "the orphan." She didn't have to ask Nurse Braulio or Nurse Patricia or anyone else what the word meant. Its meaning was as clear as dawn. Pobrecita huérfana, they said. Poor orphan.

Classmates delivered flowers, current teen and fashion magazines, and food prepared by their mothers. They gossiped about their teachers, and about one another. They couldn't stay long; their lives hadn't been upended by tragedy and medical interventions. Luz smiled and tried to keep up with their chatter but was glad when they skipped from her room back into their normal lives. It was exhausting to pretend to be brave, to deflect questions about how she felt. They were healthy and didn't really want to know about her headaches, which were triggered by bright lights, high-pitched sounds, or pungent odors and forced her to lie still for hours because even minor movements made the pain worse. Her visitors asked how she was doing, but if she told anyone except the medical staff how she really felt, she was met by uncomfortable silence, grimaces, and pitying glances. She stopped talking about the cramps that gripped her back, sizzling down her thighs to her calves, to her middle toes, the spasms temporarily relieved by changing position or rubdowns. Cold compresses, hot compresses, and smelly unguents allowed respite from the random, excruciating pain. She couldn't share any of it with those who could do nothing to make things better. So she answered their questions with "Feeling stronger every day" or "Thank you for asking" but avoiding specifics.

She cloaked her envy at the casual or careless mentions of parties and a group trip to San Juan. Apparently, she'd been a fan of La Pandilla, popular teenage singers/dancers from Spain who would be performing in the capital. Her friends were sorry she couldn't join them, but brought her a poster that Nurse Braulio then taped to the wall. Luz wondered why she'd liked the pretty boys and long-haired girl in sparkly outfits.

She swallowed her tears when someone said, "Mami said," or, "My father did that," or, "My mother told me," often followed by a gasp, embarrassment, and a muttered "sorry" she waved away. She was too young and too old to be an orphan, and feared the rest of her life would be harder because her parents wouldn't be there to help her navigate it.

⁓

She had turned sixteen while she was unconscious, the first birthday with no party, no presents, no teary toasts from Federico or extravagant gifts from Alonso, no giggly celebrations with her friends in her bedroom while the grown-ups ate and danced and thanked Federico and Salvadora for another good time. She had missed Thanksgiving, when Luz would have been helping Salvadora prepare the dinner and greeting co-workers who had no family nearby, most from the States and Europe, and who loved her pavochón, her garlicky potatoes mashed with plantain and crispy bacon, and Federico's coquito, made with fresh, not canned, coconut milk and Puerto Rican rum.

"You'll celebrate when you're well," doña Felipa said, trying to cheer her up for a future Luz couldn't envision. Every time she came, doña Felipa pointed to random photos and asked Luz to identify the people. If she didn't recognize them, doña Felipa wrote their names on the picture so she'd learn them.

⌒

Luz's memory slips frustrated and embarrassed her. What was the long thing inside the thing holding the thing that made her less thirsty?

"Straw," the occupational therapist made her repeat. "Cup. Water."

The doctors couldn't guarantee her memory would return, or that the headaches would go away, or the pains, cramps, and stiffness that kept her from considering herself normal. She felt older than sixteen, burdened with a grief she was certain she'd carry the rest of her life. Yet she was unable to be specific about what she was grieving.

"All of it," she said, incapable of identifying the greater loss: her parents' death, her injured body, her vanished memories.

Several of her teachers visited. None talked about Federico and Salvadora, as if mentioning them would trigger a setback from the progress she was making.

Co-workers from the pharmaceutical company also visited. But, unlike her school friends and teachers, they talked about nothing but Salvadora and Federico. They explained that Salvadora and Federico were chemists with advanced degrees in pharmacology who'd published scientific papers in important journals. These colleagues were from various countries, and spoke to her in Spanish, then switched to their native languages to test if she remembered them. No one was more surprised than Luz that she could easily converse with them as if nothing had happened to her.

"When you were together," one of the chemists said, "you, Federico, and Salvadora spoke a burundanga of languages no one could keep up with."

Luz loved the idea of a private language with her parents, a connection no one else could share.

The co-workers told anecdotes, and some brought albums that showed her parents at weddings, baptisms, conventions, or conferences. Luz was getting to know them through the pictures, but it was strange to believe they were her parents, especially when she was not in the images. She had to believe Federico and Salvadora were everything their friends said they were: smart and generous, trustworthy, excellent hosts, and tireless volunteers for local charities. Still, while she was getting better at recognizing their faces, the images weren't intimate enough for Luz to envision a private life as a family. Did Federico always have a loopy grin when he embraced Salvadora? There were several photos of Salvadora and two other women in a hotel room. Did she always wear foam rollers, a filmy scarf around her head not even remotely camouflaging them? In their friends' pictures, her parents looked like movie extras unlinked to the rest of the main story.

"Salva was so proud of you," one manager told Luz. "A corner of her desk was covered with pictures of you. It was her altar."

"Rico kept snapshots of you in his wallet," another chemist from the plant said. "And I don't mean the most recent. He started with you as a baby and kept pulling pictures out. It was like a magic trick. Photo after photo after photo . . ."

"You and Salva were Rico's world," another colleague said. "He was all about his family." He shook his head as if he couldn't believe he was speaking of them in the past tense.

Era, antes, hicieron, dijo, dijeron. Was, before, did, said. It didn't matter in which language she conjugated the verbs. They were no longer parts of speech but darts into her broken heart.

⌒

Alonso filled Luz in on what happened while she was in a coma.

"The doctors said you might never wake up." Her grandfather measured his words, enunciated every syllable, aware she was still aphasic. "The funeral Mass was in the cathedral. Your godfather, Pastor Josué, asked permission to speak about their time in Ann Arbor and their long-standing friendship. He's been my client for years, and nothing like the firebrand on the radio. Would you believe some people had the nerve to ask for his autograph?"

Alonso waited for Luz to agree this was appalling.

"To his credit, he refused." Another pause as he reconnected the dots in his story. "It was devastating when they brought in two coffins. I was too overcome to be a pallbearer, so their friends and co-workers did it. Every pew was filled. And the flowers! Wreaths, plants, and bouquets of every size, shape, and color. Even your grandmother was impressed by how many people came to pay their respects." He blinked away his tears. "We buried them side by side, mamita, together always, like from the day they fell in love in Michigan. I'll take you to see their graves."

Luz didn't want to see graves. She wanted them laughing and dancing, Salvadora atop a mound of snow, Federico on a stage, his tie duplicating the formula behind him. She wanted to be wrapped in their embraces, like those in the pictures on the wall.

"The doctors won't tell me when I can go home."

"The neurologist says by the middle of next month. You'll live with your grandmother . . ."

"Why there?"

"After your discharge you'll need outpatient therapies . . ."

"I don't want to live with her. She's . . . she's . . ."

"We've already moved your things to her house."

"Move them back! Please don't make me stay with her, Abuelo. I have a home. Doña Felipa said Mami and Papi left me there all the time when they traveled for work. She came every afternoon and stayed with me overnight. She made me breakfast and dinner and everything." Luz was desperate. She was his only grandchild, his niña consentida.

He scratched the back of his head as if he had to think hard about her request, then sighed. "The thing is . . ." He looked embarrassed. "The doctors said you might never wake up . . ."

"They're proud I did."

Alonso kept scratching his head as if he had lice. "You see, your grandmother can't manage her parcela, her business, you, and your parents' house . . ."

She felt faint. "What are you saying?"

Alonso squeezed the bridge of his nose and wouldn't look at Luz. "We had no idea how long you'd be . . . asleep. The doctors were grumbling that you belonged in a long-term facility."

"Like, forever?"

"Sí, niña." He paused, envisioning something she couldn't. "Your parents had excellent health and life insurance and savings, but your medical bills kept coming and your prognosis was discouraging. One of their co-workers wanted to buy the house and most of the furniture. I also sold my boat, and with all the money, I set up a trust for your needs."

"They gave you no hope for me, Abuelo? None?"

"You were in a coma for four weeks. They said even if you awoke, you'd have brain damage, hard to tell how serious. You had terrifying seizures that might never go away. The experts told us you might have to be institutionalized for the rest of your life. It was awful. I was trying to protect you, mi niña. I'm still doing that, you know." He held her hand. "It seemed like the best plan at the time."

Neither spoke for a while. Luz was on the edge of an invisible precipice, almost, but not quite, willing to jump into its depths.

"You're still a minor," Alonso continued, "and can't live on your own, even if doña Felipa checks in from time to time. In your condition, you can't be alone. Protective services would get involved and next thing you know, they'd place you in a foster home, or worse."

"I don't want to live with my abuela loca."

He smiled now. "She's not crazy, mi amor. She's religious, maybe a bit eccentric, but not loca."

"She's strange. She scares me."

"She loves you and is dedicated to helping you heal. You could not ask for a more devoted grandmother." He put his hand on her forehead and held it there, as if checking her temperature. "I know how hard this is for you. I want you to be comfortable, to have a normal life, to be happy. I'm doing my best to ensure that, mamita."

"Can I live with you? Please."

"Not right away. My condo is small but maybe I can find a bigger one." He stroked her cheek. "Don't worry, sweetheart. We'll figure it out."

A few hours later, a woman floated into Luz's room. She wore a long, pastel-colored tie-dyed dress with tassels along the hem. She was pale, her facial features angular, her blond hair pulled back into a bun decorated with rhinestone pins and combs. She'd applied her makeup as if the curtain were about to rise, her false eyelashes like tarantulas.

"Querida." She touched her cheeks to Luz's. A whiff of . . . gardenias? "What a tragedy. But I know you will overcome this."

Luz stole a glance at her wall, where there was a photo of the woman taking a bow alongside her after a performance. Doña Felipa had written her name wherever she appeared. Still, it took Luz a moment to realize this was her dance teacher. It was like watching a movie on rewind, flickers of Miss Rita in the ballet studio, dancing and laughing. In her photo gallery, Miss Rita appeared from the time Luz was four years old. She was also a frequent guest at her parents' parties. Doña Felipa had said Miss Rita had been like an aunt to Luz, but since the accident the dance teacher hadn't been in touch, not even with a condolence or get-well card.

"How was the Christmas recital?" Luz didn't know where the question came from but it made sense to Miss Rita, who pulled a handkerchief from a pocket and blotted her cheeks.

"It wasn't the same without you." She studied the room and shuddered. "Hospitals give me the creeps."

"I've gotten used to it."

"Yes, you'd have to, I suppose. How much longer do they plan to keep you here?"

"A couple of weeks, I guess."

"Then you go to your grandmother's?"

"I hope not."

"The people who bought your parents' house have a daughter. They're from New York and she's been at a performing arts school and annual summer ballet camps. Tiny little thing."

"Not an amazona, then." Again, Luz surprised herself, as if someone else were speaking.

Miss Rita peered into her eyes as if she, too, thought someone else was inside them. "They said you lost your memory . . ."

"I can't remember everything, just moments."

Miss Rita looked away. "Kyryl was a jerk. I'll never ask him back to my studio." Red splotches formed on her cheekbones.

Luz wanted to punch her. It was a stunning thought. She didn't believe she'd ever want to hit anyone, least of all an adult. She didn't know why she wanted to do it now.

"My life ended inside our car." Saying it out loud made her want to cry.

"You're very much alive, Luz, and have many years ahead. You're still a child."

"An orphan . . ."

Miss Rita pulled her neck back as if to see her from a distance. "You're not an orphan!"

"My parents are dead. That's what it means."

"You have your grandmother, your grandfather, your friends. You have me." Their eyes met again. Miss Rita looked away first, and in that moment, Luz remembered another time when she'd seen that distancing expression. But when and why? It was a flash that soon vanished, long enough for Luz to mourn whatever had bound her to Miss Rita before that evasive gaze.

Miss Rita took her hand, but it brought Luz no comfort. It felt like a theatrical gesture, not so much unfeeling as performative, required of this moment, this place, the circumstances and their history together. It didn't feel real. Or rather, too much so, a goodbye of sorts she'd not expected or imagined, like another death in her life, another orphaning.

～

The afternoon following Alonso's visit, Güela came to see Luz at her usual time.

"I understand you'd rather live with Alonso than me."

"I . . ."

"No lies." Güela pressed her fingers to Luz's lips. "He's diplomatic but I'm no dummy."

"Lo siento, Güela."

"Don't be sorry. If I were you, I wouldn't want to live with me, either."

Luz giggled.

"Mira eso. A smile." There was a gleam in her eyes that dimmed the moment it sparked. "Alonso is looking for a bigger place, but it probably won't be ready by the time you're discharged. You're stuck with me for a while."

"How long?"

"Not very."

"I'm sorry if it sounds . . ."

"I'm not offended. The way I live . . . it's not for everyone. You've probably forgotten what it's like, but you'll see soon enough. In any case, Alonso is more like Federico and Salvadora than I am." Her voice broke when she said her daughter's name, and Luz felt the tightness that gripped her whenever she thought about her parents.

They prayed, and then Güela tapped on Luz's leg to signal she was leaving.

"Hasta mañana."

Luz watched her go, but this time her sentimientos weren't for her loss. Mired in her dark mourning, she hadn't thought enough about her widowed grandparents, whose only children were dead. She was the last Peña to carry Alonso's surname and Güela had buried her eighth and most hard-earned child. Guilt nibbling around the edges of her conscience, Luz sank into the bed and curled up like a cashew, crying for them all.

Despacito

JULY 15, 2017

In the summer of 2017, "Despacito" spills from speakers on store-fronts, from open apartment windows, and from passing cars with stereos at full volume. Regardless of how many times Marysol hears the song, "Despacito" moves her. Her hips sway, her step lightens, she walks taller. When no one can hear, she sings along with Luis Fonsi's plaintive yearning and Daddy Yankee's staccato rap. The song is sexy, and each time she watches the music video, her pulse races. It helps that Warren has a passing resemblance to Daddy Yankee, so the visceral reaction to one is triggered by visions of the other. They don't have plans for this night, but she texts suggestive emojis he responds to with a clock, a racing car, and a right-pointing arrow.

In the languorous moments after sex, she presses her ear to the flag over Warren's heart.

He caresses her back. "Can I come to Puerto Rico with you?"

"It's just the five of us, mi amor. Graciela is organizing the trip. You know how she is."

He smiles. "Thorough and nothing left to chance."

"She found a rental house in the neighborhood where Mom grew up. She thought it might spark some memories." Marysol lies on her back and stares at the ceiling. "Maybe people remember her and my grandparents. They were well known in their town before the wreck."

"Puerto Rico has changed a lot since Mamá Luz left."

"I know, but there are ancianos with long memories, like Shirley's aunts in Naguabo."

"They knew your grandparents?"

"No. I mean, there might be old people in San Bernabé who remember them. We think a memory tour would be good for Mom. For me, too. I might learn something about our family."

"Some people go to great lengths to avoid theirs." Warren is often called upon to rescue one or another of his siblings from their follies.

"Ada and Shirley worked for my great-grandfather Alonso, and he told them he was the last Peña male in his line. Apparently, my grandmother Salvadora was an only child, too, so I doubt I'll be flooded with relatives. Graciela found the cemetery where they're buried. We'll bring flowers and perform a ceremony."

He leans on his elbow and caresses her shoulder. "And here I envisioned you in a bikini, romping on a beach."

"When Graciela gets something into her head, she's like a loco-motive with faulty brakes. She's designing a website for a genealo-gist and has become obsessed with ancestry. She might find more information about Mom's family. I know so little about them."

"Graciela should talk to my aunt. She's a retired reference librarian who spends hours at her computer looking for long-lost cousins."

"Has she found any?"

"More than expected, and from all over the world. The MacKen-nas got around."

"I bet they did," she laughs. "Introduce her to Graciela. She could use some tips."

"I'll do that . . ." He follows her to the bathroom.

"Mom, Ada, and Shirley will go a couple of days ahead to feed the traganíckeles."

"I don't think the casinos use coins anymore. They use debit cards."

"It's more precise in Spanish. *Traganíckeles.*" She savors the word. "Machines that swallow nickels."

Warren empties his bladder after Marysol and flushes for them. "Mamá Luz likes the casinos."

"Sure does. By the time Graciela and I arrive, las madres will have gambled all their play money."

"Or Mamá Luz could hit another jackpot."

"Mom's big payout was a fluke."

"Ninety thousand dollars is a good fluke."

"It came in handy to pay off our mortgage. I thank the spirits or gods or whatever. If I won that much money, I'd believe that's all the good luck I'm owed."

"That's the difference between you and real gamblers. They're optimistic. Even when they consistently lose, they believe the next traganíckeles will ding and flash and, presto! You're a winner."

"I'm too pessimistic to gamble, then."

"You're not. You're level-headed and pragmatic."

"Boring?"

"Never!"

"Slow to take risks?"

"Cautious, maybe, but you're brave. Even when scared, you act with courage and commitment."

"Thank you, mi amor."

"I know what I'm talking about . . ."

He follows her downstairs to the kitchen, both of them naked.

"So after las madres spend their money in the casinos, you'll visit old people with good memories and Graciela will mumbo-jumbo over your grandparents' graves? Hashtag ceremony."

"You're awful." She slaps his buttock.

"Ooh! Thank you." He caresses her bottom. "I want you to relax, mi diosa. From what you've said, you'll be traipsing around seeking memories for Mamá Luz but none of it sounds like fun for you."

"Well, fun with them is a different kind of fun from being with you." She bumps Warren's hip with hers. She turns on the kettle as he fills the teapot with chamomile flowers.

"I have an idea." He leans against the counter. "Maybe at some point Graciela can stay with Mamá Luz here for a few days and you and I can have a different kind of vacation en el terruño, just us." He frowns at the face she makes. "Don't go all enthusiastic on me."

"I'm sorry. You know Mom doesn't trust strangers."

"Graciela isn't a stranger. Mamá Luz has known her since she was a baby. And I'm sure she'll say yes, no hesitation. I've never met anyone so eager to please. Hashtag love me."

She laughs and pours the hot water into the pot Graciela gave her for her birthday, made by an artist whose online presence she manages. Marysol thinks the pot is clumsily thrown, too thick and heavy, its glaze pocked, but she feels obliged to use it.

"Do me a favor," Warren continues. He finds the plastic honey bear and two mugs. He squirts puddles of honey inside them. "At least think about it."

She does. A few days alone with Warren sounds tempting, but this isn't the first time he's made a suggestion Marysol has shut down for the same reason. She's her mother's caregiver when she's not taking care of other people. Each time she says no, she worries how long she can keep rejecting his romantic getaways and proposals before he's had enough. Warren has been second to Luz for a decade. He's the most patient, loving man she's ever met. He's skimming forty and wants marriage and a family. She's said no to his proposals, unwilling to saddle him with her responsibilities for her mother's health and welfare. He wants children, and she wants to carry them inside her. Her hormones are insistent. At thirty-five, she's teetering between do it soon or forget it. "I've never asked Graciela or her mothers to watch Mom. They live so far from here. But maybe one of them will be willing . . ."

"Yes!" He claps. "They'll do it. I know they will. And I'll show you a Puerto Rico that's fun. I'll be your guide. We won't visit cemeteries or Shirley's ancient aunts. We'll celebrate our vibrant, life-affirming isla. We'll hike in El Yunque, swim in the phosphorescent bay in La Parguera or the one in Vieques." He takes her in his arms and dances her around the kitchen. "We'll merengue to live bands in open-air dives and eat lechón from the actual varita. We'll gorge on cervezas, rum and soda, cuchifritos, and bacalaítos in Palo Seco or in roadside chinchorros."

"Now that sounds like a vacation." She pulls away. "But what about your job? Can you really get away?"

"If you say yes, I'll make it happen. We'll go in the winter, when things are dreary here."

"Yes, then."

"Really? You mean it?"

"Don't look so surprised!"

"You've never left Mamá Luz for more than a few hours."

"Are you changing your mind now that I said yes?"

"I just want to make sure, mi amor."

She pours their tea, swirls the melting honey. "I want to be more spontaneous."

They sit at opposite ends of the sofa, her feet on his lap.

"What caused this transformation? Was it the promise of cuchifritos?"

She laughs. "We have the best conversations after sex."

"I have to keep up. Don't think I believe my considerable prowess is enough to keep you interested in me."

"Because Dr. Ruth said the brain is the sexiest organ?"

"Because this"—he waves his hands over his torso as if selling it—"isn't why you love me."

"Oh, isn't it?"

"You're not that shallow."

They gaze into each other's eyes. His irises are lighter brown than his skin, his lashes longer than most women's. When he looks at her, she swims in love. "I'm so happy right now."

He rubs her feet. "Me, too."

They sip their tea, listening to the muffled sounds from the street and the television on the other side of the wall, where Luz is watching a documentary. In another hour, Marysol will go across the hall to give Luz her medications and make sure she's tucked in for the night.

"Do you remember don Jorge, my patient of a few weeks ago?"

"The Guatemalan who worked as a laborer but was really a poet?"

"So you are listening?"

"Always. What did he say?"

"He said he was dying of nostalgia because he'd never see his shadow again in the place where he grew up. Homesickness was more painful than cancer, he said."

"That's deep."

"Since then, all I want is to see my shadow in Boriquén."

"But you grew up in the Bronx—"

"Child of Puerto Ricans, raised by and among Puerto Ricans. I wasn't born there, but I've always known who I am, and proud of it, too." She removes her feet from his lap. "Don't challenge my identity. It hurts my feelings."

"I'm sorry—that was insensitive, mi reina. I know better."

"I hate it when people say, 'I'm one hundred percent Puerto Rican,' like I'm less than that."

"I hear that all the time, here and there."

"They protest too much." Staring into her tea, she wishes she'd come up with that comeback when someone said it to her. "Come to think of it, is anyone one hundred percent anything anymore?"

"That's a good question . . ."

"Think about it. Cultures are colliding against each other, especially now that social media can reach the farthest corners of the world."

"That's true . . ."

"Does a woman born and raised in Delhi who can trace her ancestry several centuries back become less Indian if she wears jeans and a T-shirt instead of a sari or salwar kameez?"

"I wonder . . ."

"Who invented the scale determining identity percentile, any-way?"

"Insecure people who raise themselves up by putting down others?"

"That sounds about right," she says.

"You know what they say, right?"

Las Madres

"Who? What?"

"Esa mancha de plátano no se despinta."

Marysol grins. "I love that phrase! My dad used to say that to me, and I asked him where am I stained by a plantain?"

They laugh. She gets serious again, and he follows her gaze. "What's up there?"

"Maybe I should tack a flag like yours to my bedroom ceiling."

Güela

JANUARY–MARCH 1976

Three months after the accident, Alonso drove up to the front doors of Doña Ana Rehabilitation Hospital. Luz was eager to re-enter the world even if it meant going to Güela's. She cried her goodbyes to nurses, therapists, and doctors, who clapped as an aide wheeled her to the curb. For a fleeting moment, she remembered what applause felt like.

A smiling Alonso ran around to open the passenger door of his Mercedes. Luz hadn't been inside a car since the wreck, and the idea of getting into one made her heart thumpity-thump. The aide touched her shoulder.

"Con calma, mi amor. Pasito a pasito," she said. "Take your time, baby."

Luz settled her breath, and with help, stepped inside the car as if it would swallow her.

⌒

Raised in an upper-middle-class neighborhood by accomplished, professional parents who showered her with resources and oppor-tunity, Luz had never lived uncomfortably. She'd had her own room with its own bathroom, her own television set, a walk-in closet that lit up when she opened the door. The house was air-conditioned, but on the rare occasions she wanted fresh air, mosquitoes and other insects slammed against metal screens. Doña Felipa came once a week to tidy and clean their house, change their beds, replace towels on racks, scrub the kitchen and bathrooms, wash and press their clothes. Salvadora had insisted Luz make her bed every morning, and her dirty clothes belonged in the hamper, not on the floor. She was to hand-wash her dance gear and lingerie. Other than those chores, Luz rarely had to clean up after herself and had been squeamish about dirt and unpleasant smells. She squealed at the sight of lizards slithering through the tiniest cracks. She flapped her arms dramatically if a bug buzzed near her.

On this day, she stood in front of her mother's childhood home with no memory of her own. Doña Felipa had told Luz she'd never spent a night at Güela's. She now walked up the steps seeing everything with new eyes. The main room was furnished with two ancient mahogany-and-reed rocking chairs, a table with four chairs, an altar featuring the Sacred Heart of Jesus, with prayer cards tacked on the wall. The plank floor creaked.

Güela's bedroom was to the left, next to what used to be Salvadora's, divided by a wall whose narrow horizontal wooden slats reached neither the ceiling nor the floor. In place of a door, a curtain, newly hung. She wanted to run away, but where? Her only family stood to either side of her, scrutinizing every move she made, as if, already cracked, she'd shatter to pieces.

"I like the flowers," she said, and Güela and Alonso exchanged a look. He must have chosen the curtain. There was nothing else remotely decorative in Güela's house.

Alonso hadn't sold or discarded everything from her parents. A dozen packed and taped-over boxes were piled against the walls. Luz couldn't imagine what her grandparents had saved from her life with Federico and Salvadora.

"I'll bring the boxes to our new place and you can go through them there," Alonso said. "You're not supposed to lift anything. Leave them alone for now."

"He insisted on a new mattress," Güela said, as if hoping Luz would ask him to return it.

"She needs a stiff one for her back." Alonso pressed the edge to test its firmness. The four-poster bed was draped with mosquito netting because there were no screens on the windows. Instead of a closet, rusty hooks on the walls were meant for her clothes, and a small dresser with warped drawers that would never close entirely awaited her intimates and delicates. She banished the thought of lizards and spiders inside them.

"There's a basin under the bed for your needs at night," Güela said. "I'll empty it in the latrine every morning."

Alonso left the room, as if dealing with one's own waste was inconceivable, but Luz had become familiar with a bedpan. Half an hour after he dropped her off, Alonso began making leaving sounds: an appointment with a client, upcoming tax deadlines, tapones at rush hour.

"I'll be back in a few days." He handed Luz a credit card and an envelope with twenty single dollars. "You'll probably need clothes and other things. She'll take you shopping."

"Doña Felipa brought me some tops and shorts."

"Good, yes, she told me. If you need anything, call."

He smiled bashfully when he remembered there was no phone in the house. He rushed through the coffee Güela offered them, kissed Luz's forehead, nodded at Güela, and climbed into his car. They stood on the porch until he was out of sight.

"My neighbor has a phone," Güela said.

"I have to lie down."

"I'll be outside."

Luz crawled under the mosquitero, making sure every corner was secured. She settled on her back with a pillow under her knees. She had strict instructions to rest, to wear a back brace, to attend psychological and physical therapy and massage sessions. The brace was stiff. To minimize chafing, she wore it over a T-shirt that was soon soaked with sweat.

A lagartijo crawled across the ceiling, and she closed her eyes. She wondered whether she'd ever been alone with Güela before her hospital visits. She opened her eyes and the lagartijo was gone. She drifted between dreams and nightmares, dozing and startling awake in the unfamiliar surroundings, so different from the only place she remembered clearly, her hospital room plastered with photographs.

⌒

Luz was unsure how long she slept. When she awoke, she panicked, disoriented, and, for a moment, thought she was hallucinating. The mosquitero waved in languid ripples, like incoming fog. Beyond it, leaves on the mango and avocado trees visible through the windows danced in the breeze. "I'm in el campo." Motors, voices, radios, and televisions in the surrounding urbanizaciones were muted by rustling vegetation, oinking, bleating, clucking, honking, braying, and trilling. She rolled over and slid from under the mosquitero, making sure that it remained tightly closed between the mattress and the box spring.

She heard Güela saying goodbye to someone at her gate. By the time Luz reached the porch, the visitor was gone, but her grandmother was walking toward her with what looked like a gray snake in her hand.

It was a bizarre, terrifying image, made worse when Luz realized Güela wasn't carrying a reptile but her thick braid, chopped from the nape of her neck. Her head was now bald and her ears had grown larger, their lobes drooping uselessly. Güela held the braid up, as if offering it to Luz, who couldn't take her eyes off her, couldn't utter a word.

Güela was twig-thin and straight-backed. As she approached,

Luz flashed on a memory. The previous summer, on their annual trip to New York, Federico and Salvadora had taken her to the Bronx Zoo. They were fascinated by the elephants, how graceful they were despite their bulk, their thick legs, ungainly trunks, and sails for ears. Güela looked nothing like an elephant, but that was what came to mind as she approached with the same heavy grace, as if she'd grown in height and width, slowing her pace but not her forward momentum. She dropped onto a rustic bench on the porch, coiled her braid on her lap, and caressed it as if it were a baby.

Luz was speechless. Up close, Güela's scalp was speckled with bloody nicks and scratches and she smelled strongly of alcoholado.

"Don't worry," Güela said. "I'll rub it with aloe and lavender. The cuts will heal."

"Why did you do this?"

"I made another vow to mi Diosito." Güela's eyes shimmered. "My prayers were fulfilled. Yo cumplo."

"You pledged your hair?"

"I have little left to give for my faith."

Luz sat stiffly on the other bench. The brace made it hard to bend or twist, and with no back support, it was an effort for her to sit for long. She pressed her hands between her thighs, narrowed her body, comforted by containment, as if her most vulnerable self were zipped inside a protective membrane. She eyed the braid, which was fastened with twine at each end, thicker toward where it had been attached to Güela.

"What will you do with it?"

Güela studied it. "I don't know. When I was young, we cut our hair and put it between the leaves and trunk of a banana tree so it would grow."

"The bananas?"

"Hair. It would grow faster and thicker. We believed it."

"Will you do that?"

She shook her head. "My pledge is to be bald. Yo cumplo."

She was mad, Luz was sure of it. Güela didn't live in the same universe as everyone else. Only a loca would do such a thing. Salvadora had grown up with her. Had she been like her mother? In photos Salvadora didn't wear strange clothes, even at Halloween. In one of the snapshots at a party, Federico was dressed like Frankenstein's monster, with bolts attached to his neck. Salvadora wore a dress with an abstract pattern, her hair no different from her everyday do, her makeup the same as always. Maybe, like Luz now, Salvadora was afraid of appearing to be as absurd as her mother. Luz wondered what had caused Güela to drop off the edge.

"What's your promesa about?"

Güela stared, as if Luz were dim-witted. "I prayed you would live, of course. That you would recover and heal fully."

"But I'm still—"

"You'll be back to normal—the doctors said so."

Güela's sacrifice was to erase uncertainties her doctors had been unable to disguise. When they talked to Luz about her prognosis, they hemmed and hawed and sprinkled their reports with "maybe," "perhaps," "eventually," "if," and "hopefully." It seemed wrong to remind Güela of their vacillations when a part of her hoped Güela was right and the doctors wrong. "Thank you."

"De nada. All I did was believe my prayers would be answered." She pointed upward with the thick end of the braid. "Mi Diosito has the power. I praise Him and hope He hears me."

"One of the nurses told me He listens to you more than to other people."

"He listens to everyone." A hen ran across the path as if late for an appointment. "Do you pray?"

"Sometimes."

"When?"

"With you."

Güela nodded. "People pray when they need something. I praise Him with every breath. You should, too."

"Uhum." Luz didn't know how else to respond. Güela's Diosito was an insecure boy requiring endless compliments.

Güela stood. "I'll make your supper."

"I'll help."

"You rest. Maybe when you're more used to this . . ." The braid was unraveling. She sat again and tightened the knots on the ends. "You and I haven't spent much time together, like other abuelas and their grandchildren."

Luz looked away.

"This is our time."

"Okay." She felt Güela staring at her, expecting more than a grunt. "That sounds good."

"Bueno." She cleared her throat. "So you know, I wake up at dawn and at the end of the day, I go into my room soon after supper. You'll hear me praying for a few hours before I sleep."

"Hours?"

"People pay me to pray."

"They do?"

A little smile. "You don't know much about me. Or maybe you forgot."

"I don't know."

"You and Salvadora were friends but I wasn't her friend, I was her mother."

"Mami and I were friends?"

"She treated you like an adult, even when you were little."

"Was that bad?"

"Parents expect children to do what they're told without complaint. Salvadora wanted you to have enough information so you could make responsible decisions. It worked, and you were very close." She was quiet for a while. "I can't lie, so you'll always hear the truth from me, even if it's different from what you've heard from others."

"Thank you." Güela waited for her to say more. "I don't lie, either."

"Muy bien." She tapped Luz's knee and walked away in the peculiar, heavy-footed but graceful shuffle that would always remind Luz of an elephant.

⌐

Güela drove like she walked, deliberate but determined, unfazed by drivers who followed inches from her back bumper, blinked their headlights, honked, and, at the first opportunity, passed her, glaring, cursing, and waving vulgar gestures. She drove at thirty miles an hour on street, road, or highway, clicking the directional lights long before she had to turn, braking frequently, as if the car would take off on its own if she didn't. She pulsed the pedals, braked, accelerated, braked, accelerated, jerking to a stop when they reached their destination. She didn't know how to parallel park and struggled with backing up into tight spaces, so they arrived at Luz's therapy and medical appointments with enough time to stalk drivers about to leave a nose-in spot. Luz wasn't sure whether Güela had always driven this way, or if her grandmother was being conscientious because Luz was nervous in a car. When they stopped, she braced before the inevitable lurch into place.

In her town, Güela was a familiar figure, but miles away, people were unused to her distinctive penitent's habit. They pointed, giggled, gawked at the tall, skinny freaks, Luz encased in a metal-and-straps medical device next to doña Tamarindo pelá como un coco, with enormous ears. Luz was self-conscious being in public, but Güela was immune to humiliation.

As in the rehabilitation hospital, Luz was usually the youngest patient at the clinics. Maybe because of her age or because Güela was such a spectacle, Luz was seen ahead of those who'd been waiting. After her treatments, she was relieved to return to the parcela, far from stares and snickers. She hoped she hadn't been like those people with their appalled expressions and odious remarks. Her experience of the past few months had made her more sympathetic than the people she saw on the streets.

With no phone at Güela's, Luz had no easy way to reach anyone she knew two towns over, although she mentally drafted letters that she never set to paper. Until she moved to Güela's parcela, everyone she cared about had lived walking distance from her home or took classes at Miss Rita's dance school. No one came to see her after she moved to Güela's.

The back brace was uncomfortable, but when she didn't wear it, spasms shot from her shoulders to her hips and down to her toes, forcing her to lie down until her muscles relaxed. When she was upright, she was often unsteady and had dizzy spells. Migraines attacked her as if her head couldn't contain what was inside her skull. She begged her doctors for pain drugs, but they were reluctant to prescribe to a teenager who might abuse them. They suggested aspirin.

"You're young."

"You're strong."

"You're getting better every day."

Luz was improving, but when her body rebelled, the aches and spasms felt like setbacks, even when Güela insisted they were assaulting her less often and were not quite as debilitating as they had been.

"Maybe I'm getting used to the pain?"

"Because you can bear it." It was scant sympathy from the self-sacrificing Güela, for whom pain was a lesson in surrender.

Luz had missed most of her sophomore year. Her goal was to stop wearing the brace by the time the next school year started in August. She followed her physical therapists' and doctors' instructions, hoping that without the device she wouldn't be singled out as a weirdo. She dreaded the casual cruelty of her cohorts, having to explain why she couldn't sit for long or why she had to get up and stretch or walk around to keep her back from spasming. She hoped her stellar report cards would prove to her teachers she wasn't stupid, although that's how she felt. She wanted to do well in her classes, but after the accident her attention drifted and her memory roamed, and it took her longer to feel confident about what she'd learned.

The physical therapist suggested Luz keep a diary of her progress.

"Someday you'll read it and be proud of how far you've come."

On a trip to town, Güela took her to the stationer's, where Luz bought a calendar, pens, pencils, more sketchbooks, and notebooks. At the bookstore next door, she found a couple of Corín Tellado novels that wouldn't frustrate her. When reading, her eyes ached or she'd get a headache if she didn't take breaks. When she looked at the page again, she'd lost track of the story and had to read the same passages several times before she understood them. Luz considered not returning to school until she was back to her former self.

She wrote down what she shouldn't forget, like the words to the Puerto Rican national anthem, "La Borinqueña." She remembered the first name of the Puerto Rican Miss Universe but not her last name or the year she'd won. She recalled doña Felipa's daughters but not her sons, unsure whether there were three or four, all living in cities she'd forgotten.

Her memory lapses were dangerous. Güela taught her how to rekindle the cooking fire from embers, but once, when Luz did it, she forgot she had to tend it and set the kitchen shed aflame. Güela was able to extinguish the fire before it spread, while Luz wailed and apologized for what she'd done.

She dressed: panties, bra, shorts, T-shirt, brace, in that order, but Güela pointed out the shorts were inside out and the T-shirt back to front. She said it was because there were no mirrors in her house. Luz thought she'd done it properly. There was a disconnect between what she intended and what she did and that, more than anything, terrified her. It was as if her body were independent of her mind.

⤚

One weekend soon after Luz had moved in, Alonso stopped by with magazines, books, art supplies, batteries, and enormous square headphones that were actually a radio.

"Your dad swore by these," he said.

His eyebrows practically flew off his forehead when he saw Güela's new look. He said nothing. She greeted him and excused herself to make coffee. Luz and Alonso sat next to each other on the porch steps.

"What's that all about?" he asked.

Luz explained that Güela had made another promesa.

"She's consistent if nothing else," he said. "I've never met anyone with so much commitment to her faith."

"I don't know how my mother grew up to be a famous scientist when Güela was her example . . ."

"When you think about it, they were both rebels on opposite shores of the same river."

"What do you mean?"

"Well, your grandmother gave up a lot so she could have children, and Salvadora dedicated her life to keeping women from getting pregnant before they were ready. It's ironic." He put his arm around her above her back brace. "Are you at least getting along?"

"She's in her gardens and taking care of her animals all day. I offer to help, but she tells me to rest or she says it's too much for me. I'm not useless. I can't lift heavy things, but, I mean, she's like, what, seventy years old? She shouldn't be lifting heavy things, either! And I could—I don't know—water the plants or something."

He chuckled. "Think of this as a special time with her. Your abuela and Salvadora weren't close but they respected each other. She loves you and has been good to you, mamita."

"I don't know where to start, Abuelo. When she takes me to my appointments, I'm afraid to distract her from driving. I don't know what to say. It's like she doesn't like to talk to anyone except her Diosito." She turned to see his face. "Did you know people pay her to pray for them?"

"I brought you the radio, so you can tune out her praying."

She smiled and leaned her head on his shoulder.

"People respect and trust her," he continued. "To you, she seems peculiar, but when I was growing up, I saw men and women fulfilling vows in ways that seem extreme to us now."

"Like what Güela does?"

"Well, definitely the habit, specific colors for each saint. Some shaved their heads, or they let their hair grow long. Some made pilgrimages or rounded the plaza in front of the church on their knees. Others fasted for long periods. I once saw a man carrying a cross on his shoulders with a crown of thorns around his forehead."

"Ouch!"

"People don't do those things anymore."

"Maybe there's less to pray for now?"

"More, I think, but fewer willing to go to such lengths."

Güela came from the back. "Why don't we sit in the shade?"

They followed her to a couple of benches and a small table that held a tin of Florecitas cookies.

"Our new place should be ready in early March," Alonso said.

"Ah! She'll be happy." Güela leaned her head toward Luz.

"I'll visit you." The adults smiled as if they knew, just as she did, that that was unlikely.

Alonso changed the subject. "Pastor Josué, your godfather—do you remember him? I told you about him."

She couldn't conjure him.

"He loved your parents and calls me often to find out how you're doing. He and his people have you on their prayer list."

"That's nice."

"¡Alabanza! ¡Aleluya!" Güela shouted, and the faintest mischievous smile crossed her lips. "They're very loud, his disciples."

"Wow, Güela, you never criticize anyone."

"It's not a criticism," she said. "That's what they do, always screaming their prayers."

Luz retreated mentally as Alonso talked to Güela. He sounded far away, not right in front of her, and she couldn't understand what he was saying until she began to surface.

"The curriculum in San Juan will be more advanced than what you're used to," Alonso said. "You'll go to a private school, with a bilingual program, in addition to French as an elective. It was important to Salvadora and Federico that you should know other languages. Josué came with me when I went to talk to the principal. She's eager to meet you."

"What if I don't want to go? I'm old enough to drop out."

"No, niña. Your parents would never allow it, and neither will we." Güela nodded. "It might be hard," Alonso continued, "but you'll get as much help as you need, whether with Ada or someone else."

"Ada?"

"Ada Gil Méndez, your tutor. She's Josué's cousin."

⁓

When Luz lived with her parents in San Bernabé, she'd paid little mind to the arc of the sun across the sky or the vagaries of weather. When it was dark, she clicked a wall switch and light brightened the room. There were frequent blackouts, but Federico kept flashlights, extra batteries, and a boxful of candles and matches in a closet with other emergency supplies.

When it rained, Luz might be awakened by spattering against the cement walk or roof, but inside, the house was dry and cozy. She stepped from her air-conditioned home, through the roofed marquesina, and into the car, which blasted cold air as one of her parents drove her to climate-controlled ballet studios, classrooms, theaters, and shops. She noticed nature and its processes only when they interfered with her plans. Overcast skies and high humidity affected her hair's texture. Seasonal Saharan Dust seeped through invisible cracks in the walls, leaving a golden powdery layer on everything their housekeeper had swept and vacuumed. They rode out hurricanes with a pantry stocked with canned goods and crackers, the tubs and sinks filled with water for flushing toilets and washing up. Drinking and cooking water were stored in stoppered pitchers, clean bottles, and lidded pots. Federico tuned his battery-operated radio to keep up with the storm's progress and Salvadora and Luz dug out playing cards and board games. The hours waiting out the storm were filled with fun and laughter.

Before the car accident, visiting Güela's parcela every other week had been an obligation Luz complained about but Salvadora wouldn't allow her to skip. Federico said the parcela was an anachronism, a rural holdout circled by urbanizaciones, less than a mile from a busy highway.

Her mother and grandmother withdrew to the cooking shed a few paces from the house. Luz spread out homework on the table to take notes from textbooks and draft essays or book reports. At home, she liked to do it in the dining room next to the kitchen, where Salvadora or Federico, often side by side, rinsed, chopped, stirred, and sizzled vegetables, meat, or fish in hot oil. The house filled with humid aromas of sofrito, oregano, cumin, tomato sauce, chicken, pork, bacalao. At Güela's, if there were savory smells, they dissipated into the open air of the shed. Mostly, she ate boiled tubers with a splash of olive oil, rice with a side of beans, funche made from coarse cornmeal, and on special occasions, vegetable broths with plantain dumplings. The simple fare was bland without the pungent flavors Federico and Salvadora added to their dishes, including the hot sauce they made with spicy red peppers in vinegar left in the sun until the flavors mingled. Güela's meals would improve immeasurably with a pinch more salt, a sprinkling of pepper, snips of herbs, a few drops of Federico's pique or spoonfuls of Salvadora's ajilimójili or chimichurri.

Federico rarely joined them on those Sunday visits to Güela. He spent the day with Alonso on his motorboat. He said he was too cheerful for Güela, and as a teenager, Luz understood what he meant.

"For someone who loves God so much," she overheard him tell Salvadora, "she doesn't talk about Him and seems to get no joy from Him."

"Ne parle pas de ma mère comme ça." Salvadora didn't like it when anyone criticized Güela. If Federico and Luz started talking about her, Salvadora set her "Don't talk about my mother" expression and warned them that what they were about to say they should keep to themselves. Salvadora considered Güela beyond reproach and tiptoed around her as if not to upset her. Luz thought it was funny how her independent and opinionated mother became humble and passive around Güela, who hardly spoke her mind, never complained or gossiped. She thought Salvadora's detached relationship with Güela was the reason she was too involved in everything Luz did.

Now Luz didn't remember that Salvadora had insisted that Luz accompany her to her Sunday visits to Güela. After they cooked, they called Luz to set the table with the mismatched dishes and cutlery. Before they lifted a fork to their lips, Güela thanked God for the food and began a litany of prayers and blessings upon Salvadora, Luz, the absent Federico, and Alonso. Her voice was raspy, as if she rarely used it. Her eyes closed, her hands pressed together, she begged God to pay special care to the poor, to the dispossessed, the sick, the lost, and those who shuffled through lives with no purpose or direction. She asked blessings for her neighbors, for her animals, for her garden and orchard, and for enlightenment toward government leaders. She thanked God for having listened to her prayers, but instead of calling him Dios, she called him Diosito, a diminutive that caused Luz to imagine Him as a boy, not as the bearded Papá Dios floating among clouds in every image she'd seen. Only after the last "Amen" could they consume their food, usually cold by then. They ate in silence. Güela believed every action should be a prayer requiring concentration and focus.

Salvadora and Luz washed the dishes and put them away while Güela watered her plants and fed her animals. The visit ended with more blessings. As soon as they were out of Güela's hearing, Salvadora tuned the car radio to a salsa station and they listened to the blaring horns and clacking timbales as if awakening from an enchantment.

Three months after the accident, and no longer isolated in air-conditioned rooms, Luz heard more noise through the open windows at Güela's house. Traffic was a distant rumble in the mornings and late afternoons as people drove to and from their jobs. Roosters crowed at all hours but loudest at dawn, going silent when the coquí began their evening serenades. "Buenos días," "Adiós," and "Bendición" drifted into Güela's yard as children and parents in the urbanización beyond her fences went off to school and work. When home, the neighbors' voices were drowned out by the chirpy tones of jingles and commercials on radios and televisions. In a dusty field near Güela's parcela, a baseball connected to a bat. *Crack!* Voices called "Run!" "Get it!" "Slide!" followed by clapping, cheering, or a collective groan when the runner was tagged out.

The hours between when children returned from school and when they were called in for dinner and homework were the noisiest. For Luz, it was the saddest part of her day, hearing parents speak their children's names, even when they were scolding them to do or stop doing something else. In the recesses of her brain, Federico and Salvadora proclaimed her lineage when she was in trouble: Luz Peña Fuentes Ortíz Argoso; but it was Lucecita, Lucita, Lulu, Lululú when their love for her encompassed every mutation of her given name. The unseen parents beyond Güela's hibiscus hedges did the same. Each time she heard them, a needle pricked her heart.

According to Abuelo, her parents' housekeeper, doña Felipa, and their co-workers, most of Luz's efforts had gone into making Federico and Salvadora proud. Without them to approve or disapprove of her actions, she had no measure of her achievements or failures. Without them, she had no compass. Alonso had said she hadn't been a rebellious child or teenager. She'd loved, trusted, and admired Federico and Salvadora and had never doubted they had her best interests in mind. Federico, his father said, had loved her in four languages. She was la luz de mi vida, das Licht meines Lebens, la lumière de ma vie, the light of my life. She couldn't imagine anyone else ever saying that to her for the rest of her life.

When she was out with Güela, Luz couldn't take her eyes off parents with children. She hoped Federico and Salvadora had turned similar loving and optimistic gazes in her direction. Her dead parents still towered over every other adult. Even though her grandparents offered Luz guidance and support, their approval wasn't the same as her parents'. Their absence was in everything she did. She sought them for comfort and confirmation, only to find fleeting memories that appeared and vanished like mirages.

☙

Another adult in her life was Ada, her tutor. Luz hadn't met her yet, but had formed an impression of a serious, exacting, but kind teacher. She looked forward to the manila envelopes with the upcoming week's work and the finished worksheets Luz had sent, returned with red circles around mistakes, question marks that forced Luz to be clearer, the exclamation points indicating Ada was impressed, and the check marks of approval.

One day, Luz had just finished a worksheet Ada had sent for penmanship practice. It was the quietest hour of the afternoon, the shadows slanting east. Birds had nested, insects had crawled under leaves and into burrows, the foliage had wilted, and the ground gasped for water. It was siesta time for those who indulged, but neither Luz nor Güela was a napper.

"Time for your merienda." Güela set a tray on the table. "You didn't finish your lunch earlier." Next to the coffee, she placed two soggy, fried empanadas stuffed with onions and peppers. Her simple meals were getting more elaborate in efforts to help Luz gain the weight she'd lost.

Luz nibbled the edges of an empanada. "The coffee smells good."

Güela had no electricity, therefore no refrigeration, so coffee was served black with three spoonfuls of sugar in enameled pocillos. Luz pushed the papers, notebooks, and drawing supplies toward the other end of the table. "I'm done with the worksheet. Look at my handwriting."

Güela studied it. "Muy bien," she said a couple of times. "Excelente." She returned the page. "Your handwriting is more legible than Salvadora's."

Luz burst into tears. Güela came around the table and awkwardly patted her back, cleaned her face with the coarse fabric of her habit, and, finally, held her up, held her in, held her against her scrawny chest, squeezing her close and speaking into her ear, the words broken into distinct syllables as if she were unused to saying them.

"Está bien, niña. Of course you miss them, querida. Cálmate, amorcito."

Luz settled into whimpers and Güela backed away but kept her hands on Luz's shoulders as if to steady her.

"¿Mejor?"

"I'm sorry, Güela."

"No need to apologize."

"It's . . . that I remember things, but the memories are so random."

What she couldn't explain and frightened her most were those moments when she recalled something, reacted to it, then came back to the present, having forgotten what she'd done or why she'd been upset or scared or lonely or happy. Now she didn't know why she was standing in front of Güela, who looked as scared as she was, but Luz sensed their fear came from different sources. She remembered sliding her worksheet toward Güela, but not why she was tear-stained and snotty, her brace chafing her ribs and one of her flip-flops upside down under the table.

⌒

Luz was unable to account for the episodes or spells that flared and dimmed without warning. Güela told her she'd seen epileptics thrashing and flailing, their eyes rolling into their skulls. Luz didn't have those kinds of fits.

"In your achaques, you disappear without leaving," she said. "You often cry or have a tantrum, but most times you look like you're thinking about something. You get really still, like you're trying to solve a puzzle."

When Luz told the doctors, they nodded, or looked into the space above her head as if the answer would pop from her skull.

"Traumatic brain injuries are specific to the individual, blah, blah, blah. Patience and time, blah, blah, blah."

She wanted to be cured. She wanted to feel normal. She wanted to return to the day before Kyryl Kyryl came to the studio. On her last visit to Luz at the hospital, doña Felipa had told her she'd heard that Mr. Kyryl was un criticón, who had humiliated her during the class.

"Your classmates blame Rita and that man for what happened

that day," she said. "Their parents were upset because Rita let him mistreat you. They don't trust her to defend their children in similar situations. I'm not the type to wish anyone ill, pero a cada santo le llega su día. Most of the parents pulled their kids from her dance school after what happened to you. She's had to close it."

Luz had forgotten so much, but sometimes she flashed on a man strutting between dancers, poking sweaty spots between shoulder blades, tapping rib cages, and lifting chins. Mister Kyryl had grown in her imagination, and she'd shrunk.

Her mind was a quilt with frayed edges and split seams. She lay in bed in Güela's house, listening to the contrast between the mysterious flutters, croaks, and whimpers beyond the windows and the human sounds outside the parcela's boundaries. She felt suspended between what had been familiar and the foreign land that was Güela's four acres. It worried her she was getting used to being there, isolated in another, slower time that encouraged reflection. Before the accident, Luz had been too busy to spend hours in bed, contemplating what else was required from a then popular and accomplished teenager.

Now, in the dark hours after she and Güela retired for the night, she followed threads of memories picked up mid-seam, seeking to mend the holes. She wrote in her journal, unsure whether the entry was a memory or a story she'd told herself to help her sleep. It didn't seem fair that the much-older Güela was sharp-minded, while, at sixteen, Luz couldn't hold on to a memory of what she'd had for breakfast.

Güela could fill some gaps, at least about Salvadora. The problem was finding a chance to ask her questions. Her grandmother's day was filled with activity and her evenings with prayer, as though she wanted to avoid spending time with Luz. At dawn, she was already harvesting produce for her farm stand at the gate to her property. Her clients came early, and other than what was in the crates she packed into her car for restaurants and bodegas,

Güela had sold everything by midmorning, including eggs and live chickens. Luz accompanied her on her deliveries but stayed in the car. They returned home in time for lunch. From what Luz could see, Güela rarely sat except when she was driving or when they had their flavorless meals.

"Can I help you?"

"No need. Your job is to heal."

"I know, Güela, but there must be something I can do. You do so much for me."

She pestered her until Güela asked her to fold clothes and bed linens still warm from the line and to light the kerosene lamps at dusk.

One morning, she called Luz outside.

"You can help water the plants. The hose doesn't reach every corner, so I'll use the bucket." She grabbed a dented can with a long spout she wouldn't allow Luz to carry because of the weight.

They worked at opposite ends of the property, each focused on her chores. Luz inhaled the earthy smell that at first was unpleasant, but beneath the tones of rot and decay, a sweetness lingered that she found intoxicating. She smiled at how leaves and flowers shimmered as the droplets of water reached them. Güela taught her to press her thumb at the end of the hose, so instead of a stream, the water fanned out as a spray. When Luz turned her wrist slightly, she was delighted by rainbows arcing over the thirsty plants. Later, she and Güela had dinner indoors, as usual, in silence. Boiled yuca, mashed plantain, or plain rice and beans with a suggestion of sofrito. Sometimes a memory flickered of more piquant meals with her parents, or her friends' families, who imbued every morsel with love.

At dusk, Luz closed the windows and lit the mosquito coils while Güela washed and put away the dishes until morning.

Güela began praying right after dinner, while Luz squinted into a paperback by the tremulous light of a kerosene lamp.

Possibly Güela heard Luz tossing in bed, or noticed light filtering through the wall slats. She realized Luz was unused to going to bed with the chickens. Or maybe she heard Luz crying or sighing on the other side of the half wall that divided them.

"Let's sit outside for a while," she said one evening. Luz followed her to the porch and pressed her back against the outside planks for support behind the creaky bench. It had rained earlier, and the air was thick, although the sky was clear. Luz studied the moon, and a word came to mind: *hemisphere*.

"I want to be better company for you," Güela said, interrupting her thoughts.

Luz emerged as from a dream. "Thank you, Güela."

"I'm unused to conversation. I need practice. What's on your mind?"

"Uhm . . . Ada sent me math worksheets. I'm learning to measure circles, triangles, and rectangles."

"A squared plus B squared equals C squared."

"Pythagoras?"

"Muy bien."

Luz grinned. "My head fills with words I can't use."

"Like what?"

"Umm . . . 'rhombus,' 'cosines.' I don't know what they are but I know they exist."

Güela chuckled. "When I was a teacher, the students dropped out as soon as the math became complicated."

"You were a teacher?"

"A long time ago."

Luz tried to envision Güela in a classroom, her habit, rope belt, and shaved head. "What kind of school?"

"One room in a barrio in San Germán before Salvadora was born."

It made more sense. There was a time when Güela wasn't Güela. "What was Mami like? As a girl, I mean."

"Always cheerful, singing when she wasn't talking. She needed three languages for all the things she had to say."

She fell silent, or so it seemed to Luz, but after a while, she heard a low hum.

"I'm keeping you from your prayers."

"Everything I do is a prayer. Mi Diosito gave me life so I can celebrate him with every breath."

"Hmmm."

Güela chuckled again. "That's what Salvadora said when I talked about God. 'Hmmm.'"

"I didn't mean—"

"I embarrassed her. She never accepted that seeming ridiculous is part of my penance."

Luz thought for a moment. "Abuelo said you made a vow so Mami would be born healthy. That's different from a penance for a sin, isn't it?"

Güela sighed. "You're too smart." She said nothing else for a while. In the distance, a car horn sounded: *da-da-da-dum, da-da-da-dum.* The melody from Beethoven's Fifth Symphony had become a popular disco tune, played at least once an hour on the radio.

"That's what Salvadora told everyone. She found romance where there was none."

"You didn't make a vow?"

"She made up stories to explain me."

"Do you mean your promesa wasn't about a baby?"

"The vow and the penance are the same thing."

"I can't solve riddles, Güela."

"I'll tell you when you're older."

"You said you'd answer my questions."

"I hoped you'd forget I said that." She shifted on her bench, making it creak. "You're so much like your mother."

"I am?"

"She became a scientist because she needed concrete answers. But faith doesn't expect or require proof."

A screech in the darkness startled Luz. "What's that?"

"Múcaro," Güela said. "There used to be more but they died off when the urbanizaciones came."

"Their call is so creepy." The owl purred and shrieked again before flapping away. As if the owl had closed a door, the hubbub from the urbanización drowned out the natural world. Plangent flutes and strings echoed from house to house as a popular tele-novela began.

"Güela, you said the promesa and the penance are the same thing."

"Again, I hoped you'd forgotten."

Luz giggled. She was beginning to get Güela's humor. "You can tell me all your secrets. They'll be gone by tomorrow." She intended it to be a joke, but Güela didn't laugh.

"It's a sad story."

"I'm sorry."

"Not your fault. You're sure you want to hear it now?"

"Yes."

Güela sighed. She took another breath and exhaled, as if measuring its length. When she next spoke, her voice sounded distant. "I was thirteen years old when I first got pregnant."

Luz gasped. "Too young!"

"Sí. I was innocent, easy to trick into doing what I shouldn't."

"Who was he?"

"He came with his family for the coffee harvest. After they left, I realized I was going to have a baby."

"He took advantage of you."

"Claro que sí, and I was afraid to tell anyone, least of all my parents. We were Catholic. I'd sinned and disgraced myself and them."

"You were a kid."

Las Madres

"Old enough to know better."

"Your parents—"

"Never knew."

"You lost the baby before you told them?"

It was too dark to see her clearly. Güela sat immobile, her hands on her thighs, her oiled pate catching what little light reached them. She lowered her head as if it were too heavy. "I'd overheard a neighbor about a doña who could make pregnancies disappear."

The air was still, and Luz thought she was in a fairy tale. If she moved or spoke, the spell would be broken.

"A couple of women in our barrio had potions and rituals if you wanted a baby or if you wanted to avoid one. It was a sin to associate with them because they practiced magic. I was desperate but didn't want to go to them in case someone would see me. So I walked to town to find doña Patty. I expected to find a bruja in a shack," Güela continued. "I was scared, imagining shaking maracas and boiling potions in a caldero on her fogón. But she was a gringa in a pretty house. I'd never met one or been where rich people lived."

"In San Germán?"

"Not far from the plaza. Behind her house was a small room with cement walls and a tiled floor. I'd never seen those, either. Inside everything was white. Another woman helped her. Doña Patty had an accent but spoke slowly and kept asking, '¿Entiendes?' I understood. I was too young to have a child."

"Was she a doctor or nurse?"

"I don't know. She gave me a muddy liquid in a coconut cup. She told me to drink it cul-cul, so I did. It was sweet at first, but after I drank it, it tasted bitter and my throat felt swollen. She said to lie on a pallet in the middle of the room. I was drowsy, but felt her and the other woman lifting my legs and poking down there, and a pinch, and cramps. They sounded far away but one held my hand and cooled my forehead with a damp cloth. Doña Patty said I should rest, and the other woman gave me orange juice. It was my first time to drink from a glass. I was bleeding and they gave me rags. The gringa said the baby was gone. I lay there until I could walk home. A farmer returning from market gave me a lift on his cart. I was back before my parents wondered where I'd been."

"So you had an abortion?" She didn't know why she whispered. For the second time in less than fifteen minutes she was reminded that Güela hadn't always been this bald woman sitting next to her on a bench.

"Sí."

In the foliage, the owl purred and screeched again. Luz rubbed her goose bumps. It sounded like a baby's cry.

"I pray for my lost child," Güela said, "and the others who came after. The next six I carried for nine months, and at the end, every one was born dead."

"So sad."

"God's will."

"Maybe doña Patty did something to your insides?"

"There was nothing wrong with me. My punishment was to carry a baby for nine months but have no child to show for it."

"Until you had Mami."

She'd had enough. "Salvadora told me you were mature, and she didn't keep things from you if you asked."

"I'm glad she said that."

"She said her job was to guide you so you could trust your choices. That's what being a parent means now." She sighed deeply again, as if avoiding crying. "She struggled with how to answer your questions. She wanted to be honest without giving you more information than you needed."

Luz heard a voice say, "It's all about timing," and was surprised when the words came from her own mouth.

"I suppose," Güela said. "Life is harder for people without faith."

"What do you mean?"

"All your questions . . . they're answered in the Bible."

"Hmmm," Luz said. She couldn't contradict Güela out of respect and because, as far as she knew, she'd never read the Bible.

Güela stood. "Let's go in now."

"Thank you for telling me your story."

"Maybe there's a lesson for you in it."

"Take birth-control pills?"

"That's against our religion."

"But Mami's job was to make them."

"The worst arguments we ever had were about that. We could never budge from our beliefs. I've never prayed for anyone as much until your situation."

"I hope she's not in . . . you know . . ."

Güela inhaled and let the air out in a long, low sigh. "Salvadora made a choice. She believed women had the right to decide when or whether to have children. I couldn't agree. Women have to suffer for Eve's sin. That's what the Bible says."

"But men wrote it, Güela, didn't they?"

Güela thought about it. "I won't argue about God with you. You know so little about Him. But Salvadora often said another woman's story is always a lesson for the rest. If she was right"— she slapped a mosquito away—"I have a lifetime of lessons for you."

⌒

In her room before Güela's prayers lulled her to sleep, Luz set down in her journal as much as she remembered of their conversation. As she wrote, she had a flash of Salvadora and Federico reading fairy tales about princesses and princes, white horses, warty witches, goblins, and magic mirrors. The stories were scary, and even though good deeds and magic attenuated the horror, Luz was glad the events took place far away and at a time when women wore long dresses and tall, pointy hats with floating veils.

After that night, Güela went from silent to garrulous.

"You've probably heard this one . . ." she'd start, and tell a story that Luz didn't remember and was glad to hear. As Güela filled gaps, Luz found herself recalling moments, echoes of conversations, images of her parents together and individually. She didn't trust they were memories and asked herself whether she was making them up because she wanted to have a history.

At the end of the day, they sat side by side on the splintery benches.

"I've never been to the sea," Güela said in the same monotone she used to voice her prayers.

"But Puerto Rico is an island."

"I've always lived in the valleys between mountains."

"You can drive there."

"I can," she said, "but I haven't done it."

"Have I seen the sea?"

"Salvadora and Federico loved it. He taught her how to swim and they often took you to the beach."

Güela always thanked Luz for listening, even when she talked about Luz and her parents more than her own history. Luz wondered whether Güela missed having someone to talk to.

"No one listens to old people anymore," Güela said one night. "When I was a girl, after our chores, we sat with our parents, abuelas, or tíos, who told stories. The older they were, the more respect they received. And we never called them 'tú.' It was always 'usted' this, 'usted' that."

"I'm sorry, Güela." Maybe her feeling about not being acceptable to her grandmother came from her use of the familiar pronoun. "I'll use 'usted.'"

"No, no. Don't change on my behalf."

"Did I say 'usted' before?"

"No. Your parents were very modern." Güela rarely expressed

emotion, but Luz was getting used to the undertones. Modern equaled not good.

If she wanted to avoid a topic, Güela promised to talk about it another time, hoping Luz would forget. To make sure she didn't, Luz kept a list she consulted before their talks.

"Abuelo said Mami was proud of her work with birth control. Was it because of your babies?"

"If she cared about them, she'd be making drugs for women to have healthy ones."

Luz shuddered, lost in the antes. When her mother was angry, she spoke in a cold, clipped tone Luz found chilling, like Güela's now.

A film hung between the urbanizaciones and the purple sky. Luz thought it was fog coming in, but realized it was ambient light from streetlamps and electrified rooms.

"Maybe Salvadora wanted to save women from babies when they were too young or poor to take care of them." Güela's tone changed again. "When she was a girl, she dreamed of being a doctor, but then . . ." She shifted on her bench. It was a moment Luz would experience often in her life, the sense that she knew more than she had any reason to know. When it happened, she assumed it was a buried memory resurfacing. But she didn't think Salvadora would have volunteered she'd had an abortion. Luz knew that was where Güela's story was going.

"Did Mami have an abortion, too?"

"Ay, nena." Güela sounded exhausted, as if she'd been carrying a weight that had suddenly become lighter.

"It's okay. It's not a surprise, somehow."

"Salvadora always said she was an open book."

"When did it happen?"

"Before she left for Michigan."

"Before I was born?"

"Sí."

"Was it my father's?"

"No, it was before they met."

"Who got her pregnant?"

"Hmph, who else? That depraved Pastor Josué, that's who."

"What? He was her novio?"

"They were in college in Río Piedras. He was a real Juan Tenorio, a rich, handsome boy, who even then could persuade others with his voice and pretty words. He was a picaflor for whom girls were nectar. Salvadora had never had a boyfriend, and was easily seduced by his flattery, confusing it for intentions. When she told him she was pregnant, he drove her to his cousin's clinic, a doctor, who did it. Then he dumped her. The man has no morals. Always talking about the devil, but he . . . Hmph! When she left for graduate school in Ann Arbor, he went sniffing around her a year later. By then, Salvadora was living with Federico, but he tried to snake into her life. Good thing by then she could tell the difference between a good man and a bad one."

◦⟶

That night, as Güela's prayers floated over the wall, Luz consulted pages in her journal. Her handwriting was improving. Her notes tended to be snippets of conversations and lists. "Josué, my godfather," she'd noted. On another page, "Good friend to our family, esp. since tragedy."

By the time she got to her journal, other things Alonso had said were beyond her recall, like his assertion that, in order to get ahead in Puerto Rico, one needed a godfather like Josué, someone con pala, who knew how the system worked and how to use it to one's advantage.

She did include that Alonso was grateful for Josué:

—connected to best doctors and specialists
—introduced Abuelo to director of my new school
—Ada, my tutor, Josué's cousin
—Josué, a godsend

Luz wondered whether Federico knew about Josué's romantic relationship with Salvadora before he came into her life. Maybe Salvadora and Josué were too young and later realized they were better as friends than they'd been as lovers. It was possible the experience with the abortion inspired Salvadora's dedication to women's health and reproductive rights. Luz had no way of knowing, and she didn't want to read more into it than that.

⁓

Alonso came to see her a few times, always rushed and antsy to get back to the city. It was late February, a fraught time for an accountant, he said. His clients who earned income outside the island were required to file federal taxes but waited until the last few weeks before the returns were due. As the date neared, Alonso looked more frazzled and tense than usual.

Ada kept Alonso up to date on Luz's progress and Luz was eager by now to meet her in person.

"Is she your girlfriend?"

Alonso stammered as if the idea terrified him. "No. She's close to your age. She's between jobs and I need help. She's packing my belongings from the condo and coordinating the move to our new place. She suggested you'll want to decorate your own room, so she'll take you shopping and be like a big sister."

"Will she live with us?"

"She lives around the corner. I'll pick you up on Ash Wednesday."

He didn't have to explain further. Güela had already told her she'd be particularly busy during Lent. She'd asked Luz whether she'd like to come with her to Mass and other religious observances but didn't force her or grimace if she said no. Luz had accompanied her a few times, but it was physically uncomfortable. She felt conspicuous with her brace but couldn't keep it off for the duration of Mass.

Her chats with Güela were now briefer because leading up to

Ash Wednesday, her prayer list had swelled. From the other side of the wall, Luz heard a hum more than a voice, a soothing monotone that caused her to slow her breathing and sleep, to awaken at dawn with Güela's quiet movements and birdsong outside the windows.

Luz was making progress toward weaning herself from the brace by the time she returned to school in early August. With the doctor's permission, she had even done some gentle stretches, using the windowsill or back of a chair as a barre. She was beginning to feel more confident, more in control of her body, but her distancing episodes still plagued her.

The day before Alonso was to pick her up, Güela brought Luz her afternoon snack, fried sweet cornmeal patties and a pocillo of fresh coffee. Usually, she left the merienda at the table where Luz was doing her homework and continued with her chores outside, but on this day she sat across from Luz.

"You know you can come back if things don't work out in San Juan," she said.

"I know, Güela. I'll visit when I can get a ride."

"Bueno." She didn't move from her spot opposite Luz. Her breathing was uneven.

"Are you okay?"

"Yes. I'm glad we had some time together."

"Me, too, Güela."

Güela picked a crumb from the table. "Forgive me. It was wrong to tell you about my sin during our first conversation."

"What sin?"

Güela was silent, but seemed so sad, Luz tried to recall what she was talking about; she had forgotten she'd written a note about that conversation in her journal. In this moment, nothing came to mind, just the vague sense Güela had had a secret. Maybe Güela expected Luz to share hers, but she had none. Alonso had assured Luz she'd been a good girl who'd managed to avoid pitfalls that changed lives. He wasn't specific, but she intuited what he was talking about. As far as she knew, she was a virgin. Surely, she'd had crushes that amounted to nothing more than longings. What was his name? The boy in one of her classes. He had great hair. He was the son of Salvadora's colleague. Sukanya? Beautiful name. What was his?

"Come back," Güela said.

Luz rubbed her temples. "I didn't realize."

"I'll remind Alonso about those achaques. You shouldn't be alone until you don't get them anymore."

"I think Ada will be a companion as well as my teacher. Sort of a hired sister . . ."

"Alonso is good at solving problems."

"He's lined up an army of specialists in San Juan."

"And I will continue to pray for you to heal fully and to have the kind of life Salvadora and Federico wanted for you."

Luz reached out and surprised them both by taking her grandmother's hands. They were large, dry, and warm, wrinkled and bony, long-fingered, with surprisingly shapely nails. Luz wanted to kiss them but didn't.

⌒

The day Luz left, Güela stood by her gate, waving at the retreating car. Luz couldn't turn around due to her brace, but watched her through the side-view mirror. From a distance, Güela did look like a tamarindo, her bald head as shiny as a helmet.

Over the next couple of months, her time with Güela faded as completely as a dream, leaving behind mere snips, scraps, flashes, and feelings she couldn't link to specific events or people. From time to time, Luz said or did something she was sure was a thread from a more complex fabric, but she was unable to connect it to the larger pattern.

Luz Peña Fuentes couldn't have known that within a year,

Güela and Alonso would be gone from her life, and there would be no one left to remind her of who she had been. Suspended in her story, Luz had little to hold on to from the past and no solid ground on which to place her feet in the future.

Ada Madrina

Had Marysol's grandparents survived the car wreck that altered her mother's life, Abuela Salvadora would have turned eighty-three years old on July 18, 2017, and Abuelo Federico would have celebrated his eighty-seventh birthday on the same day. Marysol was born six years after their deaths but observes the sad anniversary with a flame and a prayer. At six in the morning, she lights a candle next to the portraits Luz painted. The public relations department of the company where Salvadora and Federico worked provided snapshots to the media after the accident in 1975, and Graciela found them online. Because the photographs weren't in color, the portraits Luz created are in black, white, and tones of gray.

Marysol looks out her bedroom window. Luz is watering her fenced-in garden. She sings under her breath and moves her hands like a conductor at a symphony, seeking rainbows with the hose spray, childlike and delighted when she finds them.

Marysol does her morning exercises, meditates for a half hour, showers, puts on her scrubs, sets her nurse's clogs and purse by the front door. Living with Luz and her disabilities has made Marysol build habits and routines that make life easier for them both.

At eight she walks across the shared foyer of the house they've lived in since Marysol was twelve years old. A married couple, both nurses, paid a reduced rent in exchange for taking care of Luz while Marysol was in school and, later, working in a hospital down the street. After the tenants retired and moved back to Puerto Rico, Marysol took their apartment and for the first time, at twenty-five, had her own place, even if just across the hall from her mother's. Warren helped her modernize and paint the apartment. It was he who cleared and planted the backyard into a lush, fruitful garden. He also helped Marysol convert her old bedroom into a studio for Luz.

Because of her condition, everything Luz needs is within sight; otherwise, she doesn't know it exists. There are no cabinets or drawers anywhere in her apartment. The walls are lined with shelves and open cubbies, each labeled with the items that should be placed on or in them to make them easier to organize, put away, and find later.

"¡Buenos días!" Marysol calls out. Luz has already made coffee and clicks on the toaster for their bread. Marysol administers her medications.

"Angie will pick you up at Mi Casa and walk you to ballet later today." Marysol points to the giant calendar on the refrigerator. Shirley, Warren, Luz, and Marysol jointly own the six-apartment building on the other side of the driveway. Angie, one of the tenants, gets a reduced rent and accompanies Luz on a schedule. That way Marysol can work, get time to herself, and hang out with Warren.

"I defrosted the chuletas," Luz says.

"Yum!"

Luz loves to cook, a skill unaffected by her memory issues. She can also draw, sketch, paint, keep an orderly home, bathe, dress herself, do her own laundry, and read in four languages although she almost immediately forgets what she's just read. She watches the news, nature and animal documentaries, cooking and baking competitions, as well as the Yankees and the Mets without irony. Her sense of humor is minimal. Being funny requires context she can't access, although she'll surprise everyone with a clever remark or unintended pun.

While Luz fries eggs and bacon for their breakfast, Marysol peeks into the studio, which displays Luz's work in various stages of completion. If the rock is textured or contoured, Luz integrates the subject's features into the stone. She's so accomplished, she's been exhibited at the National Museum of Puerto Rican Arts and Culture in Chicago and gets commissions through the website Graciela designed and manages. She's been featured in a couple of magazines—again, through Graciela's efforts.

A family in Wisconsin commissioned Luz to paint their German shepherd.

"Wow, Mom, this is so good. You've never done an animal."

"You like it?"

"It looks almost real." The dog's eyes are bright and intelligent and the perky ears and gentle expression beg you to stroke it. In the years Luz has been doing this, not a single customer has complained or returned the work. On the contrary, they send flowers, expensive chocolates, and flattering cards and letters. Her collectors post about her on social media (#luzpeñarocks or @luzpeñarocks), again managed by Graciela, claiming Luz is a "rock star, pun intended."

Marysol and Luz have breakfast together almost every morning, usually eggs in the summer, oatmeal or cheesy funche—Puerto Rican polenta—in winter. Luz doesn't follow recipes, doesn't measure ingredients, and in spite of memory issues, senses when something should be taken out of the oven.

"I know it's done when it smells done," she says.

Marysol doesn't know when or where Luz learned to cook. Ada said she and Shirley taught her. Danilo, Marysol's father, learned from his grandmother and he might have also taught Luz. Marysol has tried to teach her things, too, like yoga, meditation, knitting, and needlepoint, all things Marysol herself enjoys. Her lessons don't seem to stick.

After breakfast, Marysol walks Luz to Mi Casa, where she's a client, like the people she cares for there. Neither Marysol nor the staff disabuse Luz of her assumption that she's on the staff. She walks with a nearly imperceptible limp but otherwise displays no symptoms of physical trauma and is, as her doctors say, high-functioning.

Upon first meeting Luz, people question why she's considered disabled but once they spend time with her, they get it. The side effects of medications to control the damage caused by her brain injury and strokes have altered her behavior in other ways. She can't access or contextualize people and experiences without constant repetition. People have to introduce themselves many times before she begins to recognize them. The same thing with events. If something happens once, it's unlikely she'll be able to recall it later.

She has no sense of selfhood. She is who others say she is. With no long-term memories and short-term lapses, she is reborn every day. There's an advantage to that. She's been more traumatized than anyone knows, but she doesn't remember what happened.

To Marysol, her mother is a barrel of contradictions and eccentricities. She speaks the four languages she learned as a child from her parents, but can't distinguish one from another unless she's asked to translate what she's just said. Marysol grew up speaking English and Spanish, and as soon as she could choose another language in school, she studied French. She's far from fluent but able to get much of what Luz says. When Luz gets too emotional or frustrated to translate her German, Marysol relies on apps to do it.

According to Ada and Shirley, who've known Luz since she was a teenager, she was a ballerina, and she still takes adult ballet classes at the Boys & Girls Club, but she can't be left alone. If she manages to slip away or is separated from the people who care for her, she freaks out. At home, Marysol installed an alarm system on the doors and windows that signals a breach if Luz tries to leave unaccompanied. She's grateful for the tracking app Graciela downloaded on Luz's cell phone and smart watch that makes it possible to locate her if she strays. Her devices are her lifeline, and Luz has learned to wear her watch and carry her phone in a pocket at all times.

Luz suffers from disassociation episodes, her "achaques." She appears to relive experiences, which she can't remember once the achaques end. Recently, better pharmaceuticals have controlled the violence that for years injured Luz and terrified Marysol. Some of Marysol's earliest memories are of her own helplessness as Luz banged against walls, seemingly defending herself from attackers. Or of begging Luz to stop as she yanked out clumps of her own hair, leaving bald, bleeding patches and dropping woolly puffs on the floor. Her close-cropped Afro looks like a fashion statement but it's a necessity. She doesn't have much to grab on to if, during an achaque, she tries to pull out her hair again.

When Marysol's father, Danilo, fell in love with Luz, his mother warned him, "She's too damaged and too needy."

Marysol knew that her father's family had discouraged him from marrying Luz and used euphemisms to point out the obvious. In addition to her "problems" and "issues," she was "muy trigueña"—too dark for a family who valued their light-skinned members. They didn't refer to her by name; they called her "esa morena."

Besides Luz, the only constant adults in Marysol's life have been Ada and Shirley and, later, Graciela and Warren. Ada and Shirley are her godmothers, and while they don't share her DNA, Marysol considers them her only living family, her mother's beloved comadres, and their daughter, Graciela, an annoying but well-meaning older godsister. Luz and Danilo were Graciela's godparents and she still calls Luz "madrina," although Marysol calls Shirley and Ada by their first names.

Luz and Marysol live comfortably from income Shirley has managed since 1976, when she was named the administrator of the trust Luz's grandfather set up soon after the car wreck that killed Luz's parents. The payouts from Federico's, Salvadora's, Alonso's, and Danilo's veterans' benefits, life insurances, and estates have been well invested, including in their home in the Bronx and the rental property next door. When Marysol was old enough, Shirley made sure she was familiar with their portfolio and had access to all the accounts. Marysol trusts Shirley's advice and integrity and feels lucky she and Ada took care of and protected Luz years before she met Danilo. They're the only people who can tell Marysol what Luz was like before she was born. They assure her she'd met them many times, but Marysol's first memory of her two godmothers is on the days following her father's death.

"Yo soy Ada, tu madrina."

"Hada madrina?"

A few days before he died, Danilo told Marysol a story in Spanish about an hada madrina he said was like the English-speaking fairy godmothers in her books. During those traumatic days, Marysol elevated Ada, a high school teacher, into a magical creature who swooped into her life when she most needed sortilegio.

With Luz in the hospital after Danilo's death, Ada provided legal, notarized documents to Children's Services that proved she and Shirley were Marysol's godmothers and co-guardians, alongside Pastor Josué, lawfully permitted to care for her while Luz convalesced. Ada took Marysol to see Luz at the hospital and convinced her she'd be okay.

"Your mommy needs to rest here for a while."

Marysol trusted Ada Madrina's assurances. A few days later Madrina Shirley and Prima Graciela arrived in the Bronx to drive Marysol to their house in Maine, while Ada took care of Luz in the Bronx. She has no memory of the car ride. It's the job of fairy godmothers to make the most unpleasant things magically disappear.

Marysol has never forgotten her first sight of their gingerbread Victorian house, nestled in a forest. It was the perfect home for fairy godmothers, with turrets and floor-to-ceiling etched glass doors leading to a wraparound porch. The outside walls were sunflower yellow, the lacy eaves turquoise. The porch ceiling and walls were cobalt. On opposite sides of a wide hallway with plush carpets were two parlors with fireplaces. Curvy balusters on dark-wood stairs led to the second floor, and a steeper staircase led to the third. There were nooks, carved doors, and secret chambers, and, at the very top of spiral steps, a small room with a bird's-eye view of the woods, the village, and the sea. Marysol had her own bedroom across from ten-year-old Graciela's. She could have been frightened of the creaky house, but she felt safe, cocooned in the clearing that was surrounded by whispering spruce, pine, oaks, and flowering catalpas.

Madrina Shirley, Ada Madrina, and Prima Graciela became the most important people in Marysol's life other than her mother. But on this day, July 26, 2017, a little more than a week after her grandparents' birthdays, she lights another candle and says another prayer, wondering whether she'll ever tell her godmothers and godsister what she saw that steamy night exactly thirty years before, when she was five years old.

It could not have taken long, but those minutes are embedded, details that disrupt her sleep as nightmares and fragments of terror. It's her only secret, carried for three decades, an encumbrance no one can move, lift, or erase. No one, not even the psychologists she saw for years nor Warren, has heard her talk about it. It's her personal millstone, her albatross, a ghost that reminds her the world is dangerous and control is futile.

On that hot July night, Marysol awoke from a nightmare about a toothy creature chasing her down a street. She called for Mommy and Daddy but there was no answer. They weren't in their room. In the living room, the gray-haired man who told the news in Spanish was frowning. When the TV was on mute at night, Mommy was helping Daddy close the bodega on the ground floor. Marysol was still scared, so she went to look for them, but she wasn't supposed to run up or down the stairs, especially at night, so she tiptoed. The door from the hallway to the storeroom was unlocked. The ceiling lights buzzed and hissed. She was about to call Mommy when she heard voices. She wasn't supposed to interrupt Mommy and Daddy when they were helping customers. She waited behind a stack of boxes next to the metal shelves where they kept extra canned beans, sacks of rice, tomato sauce. The voices in the bodega sounded unfriendly but she wanted Mommy and Daddy. She peered between the shelves and saw Mommy kneeling in front of the candy display. A man wearing a cap and a bandanna around his nose had her ponytail wrapped around one hand, and in the other, a gun pressed to her head.

Behind the counter, Daddy pulled dollars from the cash register and shoved them toward another man.

He raised his arms. "We want no trouble."

The man waggled his gun at him, but Marysol couldn't make out what he said because he was wearing a mask. "Only change here, nothing else," Daddy said. He dipped his head toward the register and kept looking from the man in front of him to the one holding Mommy. "Let my wife go. I gave you everything."

The man said something and came around the counter. Daddy lifted the cash drawer. "See? It's empty."

Mommy whimpered. "Please, don't hurt us. Please!"

The man kicked her, and she fell sideways with a scream. When the masked man turned away from him, Daddy grabbed the bat he kept behind the counter. That's when he caught sight of Marysol by the shelves in the back room. His eyes opened big and he was about to say something but there was a loud pop and he fell back, his shirt blooming red. Another pop, and he slid out of sight.

Mommy shrieked and there was another pop and she jerked and lay still. As the men ran out, the bandanna slipped from the face of the one who'd kicked Mommy. Nacho from upstairs? He looked toward the back and Marysol hid behind the shelves.

"Outta here!" the other man yelled. The bell over the door jingled.

Wet trickled down her legs. Mommy was going to be mad. She shouldn't pee her pants, and in an emergency, she should dial 9-1-1. This was an emergency. She ran upstairs and locked the apartment door so the men couldn't get inside. By the glow of the night-light, she rummaged around her dresser for clean panties and pajamas.

She changed and rinsed the soiled pants and panties in the sink, draped them over the tub to dry like Mommy had taught her. She had to call 9-1-1 and tell them a man kicked Mommy. A man who looked like Nacho who lived upstairs with his mother, Vivian, and his father, Eros. As she left the bathroom, she saw the flashing red-and-blue lights dancing against the living room walls. She peeked out the window. A police car pulled up in front of the bodega. She had to tell them that Nacho kicked Mommy. But if she told the cops, was that tattling? She wasn't to repeat what happened at home because chisme was a bad habit. Mommy said, "I've told you a hundred times. Don't be talking about me and your daddy to other people."

On the street, more police cars double-parked and an ambulance stopped in front of the building, and the doors burst open. Neighbors leaned over windowsills or sat on fire escapes. Police-car radios chattered and beeped. Cops went in and out of the bodega. People huddled on the pavement, among them, Nacho, without the bandanna or the baseball cap, and he was naked from the waist up. Maybe she was wrong; maybe the man in the bodega who looked like Nacho was somebody else. He saw her at the window, and she ducked like when playing hide-and-seek. In a little while, she sneaked a look. Nacho was staring at the window. For one frightening moment, their eyes met, and she was sure he was the man who kicked Mommy. He backed from the crowd in front of the bodega, never taking his eyes from the window. He'd hurt Mommy and was going to get his friend and their guns. Marysol wanted to hide but couldn't move.

Voices below, praying and keening, calling to Jesús and the Virgin, and "Ay, bendito, that poor child," and the screech and blare of car radios and walkie-talkies. Marysol covered her ears but could still hear them.

Someone knocked and rattled the doorknob.

"Wake up, Marysol. Let me in, baby!" It was Nacho's mother. *Thump, thump, thump.* "It's Vivian, mi amor. Open up, mamita."

Her throat was closed, and her feet were stuck to the floor. Vivian pounded and people stomped up and down the stairs. They shouldn't do that.

"Open the door!"

Marysol couldn't move, couldn't speak. She didn't know what to do.

Nacho crawled in through the fire escape window and reached her in two steps. He grabbed her shoulders. "You was sleeping, right?" He squeezed her shoulders harder. There was only one answer. Marysol nodded.

"You wasn't down there just now?" It was a question and a threat. She shouldn't lie. His eyes looked deep inside her, and his fingers dug hard into her arms.

"Did you get in, Nacho?" Vivian called from the hall.

So much banging and sirens and yelling. She wanted to run, to scream, but the scared Marysol was trapped inside her.

"You didn't see nothing." Nacho squeezed and shook her until her neck hurt. "You get that? You was sleeping." She was sure he'd break her.

She nodded. She was sleeping. She wanted to sleep now.

He let her go and unlocked the door. Vivian rushed in, followed by a policewoman. Marysol closed her eyes so she could disappear, but it didn't work.

"Gracias a Dios, you're safe." Vivian hugged her.

Marysol wriggled from Vivian and ran to the hallway. "I want my daddy!"

"No, baby, don't go down there," the policewoman said.

"Don't let her see them!" Vivian yelled.

Nacho caught her on the run and carried her to Vivian, even as she punched and kicked him.

"You stay here," he said. But she wouldn't. She screamed and scratched his face. "Mommy! Daddy!"

Nacho carried her to Vivian, who held her tightly and didn't let her go as she squirmed and cried and called for her parents.

"Come on, baby. You come with me." The policewoman took her in her arms and told Vivian and Nacho she'd take it from there. She held on to Marysol until one of the church ladies who visited her parents took her to her apartment down the street and sang her lullabies until she fell asleep. The next afternoon, Ada picked her up and returned her to the apartment. Her kindergarten teacher was there, and other women from the neighborhood had brought food and stuffed animals. A couple of days later, Marysol overheard them say that Vivian, Eros, and Nacho had moved, claiming the neighborhood was no longer safe.

No one wondered why the apartment had been locked from the inside. The keys were not hanging where Danilo always left them, on a hook by the door. They were found in the bathroom, next to the sink. No one asked why Marysol's wet nightclothes and panties were draped over the tub. No one asked whether she'd seen anything. They all assumed she'd been asleep and only woke up when she heard the sirens and the banging on the door.

Alonso

On March 3, 1976, Luz saw San Juan for the first time since her parents' death five months earlier. Her grandfather pointed to a building facing the Atlantic Ocean on Ashford Avenue. "I lived there," he said. "Remember?"

Luz nodded to please him, but it wasn't familiar, although she must have been to his condo when her parents brought her to the capital. He'd moved from the tourist-infested Condado and they were driving toward their new home. On the landward side, sleek North American air-conditioned fast-food restaurants served customers next to zinc-covered, open-air cafés featuring local cuisine. Jukeboxes blared salsa music into the street, inciting people to dance on the sidewalks. The foreign eateries were favored by Puerto Ricans dressed for work, while the cafetines lured customers wearing cut-off jeans, flip-flops, and sunburns, the only ones dancing on the avenue in the middle of the day.

Alonso turned left onto a tree-lined street. A guard stopped him, peered at them suspiciously, looked at Luz, scowled at Alonso, and asked for his ID.

"Who are you visiting?"

"We're residents," Alonso said.

The guard scrutinized Alonso's driver's license, front and back. "It says here you live in the Condado."

"We just moved."

"What address?"

Alonso told him and the guard asked him to wait, taking Alonso's license into a shed, where he entered the information on a clipboard hanging inside. He checked a second clipboard, still skeptical.

"Do you have to do this each time?" Luz asked.

"He's never seen me here before. It's a private urbanización," Alonso said. "Only residents and service people are allowed in. If we expect guests, we have to alert the guards ahead of time."

The man returned, gave back the license. "No parking on the street after midnight." He banged twice on the roof of the Mercedes. Alonso winced.

The neighborhood was flanked by high-rises facing the ocean. The single-family homes were set amid lush gardens, their driveways displaying shiny cars like trophies. Alonso maneuvered over the speed bumps as if his Mercedes were made of crystal. Luz looked up at the buildings looming over the residential enclave with the sense she was being looked down on by people on terraces accessed by floor-to-ceiling glass doors.

"They're mostly for part-timers," Alonso said, "estadounidenses and a few Europeans. You see those white metal windows? It means the owners are away, so they close up the place but leave it protected against storms and hurricanes."

She welcomed his chatter, his eagerness to educate her. He was so different from her grandmother. When she thought about Güela, tears sprouted. She didn't want to forget Güela, but feared she would. Her breathing came as gulps, and her heart ached.

"Are you all right? Do you need me to pull over?"

"No. Estoy bien."

She didn't mean to sound as annoyed as she felt. For the rest of her life, people who knew what had happened would ask, wonder, or worry whether she was okay. She was no longer like every other sixteen-year-old girl. She was the one whose parents had died. The one who'd been in a coma. The one wearing a brace. Most of the time, she was unaware she'd had an achaque, or why or what she'd been thinking when she returned to herself. She was Luz, whose name meant "light" but whose brain went dark.

"What do you think?" Alonso had parked in front of a single-story contemporary home on a large lot, the yard plantings neat and well kept. He watched for her reaction.

"It's beautiful!"

His eyes sparkled. "You're all I have left of my family," he said. "It's you and me now, mi lucero. We'll do our best, right?"

"Sí, Abuelo."

A woman was standing on the front terrace smiling as if she knew them. She was pale and freckled, petite, and, while not exactly stocky, appeared solid and grounded. Her shoulders, torso, and hips were more or less the same width, creating a soft rectangle over powerful thighs, rounded calves, and small feet. Her light-blond hair was parted in the middle and grazed her shoulders. Her hazel eyes seemed to be asking a question.

"There's your tutor, Ada Gil Méndez," Alonso said. "Oh, and right behind her is Shirley Templeton Vélez, my business part-ner."

Luz hadn't noticed another woman until Alonso pointed her out. She was a few inches taller than Ada, olive-skinned, with curly black hair bobbed to her chin and bangs accentuating star-tling blue eyes.

"Bienvenida." Ada hugged Luz. She felt pillowy. "I couldn't wait to meet you in person. Alonso said you were gorgeous, but we thought it was a proud grandpa's exaggeration. Isn't she beau-tiful, Shirley?"

"Lovely." She gazed into Luz's eyes until it made her uncom-fortable.

Luz was embarrassed by the fuss, but enjoyed their embraces, the way they squeezed her shoulders, patted her back, led her into the house by the hand. As she entered, the scent of sofrito, oregano, and cumin nearly brought her to tears. It smelled like a home.

"I'll give you a tour," Alonso said at the door.

High over their heads, ceiling fans whirred soothingly.

"It's a house for tall people like you," Ada said with a grin.

Just below the slanted ceiling, colored glass windows created a rainbow on the walls. Sliding doors at ground level led to the side yard on the left and to the marquesina on the right. The open kitchen was on the wall opposite the front door, where Ada was already rattling lids over steaming pans. Between the kitchen and the living room, six chrome-and-black leather chairs were wedged beneath a glass table. The living room was furnished with more black-leather couches and recliners. Most of the hard surfaces were glass, mirrors, or reflective chrome. The overall effect was a bachelor pad inside a disco.

"You must be hungry," Ada said.

"We'll get lunch ready while you look at the rest of the house," Shirley said. "I hope you like piononos."

Grief wrapped itself around Luz, tighter than the brace, but she didn't know why she wanted to cry.

"Piononos were your mother's signature dish," Alonso said. "People always asked her to make them. We thought it might bring back memories."

The three adults now looked uncertain.

To change the subject, Alonso said, "Come this way," and led her to the rear of the house. "Remember those boxes at your grandmother's?" He pointed to the walls, which were decorated with photographs, each labeled with names and dates. At the top were Alonso's parents and below them Alonso as a boy, as a young man, on his wedding day to her grandmother Toñita, and several formal portraits of them together, ending with one of an infant Federico on his baptism. The next two rows were images of Federico as a baby, a boy, a young man, and then a husband, alongside Salvadora in Michigan, in front of monuments and touristic sites in foreign cities, at their labs and offices in the pharmaceutical company, at conventions and conferences. There were photos of Federico and Salvadora next to governors and eminent scientists. The rest constituted a chronology of their lives in black and white and color, snapshots with scalloped edges and formal portraits, and then, Luz at her baptism, the three of them as Luz aged until her last performance, swathed in white tulle at Miss Rita's recital in the spring of 1975, *Variations on "Les Sylphides."* Inside her head now, the strains of a Chopin waltz.

She came to herself again, steps from Alonso, who had his hand on the handle of a door and was wearing an expression of such sadness she never wanted to see it on anyone ever again.

"I'm sorry," she said.

"I know, mi amor. No need to apologize. Come, here's your room." It was actually a suite, with a bedroom to the left and a study/sitting area with bookshelves, a desk, a lamp, a ceramic cup filled with pencils, ballpoint pens, and markers. "Your bathroom is behind this door." He opened it to his right. "It has a deep tub. You love baths." A rueful smile as he picked up a white plastic bucket under the sink. "Epsom salts."

"You've thought of everything."

"And these glass doors lead to the backyard." Back in the study, he stepped outside onto a covered terrace. The garden was as clean and orderly as the front, divided from the neighboring yards with neatly trimmed hibiscus hedges in different colors.

"It smells like the sea."

"One of the best beaches in Puerto Rico," Alonso said, "is two blocks away." He was proud, eager for her approval. Back in the room, he studied the blank walls. "You can decorate. Paint them different colors, if you like. The bed is bigger because this room is larger than the one at your grandmother's. If you need any other furniture or lamps, maybe a beanbag chair, different curtains . . . You had posters of dancers . . ." He ran out of options for what she might consider necessary. "Ada will take you shopping."

"I love it, Abuelo. This is perfect." She hugged him again, and he held her longer than she expected, as if she'd disappear if he let her go.

After lunch, Shirley returned to the office. Alonso handed Luz a key to the house, and an envelope with cash she didn't bother to count. He went back to work, leaving Luz with Ada.

"Rest for a while," she said in English, "and after, we can go through your schedule."

"Schedule?"

"One of my jobs is to make sure you get to your appointments. Alonso will be busy for the next few weeks. Don't worry—I won't be hovering over you when you need privacy." She finished drying and putting away the dishes. "A maid comes once a week to tidy and do the laundry." She sprayed and scrubbed the counters and cabinet doors. "When he lived alone, Alonso ate every meal out, but we convinced him you both need healthy, homemade food. You're a dancer, after all. Shirley and I are good cooks, so we'll prepare your meals. Tell me if there are foods you don't like."

Luz couldn't keep up. Ada talked like a locomotive—*prátaca, prátaca, prátaca*—a train of information and instructions she couldn't entirely grasp as it all rushed past.

"Wait." She held up her hands. "I don't understand."

Ada stopped, confused. "Alonso said you spoke English."

"I do, but it's been months since I've heard it." She didn't want to offend Ada by pointing out her pronunciation and speed made it hard for Luz to process what she said.

"It's my accent." Ada reverted to Spanish. "Shirley says I speak faster in English so I can get through it quickly."

Luz liked her. She was down-to-earth and unpretentious. Alonso had said she was a few years older, but she looked more motherly than Luz expected, and later learned that Ada was a decade older, having recently turned twenty-seven. Maybe Alonso thought she was younger than that because of her colorful clothing and youthful appearance.

"If there's anything you need, let me know. We can go shopping or I can get things for you. Shirley and I live down the street," she said. "My number is on the pad next to the phone in your room. But for now, rest. I'll be right here if you need me." She picked up a Spanish-language copy of Gore Vidal's *Burr*. "Easier to keep track of the history if I don't have to struggle with the language," she said, grinning.

Luz was glad for the chance to explore her new room. Unlike at Güela's house, she didn't need a mosquitero. There were screens on the windows and doors. The rooms were air-conditioned and the floors didn't squeak when she walked around. She felt overstuffed from the lunch Ada and Shirley had prepared, a festival of flavors that challenged her taste buds, which had been tamed by Güela's bland cooking.

It had been a long time since she'd had such lavish affection. She liked Ada, Shirley, the house near the beach, the terrace and lounge chairs so perfect for reading in the shade. It all made her happy, and for the first time, she believed a total recovery was possible and a return to the Luz she'd been five months ago.

⟋

Luz was grateful for solid walls, electricity, a tiled porcelain bathroom instead of a latrine, a deep tub with a shower and plentiful hot water instead of a hose draped over a rickety bath shed. At the end of her first day, she soaked and scrubbed her skin with a washcloth, letting the last months swirl down the drain.

The first week was one appointment after another with doctors, blood work and imaging laboratories, medical and psychological assessments, physical and massage therapists. Ada took her from one clinic to another, always cheerful, as if driving Luz around the San Juan metropolitan area were her greatest pleasure. Ada loved her Volkswagen bus, nicknamed the Twinkie because of its shape and color. She enjoyed driving, even when bumper-to-bumper, big or small vehicles crawling like caterpillars across twigs. Frequent bottlenecks didn't faze her.

"It's the price we pay for living here," she said.

She'd grown up in Salinas and couldn't imagine living far from the ocean. "As soon as I get inland, I feel claustrophobic."

Her chatter was reassuring and it kept Luz distracted while they drove around. Ada often quizzed her on her homework.

"I'm strict about academics. We'll work together so you can keep up in school," she said. "The quizzes will increase your brain power. The doctors said it's possible to recover enough from your injury for you to have an independent life. The brain seeks different paths around the damaged parts."

Ada encouraged Luz with enough praise to make her feel she was making progress. When she did well on her tests, Ada rewarded her with shopping at one of the strip malls near their appointments. One day, she took her on a stroll around the largest mall in the Caribbean. Half the stores were franchises of U.S. businesses, but there were also a number of locally owned shops and restaurants.

"Alonso told me your mom brought you to Plaza las Américas to buy party dresses and leather shoes made in Spain."

It irritated Luz that people knew more about her than she did, and, despite herself, a kernel of resentment sprouted. When she noticed negative thoughts, she tamped them down until she couldn't hear them and scolded herself for being ungrateful. Obviously, she wouldn't know what happened if others didn't tell her, but they couldn't see the world through her eyes, so the recollections they had of her life were their memories, not hers.

When they entered some shops, salespeople recognized her and consoled her with hugs and kind words about Salvadora and Federico. From them, Luz learned the accident and its aftermath had been covered in newspapers and other local media. Neither Alonso nor Güela had mentioned this. She dug out the small notebook she now carried everywhere. She wrote "newspaper clippings, accident" on a fresh page.

In the fashion stores, if she liked a shirt or dress, she held it up in front of her torso and asked Ada or the salesperson whether they thought it would look good on her. Taking off her back brace in a dressing room meant unbuckling and setting aside the contraption, without making sudden movements, until her spine settled into place without support. She had trouble envisioning what clothes might look like under the device, and covering it required a size too big for her shoulders and arms. She hated the brace and avoided looking at herself in mirrors. The few times she did, the surface reflected a younger girl than the Luz who lived inside her. She didn't look at her face, afraid of the fear in her eyes, seemingly lost before her own reflection. If she inadvertently passed a mirror, her dancer's instinct was to look, but she quickly switched her gaze to something less anxiety-provoking.

On their first trip to the mall, Luz browsed but didn't buy anything and Ada noticed she wasn't enjoying herself as much as she'd hoped.

"I'm taking you to where I spend all my money," Ada said. They drove a few minutes to Librería Vivliopoleio, a cozy bookstore in a strip mall, where they were welcomed by a tabby cat named Zeus and a white poodle who responded to Storni. Both expected to be petted and fussed over before allowing anyone to amble up and down the aisles of tightly shelved books in English and Spanish, some stacked in precarious columns on the floor.

"Is that you, Ada?" A woman with a topknot held by a number-two pencil peered over one of the stacks on the front counter.

"Sí, Minerva," Ada said. "Let me introduce you to my student, Luz Peña Fuentes."

"I know you. Salvadora and Federico's daughter."

"Sí, señora."

Minerva held her at arm's length to take a good look. Behind her round, gold-rimmed glasses, her eyes watered. "You've grown so much since the last time you were here with Federico. He'd sit on that chair at the end of the history books and watch you reading in the young-adult section."

Luz looked to the back of the store. "There's another cat."

"Yes, Hera. She likes to curl up on the pillow in the children's area. I'm impressed you remember. It's been a couple of years. I'm so very sorry for your loss."

"Thank you."

"I knew your parents well. They first met in my house."

"In Michigan?" Ada asked.

"Of all places." Minerva raised her hand and waved at a young woman who'd been dusting shelves. "Please help those customers." She pointed out a couple squinting into the science fiction section, then returned to Ada and Luz. "We were few in Ann Arbor in those days. As soon as one of us heard there was another Boricua in the area, we adopted them into our family of exiles." She shook her head sadly. "I have children of my own, but when I heard about Salvadora and Federico . . . it was like losing one of mine, God forbid." She removed her glasses and wiped them on the hem of her shirt. "I'm sorry. I didn't mean to make you sad."

"Por lo contrario," Luz said.

"She lost much of her memory in the accident," Ada said. "She needs stories about her parents."

"Oh, well, next time you plan to come, call ahead and I'll bring pictures of what they looked like before you were born. Such a great couple, and so in love."

A customer brought a magazine from the rack and Minerva rang him up. She kept talking as she completed other purchases, thanking her clients and asking them to come back soon, then returning to her story. Luz noticed some shoppers lingered, eavesdropping, but Minerva didn't seem to care.

"I met Federico through his dean. I invited him to a party at my house so he could meet the other Boricua students at the university. It had snowed the day before, and wouldn't you know, my furnace died a half hour before everyone was to arrive. Federico was the first to get there. I was on the verge of un ataque de nervios, and when I explained what was going on, he didn't hesitate. He asked for a flashlight, a screwdriver, and a hammer, and went right down to the basement as if he'd been there many times. As the other guests came in, we could hear a lot of squeaking and knocking down there, and soon the furnace clanked and next thing we knew, it was working again." She laughed, anticipating what was coming next. "Your dad was particular about his clothes. He was always well-put-together, neat, and fond of Aramis cologne. How we teased him! He wasn't prissy or a peacock, nothing like that. He was, well, like I said, particular. And that night he wanted to impress us, so he wore a new white shirt and a nice suit and tie. When he came up the stairs he was covered in soot, like a character from a Dickens novel or an Edgar Allan Poe ghoul emerging from the depths." She chortled from deep in her gut. "Guess who's the first person to see him when he opens the door from the basement? Salva! Their eyes locked and all of us in the room knew that was the beginning of something special. Oh, my goodness, what a loss." She scurried back behind the counter. "I'm prattling like I have nothing else to do. Forgive me."

The people listening nodded or smiled sadly at Luz, bought their items or left empty-handed, now that the show was over. But Minerva wasn't done. After dealing with the customers, she came over to the Local Authors table, where Ada and Luz were browsing.

"Your parents came here to buy books for themselves and for you. When they couldn't make the drive to the metropolitan area, they called, and I sent what they needed. Mostly scientific books. Federico ordered books and pamphlets in German that took forever to get here, and Salva's reading material came from France. His science books were heavy and full of formulas, but she always added novels to her list. I remember she was partial to Marguerite Yourcenar and Claude Simon but she said after a long day at work she wanted to curl up with something requiring fewer brain cells, like Harold Robbins or John le Carré. She called them her candy. Oh, my goodness, look at me. I'm a mess."

Ada hugged Minerva. Luz rubbed the older woman's shoulders. She often ended up consoling others over her parents' death or her medical problems. They couldn't cope with a reality she couldn't escape. The kernel of resentment in her heart grew. Luz was sixteen, an age for narcissism and self-indulgence, but she couldn't even look at herself without turning from her own reflection. If she mourned publicly, her own grief eclipsed other people's emotions.

⟋

"The brain is a sublime organ," her neurologist said, his hands forming its shape and contours. "It's marvelously adaptable and elastic. Your progress has been impressive, far from what I expected, given your injuries and the duration of your hospitalization."

"So I'll be normal someday?"

"Normal?" He leaned back in his chair, his exquisite fingers steepled below his chin. "Will you be the same fifteen-year-old girl you were before your injury? No, you won't." He leaned forward across the desk, as if to make sure she could hear him. "You're already six months older than the girl in the car accident, still growing and maturing. You're not the same now as then, and a few minutes from now, you won't be the same person who came into my office."

"What I mean is, will the headaches go away? Will my memory return?"

"Impossible to predict. You said the headaches are fewer and less intense. You also mentioned you can complete your schoolwork and your teacher says you're at the top of the class." He laughed. "Seriously, I'm encouraged and impressed by your progress. I'm aware that at your age, things need to happen immediately, but think of your situation as an opportunity to practice patience."

He frowned. "No, young lady, don't roll your eyes. I get enough of that from my daughters."

"Disculpe." She was embarrassed to have been caught being herself, but she was also frustrated. "Everyone tells me to be patient."

"It's the curse of the young," he said. "As we mature, we accept that events take the time they take, especially when we've been injured, like you've been."

"I feel like I'm moving in slow motion."

"That's to be expected. Respect what your doctors tell you and allow the process to take the time it requires. Anything else?"

Ada hustled her out to the next appointment across town.

"I don't like him. I can tell he's patronizing me."

"He comes highly recommended. Josué called him personally before he agreed to see you."

"Un momentito." Luz held her back. "I have to say it before I forget. Why is Pastor Josué so involved in my life?"

Ada thought a moment. "He's your godfather and knew your parents years before you were born. He and your mother were classmates, and when he met Federico, he grew fond of him, too. He's a compassionate, caring man who wants to make sure his goddaughter is well taken care of."

"Abuelo is doing that."

"Alonso is doing the best he can and he adores you, but Josué's name can open doors that Alonso can knock on but people on the other side won't necessarily open."

"Why wouldn't they?"

Ada looked uncomfortable. "Don't make me say it, Luz. You know what I'm saying."

"I have no idea."

"Get in the Twinkie. We can't be late." She merged into traffic, looked everywhere but at Luz, seeking an answer on advertising signs, walls, store windows, and billboards.

"Have you noticed that when Alonso drives into our neighborhood in his big Mercedes, the security guard stops him, asks for ID, takes down his license plate?"

"That's his job, isn't it?"

"But when it's me in my van, the same guy waves me in."

"You've lived there for a while, haven't you?"

Ada seemed annoyed. She was saying something Luz couldn't quite grasp. She glanced at Luz, pointed at her face. "Look at me. I'm white, blond with hazel eyes . . ."

"Yes?"

Ada said nothing, waited until the answer sparked, flickered, flamed. "Because he's . . . because we . . . because we're Black?" Luz asked.

"I hate being the one to remind you how awful people can be."

⌒

Luz knew she was Black, and was aware that people were different skin shades, from eggshell to ebony. Some, like Ada, were so pale a few minutes under the sun caused them to turn red and develop hives. That observation didn't mean Luz had linked skin color to behavior, at least not that she could recall. Was it another of the many things she'd forgotten? Now that Ada pointed it out, Luz was no longer race-blind.

The urbanización was among the first luxury neighborhoods in that part of San Juan, and the houses were usually passed down one generation to the next. As far as Luz could tell, she and Alonso were the only Black homeowners. When she walked from her house to Ada's place one and a half blocks away, she felt eyes on her. Neighbors on terraces suddenly needed to pull weeds closer to the sidewalk so they could watch where she was going. They didn't greet her until they'd seen her several times and it became obvious she lived in the neighborhood, and even then, it was a nod or a curious glance, indicating they'd registered her presence, not a polite "Buenos días" or "Buenas tardes" or a casual "Hola," let alone a friendly "Bienvenida."

Other than house cleaners, nannies, gardeners, laborers, the mail carrier, and a couple of the guards at the front gate, Luz and Alonso were the only Black people in the enclave. She consulted the list of her doctors—all shades of beige; the lab technicians, therapists, and registered nurses were light-brown sugar or café con a lot of leche; those lower on the medical hierarchy, like nurse's aides, orderlies, janitorial staff, were darker-skinned. The photos on the wall by her room showed her parents, a chemist and a research pharmacologist, the only Black scientists in group pictures. And in the photos featuring Alonso with his clients, he was a lone Black man besieged by faces the color of raw chicken.

Luz now saw race everywhere. The governor and other political figures, all the television presenters, the news reporters and meteorologists, the protagonists in telenovelas, the actors in commercials, the singers, dancers, and musical acts were, by and large, light-skinned with a few darker tones, like vanilla ice cream with sprinkles. She asked herself whether she'd always known the pecking order was based on skin color, or whether, like so much that had vanished into a locked part of her brain, those insights were hiding in the same place as what had happened inside the car during the accident. An Impala, she now recalled, blue.

⟋

Most days, Alonso left early and worked late. He was Catholic but not as devout as Güela. "Like her, I comply, but only with the minimum for a chance at paradise," he said with a grin. He went to Mass on Sundays and on holy days and, like Güela, didn't insist Luz accompany him.

Some evenings, he drove Luz to the Howard Johnson's restaurant on Ashford Avenue. Condado Beach was a block away, and they walked barefoot along the tide line, licking ice cream cones and enjoying the salty breeze as he asked about her progress with Ada's tutoring and her therapies.

She consulted her notebook and listed what she'd written about her activities. "What was your day like?" she asked as she stuffed the notebook back into her pocket.

"Every day is different. I can't divulge private information about my clients," he said. "But I can tell you there's a lot more wealth in Puerto Rico now than when I was growing up."

"That's a good thing, isn't it?"

"Not everyone has benefited. I'll give you an example from our family. We don't come from money. Your great-great-grandfathers were cane laborers. The next generation on my side, my father, also named Alonso, was a fruit vendor. Your grandmother Güela's father was a butcher. Are you with me?"

"They no longer worked in the fields, right?"

"In 1976, they look like small steps to us but they were huge ones for them. They were Black, they were illiterate—yes, don't look so surprised, mamita. Even today, many people can't sign their own names. It's true."

"There were no schools?"

"There were, but it was hard for poor families to send their children. Usually, the schools were in the bigger towns, and campesinos lived in rural areas. Children worked alongside their parents in the cane or tobacco fields or on the slopes where coffee grows. In the city, even the youngest were shining shoes or clearing people's yards or selling newspapers. Jobs like that were done by kids. So, no, they didn't go to school. They couldn't afford to."

"But public school is free."

"Even so, mi amor. They needed uniforms and shoes. Not sandals, like yours. They had to wear closed shoes. I knew a family with many children, so the boys and girls took turns going to school because there was only one pair of shoes among them."

Luz giggled.

"It's funny now, but it wasn't for them."

"I'm sorry, Abuelo."

"No, mi amor, I'm not trying to shame you. I've told you that story before and you reacted the same way. Federico and Salvadora laughed the first time they heard it, too, but then she thought about it. It wasn't funny for the family, she said. Salvadora was right, of course. I learned something that day. I want to help you rebuild memories. Lamentablemente, not all will be pleasant."

"That scares me, Abuelo. What if what I forgot was really, really bad?"

Alonso held her close. "That must be terrifying, amorcito, but I was there for much of your childhood. Not every day, but enough to assure you, your parents were everything others have told you about them and more. They adored you as much as I do. You had adventures and positive, magical experiences as a family. According to your doctors, your memories might come back, slowly, yes, but you know something? Bad things happen to everyone, and if some bad things happened to you, it's good those memories are gone. The important thing, what the doctors say, and I believe, and you should, too, is that you will continue building new ones. And I'll do my best that they will be good, and worth remembering."

Luz spent most of her time with Ada on lessons, visits to museums, to the Biblioteca Nacional, and hours in the Twinkie going to and from doctors and therapists.

One day after her appointments, they sat under a palm tree on the beach two blocks from the house. A few feet away, three girls stood in an intimate little group, their arms around one another's waists, aiming their giggly chatter and flirtatious glances toward the boys horsing around in the water. Luz wondered whether six months ago she'd behaved this way with her friends on the Caribbean shore. Did she wear such cute bikinis? These girls now chased one another, their ponytails bouncing against their backs as they gleefully ran into the sea and splashed one another amid happy screeches. The boys swam over, circled them like sharks, their laughter joining theirs. Had she been that carefree in her previous life? If not, she wanted to be that way now.

"I know those girls," Ada said. "I tutored them last semester. I'll introduce you."

"No, that's okay." Luz was embarrassed Ada had noticed her envious glances, but the teacher was already waving them over.

"You should meet. You'll be classmates in August."

The girls ran toward them as if they'd been waiting to be summoned.

"Hola, maestra," one said, and hugged Ada.

"Oooh, you got her all wet," another said.

"Está bien. Don't worry." Ada brushed wet sand from her clothes. "I'd like to introduce you to my student."

Ileana, Minaxi, and Perla had grown up on the same block and behaved more like sisters than neighbors. Over the next few days, as Luz got to know them, Ada made sure to be nearby, whether they were at the beach, or by Ileana's pool, or when they came over to listen to music in Luz's room. They seemed to be getting along, and Luz seemed comfortable around them, so Ada gave them more privacy. What Luz never learned was that a few days before the afternoon on the beach, Ada had run into the three friends. They'd seen Luz around and were curious.

"Is she the girl in the newspapers?"

"Pobrecita," Perla said.

"She looks like a robot," Minaxi sniggered.

The other two snickered.

"You wouldn't want to be called names if her tragedy had happened to you," Ada said.

The girls looked everywhere but at Ada.

"She seems shy," Perla said. "That's why we haven't talked to her at the beach."

"She is, but she'd love to know people her age."

"We can introduce her to our classmates," Ileana said.

"You can count on us," Perla said as if a decision had been reached.

"Loreta, who cleans our houses and don Alonso's, told my mom that Luz gets fits," Minaxi said.

"She said the same thing to my mother," Perla said.

"They're not fits. They're disassociation episodes and are the aftereffects from a brain injury. She can't control them and Loreta shouldn't be calling them that. Neither should you."

"Do the dis . . . disotion . . ." Ileana stuttered over the unfamiliar word.

Ada enunciated clearly.

"Sí, esos episodios," Ileana said. "What do we do if she has one when we're together?"

"That's a good question," Perla said. She was petite, plump, bespectacled, her blond hair dyed to match Faye Dunaway's sunny tones. Ada considered her to be the smartest of the three girls, Ileana the most social, and Minaxi the most likely to betray every secret the others shared with her.

"You don't need to do anything if she seems to flake out," Ada said.

"But if she faints or something."

"I've never seen her do that during an episode, but if she does, find me."

"How long do they last?" Minaxi asked.

"You won't even notice them most of the time. But if she seems distant or distracted, she might be having one. I usually ask, 'Are you okay?' If she's inside an achaque, she can't answer. She's somewhere else mentally, and it's as if you don't exist. She'll get through it and if she's upset afterward, it's because she relived something sad. The good thing is she'll forget it almost immediately once she's back."

"¡Qué horror!" Ileana shuddered.

"It must be awful, to have memories you can't remember unless you go into a trance," Perla said.

"She didn't call it a trance." Minaxi play-punched Perla's arm.

"It doesn't matter what it's called," Ileana said. "It's what it does. I'd hate to be her, that's for sure."

⚬‌—

Ileana, Minaxi, and Perla told their friends not to be offended if they had to remind Luz who they were several times before she remembered their names. They were popular girls, and Luz understood they had good intentions and appreciated their overtures, but it was awkward.

Not wishing to invade her privacy, Ileana, Minaxi, and Perla avoided asking the obvious, like what was with her back brace. That they ignored it made Luz invisible to herself. She was also embarrassed by the achaques, which came more often when she was anxious. The teenagers ignored them or pretended they hadn't taken place. None wanted to talk about her medical issues, although she overheard one boy talking to Ileana.

"She's like my demented grandmother."

"Shush," Ileana said. "Don't say that."

"Claudio kissed her at the movie," he said. "She let him touch her tetas and it was like nothing. She didn't even remember it afterward," he snorted.

"The perfect date." Minaxi laughed.

Later, the girls asked Luz about Claudio, and she had no memory of a kiss but tingling feelings lingered, disconnected from the events. Back home, she explored her body and relieved the pressure built up from Claudio's forgotten fondling.

Luz didn't want her friends to think she expected special treatment. On the other hand, she did have a condition that could endanger her if an episode came when she lost awareness and they weren't paying attention. She'd had achaques in front of Ileana, Minaxi, and Perla when they were shopping at a mall, playing volleyball at a local park, or hanging out at one of their homes. She'd find herself a couple of hours later in her bedroom, with no memory of where she'd been or what she'd been doing and only the vaguest sense she'd been "out having fun."

She couldn't be alone, and hated the responsibility placed on others. After Ada connected her to her soon-to-be classmates, Luz worried the teenagers, involved in their own lives and struggles, would resent having to babysit her but be too polite to refuse their former tutor.

Luz wanted to please Alonso, Ada, and Shirley, who were heartened by every improvement, however small. The girls were studying French, and when they realized she was fluent, they asked her to help them with their worksheets and translations. In time, she relaxed around them and their friends, but she never felt quite as comfortable as when she was with her adults.

Still, it was nice to have friends. The muchachos joined them at the beach, at the movies, at the mall, and at Ileana's house, where there was a pool. In the rear of the garden there was a cabaña changing room. Ileana convinced her parents to let her make it into a game room, where she could entertain friends within sight of adults but allowing them privacy. One of the boys, Kelvin Cabrera Pou, was an electronics whiz, and he wired a stereo system, a television, and, on the ceiling, a light fixture that changed colors. Two of the boys, José Juan and Juan José, were identical twins who always dressed alike so Luz could never tell one from the other. Their parents owned a furniture store, and they gave Ileana's parents a shabby floor-model sofa and beanbag chairs. They also donated an area rug with a psychedelic pattern of swirls and colored circles Luz found dizzying. Claudio Worthy Villalobos was a distant cousin of Ada's, although she wasn't close to that side of her family. His father owned newspapers and radio and television stations and his mother was a newswoman. Claudio brought a whiff of celebrity cachet to their clique. He was so pale-skinned and blond the other kids nicknamed him "El Vikingo." He was a senior and had already been recruited by a local basketball team, but he dreamed of playing for the Lakers, alongside Kareem Abdul-Jabbar. Luz liked that he was a head taller than she was. At sixteen, she was already five feet ten in flats and, when he wasn't around, she felt enormous around the other, average-size teenagers. For Ileana's game room, Claudio contributed a small refrigerator where they could keep sodas and juices.

It took Luz a while to distinguish each boy from the others. She didn't see them as often as the girls who fluttered around Ileana, Minaxi, and Perla. When they hung out in the game room, the girls shared stories of their romances and conquests. They all had novios or enamorados and had decided Luz needed a boyfriend, too.

"Kelvin likes you," Minaxi said. "But he's too shy to tell you."

"Claudio is interested in you, too." Perla danced her eyebrows but Luz didn't notice.

"Too bad for you, Minaxi," Ileana said. "El Vikingo prefers Black girls."

Minaxi gave her an "I hate you" look.

"Luz left us," one of the girls said.

"Are you okay?"

The voices faded, and in her achaque, Luz was cross-legged on her bed, facing Salvadora, who was in the same position.

"Don't feel embarrassed by those feelings, mi amor. They're natural. Mais ne confondez pas le sexe avec la procréation." Salvadora took her hand in hers. "Do you understand?"

Luz nodded. "Sex and procreation are different."

"C'est ça." Salvadora then explained that sexual urges were normal and to be expected at Luz's age. "You can relieve the pressure on your own." She crooked her index, middle, and ring fingers then wiggled them near her groin. "No te avergüences. Masturbation will relieve the pressure without the possibility of an unwanted pregnancy. When you're ready for a sexual relationship avec un homme, yo te daré la píldora."

"Pues, get me the birth-control pill now."

Luz emerged from her achaque. The girls were agape, and then screeched with laughter.

"Did you just say that?"

"What?"

"She was remembering something."

"My mother would kill me if I asked for that!"

"Don't laugh at her!"

"My dad would lock me up in my room."

"The pill is for sluts."

Luz was mortified. "What did I say?"

They laughed harder.

"What did I say?"

～

On the first Saturday in May, Luz was invited to a party at Ileana's house. She'd decided against the brace for the night so she could wear a yellow minidress Ada had convinced her to buy at Velasco. She tried on several shoes until gold block-heeled sandals looked best, even though she was tall enough without them. She put on lipstick and was about to gather and pull her hair into her usual topknot when she was startled by her natural hair blooming around her face like a soft, black cloud. In all her pictures, not one showed her with unbound hair. Did she dare leave it that way? She fluffed it with her fingers, and let it fall where it wanted to. She looked more mature, and when she walked, her mane bounced gently around her features, very Angela Davis.

She studied her image in the mirror in a way she hadn't done in a long time. She had no pimples or acne scars. Her eyes were heavy-lidded, and her sparse eyebrows were well shaped even though she did nothing to them. Her lips were full and required no color, although in this case, they were cerise, thanks to Coty. As she studied herself, she recognized features from the photos on the wall: Salvadora's eyes, Federico's nose and lips, Salvadora's hair, Federico's high cheekbones, Salvadora's long neck, Federico's wide shoulders. She was moved by the Luz in the mirror, all that was left of her mother and father, dead almost seven months ago yet living inside her.

"I'm pretty." It was a statement, not a question, not a surprise. She shook her head to aerate her hair, lifted her right shoulder, and lowered her chin to meet it. *I'm sexy.*

Warmth rose between her legs, and she caressed her breasts, glided her hands down her torso, down her belly. It felt so good, she sat on the floor against the bathtub, dipped her fingers inside her panties, and rubbed and patted between her legs until she climaxed.

Alonso knocked on her bedroom door. "Time to go, mamita."

"I'll be there in a minute."

She was glad her grandfather would never enter without knocking. She heard him walk away, and she cleaned herself, washed her hands, changed her panties, straightened her clothes. When she walked into the living room, Alonso did a double take.

"New hairdo?"

"Does it look okay?"

"Different." He dropped his gaze, looked again.

She lost some of her confidence, unsure whether his reaction was positive or negative. "I'll put it up again if—"

"No, leave it." His eyes were teary. "You look good."

"You're sure?"

"Lovely. And those earrings? You haven't worn them before."

"They're from Mami's jewelry case you saved for me. She's wearing these hoops in pictures." She pointed toward the gallery in the hallway.

He nodded. "I don't mean to make you self-conscious, Lucita. It's only . . . you look so grown up." He choked up and she sensed he wanted to hug her but was embarrassed. "I guess, until now, you've been my very tall little girl. But it's like you grew up overnight." He squeezed her hand. "Don't mind your sentimental old abuelo."

⁓

The party had been going for some time, and Luz was unsure whether she'd been given the wrong time or she'd misunderstood the invitation.

"There you are!" Ileana led her to a group of boys and girls swaying to "Disco Lady." Luz recognized a few from their outings to the movies and the mall, and they chatted for a while, munching on chips and sipping soda, checking one another out, teasing, joking, the boys shoving one another and the girls rolling their eyes at their antics. She enjoyed their easy interactions, the laughter, how certain voices rose over others, making everyone look their way.

She hadn't been in a large gathering like this since before the accident. She stood out, taller than Ileana's parents and the chaperones sending glances in her direction. She was the only Black person. A few times, she overheard guests talking about her. Accident. Dead parents. Brain damage. Weird. Loca. Una boba. No, she's really smart. Uppity. We met three times already and she ignores me. Lives in the neighborhood. Is she someone's maid's daughter? Her grandfather drives a Mercedes. Really?

She hovered by the girls and boys she knew. She felt safe around them.

When the sun went down, more people showed up. There was a salsa combo, and between sets, a DJ cranked up the music so everyone could keep moving. Luz danced with a few boys, with the girls, in groups. She had fun, but she'd been off the back brace for hours and was beginning to feel its absence.

It was fully dark now. The chaperones didn't notice teenagers sneaking liquor or smoking behind bushes or along the unlit path leading to the front yard and the street. They puckered their lips at the grind dancing but didn't see the couples disappearing into the back garden or the game room, or emerging later, straightening garments and brushing fingers through mussed hair. A couple of boys approached Luz in clumsy attempts at romance. She avoided their hungry hands. Claudio went from group to group, chatting and joking, then returning to Luz every time she was free of other dance partners. At first, she was flattered by how solicitous he was, and appreciated that, even with her high heels, he was taller.

"You guys look good together," Perla said as she passed them on the dance floor, her boyfriend attached to her like a limpet.

Claudio grinned and squeezed Luz closer.

She made space between them. The music faded into a ballad for close dancing.

"Are you okay?"

"Fine, but I have to go." She walked away before he could get fresher.

He followed her. "You can't just leave me like that."

"It's past my curfew."

"I'll take you home."

"No, gracias."

"You shouldn't go by yourself."

"It's not far."

He grabbed her hair, dragged her into the shadows, pushed her against the wall of the house, and tried to kiss her. "You know I'm crazy about you, negrita."

"Stop . . ." Luz shoved him, but he didn't even wince.

"You've teased me all night . . ."

"I didn't . . ." She screamed. No one came. He covered her mouth, pressed a forearm against her neck. Luz gasped for air, and pain sizzled down her spine, down her legs. He loosened the pressure only to grab her breast. She scratched his face and he slapped her. He pushed his forearm harder into her neck as he rummaged up her dress with his free hand.

"You're mine, mi negra. Everyone knows that."

"I don't belong to you." She kicked him, but missed his groin.

He drooled over her face. He stank of liquor and hot dogs. "All of a sudden you don't like it?"

Luz pushed him harder. He lost his grip, and it eased the pressure on her neck, making it easier to breathe. She was angry and scared. He was bigger and grunted like a frenzied animal. She screamed again. No one could hear her over a fast merengue. Luz screamed once more, louder, though her throat hurt. He attempted to drag her to the ground by grabbing her shoulders, but she turned her head and bit his arm until she tasted blood. He yowled. She shoved him hard. He stumbled and dropped heavily, face-first, into the thorny hedges along the fence. He roared. Before he could raise himself, Luz stomped his back, pressing him down into the spiny plants. When she heard steps coming in their direction, she hastened away. When she looked over her shoulder and in spite of the darkness, she could make out Kelvin and one of the twins bending over Claudio. Stabbing pain crackled up and down her back as she bolted toward the road. Streetlamp circles marked her way home like spotlights. The *slap-slap-slap*s of her sandals were out of rhythm with the muted sounds of televisions and radios bouncing against cement walls.

Rage and fear gave way to joy. Unthinking, she leaped over speed bumps. Wind whooshed past her ears, sweat sprouted on her forehead, between her breasts, down her back. She was uncaged. She ran past her house and had to turn around.

Luz collapsed on the terrace floor, panting, her back against the wall. Every cell in her body was in motion, her nerves sparking, her heart racing. The light fixture near the front door was besieged by insects. Mosquitoes swarmed her, and she smashed the ones she could catch, slapped them like she'd slapped Claudio, El Vikingo.

It had felt so good to run. It had been exhilarating, thrilling to move unfettered. She was powerful. She was strong. She was free. The ocean breeze caressed her; the floor tiles were cool. She raised her arms. It hurt, but she embraced the air. She hugged herself, rocked side to side to allow her spine to settle, her breath to slow. She acknowledged the pain building in waves, the spasms up and down her back, her calves, her thighs. She breathed.

Inside the house, the staccato voices of newscasters spread bad news. The meteorologist warned of a vaguada on Tuesday. Luz was in pain but wouldn't cry, wouldn't call for Abuelo, who was a few feet away on his cushy recliner.

A siren wailed nearby. The sound stopped, started again. Light strobed against the fences and walls down the street, then quiet and darkness descended again.

Luz stretched her legs before her. She couldn't stand without help. She counted breaths. Eight, nine, ten. She willed her calves, her thighs, her hips to relax. She stretched forward gently, breathing, counting eleven, twelve, thirteen. She stretched a little farther. Fourteen, fifteen, sixteen. Her breath slowed.

Why was she on the floor on the terrace at night? Her brain had erased how she'd gotten there but her body remembered. She'd fought. She'd defended herself. She was stiff and in pain, but her body knew what to do. She pointed her toes, flexed her feet, settled her sit bones on the floor. One, two, three, four. She crawled her fingers along the tops of her thighs, to her knees, down her shins. Five, six, seven, eight. She rested between spasms. One, two, three, four. She stretched farther. Five, six, seven, eight. She reached her ankles.

The door opened.

"Luz?"

"Hi, Abuelo."

"Are you okay, mi amor?"

"Can you help me to my room?"

"Of course." He helped her get on all fours, then stand. "Slow. That's good, hang on to me, I'll hold you up. Don't worry— I won't let you go. Despacito, one step at a time. You're doing great. Hold on a sec—let me switch the light on. Here's the bed, I'll move the blanket out of the way. Slow. That's good. I'll take off your sandals. Do you want this pillow under your knees? I'll do it." He slid the blanket over her. "Is that more comfortable? Rest now. Can I get you anything?" He clicked on the bedside lamp.

"I'm fine for a while. Thank you, Abuelo."

"Who brought you home? You were to call me to get you."

"It wasn't so far."

"I should have come to get you earlier. You haven't gone so long without the brace. Do you want it?"

"Not now. I'll lie here a bit, then take a hot bath. I'll put it on after."

"The door's open if you need me. Just shout." He flicked the overhead light off and backed out of the room.

She was faceup, with her forearm over her eyes. Where was she? She went to a party. Her neck was sore. She ran, she leaped, she stretched and now everything hurt. It didn't matter why. She had bent like a bough in a strong wind but hadn't broken.

~

On Sunday afternoon, Luz was on the terrace outside her bedroom, wearing her brace and distracting herself from the pain and soreness by reading the most recent Corín Tellado short story in *Vanidades*. She stroked her breasts and rubbed between her legs during the sensual scenes, marking them to read again at night or in the tub, when she could be free to explore and satisfy her body.

"You have visitors," Alonso called, and moments later, Ileana, Minaxi, and Perla came from inside the house.

"Don't get up," Ileana said. "And we won't stay long. Your abuelo said you weren't well."

"I overdid it last night. Maybe too much dancing." Luz grinned. The girls settled on the floor and the steps. "Thank you for inviting me, Ileana. I had fun." Luz couldn't interpret their glances. "Is something wrong?"

"No," Minaxi said, too quickly, but the others jumped in.

"It's that you missed what happened to Claudio," Perla said. "You remember him . . ."

The girls exchanged a look.

"You danced with him," Ileana said.

"A couple of times," Perla said.

A flash of the tall boy. "Claudio."

A furtive glance between the girls. They switched on the sunshine when Alonso carried out a tray with lemonade and Oreos. They oohed and aahed and made a big fuss about him. He loved it.

"You girls enjoy yourselves." He left happy.

"He's the sweetest abuelo," Ileana said.

"He is," Perla said. "We have to tell you the rest."

"Claudio brought a caneca," Ileana said. "Total rotgut. Who knows what it was made from."

"Alcohol with sugar, probably." Perla giggled.

"His cousin makes it," Minaxi said. "Calls it fruit brandy."

"He passed it around to the guys," Perla said, "and to some of the girls."

"I tasted it," Ileana said. She pretended to throw up.

"He gave you some, too," Minaxi said.

"I don't think so."

"We watched him with you," Perla said. "A bit too handsy, in my opinion."

"He was drunk." Ileana seemed desperate to justify him. "He got fresh with all of us."

"He's not usually so obnoxious," Minaxi said.

"You like him," Perla said.

"Not really," Minaxi sniffed derisively.

"I hope he didn't offend you," Ileana said. "You left so suddenly."

Another flash; her gut lurched. The smell of liquor and hot dogs.

"Kelvin saw him following you," Perla said. "He and José Juán came back practically carrying Claudio, who was bawling like a baby."

Minaxi's eyes had grown larger. "He was bleeding!" She mimed her description. "Blood on his arms, on his face. He was all scratched up, and had thorns all over. He had a gash by his left eye. It was horrible." She hid behind her hands.

"My mom called an ambulance," Ileana said.

"Is he okay?"

"He needed stitches," Minaxi said.

"That beautiful face," Perla said. "He'll probably be scarred forever."

"You're so dramatic." Ileana poked her.

"Did you see anyone as you were leaving?" Minaxi squeezed Luz's hand as if that would make her recall what happened.

Luz remembered running. Leaping. Ocean air. She shook her head. "I just came home."

"That path is so dark," Perla said.

"My dad is freaking out," Ileana said. "He's putting in lights on that side of the house."

"You won't be able to sneak out anymore," Minaxi said to Ileana.

"I only did it once," Ileana sniffed.

"Sure, you did," Perla said.

"I'm so glad you're okay." Minaxi's tone was syrupy. "We were worried about you." Cloying.

She wanted them to go away with their fake sympathy. "I'm fine, thank you. I need to rest."

"Yes, of course." Too polite.

"We didn't mean to interrupt your reading." Minaxi sniggered at the *Vanidades*.

"We wanted to make sure you had a good time. The party broke up soon after you left. Because of Claudio," she added, "not because of you."

"Is this yours? We found this on the path."

On Minaxi's palm were Salvadora's earrings, bent out of shape and missing the posts that kept them on her earlobes. Luz took them, closed her fingers around them, found comfort.

"See you soon." The girls laughed and went away, chattering and giggling. Luz pressed the earrings to her chest, hoping they could keep her heart from bursting through it. She had a flash of Claudio, El Vikingo, licking her face. Disgusting. "You're mine, mi negra," he'd said. And as the memory entered, it vanished, leaving behind the familiar yet unsettling sense the girls knew something about her she didn't remember.

Losses

2017

When Luz was orphaned at fifteen, she had affectionate Alonso, who protected and cared for her. It was a blow when, six months after they arrived in the Bronx, he died. In his will he named as her guardians Ada and Shirley, who continued to be steady and loving influences over the years of psychological, physical, occupational, and other post-brain-injury therapy.

"She was a minor when it was clear to Alonso he wouldn't survive the cancer," Ada told Marysol. "We never met the elderly grandmother who lived in el campo. He didn't trust she could advocate for Luz and her needs. He worried that when he died, Luz would be sent to a foster home or a facility for the mentally impaired, where she might not get the attention she should have."

"It was very emotional when we went to the lawyer's office to sign the papers for her guardianship."

"Was Mom there?"

"Oh, no," Shirley said. "Alonso didn't want her to know he was so sick. It was just me, Ada, and Josué, who was Luz's godfather and later became yours. He helped us a lot."

"Luz was making progress in New York," Ada said, "but it was hard for her when Alonso died. She regressed, as if all those hours of physical and psychological therapy had never happened. It took her three years to get back to where she'd been."

With them as supporters and cheerleaders, Luz strengthened her body, built new memories, and functioned well enough to fall in love, marry, have a child, and work alongside Danilo in the bodega they owned. Ten years after Alonso's death, tragedy knocked Luz down again when Danilo was shot and killed and she was seriously injured. Luz relapsed. She didn't know who she was, who Ada was, or Shirley. She didn't remember she had a five-year-old daughter.

In the summer and fall of 1987, Luz and Marysol were besieged by strangers. Danilo's mother arrived in the Bronx, trailed by men and women insisting they were Tío this or Titi that.

"They accused us of kidnapping you," Shirley explained years later, when, as an adult, Marysol wanted to talk about those terrifying days. "They wanted to put Luz away and give you to a childless couple in Danilo's family. We never met them, and they never tried to meet you. Maybe they didn't even exist—I don't know."

Social workers spouted rules and regulations as lawyers pushed documents in Shirley and Ada's direction. The biological family argued they were "doing the best for the child," that she belonged with them, and demanded legal rights, "as her blood family."

"What I remember most about those days," Marysol said, "was Daddy's mother constantly grabbing me, making me hug her. She smelled like hair spray. She smeared lipstick on my cheeks."

Ada chortled. "I remember she thought she was all that . . . a grande dame of some sort."

"Remember her jewelry? Lots of bangles, gold chains, and long earrings." Shirley laughed.

"I heard her coming," Marysol said. "And hid under my bed."

Four months after Danilo's death, a little girl was killed by her adoptive father. Her mother was on the front pages of newspapers with before-and-after close-ups of her face following his beatings. The woman was so disfigured she was nearly unrecognizable. Had they kept track of the familial violence, protective services might have intervened and prevented the child's (and her mother's) abuse. Instead, they fell through the cracks of a system that failed them. The scrutiny and criticism of their failure added tension to the battle for Marysol's custody.

She was interviewed by people from both sides. She always said the same thing: Danilo's family hadn't been in her life until after he died. At some point, a judge took her into a soothing, wood-paneled office with African violets flowering on the windowsill.

"How about some Oreos?" The judge lifted a plate toward Marysol, who took a cookie and nibbled its crunchy chocolate edges. "Do you like apple juice?" She handed her a small box with a straw sticking from the top. Marysol took a sip. It was cool and sweet.

The judge asked her about school, about her friends, about her favorite stuffed animal, about Ada and Shirley, and finally, about her paternal grandmother and uncles and aunts.

"I don't know them," Marysol said. "Why do they say I'm their family? They shouldn't lie like that. I've never seen them before." She told the judge that Ada Madrina quit her job in Maine and moved to the Bronx to take care of her while her mother recovered. "I don't want to live with those other people."

Years later, when she became a nurse and was discouraged by the paperwork and conflicting protective laws she had to follow, she again asked Ada and Shirley for more details about that harrowing experience for them all.

"The social workers were defensive and afraid to make another fatal mistake," Shirley said, "so I copied every document we had about our relationship to you and to Luz. We fought hard to keep you with your mother."

They were grateful for Pastor Josué, who flew from Puerto Rico to the Bronx a couple of times a month.

"He had the legal and political connections to fight your grandmother," Ada said.

Marysol believed that, were it not for Ada and Shirley, she'd be without a history. They were there and told her what had happened when she was too young or too traumatized or too confused to assemble her experiences. If not for them, the important people in her life might have been mere ghosts.

She was in her twenties when she learned Josué had convinced Danilo's mother to give up attempts to gain custody by paying her to leave Marysol alone.

After Ada returned to Maine, Josué arranged for nurses, nannies, and housekeepers from among his congregation. The women treated Luz and Marysol as if they had two children to care for, and their vigilance and kindness helped Luz recover from her physical injuries and regain enough neurological function to recognize Marysol. Ada, Shirley, and Graciela came frequently. When back in Maine, they called every day, sometimes more than once, to talk to Luz and Marysol.

Especially during the eight years after Danilo's murder, Marysol pestered Ada and Shirley for stories about Luz and Danilo, writing them down so she could repeat them to her mother. She knew Luz couldn't remember her childhood, but even as a child Marysol couldn't bear the thought that her mommy would forget her daddy.

"You and Titi Shirley and Ada Madrina and Gracielita," Marysol started, as they lay on the same bed, "lived across the street from a bodega."

Instead of a mother reading bedtime stories to her child, Marysol repeated what she'd learned from Ada and Shirley, night after night, sometimes rewarded by Luz anticipating a name or a place or an event. Looking back years later, Marysol is grateful for the patient little girl she had been, desperate to make her mommy better, to fix her so she'd be like her friends' mothers. They were impatient sometimes, but also hugged them, nagged and reprimanded them, then said, "You'll know I'm right someday." They showed their love with gestures.

A mother who ran her fingers through your messy hair was both loving and criticizing you for "going out looking like that." Those mothers prepared a special meal when you had a big test in school or when your report card came back with stellar grades. They squinted as they deliberated whether or not to give you permission to hang out on the sidewalk with the other kids. They oohed and aahed over your contributions to the school science fair. They sat on the bleachers during volleyball games, screaming your name. They were in the audience as you danced and lip-synched to Gloria Estefan and the Miami Sound Machine.

Marysol's mom was never where she wanted to see her. If one of Luz's caregivers brought Luz to watch her in a kung-fu tournament, Marysol couldn't do her best, worried her mother would do something to embarrass her. Afterward she felt guilty for wishing Luz had stayed home when she'd practically begged her to be there with the other moms.

Marysol will never know how her father earned her mother's trust, how he found a way to see beyond her disability. He must have introduced himself to her dozens of times before Luz remembered who he was. Marysol knows they went dancing every week, chaperoned by Ada or Shirley. When they had a babysitter for Graciela, a toddler, Danilo escorted the three sequined women on their high heels, powdered, perfumed, and coiffed, to illegal clubs where salsa blared and rum and soda flowed. He asked permission to marry Luz, first from Ada and Shirley, then from Josué.

Nine years older than Luz, Danilo was a Vietnam veteran who'd lived through a lost war. Maybe he needed to be a hero, and, according to Ada and Shirley, he was. They described the years Danilo and Luz were together as the happiest time in her life. Luz can't confirm this, but when Marysol mentions Danilo, her mother's features soften. She wishes she could see behind her mother's eyes, to know whether Danilo lives in the recesses of her memory.

Marysol tries not to romanticize Danilo but it's hard not to. She can only remember him from the viewpoint of a child. To her, he was the tallest, handsomest, kindest, funniest, most generous and loving man in their narrow circle.

She remembers riding on his shoulders, surrounded by thousands of people celebrating the Puerto Rican Day Parade on Fifth Avenue. He holds her ankles, as if afraid she'll fall, but she's secure, her fingers pressed against his temples.

They're in Van Cortlandt Park. Luz removes plastic containers filled with fried chicken, potato salad, yuca en escabeche, and, at the bottom, coconut flan. Marysol is gripping a yellow plastic bat and Danilo pitches an orange Wiffle ball for her to hit. Each time she connects, he points where she should run while Luz claps and yells, "Home run!"

Marysol nestles under his left arm, her right ear against his ribs. They're watching Bugs Bunny and Elmer Fudd chase each other around a tree. Danilo's laughter rumbles inside him, and to her it sounds like friendly thunder.

All she has left of him are such moments and Ada's and Shirley's stories. There are a few snapshots and clippings about the murder, covered in *El Diario La Prensa*. Paid off by Josué, Danilo's family disappeared from their lives, and Marysol doesn't even remember her grandmother's name. Elvia or Elba or Alba.

☙

Days after school let out in June 1994, a fire consumed the building where Marysol and Luz lived. They escaped with their lives, but lost everything they owned. The photographs, documents, sketchbooks, journals, and ephemera Luz needed to have a sense of her past became ashes. Within days of that disaster, seventeen-year-old Graciela collected photos from her mothers' albums that included Luz, Danilo, Alonso, and Marysol. Shirley and Ada added copies of letters, a few of Luz's sketches, and other papers they'd saved. Graciela organized them into a leatherette album she gave Luz on her thirty-fifth birthday. As technology evolved and Graciela's competence grew, she transferred the pictures and documents to a website she titled WeAreGLAMS. She taught Luz, Ada, Marysol, and Shirley how to find and add to the archive, although Graciela continues to be its most consistent contributor. Once, when posting about Shirley, Ada, and Luz collectively, Graciela called them "las madres."

"In that case," Ada commented on the post, "you and Marysol must be las nenas."

Las madres and las nenas write anecdotes or stories designed to keep them all abreast of one another's lives and to leave a record for Luz, including screenshots of their texts or recordings of their video calls.

During the years since she set up WeAreGLAMS, Graciela has combed through websites, seeking information about Luz's family. She searched for and downloaded birth and death certificates as well as obituaries for Salvadora, Federico, and Alonso. Censuses, phone books, and real estate records indicated where they'd lived. She unearthed medical journals in which Federico and Salvadora had published, and newspaper stories about their research at a pharmaceutical company. Following links and footnotes, Graciela was shocked when she read about the fertility experiments on Puerto Rican women.

"Did you know that was going on?" she asked Ada and Shirley. "Scientists from the United States developed and tested the birth control pill in Puerto Rico."

"I'd heard about that," Shirley said, handing her an apron.

Shirley scattered newspapers three pages deep on the kitchen table, while Ada set a small and a large bowl for each of them. Graciela lined an empty lobster pot with a plastic bag to receive the shells and bones of the steamed and cooled crabs they were picking from a mound of the crustaceans on the table.

"They went door-to-door," Graciela said, grabbing the first crab, "cajoling women into experimental trials without explaining they were being used as lab rats."

"That was in the fifties, wasn't it? I didn't hear about it until college," Ada said. "But before then, in the thirties and forties, Yanqui doctors set up clinics they said were to treat female complaints. Instead, they sterilized them. The women weren't told la operación would make it impossible for them to ever get pregnant."

"That's horrible, Mami."

"Thousands of fertile women, sterilized. When you hear the term *population control,* it always means reduce the number of children born to impoverished families, especially brown and Black ones."

"Tía Aracely recruited women for the birth control trials." Shirley snapped a crab's shell.

"Did Tía Aracely give you details about how they did it?"

"Toward the end of her life, she talked about it. She was paid to find women with at least two kids. Those with large families were desperate to avoid another pregnancy. They agreed to take a pill."

"Did she tell you some women died or were disabled from the aftereffects? They had strokes, embolisms, and cancer. They were given hormones in huge dosages, twice the amount they eventually discovered was effective."

"She never said a thing about that."

"Do you think Federico and Salvadora, like your tía Aracely, knew what they were doing was wrong?"

"If they thought about it," Shirley said, "they might have convinced themselves sacrificing a few women in a forgotten corner of the world was necessary to improve the lives of millions."

"That's so cynical, Mommy. And it's not like they were seeking a cure for cancer. They were determined to keep poor women from conceiving more children. Those people funding the research and testing also advocated eugenics. And by the way, even at that time there was a safe, effective alternative to birth control." She mimicked scissors at her groin. "Snip snip."

"God forbid men would allow a blade down there," Ada scoffed.

"Right? Instead, let's disrupt a natural but complex process with artificial hormones. And if the women have side effects, pretend they're making it up. Or, never mind, here's another pill, and this one in case the first one didn't work."

"You're turning red, mija," Ada said.

"It's infuriating to hear about those experiments on our people!"

"Well, I hope you're not planning a rant about that on WeAre GLAMS," Shirley said.

"Of course not! Luz has enough to deal with. And I'd never tarnish her parents' image, even though what they probably did was unconscionable."

"But if you think about it, Salvadora and Federico were working on safe birth control for all women, while la operación was population control of Puerto Ricans. There's a difference," Ada said.

"I guess," Graciela said. "Still . . ."

The women were silent for a few moments, each in her own thoughts.

"In the United States, we had no idea what was being done to Puerto Rican women," Shirley said. "When the pill was made available, we welcomed it."

"Your privilege is showing, Mom," Graciela snapped. "Most of those women sacrificed were brown and Black, like Luz and Marysol."

Shirley and Ada exchanged a guilty look.

"Federico and Salvadora were Black, too," Shirley said. "They knew who they were experimenting on."

"Maybe they didn't think about racial politics," Ada said in her most professorial manner. "They were scientists trying to solve a problem. It might not have occurred to them that scientific progress is built on the bones of the disenfranchised."

"I know that's true," Graciela said, "but it's so unfair. I know it can't be changed, but it still rankles."

"We agree on that," said Ada.

"I don't know where to put my rage about it."

"I hope talking about it helps."

Graciela shrugged. Her parents were silent for a while.

"If not for the pill," Shirley said, "I'd never have fucked four of the Chicago Seven."

"OMG, Mommy!"

Shirley and Ada tittered.

They'd met during the 1968 Democratic Convention in Chicago, bonded over their Puerto Rican heritage, become friends, and, years later, lovers. It was hard for Graciela to imagine them trolling for male company, but she accepted that they were different people during civil rights marches, protests, encounter sessions, and drug-fueled debates that often ended in sex on musty futons on bare floors in lead-paint-encrusted walk-ups in dilapidated neighborhoods. Graciela was the product of such casual attitudes.

"Come on, hija," Ada said. "Let it go. It's all in the past."

"I guess. But we live with its consequences. Look at Madrina . . ."

Graciela has tracked down newspapers about the accident that orphaned Luz. Marysol often sees Luz studying the fuzzy images of a car at the bottom of a ravine, tangled among trees and vines, her lips moving as she reads the dramatic descriptions of the damage and her injuries. The newspaper columns include photos of

Marysol's grandparents and bios provided by their employers, as well as testimonials from colleagues where Federico and Salvadora worked.

What's missing from the documents are Luz's experience of the events and their emotional impact. Neither Luz nor Marysol will ever fully know what Luz's childhood was like, or what caused the accident. But with the WeAreGLAMS archive, they can revisit Ada's and Shirley's versions of how, when, where, and why they met, and stories about how their relationship evolved over four decades. For Marysol, it's as if Luz were born when she met Ada and Shirley, the only people still in her life who were there back then.

Oliver

MAY 1976

Two days after Ileana's party, Luz hobbled into the living room and found Ada talking to a young man leaning against the counter. He had the same hazel eyes, light-yellow hair, and squarish body over short legs as Ada did. Luz sent a puzzled expression toward Ada.

"This is my cousin, Oliver Gil Figueroa," she said. "He works for Alonso, too."

"It's a family affair," he sang in falsetto, and half danced like Sly Stone.

Luz laughed and clapped.

He bowed. "Thank you very much," he said à la Elvis. "I dropped off some boxes from the office."

He spoke slowly, in a heavier English accent than Ada's.

"But you're also a singer?"

"I'm in a band, Los Mangoduros. You've heard us."

She shook her head.

"Even without brain damage," Ada said, "no one has ever heard of Los Mangoduros."

"Aw, come on, cuz, that's cold." He turned to Luz. "I was the DJ at Ileana's party a couple of nights ago." He was so hopeful. He shrugged. "Don't worry. I know about your problem."

"When he's not a singer, dancer, or DJ," Ada said in Spanish, "he's a driver or messenger." She disapproved of all his jobs.

Oliver glanced at Luz. "No matter what you do, some people are never satisfied."

Ada was making their afternoon snack. Oliver made no effort to leave. "Don't you have another errand for Alonso?" Ada asked as she poured cups of coffee for Luz and herself.

He got the message, mumbled goodbye, and shambled off as if he'd lost a boxing match. Ada watched him go, and as soon as he left, she chuckled, her stern face returning to her nothing-ever-bothers-me expression. "I love my cousin, but he thinks he's a teenager."

"How old is he?"

"He's twenty-two. He should find a good woman and settle down."

"But you haven't."

"I'm settled!"

"You are? Do you have a novio?"

"I don't need a man to be settled."

"But your cousin should have a wife?"

Tinkly music sounded nearby. "¡Frituras!" Ada couldn't resist the fried-food truck that came around every few days at about this time. She grabbed coins from the jar in the kitchen. "Do you want bacalaítos or alcapurrías?" She ran out as if glad for the interruption.

"I met Ada's cousin," Luz told Alonso that night while they were catching up and walking, slowly, on Condado Beach.

He chuckled. "Ah, yes, el mangoduro."

"His band."

"I don't know who came up with that one. We Puerto Ricans love nicknames." They laughed. They turned toward the winking lights next to the hotel where he'd parked his car.

"Ada was rude to him."

Alonso scoffed. "She's more like a mother than a cousin. They're the black sheep in their family."

"Why?"

"He was supposed to be a banker, lawyer, or businessman, like the men in their family, but I can't imagine him in an office all day."

"Ada wants him to settle down."

"She worries about him."

"You worry about me but you're not nasty."

"Nasty, you say?" He searched his pockets for his keys.

"Okay, *annoyed* is a better word."

"They squabble but it means nothing. They love each other."

"Why is she a black sheep? What do the women in their family do?"

"It's not what she does, it's who she is."

"What do you mean? She's so nice—except to him, I guess."

"They spar but they're close. It's them against the world."

"Like us."

"Not exactly. They're from large, wealthy families. Both were disinherited. First her, then him, when he sided with her."

"What did she do?"

He vacillated, then decided to tell her. "Her family turned their backs on her because she prefers her romantic partner to be a woman, not a man."

Las Madres

"Oh! I'm . . . That never occurred to me."

"It's not like she wears a badge," Alonso said with a smile. "She and Shirley have been together for a couple of years."

"Ada and Shirley?"

Alonso stopped walking and looked at her. "Is that a problem for you?"

"No, Abuelo. I didn't know, that's all."

He unlocked the car, made sure she was in before coming around to the driver's side. He turned to her with a serious expression. "Their private lives are not our business. They're competent, trustworthy, and generous people. They've been good to you, right?"

"Son buena gente."

He started the car. "Shirley has been the best business partner I've ever had. Josué had to let her go when he found out about them. His congregation couldn't handle it. Their loss, far as I'm concerned."

It took several tries before he could nose into Ashford Avenue. The road was like a parking lot, even in the middle of the week. With cars at a standstill, pedestrians jaywalked, waving thanks at drivers. They were dressed to party, glittering and coiffed. They seemed happy. Luz opened the passenger window halfway to catch whiffs of perfume, spicy aftershaves, and drafts of the salty sea air.

"Abuelo, do you ever see him?"

"Who?"

"Pastor Josué."

"From time to time. He's a busy man."

"His name comes up a lot in our lives."

"He's your godfather and, until recently, a client."

"He's not anymore?"

Alonso bit his lower lip, then the upper. "I've talked about retiring for years. My field is changing. I can't and don't want to keep up with the way it's going."

"Where is it going?"

"I read that accounting and bookkeeping will soon be done by computers. I doubt it'll stop the flood of paperwork. I'm tired of it, amorcito. This seems to be a good time."

"You sound sad about it, though."

"I'm sixty-seven—not ancient, but getting old. Instead of balancing ledgers and reading missives from the IRS, I'd rather spend what time I have left with you."

"I'd like that." She leaned into his shoulder.

"No more stacks of folders on the dining room table. It will look better when your friends come over."

"That's nice but I don't have many friends."

"You do! Ileana, Perla, Minaxi . . ."

"I don't trust them, Abuelo. I mean, they're good friends with one another, but I think they're nice to me to impress Ada."

"When school starts again, you'll meet other boys and girls. Don't worry."

In the hermetic, purring silence of Alonso's Mercedes, Luz heard an echo that vanished the moment she noticed it. She glanced at her grandfather, who was focused on his driving. But the sense persisted, vestiges of other conversations. As they left the Condado, the bottleneck eased, only to build up again near the hotels and casinos in Isla Verde.

"Abuelo? Have you told me Josué is my godfather before?"

"Sí, mi niña."

"And have you mentioned you're retiring?"

He took his eyes off the road for a moment to look at her. "A couple of times, mamita."

She was disappointed with herself. "This whole chat we just had, have we had it before?"

"Some of it, mi amor. I've told you about wanting to spend more time with you."

"Have I complained about Ileana, Minaxi, and Perla?"

"A veces."

"Have I known about Ada and Shirley being a couple?"

"This is the first time we've talked about it."

"Have I ever met Pastor Josué?"

"He visited your parents often. He's come to our house. The last time he was there, you and Ada talked to him for a while. He was very impressed by your progress and prayed over you. Then you had to go to a doctor's appointment."

She tried to envision what Alonso was describing, to no avail. After a while, she had another question.

"Have I met Oliver before?"

"Yes, mi niña. Several times. He's taken you to your appointments when Ada couldn't."

Luz sank into the seat. She fled into a reverie, a trip to the beach with Federico and Salvadora when she was four years old. Her father held her right hand, her mother the left, and they lifted her above the sand as they ran into the surf. They were laughing, and she squealed with joy. They ran past white, frothy waves into a calm blue sea.

"N'aie pas peur, ma petite, nous avons tes mains." Salvadora gripped her hand even tighter to prove she wouldn't let her go.

"Keine Angst, wir haben dich," Federico called.

But maybe because they were both holding on too tightly, it was inevitable she'd want to slip from their fingers. The waves surged gently but relentlessly, and she floated away from them into the pulsing sea, far from their reach. A wave cartwheeled her toward the shore, pushed her beyond the surf, deposited her, sputtering and coughing, on the sand. Federico and Salvadora ran toward her, crying, screaming in four languages, to find her laughing and begging to return to the water, where she swore she heard mermaids singing.

～

The following Thursday, Ada had an appointment, so Oliver was asked to drive Luz to her physical therapy. She studied in the morning, and, after lunch, was putting away her schoolwork when Oliver arrived fifteen minutes earlier than expected. She was flustered. She did her best to pretend she wasn't, but the effort made her clumsy. She dropped her notebook and pens, tipped a glass over Alonso's documents, couldn't remember where she'd left her handbag, or where her other sandal had walked off to. When she returned to the living room, Alonso and Oliver were chatting on the couch without the formality between boss and employee Luz expected. On the other hand, Alonso treated Ada and Shirley in the same familial manner, although they, too, were on his payroll.

"Ready?" Oliver stood and pulled his keys from his pocket.

Alonso encouraged her with a nod. Luz was ruffled, and now that she knew she'd met Oliver before and had forgotten him, she was embarrassed and shy around him.

Alonso stood at the top of the driveway, watching her go. Along the curb was a VW van, bigger than Ada's Twinkie, painted bright orange below the windows, and above them, a white rectangular roof.

"Welcome to my shoebox," Oliver chuckled. "That's what Ada calls it because it looks like . . ." He turned with a flourish, expecting her to finish his sentence.

"The box shoes come in?"

"What else? Now that's all I see." He unlatched the door and bowed. Luz wasn't sure if she should laugh, or if he was mocking her. She looked at Alonso, who smiled and waved as if to say, "Go on. Don't be scared."

There were only two seats in front. Those in the back had been removed to make way for framed canvases covered with blankets, some tied to the walls.

"While you're in your therapy," Oliver said, "I'll deliver a few paintings to a gallery."

"Like for a show?"

"Yes. They'll hang my landscapes on the walls, a sculptor who uses native bamboo gets the middle of the space, and a potter is in the courtyard."

He switched from English to Spanish easily but his English had a drawl like when he had been pretending to be Elvis. Luz wanted to ask him about it but didn't. He might not think he had an accent, for starters. "Congratulations."

"Thanks. It's a group show, but I'm the only painter."

"I thought you were a musician."

"You remembered!" He turned to her with a wide grin. "That's one of my jobs. Gotta pay the bills, you know."

"When is the exhibit?"

"It opens next Wednesday."

"Maybe Ada can bring me to see it."

"She and Shirley are coming toward the end. Don Alonso can come earlier if he can shift his plans."

"Which ones?"

Oliver concentrated on his driving. Every few blocks, he turned to Luz.

"Are you okay?"

"Yeah. What kind of plan did Abuelo have?"

"It's none of my business."

"But you know, right?"

Again, he looked at her, as if weighing whether telling her would have consequences he was unwilling to live with. She waited while he decided.

As she built memories, Luz began to connect people's behavior to their speech. Their mouths didn't always say what the rest of their bodies did. She thought they didn't deliberately lie to her, but they didn't tell the whole truth, either. She was sure those who loved her, like Alonso and Ada, were protecting her when they withheld information, unwilling to add knowledge that could delay her healing, or cause an achaque. Other people, like

Ileana, Minaxi, and Perla, said things they hoped she'd forget. She did forget a lot, but not everything. More than once she'd overheard them talking about her as "esa loca" after she'd flaked out in front of them.

"Aquí viene la loquita," she heard them say when she was coming out from an episode. They kept doing whatever they were doing as if they hadn't noticed anything unusual. The diminutive meant they didn't consider her completely crazy, only a bit.

"Don Alonso has a doctor's appointment," Oliver said.

"What's wrong with him?"

He thought for another moment. "The stress gets to him, and he doesn't take care of himself."

"Is he sick?"

He glanced at her, unsure whether to say more, but deciding he would. "He's been losing weight too quickly and working too hard. Your issues are a big responsibility. We're doing our best to take care of you both."

He was so earnest, she realized it was an echo of conversations where decisions had been made about her and about her grandfather. She had no idea how many times she'd met Oliver, but it dawned on her that he, Alonso, Ada, and Shirley had talked about her often, and at length. She resented the unfairness of not owning her own memories, of being unable to participate in her own future. In order to function, she needed points of reference. Without them, she couldn't make decisions based on experience.

He pulled over to the curb. "Please stop crying."

"I'm a burden to you all," she said. "But at least you and Ada and Shirley get paid to take care of me. You can walk away. But poor Abuelo changed his whole life, and now he's stuck with me, right?"

"I didn't say that, Luz."

"Not in those words, but I'm not stupid."

"I didn't say you were—"

"Take me to my therapy. That's what you're paid to do."

He was angry, too, but controlled it. He faced the windshield again, adjusted the rearview mirror, and attempted to enter moving traffic.

She wanted to hit something, someone. She was so upset she bit her nails. When had she started doing that? Had she always done it?

Oliver fumed in the driver's seat, and there was something familiar in his rage.

"Have you ever, before today, taken me places when Ada was busy or unable?"

"What does that have to do with anything?"

"Have you, ever, before today, taken me places when Ada was busy or unable?"

"You don't have to repeat yourself."

"I do so you get it. Have you ever—"

"Yes! You've been in this van at least ten times." He slapped the dashboard. "And before you ask, it always ends like this. Always."

"Like what?"

"You fly off the handle. I didn't provoke you or say anything you haven't heard at least a dozen times. You have these tantrums and five minutes later, you've forgotten it all, but we . . ." He looked at her. "We don't forget. We know you have a problem, and we're all trying to help you, but it's intolerable. And yes, I can say anything right now because by the time we get to the clinic, you will have forgotten we argued."

After a while, he asked whether he could turn on the radio.

"Sure." She could hardly breathe and felt tight as a knot. Her eyes itched and she had the urge to pee. He turned to her.

"Are you okay?"

"I'm okay. You?"

He found a salsa version of "Mambo Rock," and it was as if a colony of ants had climbed into his pants. His butt barely on the seat, he leaned over the steering wheel, slapping and punching the dashboard to the rhythm. "I love this tune." He danced but kept the car on the road. Luz checked her seat belt.

He made sure the receptionist knew she was there and sat next to her in the waiting room. Mostly old people slumped on the orange chairs, except for a man in a wheelchair. The patients talked among themselves in loud voices, about politics, about their medications, about their aches and pains. Others stared at Luz and Oliver. Some smiled at her, others looked mad, as if she'd done something wrong. Oliver hummed and tapped his fingers on his knees to a tune Luz didn't recognize. Occasionally, he looked at her.

"Are you okay?"

"Yeah."

He smiled and returned to humming and tapping. Outside, the sun faded. Thunder rumbled. Awnings over store windows flapped and ballooned. Raindrops plopped like tiny missiles. Within moments, the street was dark, and the rain pummeled pedestrians and vehicles, a steady drumming that muffled other sounds. Everyone in the waiting room watched the storm, as if this were the first time it had rained in Puerto Rico.

⌒

"Good work, Luz." The therapist rubbed her shoulders one last time as Luz returned from the relaxation following her session. She expected to find Ada in the waiting room, as usual.

"He's not back yet," the receptionist said.

"Right!" Ada was in Río Piedras and Oliver had brought her. She didn't remember getting here. She often had achaques inside cars. Ada said she was still traumatized by the accident.

Every chair in the waiting room was taken. Luz checked her notebook. On Thursdays after her therapy, she and Ada had a couple of hours free and they usually went to a museum or to Librería Vivliopoleio to browse, buy, and chat with Minerva, who told Luz stories about Salvadora and Federico and let her sketch photos from her albums.

Even with the air conditioner at full blast, the waiting room was stifling and smelled of wet shoes. Luz waited in the overhang outside, where a breeze cooled the air. What was left of the rainstorm dripped from roofs and branches. The gutters between the sidewalk and the road had flooded, the grates blocked by garbage at the corners, where the two avenues met. Passengers in cars, buses, and trucks were irritated, while pedestrians leaped over puddles or tried to figure out how to cross the street without losing a shoe in the rushing water that eddied and whirled with no place to go.

Oliver pulled up to the curb and leaned over to open the door. "So sorry. La Roosevelt is a beast when it rains."

"Don't worry. I checked and that was my only appointment. See? Ada wrote FUN from now until four-thirty."

"Great! Let's have some fun, then."

"We usually go to the bookstore."

"There's a lot of congestion in that direction, and those black clouds mean another squall. It's perfect for a movie closer to home."

He bought a tub of popcorn and huge sodas. There were eight other people in the theater, scattered as if avoiding one another. Oliver put the popcorn on the seat between him and Luz.

She had a hard time following the story, fascinated by the actors' lips' movements, out of sync with what they were saying in Spanish. Oliver, on the other hand, was riveted, munching the popcorn one kernel at a time and sitting on the edge of his seat. On the screen, people rushed along on crowded sidewalks. From above, a sea of yellow cabs crawled toward the sunset. The music was all trumpets and blare. A woman wearing a hat entered a hallway and started walking up a staircase. Next thing, she was wrestling with a man ripping her clothes off. He forced her into a room, and Luz had an achaque.

When she came back, she was standing outside the theater, sobbing, trying to escape from someone holding her still.

"You're okay, you're okay. My name is Dulce. Don't fight me. You're safe."

She was in a woman's arms, her voice a soothing murmur. It felt good to be held tightly, lovingly. Dulce was petite and wiry but strong. She hung on to Luz, rubbing circles on her back until she calmed down. When they separated, Luz saw Oliver screaming at two men keeping him from approaching her.

"Tell them!" Oliver yelled at her. "Tell them I didn't do anything." But it sounded like gbldguk. He was enraged, spitting, kicking, and trying to escape the men. The usher approached Luz and gave her a crumple of paper napkins from one hand and a cup of water from the other. Luz rubbed away the snot, drank the water, thanked her.

"She has brain damage and goes off with no warning. Believe me, I didn't do anything. I'm her caregiver. She's the one who went nuts. Tell them, Luz."

"Calm down, sir," Dulce said. She and the usher hovered over her. "Do you know that man?"

Gbldguk herngonz gbldguk.

When she didn't respond, Dulce stared suspiciously at Oliver and guided Luz farther away from him. "Come back inside for a while. I'll stay with you." Luz sensed a fierceness she wanted for herself. This stranger was worried about her as if she cared.

"He is . . . his name is Oliver."

"That's right! I told you! Come on, Luz. You had an episode, because of your brain damage. Tell them."

"I want to go home."

"I understand, sweetie," Dulce said. "How old are you?"

"Um . . . sixteen."

"Did he try to touch you?"

"What?"

"Inside the theater. You ran out crying, very upset. Did he try something . . ."

"I don't know."

"She had a fit!" The men loosened their grip but didn't let Oliver get closer to her. "She saw something on the screen to upset her. It happens all the time, right, Luz? Tell them!"

"I had a brain injury. I get achaques. I can't control it."

"Is he really your caregiver?"

"He works for my grandfather."

The men released Oliver, explaining they were trying to protect her. He accepted their apologies grudgingly, but they insisted he shake their hands. He was still furious. He shook, then rubbed his hands on his pants. "Let's get out of here. The car's down the street," he said to Luz.

"She's still woozy. Why don't you bring it around? I'll wait with her."

"It's not that far."

"It's best for her if she sits for a moment."

"It's not even three blocks . . ."

Dulce took Luz's arm and led her deeper into the lobby while Oliver protested. "She'll be okay with me until you return, sir." It was obvious she was used to ordering people around. "The walk will do you good, sir."

An annoyed Oliver did as he was told.

Dulce showed Luz to a bench on the far wall. She sat next to her, holding her hand, waiting for Luz to relax. "You're sure you'll be okay alone with him?"

"He drives me to my therapy and to my doctors. Usually, it's his sister but she had an appointment."

"All right, I understand. I'm glad you told me. I have a daughter your age. I'll tell you what I'd say to her if she had the same condition. Be careful around men, you know what I mean? I'm sure your mother has told you . . ."

"I think so," Luz said, wishing Dulce were her mother—a real person, not a photo on a wall, not a should-have-said-this or might-have-done-that.

Oliver drove up to the front of the theater and punched the horn as if that would raise its volume, a bleat similar to that of Ada's Twinkie.

Dulce led her outside. Oliver didn't look at them. Dulce leaned over and hugged Luz, murmuring in her ear, "You be careful, mamita. Don't forget what I told you."

As she climbed into the van, Luz apologized to Oliver.

"That was really embarrassing," he said.

"I didn't mean that to happen."

"I'd never hurt you—you should know that." He looked at her hard. "You know that, right?"

"Yeah," she said after a moment, afraid to contradict him, to say or do something to cause him to turn red again.

Irma

Luz checks the mirror, unsure whether she's this Luz or the phantom Luz. She mentally disappears while her body remains in place. Marysol told her that before her doctors changed her medications, she threw tantrums she later didn't remember, emerging bruised and bloodied. She still breaks into crying jags that leave her exhausted, puffy-eyed, and confused about what could possibly be so terrible she's sobbed in public. The staff at Mi Casa Adult Daycare, Marysol, and her friends and neighbors know both Luzes. She only knows the one who knows there is another Luz she doesn't know. After an achaque, she realizes something has happened, and when it takes place in front of people, she accepts their descriptions because the Luz with awareness has no access to the one who acts out.

Years ago, Marysol, who can tell when Luz is about to have an achaque, recorded her during episodes. Later, she let Luz watch herself banging her head against a wall and screaming at unseen people, having arguments with Salvadora, teary conversations with Federico, or apologizing to Alonso or asking Güela questions. It was eerie for Luz to see the phantom Luz puzzling out a story from her long-dead parents or grandparents. The corporeal Luz couldn't handle it. The videotaped achaques induced others, and Marysol stopped sharing them with her, although she continues to record them when she can. Marysol studies the ghost Luz, hoping she will inform the incarnate Luz. But how can she? Luz thinks she's invisible, even when the mirror reflects a woman. She's a fiction to herself.

She's had to accept she has a chronic condition. She's had to let go of shame over the behavior of the spirit Luz. She tries to be the best Luz she can be, a middle-aged woman who faces the mirror and studies the vertical lines between her eyebrows growing longer and deeper. She has no regrets that her face is no longer fresh and unlined. She believes it's a miracle she's lasted to her fifty-eighth year without major illnesses or medical interventions other than those related to the car accident and the robbery at the bodega, neither of which she remembers. Or does she? She has issues, yes, but she's luckier than the clients she talks to, plays games with, and accompanies around the backyard at Mi Casa. She's healthier than Marysol's patients, wasting away in their homes, their families unable or unwilling to usher them into their hard-earned death. The Luz in the mirror holds her gaze, approving this Luz who doesn't flinch when she sees the image. She's proud she doesn't take a single moment for granted and is confident her last breath will be one of gratitude.

She spends the Labor Day weekend finishing her most recent commission, a family of three. While the sealant on the stones dries, she joins Marysol and Warren at a barbecue next door. The building has six apartments and a yard the previous owner beautified. With Warren's encouragement and guidance, the current tenants have created vegetable plots they plant, maintain, and harvest, and they share the bounty from it among themselves and with Luz and Marysol.

The next day, Luz and Marysol are walking toward Mi Casa when the first strains of Marc Anthony's version of "Aguanile" sing on her phone. She accepts the video call and peers into Ada's worried face. "¿Qué pasó?"

"¡Ay, mija! We'll have to postpone our trip."

"Why?" Marysol asks. "What happened?"

"Haven't you watched the news?"

"I guess not."

"A hurricane is coming for Puerto Rico tomorrow or the day after. It's serious. Rosselló declared a state of emergency."

"We're not going until next week," Marysol says.

"I know, but they say Irma will hit as a Category Five."

"Is that bad?" Luz asks.

"The worst! Oliver and his wife filled every pot and jar because they always lose running water as well as electric power. He and Miriam lined up before the supermarket opened to buy enough canned and dry food. One good thing . . . nuestra gente know what to do when a storm is coming. Pero, comadre, six years after Irene, they're still recovering! Imagínate eso. Everyone's freaking out."

"So are you," Marysol says.

"Me, too." Graciela pops up on the screen from behind Ada.

"Me, tres," Shirley calls from another room.

"So, ¿cancelamos el viaje?"

"Not yet, Marysol. I'm in touch with the airlines and the hotel," Graciela says. "We might have to postpone, but ya veremos."

⌒

At Mi Casa, the staff, volunteers, and clients are aflutter over the impending hurricane. Most of the clients and staff trace their ancestry to Puerto Rico, and collectively they have relatives in almost every town. One of Luz's jobs is to greet the clients at the door and guide the ambulatory ones toward their spots in the activity room or the TV lounge. A few are wheeled in by relatives or by Elodio, an aide. Analisa, also an aide, delivers them to the physical or occupational therapy areas. Today, everyone wants to be in front of the TV, which Penny, a volunteer, switches from Telemundo to Univision to The Weather Channel with dizzying speed. Leaning toward the screen, some of the elders raise the volume on their hearing aids, others ask the person next to them, "What did she say?" or, "Can you make that louder?" No one can get enough of the updates. When breaking news interrupts the programming, everyone stops what they're doing and fixes on the latest, as if it won't be repeated every few minutes. Meteorologists and reporters grasp microphones like lifelines as palm trees sway behind them and rain pelts their shiny impermeables.

The older clients were children in 1928, when Hurricane San Felipe Segundo raced through Puerto Rico. As Luz helps doña Lina to the bathroom or opens a container of juice for don Pepo or places a bib around doña Isidora or spoon-feeds don Teo or buttons doña Calpurnia's sweater, they grab her hands or reach for her shoulder to speak about the hurricanes as if they were relatives. Felipe, Ciprián, Santa Clara, Eloise, Hugo, Georges, Irene, Gilbert, Katrina. Tears collect in the pouches under their eyes and trickle down their cheeks as gnarled, trembling fingers shape invisible losses.

"A hurricane is God's punishment," don Teo reminds them, "when we forget His power."

"The worst is afterward," doña Isidora says. "You come outside and you can't recognize your own yard."

"I lost my father during San Ciprián," doña Calpurnia says. "Our animals were howling and screeching in the barn and during the eye of the storm, Papá went out to calm them. I looked through a hole on the wall of the tormentera, but couldn't see a thing because of the rain. Then we heard a crash and a scream. When we came out hours later, there wasn't even a splinter where the barn had been. It had flown away with Papá, his horse, our milk cow, and all our chickens."

Several times, Luz zones out, to return to herself with doña Calpurnia crying with her, or don Teo with his head in his hands, or doña Isidora poking her shoulders.

That night, Marysol and Warren bring Chinese takeout and join Luz in front of the TV, riveted to the images of roofs flying off buildings and trees blocking roads in the Leeward Islands and on St. Martin. Once the electric grid fails, the networks show endless loops of the horror of the previous hours, now that reporters can't be outside to film the devastation live. The Spanish stations show residents of Puerto Rico and the Dominican Republic preparing for a siege, with long lines at the supermarkets contrasted with empty shelves, once stocked with dried beans, rice, and batteries. Business owners nail plywood over display windows, boat owners tie vessels in place or dry-dock them. Homeowners drive their cars into their marquesinas, drag outdoor furniture inside, stock up on whatever supplies they can find in the depleted stores, and charge their devices.

Luz, Marysol, and Warren are expected at work the next morning, but none of them sleep well that night. Some months earlier, Graciela had convinced them a television in the bedroom would cause sleeplessness because it would be too tempting to keep watching long after bedtime. For Luz, that means she curls up on her couch wrapped in a shawl, dozing during infomercials and awakening to the continuing weather coverage. From the frequent creaks and muted voices next door, she assumes Marysol and Warren aren't sleeping, either. Marysol's TV is in her living room, too, where she and Warren monitor the news through the night. Early the next morning, Warren knocks on Luz's door.

"Bendición, Mamá Luz."

"Dios te bendiga, hijo."

"I had to get away from the news, so I went for bagels. Still warm." He unbags more bagels than three people can eat in one sitting. "Cream cheese and butter?"

"Claro que sí."

Marysol brings a party-size coffee carafe. "We figured you were up all night, too." She's in her scrubs and keeps checking her watch even though it's six-thirty in the morning and she isn't expected at her patient's bedside until ten.

One eye on the TV, they set dishes, mugs, cutlery, and napkins on the coffee table, while Warren arranges platters with two kinds of cheese, smoked fish, capers, sliced onions, and the bagels. They sit side by side, appalled as the overnight reports come in. Hurricane Irma is battering Barbuda and St. Martin, the shell-shocked meteorologists explain. It's expected to cause devastating damage in the Virgin Islands and will reach Puerto Rico that evening, with winds over 150 miles per hour.

"You're trembling, Mom. Lie down."

"I'm fine, just cold."

Warren retrieves a blanket and drapes it over Luz's shoulders. "Is that better?"

She nods and disappears into an achaque, this one like a trance, quiet and intense, her eyes shut, her breathing ragged, interrupted by gasps and sighs. Marysol puts her arm around her mother and squeezes her closer. Warren mutes the television. Luz's breath settles into a normal rhythm. A few minutes later, she opens her eyes, and as often happens following an achaque, momentarily panics until she recognizes where she is. She fixes her gaze on the bottom of the TV screen. A ribbon glides leftward below the newsreaders, correspondents, historians, weather experts, and scientists, who elaborate on the events, their opinions captioned, often misspelled.

"Maybe we've seen enough of this." Warren scrabbles for the remote.

"Let me help you to bed, Mom," Marysol says. "You have a couple of hours before work."

"I want to do something," Luz says.

"We can donate to the Red Cross." Warren's thumbs fly over his phone screen. Luz and Marysol pick up theirs and he guides Luz through the process. They each send fifty dollars.

"It doesn't seem like much," Luz says.

"Every cent helps." Warren stands. "I have to go. Will you be all right?" he asks Marysol.

"Gracias for las bagels de blueberry," Luz says.

"I'm happy you liked them. Bendición."

"Que Dios te cuide, hijo."

Marysol walks Warren to the hall, where they whisper before he leaves.

In her most painful moments, Luz understands what Marysol will never say to her face. Her impairments affect Marysol and interfere with the life she deserves. She loves Warren, he loves her, but Marysol won't leave Luz, and, without discussing it, she has chosen her mother over the love of her life. When Luz follows this thinking, she's afraid she's ruining Marysol's future, her emotions bubble to the surface, and she flakes out.

When Marysol returns from saying goodbye to Warren, she finds Luz standing between the living room and the kitchen, holding the tray of leftovers. She gently removes the tray, sets it on the counter, and leads Luz back to the couch, where she sits with her face in her hands, not quite crying, heaving breaths interrupted by groans. Marysol helps her lie down, and caresses her mother's hair, forehead, her cheeks. Luz closes her eyes, and in minutes falls asleep. It's Marysol who now presses her elbows into her knees, her fingers gripping her face, as tears form at the corners of her eyes. By the time Luz wakes up, she'll have forgotten the vigil, the bagels, and the fifty dollars whooshing away on her phone screen.

⟋

Five of the thirty clients expected at Mi Casa are too distraught to spend the day in the facility as Hurricane Irma's path hurtles toward what they consider home. Sons, daughters, or spouses take the day off from jobs to care for their anxious relatives. They can't focus on anything but the impending disaster, either. One of the elders died overnight, and while the Mi Casa staff didn't make an announcement about his passing, some of his friends have already heard about it and their lamentations add to the tension. By the time Luz places doña Calpurnia's lunch in front of her, the news stations are feverish with the near-total devastation in Barbuda. Don Teo, terrified of his vengeful God, collapses and is taken away by ambulance.

On television, the governor of Puerto Rico, Ricardo Rosselló, reminds estadounidenses that they're being threatened by a hurricane as powerful as Harvey, which only two weeks earlier caused extensive flooding, destruction of property, and the death of more than one hundred people in Texas and Louisiana. Some of the viejitos at Mi Casa jeer at Rosselló.

"Mamao," snarls doña Isidora. "Why is he talking about Harvey?"

"Porque tiene que lamer los culos a los gringos," don Chipe grumbles, hoping his vulgar words won't reach the women nearby.

"That's true," doña Amelia says. "If he doesn't lick the gringos' butts, they pretend Puerto Rico doesn't exist."

"Let him talk," doña Lucía shushes them.

Rosselló, the son of a former governor, has yet to develop the confidence and gravitas expected from a leader. He looks younger than his actual age and seems to be begging to be taken seriously. It doesn't help that during news conferences his voice registers higher than expected from the size of his body.

Some of the elders at Mi Casa, who, like Rosselló, are pro-statehood, scowl at anyone who disparages the governor.

"Esa es una falta de respeto," don Monche complains. "He was elected by the people."

"Like him or not," doña Amelia says, "he's in charge."

"Maybe he'll surprise everyone," don Chipe says, "and do something good for a change."

⌒

Throughout the day, Luz receives numerous calls and texts from Ada, Shirley, Graciela, Marysol, and Warren. Surprisingly, Luz is nervous but not, as they expect, a mess. As Marysol often says, there's a bright side to a compromised memory.

By midafternoon, Hurricane Irma is veering northeast of Puerto Rico and it's reported that the island might not take a direct hit; nevertheless, the authorities predict heavy rains and say the electric grid has already failed. This news, while not great, is a relief to everyone at Mi Casa. They consider the loss of power inconvenient compared to the razing of Barbuda and parts of St. John, St. Thomas, St. Martin, and other islands in the Antillean Caribbean. By the time Angie, Luz's neighbor, comes to walk her home, Luz isn't as anxious as she was in the morning, when Marysol dropped her off. She turns on the TV while she and Angie prepare dinner. Meteorologists and news reporters keep saying "seems as if," "might," "could," "expected to," and the tension returns, but neither woman can bring herself to turn it off. Angie keeps expecting developments, while Luz experiences each report as if she's never heard or seen one before.

Marysol and Warren join her for dinner on what will be another sleepless night until Irma whirls out to sea.

"They have no idea how worried we are here," Marysol says as she sets the dinner table.

"We're the last thing they need to think about right now," Warren says. He drops ice cubes into tall glasses and pours fresh-squeezed lemonade over a jigger of lemon Don Q.

"Yes, but I wonder, do they ever think about us, the exiles?"

"They have their own problems," Luz says, ladling arroz con pollo onto the serving platter.

"Yo entiendo, pero . . . they have the one thing we don't have. Do they suffer from an absence of . . . I don't even know what it is . . ." Marysol seeks the words on the ceiling and, while they're invisible to Luz and Warren, she finds them. "Do they miss Puerto Rico like we do?"

"I don't think you can miss what you have. Maybe they're wistful for the historical Puerto Rico," Warren says. "They romanticize jíbaros, life in el campo, the rhythms of la plena, and what they believe was a less hectic life."

"Homesick for their parents' and grandparents' times," Marysol says.

"And those days weren't all that great, either," Luz adds.

Warren and Marysol wait for her to say more, but she's moved on to decorating the platter with roasted red peppers.

Warren wraps his arms around Marysol and she burrows into him. "You're exhausted, mi reina. No TV tonight. There's nothing we can do until the storm passes."

"Good thing we have the Spanish stations," Luz says. "Los meteorólogos here only report hurricanes that reach Florida or—¿cómo se llaman? Ah, sí, los Outer Banks. ¿Dónde queda eso?"

Marysol reluctantly disentangles from Warren. "They're off the coast of one of the Carolinas."

"They worry about esos Outer Banks. They must be very important to the gringos."

Warren and Marysol snort.

"We're not supposed to call them gringos, Mom."

"El Trompo calls us criminals and rapists, I can call them gringos."

"Of all the things to remember," Marysol says, "why clutter your mind with anything that man says."

"I can't control it, hija."

"Don't worry, Mamá Luz. *Gringo* isn't an insult. It means foreigner, including, but not exclusive to, estadounidenses—"

"Who think everything is about them." Luz shapes a red-pepper strip into a circle atop the mound of rice.

"Mamá Luz, the political pundit," Warren laughs.

"Let's eat before it gets cold." Luz places the steaming platter on the table. "Und schalten Sie den Fernseher aus."

"I beg your pardon?"

"Irma will do what it does, whether or not we watch it on TV."

⁂

The past two days have been stressful, but when Luz walks into Mi Casa, relief seems to be dripping from the walls. The clients arrive smiling, as if their will and prayers altered the course of the hurricane. They joke, high-five one another, and celebrate the close call. With the next breath, they speak of the tribulations their Caribbean neighbors will face as they rebuild.

While Irma didn't turn out to be the catastrophe scientists and news anchors predicted, it ravaged the easternmost parts of Puerto Rico and Vieques and Culebra. Four people died. Floods and winds leveled homes, and thousands were displaced. By Thursday morning, more than a million households and businesses were without power, with no idea when it would be restored.

"The good news," Graciela says over FaceTime, "is that you

won't have to postpone your trip. Your hotel has generators and they expect things to be normal in a couple of days."

"They connect the tourist areas first," Ada says. "Que se chave el resto del pueblo. Gotta keep the turistas happy."

"Turistas like us." Graciela talks over her mother, who appears to be in bad temper. "The airline expects to be on schedule by the time you fly. So, light your good-luck candles and rinse your amuletos. The casinos want good news coming from Puerto Rico. They'll probably rig the machines for someone to win big. That could be you."

"I'm bringing the shawl with the dollar signs all over it," Shirley calls from offscreen.

"I'm wearing the same outfit I wore the day you won the jackpot," Ada says to Luz. "And I hope you kept your lucky hoodie with the rhinestones."

"It's hanging on my door, comadre," Luz says.

"We're all set, then." Shirley appears on the screen for an instant. "¡Pa'alante!"

The Gallery

MAY 12, 1976

On Wednesday, a scorching morning in San Juan yielded to crackling lightning, explosive thunder, and torrential rains in the afternoon. The vaguada caused flooding, and a symphony of horns disturbed the evening as frustrated drivers attempted to get home in time for dinner.

Luz and Alonso waited until the heavy rains became sprinkles. The mist around headlamps, streetlights, and billboards dissolved angles and created deeper shadows. The shimmering surface of puddles disguised huge potholes. Alonso dodged them as if one would swallow the car.

They arrived at a Spanish colonial-style house converted into a café and gallery in Hato Rey. Alonso helped Luz from the car and kissed her hand. They linked arms and he patted her forearm reassuringly as they entered the foyer. Oliver was shaking hands with someone who looked like a younger version of former governor Luis Muñoz Marín. This man had the same florid complexion, hair parted on the right, thick eyebrows shading astute eyes, full mustache, and a not-quite-portly-but-on-its-way belly as Muñoz Marín did. And like the former governor, the man dominated the room. His image was on Luz's wall at home, and she'd copied his features into her sketchbooks, usually next to Alonso or Federico or with his arm around Salvadora's waist.

"That's Josué with Oliver," Alonso said.

Josué approached as if he were about to do them a favor.

"Alonso Peña Ortíz and his lovely granddaughter, Luz Peña Fuentes," Josué said. Other guests eyed them as if they were part of the exhibit. "How good to see you." He embraced Alonso and slapped his back. "You're looking well."

He turned to Luz with an exaggerated bow, took her hands, and brushed his mustache against her fingers. She was put off. She'd been kissed on the hand moments earlier, and could tell the difference between Alonso's gesture of love and Josué's, meant to bring attention to himself. She rubbed her hand against the side of her skirt to clear the tickling sensation of his wet lips behind his bristling mustache. She felt herself falling into an achaque. Alonso and Oliver exchanged a look, and her grandfather took her elbow.

"Let's look at the paintings." He led her across the courtyard to a bench.

"Don't worry, Abuelo. It's passed." She rarely had a warning of the achaques, but this time she had felt one coming, and was grateful for Alonso, who also, somehow, detected she was on the edge and kept her from dropping over it. "How did you know I was about to flake out?"

"Your lids fluttered," he said. "Ada has noticed it and told me to look for it."

"So it's obvious something's happening?"

"Not always, and only if you know that's one of the signs. Ada, Shirley, Oliver, and I look for them."

"There are more?"

"When your brow sweats, or your fingers scratch the air. But most times you go inside, as if you're dreaming. Even when we can tell what's happening, we don't interrupt it. You shouldn't wake a sonámbula."

"So, I'm like a sleepwalker?"

He stroked her forearm. "It's unsafe to disturb people in that state, so, just in case, we make sure you're safe and wait it out."

"How long do the achaques last?"

"It depends. Usually a few seconds or minutes, other times an hour. A couple of weeks ago Ada dropped you off at your therapy. She had to go to a political rally in Río Piedras, so Oliver brought you home afterward. You were in an achaque for almost two hours, more spaced out than I'd seen. I was dialing your doctor when you came out of it as if nothing happened."

"Have you told me this before, Abuelo?"

"It doesn't matter, mamita."

"But I want to know if what I hear is new to me or not."

"I understand, mi amor. I told you about that one because it lasted longer than the ones I'd seen. You were fine. Ada was aware some lasted longer than others. She mentioned it to your neurologist and he didn't seem concerned."

"I'm such a burden."

"Not at all, mi niña consentida. It's a privilege to be your grandfather, to care for you like you deserve. You've brought joy into my life. But I'm an old man who forgets to tell you things." He grinned, and she giggled and touched his arm to let him know she understood the joke.

Later, Luz was standing in front of a painting. She'd seen ones like this on the plazas in Old San Juan, where men set up easels in front of La Catedral, or the view of the governor's mansion from Calle de la Fortaleza, or a garita facing the Atlantic Ocean from El Morro, or the too-friendly pigeons at the Parque de las Palomas. Tourists bought the factory-stretched canvases still smelling of acrylic paint, the edges sticky. The artists reminded the buyers to let them dry. But unlike this one, those paintings were no bigger than what could be carried aboard a plane. Ada had told Luz she'd bought a few as gifts for people in El Norte to brighten their short winter days.

"Those pictures are frivolous and don't show the real Puerto Rico. I should be ashamed."

"Why do you buy them?"

"Mostly to support the artists, but actually because in spite of years of reading and study, I'm mentally colonized and blinded by years of oppression."

"Wow, that sounds heavy," Luz said.

Ada laughed. "You have no idea." She became serious again. "I was being sarcastic. We can't escape the effects of colonization and oppression. Whether we notice it or not, we're influenced by them."

Luz now wondered whether this painter was also mentally colonized. It explained why the images were trite. They were about the viewer, not the painter. Was that what being colonized meant? To see through the eyes of others, not your own? Wasn't that what her own life was like? She was what other people told her she was. On the other hand, she had an injured brain. How did a healthy brain get un-colonized? Or was it *de*colonized? She scribbled a note to ask Ada next time she saw her.

"What do you think?" Oliver came over to stand next to Luz.

"It has energy and movement," she said.

"You're the only person to make a useful comment on my work."

Luz had a flash of canvases in back of Oliver's car. "These are yours?"

"You're right to be skeptical . . ."

"I didn't mean—"

"It's okay. I know I'm not very good."

"But there are many people here who disagree. Abuelo said those dots mean they're sold."

"Bought by my friends and neighbors. That woman with the long braids and the guy wearing the caftan? They're talented painters who came here to check out the competition. They need not worry."

"You're hard on yourself," Luz says.

He dropped his gaze, as if to avoid looking at his own work. "People say, 'I like it,' or point to another they like better. As if that's all that matters in a work of art. As if all the artist cares about is whether the viewer likes it or not."

"You don't?"

"I want the viewer to see beyond 'like' or 'not like,' to be moved and to ask why they're emotional, to realize something about me and about themselves."

"That's a lot to ask."

He smiled. "You see energy because you're a dancer. The work moves you because you understand movement and you're in touch with that part of yourself."

"I was a dancer. I can't do that anymore."

"I'll sell as many of these as I can," he continued, dismissing her doubts, "and burn the rest."

"That's extreme. Wouldn't you miss doing it?"

"I might. I do love the process."

"You shouldn't give up yet, then." She looked at the next canvas. "You can always get better by practicing."

"Nah. I don't have the commitment or the discipline."

"I've seen pictures of me as a dancer," she said. "It makes me sad because I can't dance at that level anymore. That girl in the photos in our hallway? She's me. Was me. I wish I could remember her. I wish I could be her. I can't but, you . . . Maybe, someday, you'll see one of your canvases and remember who you were when you painted it."

Oliver was about to say something when Josué approached with his ingratiating smile. Luz couldn't make sense of why he gave her the creeps. He was polite and admired Oliver's work, but she distrusted his flattery.

"I like that one best." Josué tapped the wall next to a painting. "It's not too big. The others won't fit in my living room." He chortled as if he were joking but bought the one he'd pointed to, not so small that it required close scrutiny but not so big it couldn't fit over a sofa.

Piñones

SEPTEMBER 15, 2017

Once the plane rose above the Rockaways, Marysol could see nothing but the blue-gray Atlantic Ocean, soon covered by clouds, the remains of Hurricane José. Like Hurricane Irma, José spared Puerto Rico and is now whirling toward the Outer Banks while Marysol flies in the opposite direction. As planned, Shirley, Ada, and Luz arrived in Puerto Rico four days ago so they could feed the traganíckeles. Their daughters weren't interested in casinos. Las madres have been rewarded with blinking lights, bells, dings, jingles, and more than eight hundred dollars so far. Graciela arrived in San Juan last night, but Marysol could only get away this morning.

The plane thrums, thumps, and dips toward the green patch floating in the ocean blue as a tinny voice announces turbulence over Puerto Rico. Marysol tightens her seat belt and pushes her bag under the seat ahead of her. She's been on an airplane only twice, to and from Orlando. Those flights hugged the coast but her assigned seats had faced landward. She assumed vast green patches broken by gray squiggles were roads, the silver snakes indicating rivers, and mirrorlike sparkling lakes or ponds. Between swards of vegetation, rectangles and squares defined the roofs and parking lots in towns and cities.

Now, bouncing toward the airport, she recognizes the telltale signs of human habitation along Puerto Rico's Atlantic coast. The ocean isn't gray, as it is at Orchard Beach or in Maine. It's a deep marine blue. From the air, the landmass appears to be mostly rich, green forests.

The pilot guides the aircraft inland, then turns again toward the sea. It feels as if the wings are flapping and might at any moment separate from the sausage-shaped aircraft descending and bobbing toward the runway. It's early afternoon, and the sun plays on water, glass, and metal, flashing like a thousand winks. Marysol makes out roofs in various sizes and shapes, some areas packed like a Tetris board, others surrounded by empty lots bordered by vegetation and roads curving to and from commercial centers.

"The roofs are blue," the woman behind her says to her companion.

"After Irma, the government handed out tarps for people who'd lost their roofs," he says.

As the plane gets closer to the airstrip, Marysol is surprised by the upended trees, their exposed roots like arthritic fingers reaching for the sky. Lampposts and telephone poles lean dangerously over buildings and roads, their wires draped over one another like black spaghetti. Clusters of people queue in front of tents and buildings.

"They're waiting for potable water and food," the man behind her says.

As they approach the runway, the ocean is screened by a long line of tall buildings.

"The Condado and Isla Verde look normal," the woman says.

The passengers applaud the landing and Marysol relaxes, as the amens of those who've been praying since the turbulence started echo throughout the cabin.

She texts Graciela and Warren—"Landed!"—and almost immediately a thumbs-up and a heart-eyed face emoji appear.

Travelers stand the moment the seat belt light dings off. Tall Marysol is called upon to help shorter passengers retrieve suitcases and zippered plastic bags from the overhead bins.

When she enters the tunnel toward the waiting area, a hot wave envelops her like an embrace. A knot forms in her throat. Inside the terminal, the air-conditioning is colder than she expected, and she shudders at the contrast.

It's not until she reaches baggage claim that she feels she's no longer in the United States. Three men wearing crisp guayaberas and narrow-brimmed jipijapa hats are singing jíbaro music accompanied by a cuatro, a guitar, and a güiro. They play the jaunty music with such commitment that passengers stop to listen before lining up around the baggage claim belts. Marysol drops five dollars into the basket in front of the musicians.

While waiting for her suitcase, she reads the pdf Graciela posted on WeAreGLAMS with the itinerary for their vacation. Marysol is neat and organized but Graciela beats her by miles.

She retrieves her bag, and a couple of steps outside the terminal, the heavy, humid air takes her breath away. The thunder of airplane, truck, and bus engines competing with car horns, rolling suitcases, voices echoing off the cement walls and sidewalks stops her in her tracks, forcing the large man behind her to crash into her. They tumble to the sidewalk in a jumble of suitcases, legs, and packages.

"Disculpe, señora," he says, although it was her fault. She wonders if flying over the Atlantic has aged her. No one has called her "señora" in the Bronx.

She jumps to her feet and helps the man stand while his companions gather his belongings. She's too hot, ruffled, chagrined, and thinks she's imagining the voices of Shirley, Ada, Luz, and Graciela clucking around her. But there they are, fussing and apologizing to the man and his family who thank them and assure them he's okay and they know it was an accident. They scamper away as if they've been assaulted by a coven.

"Why are you here? The pdf says I should take a taxi."

"Change of plans." Graciela grabs her suitcase and rolls it toward a white limo. The driver drops it inside the trunk and runs to hold the door open for them. He smiles as if he can tell Marysol has never been inside a limo. Shirley, Ada, Graciela, and Luz are giddy and might be drunk or high or both.

"Vámonos." Ada settles at the far end of the vehicle. It's cool inside and the stereo blasts Gilberto Santa Rosa and his band's "Que Manera de Quererte." An open bottle of Champagne sweats in an ice bucket.

"What's all this?"

"You've heard me mention my cousin Oliver," Ada says.

"Mucho gusto." He waves from the driver's seat.

"His wife, Miriam, owns a limo company," Shirley explains.

"It's only one limo," Oliver corrects her.

"The people who rented it for today canceled," Graciela says. "Miriam and Oliver sent it as Mami's birthday present."

Luz pours Champagne into a glass flute for Marysol.

"You must be hungry. We're going to Piñones," Ada says.

"In a limo?" Marysol has seen images of the beachside kiosks and open-air restaurants that look casual, even rustic.

"Why not?"

They laugh.

"I don't turn seventy every year." Shirley grins.

"¡Wepa!" Las madres clap and dance on their seats.

"How long have you been celebrating?"

"We had a couple of mimosas before Oliver came." Shirley tops her Champagne.

The darkened windows, the excitement, and the throbbing music are making Marysol queasy. She's about to ask Oliver to lower the windows for fresh air, when he stops in front of what looks like a thrown-together, palm-roofed rancho on the beach. He opens the door with the ceremony of a presidential staffer, his free hand outstretched toward the impaled pig roasting behind a glass case. The ocean air revives Marysol, and the nausea dissipates, to be replaced by hunger pangs.

"You wanted lechón," Oliver says. "This is the best." A man approaches. "This is my nephew Lucho. Miriam's brother owns this place and they'll take good care of you. I can't park the limo here. Text when you need me, or Lucho will."

Lucho could be a contender for the Sexiest Man Alive. He's fit, and obviously proud of his chiseled shoulders and arms, which make the most of his sleeveless shirt. His well-moisturized carob skin enhances his turquoise irises.

"Ay, mi madre," Graciela says between a sigh and a gasp. "¡Qué macho!"

Marysol elbows her. "Down, girl!"

"Can't be real," Luz whispers as Lucho guides Shirley and Ada toward a picnic table in the shade.

"Oh, it's real," Graciela giggles.

"She means this." Marysol points to her eyes.

Lucho fawns over Shirley and Ada, ensuring they settle on the benches facing the ocean, and that plastic cups and a pitcher with ice water are placed before them. He treats them as if he were their favorite son and they his beloved mothers.

Marysol stands under the sun for a moment and seeks her shadow. The knot in her throat comes back, and her chest fills with emotion. Luz leans her head on her shoulder.

"Bienvenida a tu patria," she says.

"We won't tease you if you kiss the ground," Ada says.

"That's all right," Marysol says, but she takes off her shoes and digs her toes into the sand.

It's impossible to ignore the damage caused by Irma. Abandoned heaps of wood, broken plastic tables and chairs, and equipment beyond repair litter the beach like fractured dreams. In spite of the damage around them, some of the restaurants are being rebuilt in time for the lucrative weekend crowds. Marysol's chest fills with pride at Puerto Ricans' optimism in the face of destruction.

Over the next few hours, Lucho delivers food and drink to their table. Most offerings come from the fryer or in chunks from the lechón asado. There is no printed menu or a list of offerings on a board. Hot, crispy bacalaítos, crunchy fried yuca with garlicky mojito, tostones to be dipped in mayoketchup simply appear before them. Lucho purrs, "You look like you need alcapurrías," as he places a newly fried stack before them.

Graciela gushes over the mango juice Lucho puts in front of her. The women sit at the picnic table eating what Lucho and a tattooed young woman deliver. Las madres and las nenas alternate eating with walks along the sand. Luz finds a couple of rocks she wants to paint in her studio back home. She also sketches their smiling faces, the landscape, the lechón becoming mere bones on the stick before another, plump and golden, appears.

From time to time, the women splash into the ocean up to their knees, unconcerned about their wet clothes.

"It's so warm," Marysol squeals when she first steps into the water.

"Just wait until you get to the Caribbean beaches," Graciela says. "They're like a bath."

❧

Marysol awakens to stifled moans and someone shushing someone else on the other side of the wall. Her head is filled with pebbles, and she has to use her hands to lift it from the pillow. She's been facedown in the trough of a cheap mattress on top of a polyester quilt in a dimly lit room painted shades of blue and brown. The drapes are closed. A scarf has been placed over a lamp next to another bed, unoccupied but with clothes on it. Each detail makes more sense than the one before it. She's in Puerto Rico, sharing a room with Graciela. She blinks to focus on the red numbers on the bedside clock: 11:37 p.m. With effort, she turns on her side, attempts to sit up, and is overcome with the sour taste of too much rum. Her sunburned shoulders, chest, nose, and forehead hurt. She manages to roll to the edge of the mattress, drops her feet to the carpeted floor, and has the urge, no, the necessity, to move her churning bowels. Light seeps under the bathroom door and she shoves it open. An ecstatic Graciela is braced on the counter, facing the mirror, her breasts cupped in the hands of the Sexiest Man Alive in the throes of an orgasm between her buttocks.

"Out! Out!" Marysol screeches. "I need the toilet. Now!"

Lucho and Graciela gather themselves and scurry while Marysol relieves herself of alcapurrías and bacalaítos, yuca, lechón asado, and too many tostones with mayoketchup.

❧

She showers, alternating hot streams with cold water, holding on to the senior handrail throughout, trusting it will hold if she falls. By the time she's steadier, Lucho has left, and Graciela is sitting on her bed, fingers racing over her laptop keys. She looks up, smiles bashfully.

"Your suitcase is in the closet." She returns to her typing.

Las Madres

Marysol retrieves it from behind the mirrored doors and unzips it atop the desk against the wall. She's not sober but not so drunk she can't perform routine tasks like brushing her teeth and moisturizing her face and body. Her movements are deliberate but clumsy, sentient but mentally muddled. She's annoyed with Graciela, whose keystrokes sound like jackhammers.

She opens the curtains to a four-lane highway, flashing billboards above flat-roofed houses and stores. Planes arriving and departing rumble in the nearby airport, the sound of their engines only slightly dampened by the humming air conditioner in the room. Graciela's *clickity-clickity-clack* recalls the number 6 elevated train over Westchester Avenue.

She removes the scratchy quilt on her bed, punches the lumpy pillows, and settles into the trough, hoping to sleep through Graciela's relentless keyboarding. Instead, she stares at the pocked ceiling, unable to relax until she says her piece.

"What were you thinking?"

"About what?" Graciela snaps her laptop closed.

"Lucho."

"What about him?"

"Do las madres know you and Lucho were doing the nasty in our bathroom?"

"They were—how do you say—inebriated."

"We were all borrachas."

"Not me. Oliver and Lucho practically dragged las madres into their room, singing 'Cielito Lindo' at the top of their lungs. You were no help. Lucho carried you like a fireman rescuing a victim. I should have snapped a photo for Warren."

Marysol has no memory beyond the spectacular pastel sunset behind distant mountains. "How long did I sleep?"

"Two or three hours, at least."

She turns on her side to Graciela's grin. "Hours?"

"Lucho wasn't drunk, either." Graciela blushes.

"You've been in the bathroom for two to three hours?"

"Mas o menos. We didn't want to wake you."

"That was considerate."

Graciela ignores Marysol's sarcasm. "We showered and everything . . ."

"Spare me. I saw more than enough."

"I hadn't had sex in months."

"Oh, that explains it . . ."

"It just happened. I didn't exactly plan it."

"If you had, you'd have added it to the itinerary, right?"

"What are you talking about?"

"Well, you're always so . . . methodical."

"Oh, thanks, but no. I made it clear I was available. And before you ask, yes, I had condoms and insisted he wear them."

A Problem

SEPTEMBER 16, 2017

The next morning, Marysol rouses again, facedown on the mattress trough. Graciela is punching keys into her laptop. Marysol groans at the clock: 6:27. "Too early!"

"Sorry. We have a problem." Graciela has canceled Shirley's birthday party in Naguabo because the eastern shore of the island is still without electricity. The restaurant owner couldn't get a message to her until a couple of hours ago from another town. "Mom's cousin Edith got a cell signal day before yesterday, an hour away from her house and she couldn't connect by voice, only texts. Things are terrible there."

"We're not leaving Puerto Rico? I just got here!"

Graciela chews on a hangnail. "Las madres said they've had blackouts since they got here, but the lights came back."

Las Madres

"If we stay in this hotel, they'll spend our vacation in the casino."

"I'll look for a condo nearby." Graciela resumes keyboarding. "They can walk to a casino if they want to, while you and I hang out on the beach."

～

Las madres stumble into the restaurant shortly after nine-thirty, when Graciela had scheduled them to meet for breakfast.

"I don't remember the last time I drank so much," Shirley says as she takes her seat.

"Last month, at your retirement party?"

"Nothing like yesterday, though. I was still upright at the end of that night."

Marysol's hangover makes it hard to focus. Her headache is only slightly relieved by coffee and lots of water. Like her, Shirley, Ada, and Luz are not as sharp as usual and a perky Graciela has to explain the situation several times before las madres understand why the plans have changed.

"We couldn't have known more than one million people would still be without power ten days after the hurricane."

Ada squeezes Shirley's hand. "We'll celebrate your birthday at a nice restaurant."

"Don't mention food right now." Marysol is seated with her back to the buffet and keeps sipping coffee from the mug the server refills from a thermal pitcher. The strong aroma masks the breakfast smells.

Luz drapes her arm over Marysol's shoulders and squeezes her closer. Her headache vanishes.

Graciela turns her computer screen toward las madres. "I bookmarked places that look promising and might let us check in later today or tomorrow."

Las madres lean on their forearms, focused on Graciela as if she's creating, rather than seeking, a place for them. Marysol has no interest in watching her opening and closing tabs on her browser.

"I need some air."

The glass door to the pool area scrapes against the cement walk as she pushes it open. Speakers blast Olga Tañon merengues in the management's attempts to mask the noises from a highway a block away. The beach is in the opposite direction, and neither soothing waves nor salty breezes reach this patio. Skinny brown lizards scurry into the shadows beneath plants. Three children play in the pool with their dad. Their screeches float over the fast-paced merengues, and at first they get on Marysol's nerves, but soon their delighted squeals force a smile.

She was a child once, and she adored her father, Danilo. His friends in Yonkers had a pool surrounded by flagstones. The couple hosted barbecues almost every summer Sunday, children invited. Their two teenage sons were lifeguards so the adults could drink, eat, laugh, and dance on the deck. The dad in this pool lifts his youngest girl high above the shallow end, launches her into the deep end, then swims as fast as he can toward where she's dropped into the water, diving below if she doesn't pop up quickly enough. This was one of Marysol's favorite games with Danilo on those Sundays when he and Luz needed a day off and left the bodega in charge of their upstairs neighbors, Vivian and Eros.

Breathe, she tells herself. Memories are stored emotions, and to return to this moment, Marysol counts to ten, to twenty, to thirty. Inhale. Exhale.

The door to the restaurant opens, and Ada beckons her inside.

⌒

Las madres and las nenas check out of the hotel and Oliver picks them up in a six-passenger van, cooled to arctic temperatures and blasting Marc Anthony on the sound system. He's dispensed with the formalities of the previous day and now wears jeans, a Hard Rock Cafe T-shirt, and sneakers. He and Shirley, in the front passenger seats, narrate the sights.

"That sushi place," Oliver says, "opened a month ago. I can't get into raw fish. Their tempura is really good, though."

"It used to be La Nonna, the best Italian food in the city." Shirley turns to Ada and Luz in the middle seats. "We loved that restaurant."

"Our favorite was the eggplant parmigiana," Ada says. "And grilled pulpo."

"Ummm . . . eggplant," Luz adds.

On the seats behind their mothers, Graciela and Marysol can catch only parts of the conversation because of the bass-heavy speakers on the side panels.

Marysol leans closer to Graciela. "This house we're staying in . . . does it have anything to do with being closer to Lucho?"

"No. I've no idea where he lives. FYI, he was a diversion. It had been a long time and, well . . ." She shrugs. "All I can say is he was worth the wait."

"You don't need to apologize."

"It's not an apology. It's an explanation. Oliver found this place for us. He knows a lot of people. His cousin's a Realtor."

"Another cousin!"

Graciela laughs. "Everyone's someone else's cousin here, don't you know?"

"I know, I know. Island. Everyone's related, blah, blah, blah. But think, Graciela. You do realize that Lucho is your cousin if he's Oliver's nephew."

"On his wife's side."

"Oh, in that case . . ."

"Stop judging me, Marysol," Graciela snaps. "My private life is none of your business." She turns toward the window opposite Marysol's and huffs.

Marysol glares at the businesses packed close together on her side of the street. Much of the signage is familiar from the Bronx. She can't let go of her disappointment that so far the trip hasn't been fun. Then she remembers Piñones, and her feelings ricochet. That was fun. But Irma had taken many of the kiosks and open-air restaurants. The beach was littered. But the water was so warm! When she first stepped in, she thought someone nearby had peed in the ocean.

Inside her head is a pinball machine, the ball pinging against bumpers and targets. Ping! *Puerto Rico isn't what I expected. What does that mean? I hoped it would look more traditional. What does that mean? Exotic? That's a stereotype.* Ping! *This is my first trip here and I'm sorry I came so far to feel bad about myself.* Ping! *I miss Warren. He's pointed out that liquor makes me irritable.* Ping! *Graciela's right— I judged her. It's Graciela's body and her choice to use as she wants.* Ping! *Still, she knew we were sharing a room. Why didn't they go to his place?* Ping! *Why should I care what she does where?* Ping! *Knowing what sets me off doesn't help me get over it.*

When she doesn't want to be where she is, Marysol closes her eyes and envisions Everest, goddess mother of the world, looming over lesser mountains in Nepal and Tibet, snowcapped and serene. Or so it seems in pictures. Conjuring mountains like Everest, Mount Fuji in Japan, and Kilimanjaro in Tanzania usually soothes her. They're so unimaginably far from where she finds herself. This particular moment isn't only happening in a van in Puerto Rico. It's ticktocking across oceans, valleys, and deserts in places she'll probably never visit, at least not so long as she has to care for her mother. Ping! This line of thinking is guilt-inducing, so she whiplashes to what's happening now, scrunched up in the back seat of a van with four of the most important people in her life. She has to call upon her own reserves.

She pokes Graciela's shoulder. "I didn't mean to judge you."

Graciela doesn't turn around. "Don't apologize. It doesn't suit you."

"What do you mean?"

"You always do that."

"Do what?"

"This, what you've been doing since . . . forever. Always having an opinion about everything I do. I'm sick of it."

Marysol is taken aback. "Always?"

From the van's middle seats, Luz and Ada eye each other, aware las nenas are bickering about something they can't quite hear, what with the stereo vibrating and Oliver and Shirley exchanging before-and-after stories up front.

"And if you don't say it, it shows on your face. You need to work on that."

"What are you talking about?"

"You don't even notice it. Like your expression when I walked down the aisle . . ."

"What aisle?"

"You were upset because you couldn't be a bridesmaid. And you made a face, like, like——"

Marysol has to rewind. "Wait. Are you talking about your wedding, uhm, twenty years ago? With the Princess Diana dress with a bolt of tulle on the skirt and a twenty-foot train?"

Graciela gives her the side eye, clicks her tongue, and fixes her gaze on the slow progress of traffic.

"You're telling me I made a face twenty years ago and you haven't gotten over it? Is that what you're saying?"

"What's going on?" Ada calls. "Are you arguing?"

"We're talking," Graciela says. "There's the drugstore. Can we stop for a minute? I need something."

"What? Toothpaste? Shampoo? Deodorant?" las madres call out, like hawkers at a fair.

"No, it'll take a minute. You can wait in the van."

Oliver signals left as a stream of cars from the opposite direction try to beat the green light on the two-lane road. The drivers behind the van honk and gesticulate from open windows as the light ahead turns yellow.

As soon as Oliver pulls into the parking area, las madres open the doors and spill out, slinging purses over their shoulders, adjusting bra straps, straightening garments, fluffing hairdos. They've been in the vehicle for less than half an hour and are eager for another adventure.

"So are we all going to Walgreens?" Marysol's flip-flops are too thin for the hot tarred pavement. Las madres are already halfway to the door, chattering like teenagers.

Graciela waits for Marysol.

"Can you do me a favor?"

"If I say no, will you be throwing it in my face twenty years from now?"

"Come on, Marysol. We're going to be together for another week and a half. We're all . . . Well, they're not . . ." She looks toward the door closing behind las madres. "You and I are stressed for different reasons. Can we talk about it later? Let's not spoil this for them."

"Okay. What do you want me to do?"

"Keep las madres busy while I shop."

"What are you looking for?"

"None of your business!"

"Which part of this huge drugstore should we avoid?"

"I don't know. I don't know where they keep them." Graciela blushes so red, Marysol thinks she's about to pass out.

"Condoms? You're here for more condoms?"

"Yes. I ran out. And no, it's not for Lucho. He's not the only man here. Aha! There's that face again!"

"I can't help what my face does," Marysol retorts, but Graciela is sprinting toward the front counter, where a display provides every size, color, and texture.

Las Madres

Las madres have found their way to the grocery aisles. Their cart overflows with chips, cereal, crackers, and the last three cans of Vienna sausages.

"We don't want to run out of snacks when we get the munchies," Ada says with a mischievous smile, and the others giggle as if . . . Is it possible? She and Shirley are already high.

They set off toward the refrigerated cases, Luz between Ada and Shirley. Las madres always arrange themselves this way, with Luz in the center. She's tall, mahogany-skinned, her close-clipped salt-and-pepper Afro accentuating her perfectly shaped skull. Her flowing midi-dress in a polka-dot pattern seems designed for dancing. Olive-skinned Shirley has the same bangs-and-bob hairdo she's worn since junior high school, her hair as black as it was then, thanks to drugstore dyes. She wears Capri pants, a camp shirt, and platform sneakers. Ada might have recently arrived from Coachella, her long gray hair braided to her waist. It occurs to Marysol that the pyramid they form can also recall a mountain, Ada and Shirley the lesser mounts that make the peak possible.

Oliver approaches a wrought-iron fence meant to appear ornamental but intended to discourage anyone from scaling it and being impaled on the arrowheads along the top. The house behind it is in the middle of the block and fronts the end of a T-intersection with a good view of the street leading to a park several blocks away. The sidewalks are blocked by branches, abandoned furniture, and discarded appliances.

The gates are open, and Oliver rolls into the carport. As las madres help one another climb from the van, an elderly woman leaves the house, carrying a broom, mop, and bucket she then sets against the wall.

"¡Aquí están! ¡Bienvenidas! Welcome!" She's under five feet tall, sinewy. Her mustard-colored hair is pulled back and held in place with rhinestone clamps. The lines and wrinkles on her small face recall a crumpled paper bag.

"Loreta?"

"Claro que sí." She grins as she hustles down the steps. One arm around Ada, another around Shirley, Loreta pulls them into a huddle of tears. "¡Tanto tiempo!"

"I guess they know each other," Marysol says to Graciela.

"And here are las nenas, now grown women." Loreta greets Luz, Graciela, and Marysol with the tight hugs and smooches she's bestowed on Shirley and Ada.

"Mucho gusto," Luz says.

"Ay, mamita. Don't worry. I know about your problem." Still, she waits for Luz to recognize her. Luz smiles noncommittally. "When you lived down the street I cleaned don Alonso's house, but it doesn't look the same. It's an apartment building now." She waves it into the past. "Some of your neighbors are still around, though."

Ada and Shirley share a look that Marysol can't interpret. Graciela is focused on her texts, which seem to have exploded in the last few minutes.

"Why are we standing out in the sun?" Loreta takes Shirley's and Ada's hands, and nods for the others to follow. "I'll show you around."

"Wow!"

"It's bigger than our house!"

The ground floor is arranged into a living room that leads to a dining room, and a kitchen with an island, the discrete areas separated by half walls and cleverly positioned furniture.

"Aren't these paintings yours?" Ada asks Oliver.

"From years ago." He doesn't look at them. "I don't paint anymore, but they show up here and there from time to time."

Luz studies one over the sofa. "Why did you stop?"

"I wasn't good enough," he says. "You were there when it became obvious to me."

"I was?" Luz seems to be grasping for a memory. They all lean toward her, expecting something she doesn't deliver.

"You were kind," Oliver says.

Marysol feels a shroud of sadness enter the house and, instinctively, moves to protect her mother, who now examines the largest canvas. Marysol can tell she's reliving a memory she's unable to share. Luz turns her back on the painting, with the familiar expression of someone who's been lost and is beginning to make sense of her surroundings.

"I'll get the rest of the stuff." Oliver returns outside, but Marysol notices he slams the van's doors with more force than necessary. Has he just realized he was a better painter than he gives himself credit for? Or is he embarrassed to face his failure as a painter in front of people whose opinion matters? She looks at the picture. Three wooden houses face a surfy sea and a marine-blue horizon under an azure sky. In the foreground, a rowboat with the Puerto Rican flag on its bow seems to have been beached among unidentifiable weeds.

Marysol has always admired the precision in Luz's paintings, and thinks she knows what Luz might say about the messy edges around the rustic buildings, the boat, the lumpy human figures, the muddy colors, and banal imagery. Luz is kind and rarely criticizes anyone, but Marysol thinks Oliver hoped she'd say something about his work. It must have been disappointing when she turned from it without comment.

Down the hall, Loreta opens the door to a narrow utility room with a washer and dryer. Behind it is a screened-in porch with a glass table surrounded by six chairs. On the patio outside is a propane-fired grill.

They trek upstairs to four bedrooms, each featuring views of the sea. Las madres and las nenas choose their sleeping quarters. Marysol and Luz share a bathroom. Graciela claims the bedroom across the hall from Marysol's. Ada and Shirley settle into the one with a king bed.

Downstairs again, Loreta opens and closes kitchen cabinets. "I bought you a comprita." She points to cans of tomato paste, pinto beans, and ground coffee near a sack of rice and a box of cubed sugar.

She opens the refrigerator. "I made you fresh sofrito."

Shirley hugs her.

"Ay, mi amor, when Oliver told me it was you coming, I was so happy." Loreta returns Shirley's hug. "You left so suddenly, we didn't get to say goodbye."

"But we're all together again," Ada says. "No más lloriqueos. Crying won't reverse time. You're good, we're good, everything's good."

Shirley's Birthday

SEPTEMBER 17, 2017

Once Loreta and Oliver leave, las madres and las nenas settle into their rooms. In the early evening, feeling refreshed, they walk to a restaurant down the street. As they leave, Graciela receives a text from Oliver, inviting them to a nearby club with live music.

"I'm too tired," Marysol complains. "You guys go ahead."

"Aw, come on. Just for a while," Graciela begs.

"You can sleep late tomorrow." Luz hooks her arm around Marysol.

The club is in the basement of an old building on the main drag. It's hopping with locals who prefer salsa and merengue to reguetón. Most of the customers are about the same ages as their little group. Oliver is there with his wife, Miriam, and her brother Pipo. They seem to know everyone else there. As soon as they order drinks, unpaired men appear with hands palm up, asking them to dance. Sometime after midnight, the band breaks into the happy birthday song plena-style, as the servers roll in a cake decorated with lit sparklers.

"Happy birthday, dear Shirley," the musicians sing to the shocked madre, who is both laughing and crying into Ada's and Graciela's shoulders. Everyone joins the band's version of "Feliz, feliz en tu día." The cake is followed by more rum and colas, more dancing, and maudlin toasts by strangers.

By the time Oliver drops them stumbling into the house, the last stars are fading into a reddening sky spotted with flocks of birds flying west.

⌒

It takes Marysol a moment to identify where the insistent buzzing is coming from. She groans as she reaches for the phone on the nightstand. It's almost two in the afternoon but the light-blocking louvers create a pleasant twilight, and the purring air conditioner masks street sounds.

"Looks like you had a good time," Warren laughs.

She plops onto her back. "What do you mean?"

"Ten text messages with pictures between one and four in the morning. Las madres look as wasted as you do."

"I texted you?"

"Graciela did, too."

"They're a bad influence."

She fills him in on what she recalls from the previous day and night. A knock on the door is followed by a smiling Luz with a tray: hot coffee, buttered toast, and a glass of water. She slips out as quietly as she slipped in.

By the time Marysol has made herself presentable, it's 3:30 p.m., and Luz and Ada are sipping lemonade on the front porch.

"Where are Shirley and Graciela?"

"Supermarket," Ada says.

"There's a storm on the way," Luz says.

Ada waves the thought away. "Just a vaguada with a lot of wind and rain."

Ada and Marysol lower their voices, aware Luz is lost in an achaque. Regardless of how many times they've been with her during episodes, there's something holy and otherworldly about the way she transitions from the present into another place, another time.

Marysol watches Luz's lids quiver and her fingers moving as if saying the rosary.

"She's okay," Ada says. "I'll stay with her. Why don't you walk on the beach for a while? I know you miss your exercise."

⌒

Marysol has been in Puerto Rico for forty-eight hours but until now hasn't studied her surroundings without the distractions of Graciela's shifting moods and their mothers' high spirits. She follows the sound of the ocean a couple of blocks to the left of their rented house. The homes are one or two stories high, surrounded by tall buildings on the landward sides. Newer, shiny ones face the beach, blocking the views of the older homes. Every few minutes, engines roar above the ocean as planes lift into the sky from the nearby airport.

Even with sheared leaves and broken branches, the trees seem to be recovering from Irma's winds. Some flowering bushes and plants survived around houses with broken windows and downed fences. The beach itself is as crowded as Orchard Beach in the Bronx, but the water is at least twenty degrees warmer and also bluer. The sun is intense, even in late afternoon, but Marysol relishes the breeze. A labyrinth of family groups have set up boundaries with coolers and beach chairs. Several women wear T-shirts and shorts, but the majority choose the smallest bikinis they can fit into. Men prefer loose nylon shorts. A boom box is playing

"Despacito," and even though Marysol has heard it a lot, she thinks it's a perfect song for this place and this time.

She starts back to the house, but a couple in the water catches her eye. A young woman with lavender hair stands in the water up to her knees, next to a man raising a naked baby boy as if offering him to the sun. She scoops seawater and lovingly rubs it over her man's back muscles with the intimacy of a wife or romantic partner. Marysol recognizes his round glutes, which are barely covered by a red Speedo. As if aware of her gaze, he turns, and the Sexiest Man Alive pales and nearly drops the baby into the surf. Thankfully, the woman catches the scared child while Lucho stands motionless.

Sí, pendejo, you're busted.

"¿Quién es esa?" the lavender-haired woman says loudly enough for Marysol to hear, a warning not to come nearer to her man. The baby wails and squirms. Marysol gets the sense the lavender-haired woman assumes Marysol is more than a bystander. Lucho says something Marysol can't hear, and the woman continues to question him in language unfit for a child's ears.

Before she reaches the pavement, Marysol looks back at the couple, who are now gathering their things on the beach. Lucho is still explaining as the woman berates him. Marysol wonders what he could possibly be telling her. On her knees on the sand, the young mother dresses the baby in quick, rough movements and Marysol can't help but feel sorry for her.

⌒

Graciela is reading on the porch and smiles when Marysol opens the gate.

"Did you have a good walk?"

"It's a gorgeous beach."

Las madres call out hello and continue their chatter in the kitchen. The aromas inside remind Marysol she's hungry.

Graciela takes a whiff. "It's like being home, except we're

'Home.'" She pours Marysol a glassful from a pitcher on the side table. "I made fresh lemonade with a bit of sugar. Do you want Don Q with it?"

"It's delicious without it." She takes the other chair. "Gracias, Graciela," she says, after a while.

"What did I do?"

"You organized this trip. When things didn't go as planned, you pivoted. It was impressive how you organized a surprise birthday for Shirley with cake and everything."

"That's nice of you to say that. Thank you."

Marysol is about to tell Graciela about Lucho and the lavender-haired woman, but decides there's no point. For Graciela, he was a vacation perk—why spoil it for her? Marysol finishes her drink, jumps from her seat, and calls into the kitchen. "Do I have time for a shower before dinner?" A chorus of yeses follows her upstairs.

      ◦—

When she returns, Shirley is talking to her cousin Edith. She and her husband went to check on the aunts and got a cell signal in their building. Shirley puts the phone on speaker so everyone can hear and help her interpret the garbles from the poor connection.

"The last eleven days have been un martirio," Edith says. "And now we hear another hurricane is coming. If I were you, I'd get the next plane home before things get worse."

"Should we leave?" Shirley asks.

Graciela looks up from her phone's screen. "Some governors have issued storm warnings. Not Puerto Rico's."

"Maybe they know something we don't know," Marysol muses.

"The food is on the table," Ada calls. She's unbothered about the alarming news. "Let's talk about it after dinner."

Warren calls as they're about to sit down.

"Mi amor, there's a hurricane heading for Puerto Rico." His voice is tight with worry.

"We heard about it."

"Tell him it's a tropical storm," Ada calls.

"It's a hurricane," Warren insists. "You should come home before it hits."

"Aw! You're worried about me . . ."

"And about us, too, I hope," Shirley adds.

"This is no joke," Warren says.

"Let me talk to him." Ada takes the phone. "Hi, cariño! Don't forget that this time of year we get vaguadas with a lot of rain and wind. We welcome the moisture that keeps our beautiful Borikén so lush and fruitful. ¡No te aflijes! Your three mothers-in-law get along and know how to handle themselves in a storm—and Graciela and Marysol know when it's time to leave each other alone! If a storm comes, we'll dance in the rain. It's good luck, you know." She returns the phone before Warren can argue with her.

Marysol steps to the farthest corner of the yard, where she has a modicum of privacy. "We're fine, mi rey. Las madres are having a blast. Graciela had a fling. I had a long walk on a beautiful beach. We settled into this house and are making the best of the changing plans. When it rains, we'll stay inside reading and eating. Las madres bought enough food and rum to open a bistro."

None of her assurances decrease his anxiety. "Do me a favor—go online and get updates. Irma skirted the island but that doesn't mean this one will do the same."

"Okay, mi amor. I'll call tonight and we can talk longer."

Before returning inside, she searches the weather and confirms the storm is now a hurricane with a name, María. It's still forming, and governments south and east of Puerto Rico have issued storm watches.

She remembers the heavy rains and winds during Superstorm Sandy in 2012, when parts of the Bronx flooded. Sixty-five-mile-per-hour winds sheared off part of her roof and some of the siding from their building next door. In Maine, Shirley and Ada lost a shed, with all its contents. Graciela's garage roof collapsed onto her car.

They were properly insured, but friends and neighbors had to move when the damage to their houses or apartments made them unlivable. Remembering that time, and the stressful days around Irma, Marysol wonders whether Warren is right and they should leave while they can. Las madres had a win at the casino, and while Shirley's birthday party wasn't exactly what Graciela had envisioned, it was joyful, and Shirley was celebrated. Maybe that should be enough. They can always return. Marysol decides to stay abreast of the weather and to discuss an early departure with Graciela after dinner.

The meal is interrupted by frequent pings and buzzes on their phones. None of them want to show how unnerved they are by the hysterical messages from the U.S.

"Be careful. Hurricane coming to Puerto Rico."

"Praying for you."

" 🎵 Temporal, temporal, 🎵 allá viene el temporal. 😱"

"Worried about you. Take care of yourselves."

The screened porch overlooking the garden is bordered by plantings that block the neighboring yards. Between bursts of airplanes taking off and horns from impatient drivers in the avenue three blocks away, the sea is a soothing background to the cheerful coquí frogs and the women's own chatter and laughter. They finish two bottles of wine. Ada passes a joint around. Just as Marysol begins to feel mellow, Graciela jumps from her chair.

"Time for presents!" She hurries upstairs.

"I thought the trip and the party were my birthday gifts," Shirley says.

"You know how she is," Ada says. "Ella pone y ella dispone."

Marysol doesn't bother to comment, but it's true. Graciela spends hours planning and organizing get-togethers and activities, preparing formatted and decorated pdfs of itineraries and agendas on the blog, but often goes off script, although she's not happy when anyone else does.

She comes down balancing five identical boxes wrapped in shiny paper with neat bows.

"We all get a present?" Ada is puzzled.

"Yeah, including me," Graciela chirps. "Don't open them until I sit down. Okay, now!"

"What's this?" Shirley holds hers as if it's radioactive.

"It's a DNA test kit."

"What?" Ada's buzz has left her.

"It's part one of your Christmas present."

Shirley and Ada look distressed. Marysol and Luz are confused by the gift.

Graciela leans over the table. "I've been on the ancestry sites, right?" They nod. "That's how I found those new documents for Madrina's blog and the cemetery where her parents are buried. So I thought if we do the DNA test, we might find more relatives for her and for us. I also thought . . ." She blushes, as if she's been caught doing something naughty. "Don't get the wrong idea, Mami. This wasn't the reason I want to do it, Mommy. It just . . . It also occurred to me that maybe, if any of his relatives are also on the site, they might connect me to my father."

Shirley puts the kit in the middle of the table. "I'm not doing this."

"Me, neither," Ada says.

Luz adds hers in solidarity.

"But it's not a big deal," Graciela argued. "It's not just about finding my father, I swear. I wanted to draw family trees for us and for Madrina and Marysol, and the other thing is a bonus." She rubs her eyes. "The family trees will be your Christmas presents. I thought you'd love it."

"It's a sweet idea," Ada says, "but for us, it's about privacy."

The sounds beyond the fences were dampened by their laughter—now the noise outside is amplified by the silence around the table.

Shirley rubs the goose bumps from her bare arms. "It's a bit cooler than I like and it's been a long day. I'm going to bed." She doesn't wait for permission, and pushes her chair back. She struggles to stand, falls back on her seat, and has to press against the armrests to help herself up. To Marysol, she seems ten years older.

"I'll come with you." Ada, too, is unbalanced. Neither looks at Graciela, and Marysol assumes it's because they hate saying no to her.

"You go up, too, Mom," Marysol says.

"You don't mind?"

"Of course not—you three did all the cooking."

"I'll make sure she takes her meds," Ada says.

Las madres look weary and, heads bowed, go without a word. Marysol watches them go upstairs in order—Shirley, Luz, Ada.

"Ahí van nuestras ancestras," Marysol says out loud.

Graciela, smarting from hurt feelings, doesn't hear. She's gathering dishes and cutlery. She empties scraps onto a plate, and stacks the others at the end of the table. She takes the dessert bowls and sets them by the plates. She groups the wineglasses. She picks up the forks, then the knives, then the spoons used for the flan, and finally a column of water glasses. Marysol is moved by how methodical she is, yet she can't help but notice how inefficient it is to go around the table more than once, picking up one group of items at a time. It saddens her to see Graciela so dejected.

"I'll do it with you," Marysol says.

"What?" Graciela is in another world. Maybe not exactly where Luz goes, but definitely not here.

"The DNA kit."

"Oh, you don't have to."

"I want to. Maybe it will find people on my dad's side who aren't racist assholes like his mother and sisters and brothers."

Graciela smiles dispiritedly. "It upset las madres." She picks up the five boxes, the wrapping paper, the bows. "I thought it would be fun . . ."

"They'll change their minds. They hate to let you down."

"You think so?"

"They resist technology, but you manage to keep them one step from being Luddites." Marysol is glad to hear her chuckle. "Go ahead up. I'll do the kitchen. So far, I've contributed nothing to this evening's meal and entertainment."

"I won't argue. I can't wait for a hot bath."

She goes up, and moments later Marysol hears the tub filling.

She brings the dishes to the sink and, overcome, leans against the counter. The sight of Shirley, Luz, and Ada climbing the stairs has upset her. She covers her face, as if she could erase what she saw, nuestras ancestras, their heads seemingly too heavy for their necks, facing the ground, ever so carefully stepping up the stairs. It takes some effort for Marysol to settle her breath.

She often tells Luz she's lucky to have memory issues. Luz is the only person she knows who lives unencumbered by the past. But her tribulations and misfortunes reveal themselves only to herself, and as soon as a memory appears, it withdraws, making it impossible to share with anyone else. Marysol thinks it must be a lonely existence.

She recalls one patient whose memories of his childhood in Guatemala were his only treasures. Remembrance is a noble act, an honor as well as honorable. Ping! Her restless mind searches for the last time she heard the word *noble* used in a context beyond self-sacrifice and honor, as behavior without expectations. Her ancestors understood nobility and honor to be virtues that guided their lives, not words engraved on plaques and medals. As she washes dishes, Marysol continues to connect her thoughts and comes back to her mother, who is noble and honorable in the old-fashioned sense, but doesn't know it.

To Marysol, Luz is as much a mystery as the ancestors Graciela posts about on WeAreGLAMS. It occurs to her that even though Luz is here now, she's become as much history as her forebears. Beyond the circle of her family and friends, she's been reduced to name, dates, and racial and geographical data. So has Danilo, who read Marysol books in English and in Spanish, who made peanut butter and pickle sandwiches, who danced her and Luz around the apartment. That man they both adored has probably been erased from her mother's memory and is fading from Marysol's. They have photos, but she can't recall her father's voice and has forgotten how often she fell asleep on his shoulder, soothed by his scent.

When Luz has an achaque, Marysol wonders, does she revisit those intimate moments, unremarked by anyone else, unrecorded in databases and electronic archives? Marysol has no answers, only questions.

She steps into the yard and stands in the center, grateful for the cooling, salty air. She judges herself, and doesn't know what to do with maudlin moments like this one. She refuses to cry, even when her chest fills with emotion and her eyes itch for the relief of tears. Ada and Graciela have criticized Marysol for being more stoic than Shirley's stern and imperturbable New England ancestors. Graciela and her mothers say she's a skeptical Scorpio who needs time to process emotions. Marysol finds astrology and their other woo-woo stuff grating. They include her in ceremonies involving incense burning, drumming, chanting, tarot cards, crystals, aromatherapy, and bundles of feathers. Marysol goes along to be agreeable and because she loves and respects them. She's not traditionally religious and avoids describing herself as spiritual in the New Age jargon that sounds like hedging your bets in case God exists. If anything, she's agnostic but understands the need for higher powers. She does feel things deeply without the aid of magic or incantations. She has her own way of dealing with them without fuss or public displays, mostly by focusing on her breath.

She's moved by the thought that more than forty years ago las madres walked these streets, and tries to imagine Shirley and Ada as young women, Luz as a teenager. She has snapshots of them in their mid-1970s hair and clothes. Shirley in buttoned-down blouses, A-line skirts, and closed shoes. In 2017, Ada still dons the same styles she wore in the late 1960s: paisley, flowers, Indian prints. In the few photographs of Luz as a teenager, she's in T-shirts and shorts. Her expression makes her seem lost in her own world, as she was. Again, sentimientos compress Marysol's chest. She closes her eyes and breathes. She presses her bare feet into the ground while imagining herself floating toward the heavens. She listens. Beyond the human-created sounds of vehicles, televisions, airplanes, and distant voices, Marysol hears the coquí's song, the murmur of the eternal sea, a tender breeze, unaware of the clouds gathering to the east.

A Walk

SEPTEMBER 18, 2017

Steeping in her bubble bath, Graciela reproaches herself. She should have known how Shirley and Ada would respond. Both are intelligent, savvy women who worry about how deeply technology reaches into private lives. They don't participate in social media, and until five years ago, insisted on dumb phones because they believed they couldn't be tracked by a mysterious, unnamed "they." When Graciela explained that, dumb or smart, their phones could tell where they were at any given time, and then their carrier advertised a two-for-one promotion for the latest models, they switched. There was no going back, once the devices were in their hands.

Graciela taught them how apps worked, and they downloaded games and sites related to their interests. They became snobs about audio-only calls now that they knew there was a possibility they could see the other person on their screens. They delighted in the electronic assistant they could ask to find a recipe, directions, or good restaurants nearby. They invested in cute cases and Bluetooth earbuds, and learned how to borrow e-books and audiobooks from the library. They thought they were cool, with their shiny phones like the ones "the kids" carried. Maybe sharing their DNA was too much of a leap into modernity.

She chastises herself. She should have prepared them, she says to herself, as she dries off. *I should have said my DNA might connect me to my father but nothing would change between me and them. I blew it.* She'll apologize in the morning.

She fluffs her pillows behind her and checks the weather app for news about the storm. With every click she sinks farther into her mattress, her back pressing against the bed frame as if weighed down by an invisible force. She gasps as she follows the text and image links, the chilling news that María is intensifying faster than experts predicted. It becomes clear that they should have taken Edith's and Warren's advice to leave while they could.

Graciela peeks into the hall, hoping for light from the bedrooms. Las madres and Marysol are asleep. She decides to make travel arrangements and explain the next morning.

There are no available flights from San Juan to New York or Boston. She expands the search to any city in the Northeast. No luck. She adds their names to waiting lists she thinks are hopeless. The Luis Muñoz Marín Airport is an international hub that connects the smaller Caribbean islands. Tourists and residents are probably decamping from the threatened areas in a hurry. She compulsively checks the National Oceanic and Atmospheric Administration feed, The Weather Channel, and online local radio and television stations. Her tension increases, and when Graciela panics, she makes lists.

By first light, she has over one hundred checkboxes organized into categories. She emails Oliver, hoping he can take las madres to the market for supplies she enumerates in a separate file. The Red Cross and insurance companies provide detailed preparation lists Graciela adds to her own. While their mothers are shopping, she and Marysol will drag inside anything that can become missiles from the expected cyclone winds. They will also fill every vessel they find with water, and make extra ice to keep in the freezer and in a battered cooler in the utility room. Finally, she creates a pdf with personal and emergency phone numbers, including the nearby hospital, police, and fire station, and uploads it to WeAreGLAMS. She also sends them as emails to Oliver and Warren so everyone will know she's on the case. By the time she sleeps, a leaden sky is beginning to brighten and the neighborhood to awaken.

⌒

Las madres love breakfast, so Graciela isn't surprised to smell bacon, fried eggs, strong coffee, and toast. She turns over, soothed by the muted voices downstairs, and dozes until she hears a man speaking. She dresses quickly and runs downstairs.

"I got your email," Oliver says as soon as he sees her.

"You wrote to him at five in the morning?" Shirley frowns.

"I wanted him to see it first thing . . ."

Oliver points to shopping bags. "I brought you flashlights and extra batteries. Also those tall candles with saints on them."

"Is it going to be that bad? I mean, we were here on vacation during Georges—when was that, Ada?"

"September 1998. That was a two-disaster year for us. In January we'd had the great ice storm."

"Yes! Everything was covered with ice—"

"So heavy it broke the branches—"

"We heard them cracking and trees falling—"

"Whole forests went down—"

"And we had no power for a couple of weeks—"

"In January," Ada said.

"In Maine!" Shirley added.

"I thought you were talking about an ice storm in Puerto Rico," Marysol laughs.

"Nothing like that here," Oliver says. "But María is gaining strength. It's still far away and might lose power or change its course as others do, but it's smart to get ready." He's printed out Graciela's email and made sure she notices he's already checked off some items. "The supermarkets aren't usually as well stocked on Mondays and were depleted even before the weekend. We all went crazy buying everything in sight for Irma." He places the shopping bags on the counter and empties them. "I brought you what I could find and three more gallons of water. Miriam added tins of corned beef, a couple of cans of cooked spaghetti, and these." He stacks six cans of Vienna sausages. "You can't go through a hurricane in Puerto Rico without salchichas."

"Claro que no," Shirley laughs.

"Here's a box of saltines, and some dry pasta. Don't cook it in tap water until they announce it's safe. I can help you bring in the furniture from the porch and terraces."

"We'll do that later, Oliver," Marysol says.

He riffles through another bag. "Here's a set of dominoes and a deck of cards to entertain you when the power goes off."

They smile because he's grinning, but no one thinks it's funny.

"That's considerate," Shirley says, cutting the tension.

"I should go. I have to prepare my house, too. Irma flooded a couple of inches of water on our first floor, and we're still cleaning up the mess." He stops at the door for more instructions. "Keep away from glass doors and windows. They're safety glass but something could fly and hit the one weak spot. It's meant to shatter like car windshields but . . ." He shrugs.

Graciela flinches.

"Don't go outside when it sounds like it's over," he continues. "That's the eye."

"Don't worry," Ada says. "We'll be okay. We've been through it. We know what to do."

"Sorry to wake you up so early," Graciela says.

"No problem. Take care of yourselves," he says, and hugs them all goodbye.

"So, what do we do now?" Marysol is sure Graciela has already looked into their escape without results, or she wouldn't have sent Oliver instructions before dawn. In one of her folders she must have a plan with bullet points and links for further information.

Sure enough, Graciela explains she's been up all night. She tells them about the NOAA reports, and her fruitless efforts with the airlines. "If the surge is as bad as they predict, we're likely to be flooded. Hotels have no vacancies. Our only options are to stay here or go to a shelter. I think the closest is an enclosed stadium."

"We lived in this area during Eloise in 1975," Shirley says. "We had a lot of wind and rain, and the surf was wild."

"Some of the houses along the shore flooded," Ada adds. "But it wasn't that bad. No one drowned or got washed away. Power was restored in a couple of days."

"So no shelter?" Luz asks.

"We'll be safe here," Ada says. "This house is well built."

Luz is unconvinced and Marysol stands closer to her.

"The shelters keep people safe in case of floods and flying roofs," Graciela says.

Ada glowers. "Remember Katrina? The stadium in New Orleans lost its roof, and those people had to be rescued."

"So we stay here?" Graciela's fingers are poised over her keyboard. She looks at each of their faces in turn, and waits for confirmation. In varying degrees of certainty, they nod. "Got it." Graciela ticks off items below the "shelter" category on her list. "In that case, we have the rest of the day and part of tomorrow before the weather changes."

༄

They walk around the neighborhood, Shirley and Ada pointing out houses they recognize. Every few minutes, Luz stops to sketch a gnarled tree, or bougainvillea spilling over a fence, or the vista from the corner down the street to the park. As she sketches, she hums one of her favorite boleros.

Las nenas lag behind their mothers.

"Do you think we did the right thing by not going to the shelter?" Graciela asks.

"Your mothers have the most experience with hurricanes, so I'm following their lead. I also think Mom would be more anxious around a lot of strangers."

The day before, the neighborhood was relatively quiet, but today a staccato of hammers and power tools overtake other sounds as residents attach plywood sheets to glass doors and windows. As las madres and las nenas pass them, people wish them buenos días.

"Do you worry everyone is preparing for the hurricane and we're not?"

"You've done all you could do," Marysol says. "We can't do anything about the storm except survive it. Can you relax?"

"I'm sorry. I should take my own advice, right?"

The air is heavy, the sky alternating punishing sun with filmy clouds.

"It's strange to imagine a hurricane when it's so bright and not a leaf is stirring."

"The calm before the storm?"

"I guess," Marysol says. Lagartijos scuttle from shade to shade as they near them.

"Have you ever been in this neighborhood with Ada and Shirley?" she asks.

"No. And they're unhappy about being here now."

"I wonder why."

"They didn't explain, and I wasn't about to get into an argument with them."

Marysol thinks for a moment. "Are your mothers upset about being here for themselves or for Mom?"

"What do you mean?"

"Well, she lived here, too."

"That's true."

Ahead, las madres cross the street and stop in front of a building. They're unusually quiet. Graciela often marvels that las madres always have something to say to one another, even after decades of friendship. They laugh, touch one another's shoulders, hold hands, or walk linked by their elbows. Now they stand several feet apart, studying the structure as if considering buying it. Graciela hopes they aren't. In this pretty residential street, the spare, unpainted cement building seems to be giving the finger to its neighbors.

As Graciela and Marysol approach, Luz reaches for Marysol's hand and they step a few feet from the others.

"Ada came," Luz says.

Marysol waits for Luz to say more. Just as she's about to ask, Luz shakes her head. "Le tapis m'a fait étourdir."

"The rug made you dizzy? What rug?" But Luz has disappeared into an achaque.

Loreta Frías Hernández had worked for Ileana's parents for ten years every Monday and Friday. On other days, she took care of other houses in the neighborhood, including Alonso's.

During the 1976 summer break from school, Ileana had more time to hang out with her friends Minaxi and Perla. The girls included Luz in their outings to the mall, to the movies, or for impromptu pool parties. Ileana's parents worked during the day, but allowed her to have boys over only on those days Loreta was there.

Loreta was expected to keep an eye on the teenagers, but as far as she was concerned, she wasn't paid to babysit. Whenever she passed the kitchen window, she checked to make sure no one had drowned in the pool before returning to her duties. She prepared their lunch or snacks, and after serving and picking up the used plastic dishes and utensils, Loreta closed the door to the laundry room and listened to her favorite radionovela while ironing the family's clothes.

On the days the boys came, they arrived in twos and threes, carrying liters of soda, bags of chips, and, unbeknownst to Loreta and Ileana's parents, joints or purloined liquor. They swam and horsed around, then slouched on the beanbags in the game room to listen to records. Out of sight from Loreta, some couples had sex on the shag rug while the others splashed in the swimming pool and acted as lookouts in case an adult showed up unexpectedly.

On a muggy Thursday afternoon in mid-June, when the boys were not supposed to be at Ileana's, Ada dropped off Luz while she went for groceries. When she returned to Alonso's, Loreta was still finishing up cleaning the house. As Ada was putting her purchases away, Loreta came from the bedrooms.

"Disculpe, maestra."

"Is everything all right?"

"I don't want to ask don Alonso," Loreta whispered, even though no one else was home. "This is women's business, and the girl has a condition . . ."

"What's wrong?"

"It might be nothing, but, you see, I always check the cabinets to make sure there's enough toilet paper and soap . . ."

"Just write whatever's missing on the list." Ada tipped her head toward the notepad on the bulletin board by the door.

"It's not that, maestra. I was emptying the trash in her bathroom and there were no used sanitary napkins."

Ada stuffed her shopping bags in the drawer. "She might have thrown them away, Loreta. You know how neat Luz is."

"Well, that's the thing. I checked the box, and she hasn't used any in a while."

Ada stopped midway between the counter and the refrigerator. It was one of those moments when time disappeared. Ada, suspended in time and place, saw herself from a corner of the slanted ceiling, watching the other Ada listen with her entire body as Loreta spoke.

"I'm worried because, well, I'm at Ileana's two days a week, and she's not to have boys when I'm not there, but those kids are no angels—you know what I mean? The boys come whether I'm there or not. And Luz, well, with her problem . . ."

Ada didn't hear the rest. She ran. The two city blocks to Ileana's house felt like miles, and she couldn't get there fast enough. In years to come Ada would revisit that race many times, asking herself why she hadn't seen what was going on sooner. Loreta's words, "those kids are no angels," would echo through four decades of remorse, self-reproach, a guilty conscience, and self-condemnation.

Her job was to take care of a vulnerable young woman who trusted her. Instead, she'd delegated her responsibility to kids.

She'd never forgive herself if her negligence had endangered the girl entrusted to her care.

She didn't bother to knock on the front door, but went around the side, as she often did when she picked up Luz at the pool. Ileana, Minaxi, and Perla were splashing in the water while Perla's boyfriend and another boy tried to keep them from getting out. They froze when they saw her and looked guiltily toward the game room, where, in fact, they hoped she wouldn't go. But Ada did. And she saw Claudio, the aspiring professional basketball player, rutting an inert Luz, who was obviously in an achaque.

Luz came to herself slowly in her bedroom as the sun was setting. She ached all over. Disconnected images were fuzzy: Ileana's shimmering swimming pool, Perla passing her a joint, Kelvin cannonballing into the water, Claudio putting on a record, the fan on the cabaña ceiling spinning, Ada screaming. She became aware of a hushed conversation in the living room. Ada, Shirley, Alonso, another man. She struggled to identify that mellifluous, theatrical voice. She didn't know he'd trained as an actor. Even his whispers carried. She caught his phrasing in response to the others' swallowed syllables. Her mind was like a ticker tape, random names floating horizontally between her ears. Then she recognized one. It was the radio preacher, who at times screamed Jesus's name in exultation, while at other times he caressed the *J* and lengthened the sibilants into hisses.

"I agree, compadre. The boy will be dealt with by his parents. But our first obligation is to Luz," Josué said.

She could catch only phrases as the other urgent voices rose and fell. Ada. Shirley.

Alonso: "No, not that. Never!"

Ada and Shirley reassured him in murmurs.

"It's your decision," Josué said.

Ada: ". . . but then . . . ?"

They were puzzling over something, arguing, exchanging opinions, words riding over one another's, a mishmash of questions. Luz guessed they were trying to convince Alonso.

Shirley: ". . . your cancer?"

Ada: ". . . treatments . . . options."

"I have solid contacts," Josué said, "with the best doctors."

Alonso: "Can she handle another move?"

Ada: "I'll be with you both."

Shirley: ". . . here . . . the office."

"You say the word and we'll take care of the rest," Josué said.

More assurances from Ada and Shirley. A long pause. A sob.

"No, Alonso. There will be no scandal—I give you my word," Josué said. "She's been through enough. I'll talk to his father in private. The last thing the Worthy family wants is bad press about their golden boy."

Alonso spoke. Ada spoke. Shirley spoke. Shuffling feet. The front door opened. Closed. Steps toward her room. Luz turned to her side with her back to the door.

⌒

Luz often wondered where her memories had gone. Her doctors said they were stored in her brain, and if she followed their instructions, new pathways would grow and she'd remember again. Once they moved to New York, her new doctors prescribed medications that Ada dispensed. Luz kept asking what they were supposed to do, Ada told her, Luz forgot, and then she concluded the drugs weren't meant to restore her memory. They relieved back pain and migraines or controlled her seizures. But the pills, tablets, and new therapies did nothing about the experiences that emerged from the fog that came, went, and obscured her earliest and most recent memories.

It felt to Luz that one day she was in Puerto Rico and overnight, she, Ada, and Alonso were in New York. She thought they were there to find neurologists with modern technologies that might treat her brain injury and restore her memory. Actually, they were there for Alonso, whom a platoon of doctors couldn't save from the cancer he'd been living with before her accident. She didn't know whether he'd told her about his illness and she forgot, or whether he'd kept it from her until it was clear he wouldn't recover. She had no memory of those early years in the Bronx, as if a huge eraser had wiped them away. She consulted her journals, where she found more questions than answers. When she first began writing things down, she didn't enter dates on the pages decorated with drawings and doodles, phrases, short lists, or queries for Ada, Shirley, Alonso, her doctors, and a slew of other names she couldn't recognize. There were no lines across entries or x's next to what she'd hoped to learn, no side notes about who the other people in her life were at the time. She didn't know whether a few sentences strung together were things she was supposed to remember, part of a story she'd heard, or one she'd made up.

One entry read "Mayflower Avenue, Bronx, New York," accompanying a drawing of a five-story building with a stoop. A woman leaned out a window, her head studded with pink rollers. On another page, she'd pasted a postcard from Our Lady of Lourdes Grotto, St. Lucy's Church. On the back, where the greeting would go, she'd written, "Abuelo prayed here." She had no idea whether and when she'd been to that holy place, which was a few blocks from where she still lived in 2017. A clipping from a newspaper showed a gymnast wearing a long-sleeved white leotard, her face and muscles tight as she prepared to do something on a balance beam. Around the picture, Luz had written "10" and "Nadia" in fancy script, every letter in a different color. Months later, when Luz came across that page, she couldn't figure out who that girl was and what the numbers meant. Decades after that, she flashed on that black-and-white image, floating with no context, like a ghost.

She must have recorded what her life had been like in the Bronx, including Danilo's courtship, their marriage, the time when she felt like every newlywed in love with her husband, Marysol's birth, motherhood. Danilo's murder and the gunshot that almost killed her caused a relapse that lasted much longer than the aftermaths of her previous tragedies. While she was still recovering, her journals and sketches, the photographs Ada and Shirley had brought from Alonso's house in Puerto Rico, everything Luz and twelve-year-old Marysol had collected and owned, burned in the fire in 1994.

Kind neighbors, Ada, Shirley, and Graciela helped them find another place, and furniture, clothes, and other necessities to fill it. Luz and Marysol resettled into one side of the two-family house around the corner from Mi Casa Adult Daycare, where Luz had been spending her days as she became more functional. Graciela gave Luz a stack of blank diaries and sketchbooks, insisting she begin each page with a date. She suggested she title the lists or notes, and include a few words about what she'd done that day and how she'd felt. By 2017, Luz could go to a shelf in her living room, slide out a volume, and read what she'd written since 1996. But her childhood and the years between 1976 and 1996, when she began again in earnest to write and draw, were as blank as empty pages, her memories held by Ada, Shirley, Graciela, and Marysol.

En mi viejo San Juan

SEPTEMBER 18, 2017

On the commercial avenue lined with shops, cafés, hotels, and condos, residents are either preparing for the storm or ignoring the weather reports. Some merchants have already covered their windows, while others will roll down metal garage-size doors when the rains begin. Las madres and las nenas take a bus to Old San Juan and walk its cobblestoned streets, browse the outlets, and rest inside the cool, ancient churches. In one of the plazas, a guitarist accompanies himself singing "En mi Viejo San Juan." The women join the sparse audience, everyone swaying to the melancholic tune. Ada drops a few dollars into his hat.

"Puerto Ricans love the lyrics to that song more than the national anthem," Shirley says as they walk away.

"Their sentiments are completely different," Ada says. "'La Borinqueña' is about how beautiful Borinquen is. 'En mi Viejo San Juan' is about being elsewhere but yearning to return."

"El lamento de los ausentes," Graciela says. "It always makes me cry."

"My Puerto Rican patients play it over and over again," Marysol adds.

"You'd think a song about the singer's old age and imminent death would make sick people feel worse," Shirley says.

"Maybe it helps them come to terms with their lost dreams and ambitions," Marysol says. "Everyone has regrets, and nostalgia can be healing."

"Only if what you remember is positive," Graciela says, with a sidelong look at Luz, who has stopped to sketch the tiles on a building's façade.

"We can't appreciate joy until we've known sorrow," Ada says.

"Truth," Marysol says.

As they amble up and down the streets, in and out of stores, everyone they talk to says something about the hurricane. Most of them are annoyed that, again, they have to prepare for a storm that might veer into the Atlantic Ocean.

"The thing is," a store owner says, "if I don't, I could lose everything I've worked for. If I do, and the storm doesn't hit, I've spent a lot of time and money for nothing."

Residents roll up awnings, bring potted plants and outdoor furniture in from their patios.

"I feel guilty having fun," Marysol says. "It doesn't seem right when they're working so hard."

Ada insists they tour the forts and, in the late afternoon, exhausted and overheated, they sit on the grass as children fly kites on the lawns. Down the hill, the sparkling Atlantic is dotted with whitecaps under a graying sky. An oppressive air is weighted with expectation.

Marysol is desperate for a cool shower, but Ada is determined to have dinner at a white-tablecloth restaurant Graciela found on the Internet. When they get there, it's closed.

"It's Monday," Ada says. "That's why."

A young man passing by stops. "Haven't you heard? The government just announced a hurricane warning," he says. "Businesses are closing."

"I thought it was coming in two days," Graciela says.

"María is moving faster than expected," he says. "They're calling it a possible cyclone. That's stronger than a hurricane. Take care of yourselves." He continues down the street.

"He assumed we're turistas," Marysol says.

"That's all you got from that exchange?" Graciela is appalled.

"He wasn't being condescending," Ada says. "He was being kind."

"It's getting dark. We'll cook at home," Shirley says.

They're the only pedestrians on the dimly lit street. They hurry to catch a bus about to pull away from the citadel. Graciela herds las madres on board. They sit up front so they can listen to the dashboard radio. Hurricane María has intensified and is racing toward Dominica as a Category 5 hurricane.

"Eso es algo grande," the driver says, and the women nod but say nothing. Graciela and Marysol exchange a panicked look. Las madres are silent. Marysol holds her mother's hand, and Luz squeezes her daughter's fingers as though they're a lifeline.

"Es obvio que esta situación se está poniendo grave," the driver says, "I have five Puerto Rican women in my bus and none of them can say a word."

Marysol is about to challenge his misogynistic comment when she notices that Graciela is so pale, she appears bloodless. Shirley and Ada are stoic as the news unfolds. Graciela chews on the nail of her index finger as if she were a starving animal. She's obviously terrified at what she's hearing, and Marysol is sure she's playing scenarios in her head. Graciela becomes aware of her gaze, and unwilling to articulate what she's going through, pulls her phone from her pocket and attacks the keyboard. Without seeing what's on the screen, Marysol envisions more items being entered onto another endless list.

Preparations

SEPTEMBER 19, 2017

Marysol's phone has been vibrating so often, it's slid to the edge of the night table and now clatters to the tile floor. She finds it under her bed.

"I've been trying to reach you since six a.m.," Warren says. "Have you seen the news?"

"No. I've been sleeping. What time is it?"

"Almost nine. Hurricane María has devastated—I mean, this is no exaggeration—it has destroyed Dominica overnight. And it's heading for Puerto Rico."

"I told you yesterday," she says, wanting to calm him, but instead going into a cold sweat, "Graciela tried to get us out, but there were no flights." The call is interrupted by the Mi Casa administrator, who is in a panic, and alarming texts from friends. She has to get off the phone, to settle her nerves, to brush her teeth, and see what's going on in the bathroom she shares with Luz. "I have to go, mi amor. Mom is sobbing."

Luz is leaning over the counter watching the images on her phone.

"Everything's gone! Those poor people."

"Put it away, Mom." Marysol tries to take the device.

"Look at this! ¡Ay, bendito, mira qué horror! Regardez ça!"

Marysol looks. Cement floors with no homes over them. Vehicles bunched up against one another or floating in muddy ponds. Dazed residents, disbelieving the destruction around them. Graciela comes in through Marysol's room. Ada and Shirley enter from Luz's room, and the five women huddle in front of Graciela's laptop, which is between the double sinks, surrounded by the rocks Luz has collected since their arrival.

"C'est tellement terrifiant," Luz says, and they can't pretend it isn't terrifying and can't convince her to look away because each is thinking the same thing: *María is coming for us.*

~

The day is overcast, the air dense. Marysol and Graciela drag the furniture and grill inside while las madres put items that might be damaged from flooding atop counters and tables. They fill the tubs and every vessel they can find with water, including the washing machine. In the early afternoon, they walk on the beach. The whitecaps they saw the day before from El Morro now crest like whipped cream over crashing waves. None dare go near the tideline.

"At least it's not a full moon tonight," Graciela muses, "so the tides won't be as high."

"Merci, mon Dieu," Luz says.

By the time they start home again, the wind has picked up and flings sand against their bare legs. They reach the house as sprinkles begin. The street is deserted.

"Let's leave the gate open, like the neighbors have," Marysol says.

Las madres cook, interrupted every few seconds by calls and texts from friends and family in the U.S. Oliver calls Ada. They reminisce about other storms and he assures her he'll stop by as soon as the hurricane has passed. Every so often, the lights blink, and at first, las madres and las nenas stare at the fixtures as if their will alone can restore the power. Wind-driven twigs and hard rain clang against the metal louvers. Heavier objects slam against the outside walls.

"Someone forgot to dismantle an awning," Ada suggests.

"Satellite dishes," Marysol says.

Graciela reports the meteorologists don't expect María to change its course, and it will certainly make landfall in Puerto Rico early the next morning, Wednesday, September 20. It's still possible to stand in the covered front porch, and las madres and las nenas are mesmerized by the solid sheets of rainwater forming halos around blinking streetlights. Some trees have already lost branches and one of the two palms at the gate releases the fronds damaged by Irma. They whirl like the kites the women saw the day before in El Morro, then disappear.

Luz trembles. "Je ne veux plus regarder. Je ne peux pas."

Marysol leads her inside and sits by her until her shaking stops. In the past few years, with new medications, her mother's violent episodes have come under control, but she's noticed Luz seems to be regressing in other ways. Marysol believes her mother is in early dementia, but she hasn't shared her concern with the others, although she guesses they may have noticed the changes and think the same thing. She's made appointments for Luz to be evaluated when they return to New York. It pains her to imagine her mother edging toward the fatal kind of forgetting. Marysol has cared for hundreds of patients at every stage of dementia and Alzheimer's disease, but the idea that Luz will deteriorate until she can't recognize any of them causes her throat to tighten, as if her fear lives there and she can neither swallow it nor bring it up.

The temperature has dropped. Shirley and Ada find hoodies for everyone. Graciela can't stay away from her computer.

"Let's play dominoes." Ada spills them onto the dining room table and shuffles the tiles. Shirley, Luz, and Marysol join her until they all begin to yawn.

Marysol puts Luz to bed. The others return calls and texts as a distraction from the thunder above and bumps against the walls.

"Is it dangerous to be on the phone when there's lightning?" Marysol asks Warren.

"You're not on a landline, so you're okay."

"Remember Sandy? It's like that, with lots of thunder and lightning. We realized how many cracks we had around our windows then."

"Is rain leaking through there?"

"No. This house is concrete, and the windows are aluminum slats. It's solid, not like ours."

"How's Mamá Luz holding up?"

"She's in and out of achaques more often, speaking in French or German most of the time. I'm worried about her, but right now she's asleep."

"How are you?"

"Trying hard not to panic."

"I wish there were something I could do to help you, mi reina."

"It helps to know you're concerned, papi. Let's talk tomorrow. Graciela told us to turn off our phones to conserve the charge for when we lose power."

He laughed. "She sent me an updated itinerary with your address, in case I need to rescue you."

"My hero!"

A few minutes later, just as Marysol is on the edge of sleep, Luz tiptoes in.

"Is everything all right, Mom?"

"J'ai peur."

Marysol moves over and Luz crawls in beside her. They hold each other, sleepless, while around them, María howls.

～

Before bed, Graciela helps Ada and Shirley set up their devices with "Do not disturb" automatic responses in English and Spanish: "We've prepared as much as possible for María and are aware we're likely to lose power for a few days. Thank you for your calls and messages. I'll be in touch as soon as power is restored." They turn off their phones and tablets. Shirley and Ada cozy up in their room, and even with the turmoil around them, they soon fall asleep.

In her room, Graciela can't take her eyes from her computer screen. She posts on social media, describing the winds and noises, until the connections break around three in the morning. Then she lies on her side, a pillow over her head to muffle the clamor.

～

Through the bumps and booms, the whistling wind and pounding rain, a new noise begins above Marysol's and Luz's heads. At first, it's a squeak, followed by scratching that soon develops into scraping, as if an enormous animal's claws are digging on the roof, trying to get inside. Marysol and Luz jump from the bed.

"Está más oscuro que la boca de un lobo," Luz says, the first Spanish phrase she's uttered in several hours.

Marysol finds the wall and feels for the switch by the door. She clicks it several times. "Power's gone."

Graciela comes in, wielding a flashlight. "What's that noise? Are you okay?"

"Irgendwas versucht, reinzukommen," Luz whimpers.

Las Madres

Marysol and Graciela don't ask. Her expression is enough to scare them as Ada and Shirley come running.

"Let's get out of this room." They each take one of Luz's hands and lead her, Marysol, and Graciela to their bedroom across the hall, at the front end of the house. They climb into the king-size bed, unable to hear one another over the clatter. The sounds from Marysol's room increase into spooky, metallic screeches over the clangs and clunks pummeling the back of the house. Once they turn off the flashlights, they can't tell whether their eyes are open or closed. They're caught inside the wolf's maw, unable to decide whether it's more frightening to close their eyes or to surrender to their imaginations.

María

SEPTEMBER 20, 2017

While las madres and las nenas cower in one bed, Hurricane María swirls toward Puerto Rico. Overnight, it demolishes Vieques and Culebra, which were already struggling from Irma's ravages two weeks earlier.

María makes landfall on the big island on the southeastern shore at 6:15 in the morning. As it churns northwest, the storm surge pushes the sea into mangroves, where boats were anchored by owners intending to ride out the hurricane in their vessels. The hulls bump against one another, their lines tangling or severed. Masts break in half. Sailors bail water as the relentless waves sweep over the gunwales. A couple are forced to abandon their capsized boat to brave the sea on an inflatable dinghy. Harrowing hours later, a local fisherman in a more sea-worthy boat rescues them. They make it to a marina far from where they all started.

Another boat flies through the air and crash-lands feet from a house that is miles from shore.

In bays, harbors, and coves, brackish water enters wetlands, altering the delicate balance upon which numerous species depend.

In Humacao, a news photographer sets up his camera in front of his hotel room's glass sliding door. He films a line of trees on the main road to the resort, their trunks bending so far, they seem about to snap as their leaves whirl off and the bark peels into strips. Palm fronds wave like ostrich feathers in increasingly sharp angles from the stems until they finally fly off like errant birds. As the wind and rain batter the doors, the glass rattles against its casing and appears about to burst into the room. It holds. His neighbor knocks on his door, begging for shelter for herself and her traumatized six-year-old twins. Their doors shattered, she says, exposing them to the wind's fury. They hunker in the bathtub until the storm abates.

In Naguabo, Shirley's cousin Edith has convinced their two aunts they'll be safer at her house than in the senior-housing apartment building where they live together. Unable to sleep through what sounds like a locomotive circling the house, and clinging to their rosaries, the tías sit in their wheelchairs in the center hallway with the rest of Edith's family. María collapses the carport over Edith's van. The winds push an air conditioner into the room and torrents of water rush inside through the opening. The kitchen window implodes. Shards fly against walls and furniture. More water floods the ground floor. Edith and her husband carry the tías, their wheelchairs, their adult diapers, oxygen tanks, and medications to the second floor. The old women pray, trusting the Trinity will detour the winds that threaten to take the roof and everyone under it.

María reaches the Puerto Rican foothills of the Cordillera Central. A hurricane racing through a landscape can be less destructive than one that hovers over the terrain. Strong winds damage structures and vegetation, but floods are a greater threat to humans and fauna. María's winds slow over the mountains. Its rains soak the land, causing mudslides and sinkholes. In San Lorenzo, a house perched on a hill skids into a ravine when the saturated ground can't support it. Inside are a family of seven.

In Aibonito, a farmer has spent two days securing the buildings where he's raising sixty thousand chickens destined for market. Over the next thirty hours the fowl drown or are crushed under the collapsed structures meant to protect them.

In Toa Baja, Oliver and Miriam have fortified their doors, windows, and enclosed garage, with their limousine and Lucho's car inside. Lucho has borrowed the van to drive other family members to higher ground near Caguas. He's done one trip already, but the road becomes impassable, and he has to retrace his steps to safety. It is still possible to make cell calls, and he alerts eight other relatives to make their way to Oliver and Miriam's just in case the nearby river overflows its banks. None expect Oliver and Miriam's doors and windows to fail against the onslaught of wind, water, and mud. Their screams bring neighbors, who rescue them, but Miriam's sister and her grandson are swept away by the whirling currents.

In Aguas Buenas, a man living alone has nailed plywood to the outside of his windows and pushed a sofa against the front door once he's made himself comfortable inside. He's lived through enough tropical storms and hurricanes to be confident he's well prepared. He has plenty of water, food, liquor, and oil lamps for the inevitable power outage. He drinks enough rum to pass out, his chosen method to pasar la tormenta. But he wakes up and quivers in terror during an onslaught of lightning and thunder that sounds like giants marching toward him. He dies of a massive heart attack.

The sea inundates the swimming pools at a resort in Ponce. The wind rips the roof from guest rooms and from the convention center, where several hundred visitors are sheltered. Perla has been a concierge for eight years and knows her way around the complex. She's guiding guests away from the damaged area when a wind blast picks up her petite body and slams her against a wooden podium, breaking her spine. Her flashlight whirls in erratic circles, causing those who've been following her to panic. No one sees where she falls and the crowd loses their way in the darkness and confusion, finally following lights from phones held aloft by other guests who've found a way toward safety. Perla's mangled body is left behind.

In Jayuya, Adjuntas, Ciales, and surrounding towns, bridges fracture into rivers and canyons, isolating residents, who have no possibility of escape from the mountainous area. Mudslides take out roads, and the unpaved rural paths and local lanes become gullies between gorges.

In Guares, the cemetery gives up its dead, the coffins rising from the sodden ground, their tombstones tipping over and scattering, separating the dead from their monuments. Salvadora's and Federico's caskets, among others, are bobbing in fango.

In the coffee-farming regions of Yauco, Lares, and their environs, María uproots the lovingly tended plants and the tree canopy that shades them from the harsh sun, razing the entire 2017 harvest. The crop will not recover for years.

Close to the shores, buildings surrender to the waves, which also claim docks and warehouses filled with food, water, medicines, and other lifesaving supplies.

In Morovis, a seventy-four-year-old woman named Gladys was discharged from a hospital two days before María formed in the Atlantic. Recovering from abdominal surgery, she's well enough when the storm is announced, and she helps her adult children prepare their home. As María rages, Gladys feels discomfort, but she doesn't want to worry her family members until the pain becomes unbearable. Her children are unable to get her to a hospital and she dies from internal bleeding before their horrified eyes.

In Utuado, a teenager goes into labor soon after her in-laws secure their home. She delivers her first child into her mother-in-law's hands while her husband and father-in-law struggle to keep their roof from flying away, to no avail. They all perish.

In Maricao, a tree crashes into a bedroom, killing a sleeping baby.

Claudio, El Vikingo, hasn't thought about Luz in years. His dreams of a professional basketball career ended with injuries made worse by hard partying after he came into an inheritance. He's now a tractor-trailer driver hauling appliances for a big-box retailer, and has driven heavy rigs through dozens of tropical storms for decades. Beyond Guánica, María's winds tip his rig over onto its side and it skids into a trench filled with rushing water. Claudio loses consciousness momentarily. When he comes to, he manages to open the driver's door facing the sullen skies, and with effort, climbs out and drops into the water below. His headlights illuminate some buildings ahead, and he fights the current, grabbing whatever he can hold on to until he slithers from the trench. For every step he takes on what is left of the road, María sends him back three. Claudio bangs on doors and windows, yells for help. Either the residents have fled or they can't hear him as he goes from house to house. Increasingly desperate, wet, bleeding, wild-eyed with terror, El Vikingo battles María, but with one violent gust, the storm smashes him against the cement wall of a sporting-goods store, where he stops moving.

In each of the seventy-eight Puerto Rican municipalities, walls crumple and roofs slump into homes or fly off in crazy patterns over the transforming landscape. Trees that have survived generations of the ravages of tropical storms and hurricanes challenge María's gales coming from the east, from the west, from the east again, from the west, gusts twisting their trunks, unscrewing them from their roots, and dropping them atop vehicles, barns, schools, factories, restaurants, hospitals, middle-class homes, housing projects, and mansions, into swimming pools, ponds, creeks, brooks, and rivers, alongside roads, down the leafless hills, and into flooding valleys.

María's fury batters the land during the day, but even those who dare look outside can't see much. The light is filtered by rain opaque as a lace mantilla.

For las madres and las nenas, hour after hour of the screeching coming from the roof makes it impossible to hear one another—to think, even. They wrap pillows over their heads with little effect. At the height of the winds, a thump vibrates the house, and the metal grinding and animal sounds stop. They're certain a wall in Marysol's room has collapsed.

"I'll check whether water is coming in."

They can't dissuade Marysol. Ada follows her. It's midday, or at least no longer as dark as the inside of a wolf's mouth. A thick, humid mist smells of seawater. The flashlight beams can't break through the fog enough for them to see what's ahead. They touch the walls, and a slimy moisture makes them rub their fingers against their clothes. It's raining inside, water creeping through invisible crevices and closed window louvers. The ceiling in Marysol's room appears to have held and, mercifully, the infernal noise has stopped, but the tempest has not abated and will not do so for hours. The women use towels to sop up the puddles forming in corners. The concrete house shakes as if trying to take flight. Las madres and las nenas tiptoe around it like mimes, as if their voices will unleash more rain, more wind, more devastation.

❧

The winds diminish, and an eerie calm descends like a heavy quilt. The rooms are stifling, and Ada announces the eye of the storm is passing over them.

"I don't know how long this will last," she says, "but we can see what's happening outside before the winds hit us from the other direction."

With effort, she opens the front door and, holding on to one another, las madres and las nenas step onto the slippery front porch. The floor tiles have separated from the grout, forming peaks and valleys covered by leaves and twigs. The palms at the gates have resisted the gusts, but their fronds have disappeared, making them look like enormous fence posts. Fractured and uprooted trees litter the yard. Wrought-iron fencing leans in every direction, and nearby homes have lost roofs and walls, exposing bedrooms and living rooms, their contents in disarray. Black wires weave and flutter like tassels.

"C'est un désastre!"

Ada, Shirley, Marysol, and Graciela huddle around Luz.

"We'll get through it," Ada says. "We will! We just have to ride it out."

It sounds to Marysol as if Ada is talking to herself.

She's unsure of the time, but knows it's daytime, maybe late afternoon. Breaks of sunlight play on the streets, now canals, in which all manner of objects float and bob. When the clouds return, a steamy gray haze, thicker than fog, surrounds them.

"Floodwaters are more than halfway up the driveway," Shirley remarks. "Hopefully it won't keep rising."

"Ich will nicht in schmutzigem Wasser schwimmen," Luz whimpers.

"What does that mean, Mom?"

"Je ne veux pas nager dans l'eau sale."

"You won't have to swim in dirty water," Graciela says. "If it continues to rise, we'll go upstairs, where we'll be safe."

The calm air isn't reassuring. Neighbors take stock of the damage so far, aware la virazón, the other wall of the hurricane's eye, will bring more wind, more rain, thunder, lightning, more destruction. Having been through the first stage of the storm, they dread another night of terror.

Their next-door neighbor sloshes around his property. When

he reaches the side of the house facing theirs, he stops what he's doing and calls out, "Is everyone okay in there?"

"We're good," Shirley says. "And you?"

"Gracias a Dios." He's about to return to his chores when he catches sight of Luz. "Is that you, Luz Peña Fuentes?"

"C'est moi. Comment allez-vous?" she asks politely, with no flicker of recognition.

"Yo soy Kelvin Cabrera Pou," he says. A ray of sunshine clears the gloom. Kelvin takes a good look at Ada, Shirley, Graciela, and Marysol. "You're the teacher," he says, "and you're the accountant. Am I right?"

"Para servirle," a tight-lipped Ada says, not at all eager to be of service.

"The wind is picking up again," Shirley says, and hustles Luz toward the door.

"Take care," Kelvin says. "If you need anything, don't hesitate to call on me."

A preoccupied Ada locks up and goes into the kitchen. She studies the electric stove, a sheet of glass useless during a power outage.

"I need coffee," she says.

Las madres and Marysol are suffering from caffeine withdrawal, feeling irritable and their heads achy. Graciela isn't physically suffering quite as much. Her particular addiction is to the Internet but it's been more than twelve hours without Wi-Fi or cell service with no hint of when it and electricity will be restored.

"I'm jumping out of my skin," she says to no one in particular. She goes upstairs, she comes back downstairs, makes notes in one of Luz's sketch pads, with plans to post when the service is restored. She adds to her lists.

They can't hear one another over the renewed banging and crashing. They play dominoes by candlelight. They eat leftovers and play more games. They open a couple of tinned sardines in olive oil, which they mash with a fork and mound on crackers.

Graciela makes more sweetened lemonade. They have ice, a couple of bottles of rum and soda. They drink. Their dinner is cold canned spaghetti with tiny meatballs, a far cry from lechón asado at Piñones.

The booms and thwacks increase as the opposite wall of the storm passes. Las madres and Marysol are tired of dominoes. They settle around the living area. Before leaving the United States, they loaded their tablets and phones with books and games. Graciela reminds them not to exhaust their batteries.

The winds now coming from the other side of the storm's eye whistle through cracks. Flashlight in hand, Graciela runs up to check the bedrooms. Rain is seeping through the windowsills. She rolls up towels, stuffs them in the cracks. Within moments, she's squeezing water from soaked towels into nearly full tubs. When she goes downstairs, she slips and falls on her butt.

The others run to help and notice the moisture on the floor tiles. Water is leaking through the back-porch doors. By the time Ada finds the mop and bucket in the utility room, streams are forming along the channels between tiles. They upend their chairs on the table and clear the floor, as rivulets creep through the front door as well as the door in back. The mop is useless. They use the rest of the towels, which are soon soaked through. The relentless wind-driven rain makes its way through vents and openings for power, cable, and long-abandoned phone wires.

They can't squeeze the towels dry enough to make much difference as the water rises. Las madres and las nenas stop trying to keep up with the flooding on the first floor. They grab bottled water and food supplies to take upstairs. The seams along Marysol's and Graciela's ceilings have been breached. They push the beds away from the outside walls, grab their belongings, and for the second night, the five women climb into the king-size bed and huddle together as wind and rain pound the walls and flood the lower story.

The Cleanup

On Thursday afternoon, las madres and las nenas are standing on the ground floor in sand and mud above their ankles. The apocalyptic noises have diminished, replaced by barking dogs and human voices in lamentation. As Ada opens the front door, the sludge drifts outside. On the street, people splash through knee-high muck, checking on neighbors and taking stock of the damage. Caved-in walls, blown-out windows, and missing roofs on half-submerged homes form an archipelago of calamity. Splintered telephone poles have crashed into porches and crushed vehicles. Others lie across roads and sidewalks. Metal light posts are bent like drinking straws. A forest of wires is knotted like moth-eaten curtains.

"Where did all those wavy metal sheets come from?" Marysol asks.

"Planchas de zinc," Ada says. "They fly like kites from people's roofs. Not everyone lives in neighborhoods like this one."

Marysol is abashed. Her experience in Puerto Rico so far has been in tourist areas, where poverty has been made invisible. This area is middle-class, the houses built from concrete and most, like theirs, two stories high, with a floor above the flood line. "I can't imagine what María did to people who lived under zinc roofs."

"They pass the storm with relatives or friends," Shirley explains.

As las madres and las nenas watch from the porch, more men, women, and children stagger from their homes, stunned and disbelieving the wreckage around them. Some burst into sobs, others call out they're okay and stoically begin clearing debris. A

Las Madres

weeping Luz leans into Marysol's shoulder alongside Shirley and Ada, their arms wrapped around one another. Graciela waves her phone around with no results. She isn't the only one desperate for a signal.

"It smells like the sewers overflowed. We shouldn't be standing in this slurry," Marysol says. "It's a soup of communicable diseases."

Shirley grimaces, but she leads the way inside again. Marysol makes Luz sit on the steps to the second floor and scrubs her mother's feet and legs, suggesting the others do the same to theirs before returning upstairs.

"Merci, ma chère," Luz says.

Shirley, Ada, Graciela, and Marysol are worried that her utterances have almost entirely been in German or French since the hurricane began.

"I love you, Mom," Marysol says now, as she helps her upstairs.

⸎

In the fading daylight, they wipe down Marysol's and Graciela's rooms.

"This doesn't help," Graciela says. "The more water we mop up, the more water dribbles in."

They clear the terraces of leaves, branches, and dead animals.

"Look what I found." Marysol raises a satellite television dish that has been wedged in the corner of the back terrace. "Must have whirled like a Frisbee."

The sun fades and clouds part theatrically to a void.

"Wow!"

Marysol follows her mother's gaze. "I've never seen so many stars!"

Las madres and las nenas look up as Graciela pulls out her phone and snaps pictures.

⸎

By the next morning, the waters on the ground floor have receded, leaving a brown, slippery batter on the tiles, which Marysol and Graciela push outside with brooms. They collect the wet towels to mop the floors. No matter how many times they swab the tiles and walls, they can't erase the abstract patterns of muddy smudges.

Branches, leaves, broken chunks of plastic, wood planks, and parts of a billboard are pressed against the rear doors. Slime the color of feces continues to leak inside. It rains intermittently and Shirley cranks open the louvers, hoping to get a breeze moving through. During the hurricane, they hadn't felt the heat indoors quite as much as they do now.

Las madres discuss what to do with the food in the refrigerator.

"Ich hasse es, Essen wegzuwerfen." No one has any idea what Luz says. She studies, sniffs, and squeezes the meat and vegetables, and they figure she's determining whether they're still edible.

A whine and a roar startles Marysol. "What the hell is that?" It goes on, off, on again.

"People starting their generators," Ada says.

Two teenage boys knock on the front porch gate. One carries an industrial broom, the other a shovel. They introduce themselves as Felipe and Jason Cabrera Rubinate, and point to Kelvin, who is waving from his roof next door. "Papá sent us over to clean the leaves and branches from your roof."

"The water isn't draining," Kelvin calls. "Another aguacero, and the roof might cave in."

"Oh, no! Entiendo, gracias. Please, thank you . . ." Shirley is scared. "It's so kind of you."

"I want to see." Marysol follows the boys up the rear stairs.

Like the roof on her house in the Bronx, this one is flat. A low parapet surrounds a channel to guide rain through scuppers into downpours. A nearly imperceptible slant toward the rear of the house encourages draining, but junk has blocked these scuppers, converting the storm-driven rain into an enormous puddle that dribbles rather than flows.

"Oh, my God!" Marysol gasps. "It's like a swimming pool."

With nowhere to go, rainwater seeps through the inside walls and ceilings, which under normal circumstances wouldn't happen, since the house is made from concrete. From his roof, Kelvin calls instructions to his sons about where to dump the debris.

The roof provides an expansive view of the neighborhood and the ocean. Marysol takes a few moments to survey the devastation below. It recalls images from war-torn cities and earthquakes on the evening news. Many of the windows and glass doors to terraces on the nearby condominium buildings have shattered. Metal storm windows have been ripped off their frames, forming tormented origami shapes. A tree is impaled through one window, and from another, a forlorn curtain flutters like a white flag of surrender.

"Yoo-hoo!" Graciela comes up. "This is nice here," she says before she sees what's below. She gasps, covers her mouth. "This is . . ." She can't articulate it and falls into Marysol's arms.

Behind them, Felipe and Jason don't know which way to look in the face of her emotion. They back away to the farthest corner and inspect the roof over Marysol's bedroom.

"Those screeching sounds we all heard," Jason says, "were the solar heater detaching from its metal bolts."

"It probably landed in Arecibo," Felipe says with a sidelong glance at Marysol and Graciela, hoping they'll laugh. They smile.

Marysol and Graciela join them to clear the scuppers. Soon the roof is draining properly and the boys go down to remove the mound of debris against the back door.

"I've got to post about this." Graciela pulls her phone from her pocket.

Marysol watches her snap one photo after another from different angles as she tries to encompass the devastation. There is no way, Marysol thinks, anyone will believe how bad it is, even with pictures.

"No, señora," Jason and Felipe say, refusing the money Shirley wants to give them. "That's unnecessary."

"But you've spent all morning—"

"No se preocupe."

They shuffle off.

"I might have offended them," she says to Ada.

"We'll do something for them," Ada says. "I'm sure they'd take your money if their dad weren't watching."

Graciela and Marysol wheel the gas grill outdoors. They have similar ones at home, and in no time, Marysol has it going and makes coffee using the aluminum moka pot.

"I feel the caffeine entering my veins," Shirley says.

Luz breathes in the aroma and grins. "Ma migraine est partie!"

"Her headache is gone," Graciela translates.

"You haven't even tasted it," Marysol laughs.

They don't know how much propane is left in the canister, but they're all hungry for hot food after a couple of days of canned spaghetti, tuna, and sardines with saltines.

A rumble startles them and they look toward the ocean. A plane is rising into the sky.

"I forgot how close we are to the airport," Marysol notes.

"It must be open again," Shirley says.

"Maybe that means things will be back to normal soon."

"Können wir nach Hause gehen?"

"House?"

Luz nods.

"Our house?" Marysol asks.

Luz nods vigorously.

"Wednesday, five days from now." Ada shows her fingers.

Luz sighs. The others exchange sad looks. It's obvious she's been traumatized by María. Since the first night of the storm, her achaques have been frequent and last longer.

Las Madres

Ada collects their mugs. "Back to work." Her voice is strained, and Marysol knows Ada is worried about Luz but doesn't want to talk about it. At least, not now and not in front of her. "We have to keep everything as dry as possible," she continues. "Mold and fungus build up fast. We'll take care of the first-floor rooms. You girls do the upstairs."

As they clean, they find leaves, twigs, sand, and dead animals inside closets and dresser drawers. Over the next few hours, they use all the chlorine bleach and cleaning fluids Loreta left. They scrub the floors again, but they remain grimy despite their efforts.

"Maybe when you get through to Oliver, ask him to bring supplies," Marysol says.

"I've been trying." Graciela hates being reminded she has no communication. She travels with a panoply of devices that are now useless without power or cell signals.

"Do you think people in the U.S. have any idea Puerto Rico looks like a bomb went off?"

"The rest of the world could have exploded," Graciela says. "We could be the only survivors and we wouldn't know it."

"That's an uncharacteristically depressing thought coming from you."

"I've never seen anything like what we saw from the roof, and we haven't even stepped beyond the front gate." Graciela pulls clothes from her chest of drawers and sniffs a shirt. "¡Ay fo! Everything's damp and smells like low tide. How's that possible? It didn't flood up here."

Marysol shrugs.

They drape their clothes over the porch furniture. The day is overcast, and sweltering heat alternates with rain showers. By late afternoon, Graciela realizes they've used most of the water in the tubs and sinks for cleaning and haven't saved much for bathing or flushing toilets. Her chipper attitude is fraying.

"Laissons des pots et des casseroles dehors," Luz suggests.

"Something about leaving the pots outside," Marysol interprets.

Luz nods.

"Why?"

"Pour attraper la pluie pour les toilettes."

"Ah! Great idea, Mom. We catch rainwater for the toilets."

Ada grins. "We'll be resourceful like our grandparents."

"I don't have to go back two generations," Shirley says. "We didn't have a refrigerator until I was a teenager. We had an icebox. Mamá cooked what might turn bad before the next ice delivery. If we had more than we could eat, she'd send me with it to a neighbor, who was usually happy to take it."

"Then we'll do what our madres y abuelas did," Ada says. "We won't let food rot and we'll share."

They make a hearty sancocho with meats and vegetables. Shirley and Ada deliver half of it to Kelvin and his family next door. Coming back, they huddle for a moment before going inside. To Marysol, they seem nervous.

"Is everything okay?"

"We're fine."

They take their customary places around the table on the porch. It's minutes to sundown.

"Ada had a blast-from-the-past moment," Shirley says as she lights a candle in the center of the table. "She forgot she'd tutored Kelvin back in the seventies."

They watch Luz, as if expecting her to recognize the name. She doesn't.

"Kelvin grew up in that house." Ada again checks for Luz's reaction. Nothing. "But his wife is from Utuado. Her elderly parents survived Hugo and Georges with minor damage, and decided to stay in their home for María."

"He heard the mountain towns were hard-hit," Shirley adds.

"At least their youngest son and pregnant wife live with them."

Ada glances toward Kelvin's house. "Her baby is due any day now."

"Ich hoffe Sie sind okay," Luz says. The others understand only the last word.

In the background, generators thrum and their fumes mix with the stench of dead animals and sewage.

"I miss the coquí," Marysol says. "I hope they didn't all drown."

Luz shudders. "Puerto Rico sans coquí est inconcevable."

"They'll come back," Ada says. "They always do."

They're all in contemplative moods. Shirley thinks about her aunts, hoping Edith convinced them to stay with her and that they're all safe. Ada wonders whether Oliver and Miriam are okay in Toa Baja, where there was major flooding, according to Kelvin. Marysol watches Luz sliding in and out of achaques, babbling incomprehensibly. The others notice it, but don't comment. Graciela checks her cell phone for a signal, just in case. No bars, and the battery is nearly exhausted. She makes a mental note to connect the phone to her backup charger. The candle sputters and Ada lights another.

Injuries

SEPTEMBER 23, 2017

On Saturday morning, las madres and las nenas join the brigades clearing drainage grates and driveways and unblocking streets. Neighbors have tied up the dead wires for the professionals to deal with later. With their machetes or hand saws, they trim branches obstructing driveways, roads, and sidewalks. Other volunteers stack them. The government crews will come eventually, but they're all aware the mounds left by Irma weren't taken before María scattered them all again.

"¡Ay!" a boy screeches. He's been helping with the cleanup and gets a cut on his hand. Several women converge on him.

"I'm a nurse," Marysol calls. The boy's mother focuses on reassuring him while Marysol examines the bloody but superficial wound. "I have a first-aid kit inside." They follow her, the boy now calmer. Luz offers them a seat on the porch while Marysol finds her supplies.

When she returns, there are other people waiting outside.

"We heard there's a nurse here," someone says.

Most have cuts, scrapes, and sprains. Marysol and Luz always carry first-aid kits, and when the neighbors realize she has no other supplies, they bring alcohol, gauze, antibacterial creams, and compression and adhesive bandages of every shape and size. Anything remotely medical ends up on the kitchen counter, where Luz organizes them. The living room becomes an impromptu clinic.

As more patients appear, Luz goes in and out of achaques, distracting Marysol and the injured, who can tell something is off with her, but are too polite to ask.

"Where is she from?" a woman asks, upon hearing another language. "Is she Haitian?"

"She's Boricua, but she speaks three other languages as well as Spanish."

"¡Impresionante!"

"¿Verdad?" Marysol grins.

Ada drags in a red-faced Graciela. "You come with me," she says to Luz. "She's taking over," she says to Marysol.

"I forgot my cap and the SPF." Graciela's nose and forehead are sunburnt.

"There's aloe in my room." Marysol points with her lips.

When Graciela comes back, the line of people waiting for Marysol is longer. Some are bloodied, others moaning in pain, but all have the resigned attitude of people used to waiting in line. Within minutes, Graciela sets herself up on the porch and creates a database on her laptop.

"What happens when your battery runs out?" Marysol asks from the living/treatment room.

"She can charge up in my house," a man says. "We have a generator."

"Or in our car," a woman offers.

Someone brings them coffee and Ding Dongs. "I hope you don't mind it's black. Our milk went bad. We do have sugar."

"That's so kind! Don't worry—we like it black and unsweetened," Graciela says.

"We heard you're here on vacation," Otto, Marysol's next patient, says.

"Sí, señor."

"Your Spanish is good, but you don't sound Boricua."

"What do you mean? Who do I sound like?"

"Like you learned it afuera," his wife, Felicita, pipes in. "You're Nuyorican, aren't you?"

"Do you mean that as a compliment or an insult?"

Felicita and Otto blubber. "Oh, no! Please don't be offended. Disculpa."

"Okay." Marysol is unable to hide her annoyance. "I'm Puerto Rican, born in New York. Nuyorican."

"And I'm Mainarican," Graciela calls from the porch. When Felicita looks puzzled, she explains, "A Puerto Rican in Maine."

"That sounds like a reality TV show," a woman scoffs, and everyone laughs.

Graciela counts twenty people waiting for Marysol to see them. The hospital is four blocks away, but the injured say the doctors and nurses can't keep up.

"When Otto cut his arm, it bled a lot," Felicita says. "I poured a whole bottle of Agua Florida over his arm."

"That's why you smell like flowers." Marysol smiles.

"It burned, but I was afraid to lose my arm."

His wife flutters her hands around her face. "Ay, this infernal heat!"

"It's always like this after a hurricane," Otto says. "All the leaves are gone. No shade."

The next patient is an obese man in his forties.

"I'm diabetic but don't need insulin, gracias a Dios. I take pills and have enough for a couple of weeks."

She checks and cleans the lacerations on his scalp and down his back. "How did this happen?"

"My ceiling went ¡Fuá!" He windmills his arms and pretends to duck falling debris. "As you can see, yo soy gordito." He pats his belly. "Mamá said she's never seen me move so fast!"

Another man has a sprained ankle. "I fell off a ladder while taking down plywood."

"Do you have any ice left?"

"I wish," he sighs.

A teenage boy has a cut on his thigh. His grandmother rubbed Vicks on it and made a bandage with a shirt. Clotted blood is stuck to the wound and the improvised dressing. Marysol works slowly to avoid ripping off the scabs along with the rags. She's relieved the cut hasn't festered, although he was injured on the first night of the storm.

During a break, Graciela shows her a list she's compiled on her computer. "People heard there was a nurse here and begged me to ask you to visit their relatives in their homes. Most of them are elderly, bedridden, and dependent on respirators and other machines."

Marysol covers her face, rubs her temples, sucks her lips into her mouth, and holds them there, swallowing sorrow.

"Take a breath," Graciela says.

"I don't have a stethoscope, a thermometer, medical gloves, or masks. All I have is a small bottle of hand sanitizer. I don't know how much I can do for people confined to their beds and dependent on medical equipment. What do I do if they need a doctor, a hospital, or oxygen?"

"You'll comfort them."

⌒

To thank Marysol, Felicita and Otto drop off enough ropa vieja with a side of white rice to feed the five hungry, exhausted women. They dine by a flame sinking into a waxy puddle. Marysol worries about Luz, who is weirdly passive, as if she isn't emerging fully from her achaques. As soon as they finish the meal, Marysol encourages her to go to bed. Luz doesn't argue. Marysol leads her upstairs and cools her down with a hand towel dampened with bottled water.

"Das ist so erfrischend!"

"Feels good?"

"Oui, c'est bon."

Marysol helps her settle in. The room is stifling, but Luz doesn't seem to notice or care. She's asleep within moments.

Ada and Graciela are washing the dishes by flashlight and Shirley is on the back porch, listening to the intermittent rain showers taking the edge off the clamoring generators. After a while, Ada and Graciela join Marysol and Shirley there.

They've adapted to the darkness and its intimacy.

"I want to go home." Shirley sighs.

Graciela harrumphs. "The airport is as much in the dark as we are."

"We heard an airplane earlier," Marysol says.

"I don't know how they took off. The control tower was wrecked."

"Who told you that?" Ada asks.

"The neighbors talk while waiting for Marysol."

She's heard some neighbors with battery radios can get news from the only station on the air. All the others lost their antennas and can't broadcast. People complain the local governments don't communicate with one another in the best of times. Public officials spend more time wrestling for power and resources than fulfilling campaign promises. The neighbors are particularly scornful of the utilities and public services. They're politicized and don't share information with one another. Their lack of transparency and poor communication means it's difficult to coordinate needs and organize teams responding to emergencies or natural disasters.

"This has been going on for decades," Shirley says.

"That doesn't make me feel better."

"Graciela showed me a list of people who want me to visit the infirm," Marysol says. "A few are on dialysis. Others need ventilators. Insulin and other medications have to be refrigerated. I can't help them!"

"No te afliges, nena," Ada says. "They know you're not a miracle worker."

Graciela continues her litany of grievances. Businesses have been looted. The hospitals depend on diesel, which is in short supply. The rumor is that thousands have died. Morgues are full, with no place to store the dead until their families can claim them.

"No one knows how many died. Probably thousands."

"No, hija, it can't be that many." Shirley reaches into the dark to touch Graciela but can't find her.

Ada is closer and caresses her daughter's arm.

"Here we are, smelly, uncomfortable, and stressed," Graciela says. "But when the airport opens, we can go home. Tens of thousands of Puerto Ricans lost everything and have no other place to go."

"Reporters must be covering it for the outside world," Marysol says, "like they did for Irma."

"Don't get your hopes up. The media focuses on the most dramatic, visual images, but María is happening here." Graciela slaps her chest, a shocking sound that echoes against the concrete walls.

"Nobody can see inside, not here." She slaps her chest again. "For the media, we're sound bites between commercials."

"Ay, hija." Ada stands to wrap her arms around her daughter. Shirley, too, finds her way to her. "We have to be strong."

"We can't fall apart now," Shirley says, "not after what we've been through."

Marysol kneels in front of Graciela, takes her hands, and presses them between hers. "Breathe."

Graciela tries to control her emotions. Her mothers find their chairs again, bring them closer to their daughter, and each places a hand on her shoulders and holds it there, as if to keep her from flying away.

"If we were home," Shirley says, "we'd be collecting donations from our friends and families to help Puerto Rico, like we've done after other storms."

Graciela gives up all semblance of restraint. "This was not a storm, Mommy. María is a calamity. Puerto Rico has been ravaged and will never be the same." She takes her hands back from Marysol's, shakes off her mothers, and breaks into unbridled sobs. There's a silence, interrupted only by the coughing of generators in the near distance. One by one, Shirley, Ada, and Marysol also weep in the dark.

Media Moment

SEPTEMBER 24, 2017

"I've never cried so much in my life," Graciela says to Marysol the next morning as they walk to the home visits on her list.

"Me, neither, but a good cry relieved some of the tension."

As las nenas pass, neighbors wave, and some stop to chat before continuing the cleanup of their yards and sidewalks.

"It's as if we've lived in the neighborhood forever," Marysol says.

"Nothing like a disaster to bring strangers together."

They turn the corner. Mounds of soggy furniture and battered appliances are piled in front yards and on sidewalks. Puddles reflect passing clouds that then reveal infinite azure skies. The major flooding has receded, but the odor of sewage, mildew, decomposition, and gasoline follows them everywhere.

Having cleared the local roads, drivers brave the avenues and highways, hoping to reconnect with loved ones and seeking depleted supplies. They stop to share news with Graciela and Marysol. One informs them a dusk-to-dawn curfew has been imposed and the sale of alcoholic beverages banned.

Another tells them the lines at the groceries are hours long and those at gas stations are even worse. A married couple were at the supermarket by four in the morning, and found fifty people ahead of them. When the store opened, they let in only a few shoppers at a time. The shelves were mostly empty, they report. They went to another grocer but weren't allowed inside. They had to give them a list and if the employees found the items, they brought them out. On top of that, cash only. The registers don't work without electricity and neither do the ATMs. Banks are closed. People are confused and enraged.

Another woman is in tears. She ran out of diapers and can't find more. She's been cutting up T-shirts to make some. "But who has those big safety pins anymore?"

A man and his wife went to Loíza and burst into relieved sobs when he reached his mother's house. She'd survived and her house had only minor flooding, but the trip there and back was harrowing. It took them hours when it should have taken less than forty-five minutes. His wife leans over from the passenger seat.

"The trees are the color of smoke. You think if you touch one, it will turn to ash."

Bridges and overpasses have collapsed. Motorists have to help people clearing trees or boulders from the roads before they can continue.

"And traffic lights don't work," his wife says. "Every intersection is an adventure."

It takes a long time for Marysol and Graciela to reach their patients. Between the visits and chats with the neighbors, las nenas talk to each other in a way impossible when they're around las madres.

"Madrina seems more confused now," Graciela says.

"Mom's in shock."

"Are you worried about her?"

"I always worry about her." Marysol scratches her scalp. "¡Ay! I need a shampoo. And a hot shower."

"You always do that."

"What?"

"You swerve." Graciela gestures like a fish darting through water. "You don't have to change the subject every time you're upset about Madrina."

"I do that?"

"I notice that and other things. Like how Mommy and Mami have also been swerving since we got here."

"When? How?"

"Yesterday, when you and Madrina were helping the injured, we were working on the street with women who recognized them. They went pale, were nervous, and Mami dragged me away. She said I was getting too much sun and brought me inside to work with you. She swerved." Graciela's hand pretends to be a fish again.

"You were sunburnt, Graciela. Don't get paranoid."

"You don't believe me, but I know them, and something's

bothering them. Haven't you noticed Mami is . . ." She searches for the word. "She's testy. With me. All I've done is try to make a bad situation bearable. It's like she blames me for the hurricane."

"Come on, Graciela. She doesn't. I think she and Shirley are disappointed about not being able to walk down memory lane with Mom. Old people do that. They like revisiting the past."

"So why didn't they mention this neighborhood as a destination? And why are they so skittish about being here? This is where they lived for years. You'd think they'd want to see how it looks now."

"They're not as romantic as you are," Marysol teases.

"There's something going on," Graciela says. "They're not like this."

"Like what?"

"Anxious. Whenever they're recognized, they get uptight."

"Can you imagine what it was like to be openly lesbian in the seventies? People they're running into were probably not quite as enlightened as they might be now. My guess is your mothers are triggered when they see them again, remembering the bullying, the bochinche and chisme they surely endured. They've told us about that, Graciela. But talking about it and knowing that things are somewhat better now doesn't erase what happened then."

Graciela is unconvinced. She checks her list and looks at the house in front of them. "This is the place."

"Who's swerving now?" Marysol mutters, following her up a driveway.

⌒

Marysol is unused to having someone with her on her medical visits, but Graciela is helpful. With the batteries on her devices expended, Graciela has gone analog until she can charge up again with a neighbor's car or generator. Until then, she carries one of Luz's sketchbooks and a pen everywhere.

After a couple of visits, they establish a routine. Marysol talks to the caregiver and learns about the patient's condition and medications. While Marysol examines them, Graciela keeps the rest of the family in another room or outside to give the patient privacy.

Marysol needs as much quiet as possible to hear the patient's sounds, complaints, or questions. If generators are running, she insists they be turned off until she's ready to leave unless they're running life-support equipment. As Graciela said the day before, she can do little but comfort the sick and provide solace to their relatives. She can't do much about her patients' medications degrading in the heat, or the lack of power for their medical devices, or generators that have to be refilled often at a time when gas stations are closed or limiting how much fuel a customer can buy.

Graciela keeps track of who is seen and where. She asked Ada and Shirley to draw a rough map of the area and seems to have memorized it. After the visits, Marysol adds notes if there is to be follow-up. She'd love to record her patients' stories, to add their narratives to the others she has neatly filed in labeled thumb drives inside a locked box in her clean, cozy, comfortable house in the Bronx. She blocks the longing from her recollection. *Be here now,* she tells herself.

As they leave the house of a man likely to die within days without his dialysis, they see people running toward the avenue.

"There's a news van." A young man points in the direction of the stampede. "They're filming people!"

Without hesitation, Marysol follows, Graciela doing her best but failing to catch up. Marysol turns the corner and catches sight of the antennas atop a van, the logo of a major television network on its side panels, the harried, vested videographer besieged by desperate people, and the reporter, whose wrinkled shirt and rumpled hair will present a version at odds with his usual unruffled self to viewers. She can't remember his name. Marysol notes he's much shorter and skinnier than he looks on TV, but his sonorous voice sends a familiar shiver through her. Next to him, a woman takes notes on a clipboard and translates for the people he interviews. Marysol has the same idea as everyone ahead of her: If she can get before the camera, maybe, just maybe, people who know her in New York will see she's survived María and they'll alert Warren and their friends.

"I'm a nurse," she yells over the other voices trying to get the reporter's notice. "I've been treating injuries."

She's speaking English while most of those around her are clamoring in Spanish. The reporter is relieved to hear the only language he understands. He waves her closer. Marysol is conscious of the resentment she creates as she moves toward the newsman. Some people step aside. Others deliberately jostle or trip her. Marysol has quick reflexes and swats away those who block her path. She doesn't care that they call her a pushy Nuyorican. She runs her fingers through her unruly hair, smooths the front of her top, and stands as defiantly as an Amazon.

"Please tell us your name," Scott or Matt or Tom asks.

She leans into his mic and looks straight into the camera lens. "I'm Marysol Ríos Peña from the Bronx. I came here with my family and we were stranded by the storm. We got through it, though, and we're all safe. Safe!"

"You said you're a nurse?"

She nods. "There are many injured and the hospitals can't keep up. I've been treating wounds with whatever people donate from their medicine cabinets. We have no electric power, no clean running water, no access to medications for the most compromised patients. People are dying."

"Thank you." The reporter begins his wrap-up.

"Dile que somos ciudadanos," a woman calls from the crowd.

"Yo soy veterano de Desert Storm," a man yells.

"Wait, wait." Marysol stands closer to the reporter and points to the crowd. "Let me translate what they said." She again faces the camera. "Puerto Ricans are United States citizens. Like that man over there, many men and women here are veterans who've served in the United States military."

"Korea!" someone shouts.

"Vietnam! Purple Heart!"

"I served in Iraq!"

"Y yo en Afghanistan!"

"I fought fires in California," a man shouts.

"I rescued people during Katrina," a woman says.

Marysol is moved by the emotion in the voices and turns to the reporter, who also seems stirred. She faces the videographer again. "Puerto Ricans have stepped up in every war and disaster in the States. We're your fellow citizens, in desperate need of help. Please don't turn from us now. Thank you."

Her throat is tight and her chest full of emotion she doesn't know what to do with.

"Well done." The reporter backs away as if worried she'll commandeer his microphone.

She stands in the same spot, stunned by her own daring, on the verge of tears.

The videographer follows the reporter toward the van. People who hoped to be on TV surge, begging them to lend them their phones, or to record their faces and show them on the news so their families will know they've survived. When it becomes clear the news crew is done with the interviews, people call out their names:

Joaquín Hernández Santos
Angela Muñiz Torres
Adam Alvarado Jimenez
Teddy Bravo Martínez
Clara Echevarría López

The journalist and his cameraman are cornered. They're no longer filming, the microphone has been turned off, but a chorus of names follows them.

Efraín Coto Fernández
Silvia Díaz Colón
Zoraida Pérez García

Marysol feels guilty for having been so assertive but it passes when she finds Graciela on the periphery, sobbing. "I'm so proud of you!"

Minaxi

It's long after lunchtime and they're hungry. Marysol wants to check on Luz. While she and Graciela were visiting patients, las madres were out with the brigades, and while they're tired and grubby, they're in good spirits, as if the circumstances are mere blips in a continuum.

Graciela tells them about Marysol's media moment. "Marysol Ríos Peña for Congress!"

"¡Wepa!" Ada and Shirley call.

They haven't laughed in days, and it feels good.

The neighbors with propane stoves have opened their kitchens to those with supplies but no easy way to cook hot meals. They've organized, shared what they had, and distributed portions. Las madres have been part of that effort and have saved lunch for their daughters. They reheat the food on the gas grill and make their afternoon cafecito.

After las nenas rest for a while, Shirley hands Graciela a scrap of paper.

"A little girl delivered a message earlier. Someone in her house is sick. They wrote their address but didn't include their names. They're in a new development by the park."

They have no choice but to walk there in the afternoon drizzle.

"It's a relief from the heat, at least," Graciela says.

Marysol rubs the sprinkles into her skin. "I'd give my queen-dom for a long, hot shower."

"Sorry, your majesty. No can do."

They turn left from the main street and stop in front of a mound of rubble.

"This can't be it." Graciela checks the address.

A girl comes from the rear of the house. "We're back here!"

She's about ten or eleven years old, her hair haphazardly plaited to her waist. She waits for them to climb over chunks of concrete blocks, splintered window frames, massacred ceramic planters still containing improbable geraniums in the shallow dirt amid the shards. To their right, a woman nods as they pass her, and continues going through a jumble of soaked clothes inside a cracked suitcase. She holds a stiletto shoe against her breast as she scrounges around in the clutter.

"Is that a Louboutin?" Marysol says to Graciela, who maybe does or does not know or doesn't care about brands. She's more concerned about the tree sitting roots-up inside the swimming pool and the SUV taillights next to it. "A tornado hit here."

The one-story house was a horizontal squat capital I with a walled, glassed-in breezeway separating the front and rear sections.

A woman comes around the corner from the part of the house still standing. She's dressed and coiffed in the style of a cast member from the *Housewives* reality-TV series—albeit one who's been through a hurricane. Her big eyes are black-rimmed and, because the lines are so precise, Marysol guesses they're tattooed. She fixes her gaze on Marysol as if she recognizes her and decides she doesn't care.

"Which one of you is the doctor?"

"Neither." The woman's imperious tone grates, but Marysol prides herself on being professional. "I'm a nurse, and she's helping me." She introduces herself and Graciela formally, using first, paternal, and maternal surnames. The woman does a double take, peers at Marysol, at Graciela, at Marysol again, and stows the memory behind her ragged eyelash extensions.

"This way." She leads them through the back door. The niña scuttles between them and disappears down the dark hall. The kitchen is crowded with furniture and knickknacks apparently salvaged from the ruined part of the house. Next to the refrigerator is a stack of plastic-wrapped boxes of bottled water.

"I didn't get your name," Graciela says.

"Minaxi Otero Polanco."

"Can you spell it?" Graciela poises her pen over a blank page. "I record the patient's—"

"Oh, you're not here for me. It's for my housekeeper. Her name is Yanet, spelled with a *y*, not a *j*."

"¿Apellidos?"

"Ortíz Solís. She's about seventy years old and lives with us Monday to Friday, but with this situation"—she waves a limp hand to encompass the disarray—"she couldn't go home and now can't get out of bed."

"How long has she been bedridden?"

"She was mopping the water coming through the front door when, shash! Have you seen *The Wizard of Oz,* the movie?"

Marysol and Graciela exchange a puzzled look. "Yes."

"It was like that," Minaxi says. "We were back here when the wind lifted the front of the house and dropped it. We pulled Yanet from the rubble."

"Can you take me to her?" Marysol picked up a malodorous scent when the girl opened a door at the end of the hall. "Graciela has more questions you can answer while I examine Yanet."

Minaxi grabs a flashlight and goes past more chairs and side tables, a sofa, and paintings and rolled-up carpets pressed against the walls. She walks like a model on a runway, hips leading the rest of her body, lighting her own way but leaving Marysol in the dark.

"Excuse me," Marysol calls. "It's hard to see where I'm going." She has her own flashlight, but it's almost out of power.

"Oh." Minaxi's affect is flat, as if she's expended every emotion over the past five days and has run out of energy to feel what's still happening. "We had to move this stuff here from the front wing of the house with no other help. Just me, my daughter, Nadiya, and my granddaughter, Lisi. My husband is stuck in Barcelona with our son-in-law."

"They missed the whole thing?"

"They were at a conference, and I expected them the same day the airport closed. They have no idea . . ." She opens a door. "She's in there." She lets Marysol through. "Call if you need anything," she says as she walks away.

The room is gloomy. A candle has been recently lit on the side table. Marysol hopes her flashlight has some juice left. Replacement batteries are impossible to get.

Lisi is on a rocking chair next to Yanet's bed. "I keep her company. I put alcoholado on her forehead."

"That's sweet of you." Marysol touches Yanet's hand. It's cool and dry, even though the room is stifling. Yanet isn't sweating, most likely because she's dehydrated.

"She cries a lot," Lisi says. "It was scary when the house fell on her."

"Did you see it happen?"

"No, a big noise woke me, and Mamá and Abuela were screaming. They were scared because Yanet was trapped in the living room and they had to wait until it was safe." Lisi rocks the chair a couple of times, and Marysol is about to ask her another question, when Lisi continues. "I heard her calling, 'Help! Help!' Abuela and Mamá were afraid to go outside but I wanted to help Yanet.

She's really nice. It was hard to open the door because Mamá and Abuela had rolled up towels underneath so the water couldn't get in. It was raining so hard! They were cursing and yelling, 'Close the door, close the door!' I saw the roof was down. And even with the wind and with them yelling, I heard 'Help!' " Lisi yelps like a wounded puppy. "I ran across the breezeway. There was stuff all over the place and the water was like a river. I heard Yanet: 'Jesus, help me,' and 'Virgencita, ayúdame,' and 'Todo poderoso, sálvame.' 'It's me, Lisi,' I said."

Marysol is mesmerized by the little girl's composure. "Where did you find her?"

"Under the piano. There was so much water! We almost drowned." Rock, rock, rock. "I called to Mamá and Abuela, 'Here she is! I found her!' They came then. We brought her here. I was soaked and had a lot of cuts." She points to scabs on her legs and arms. "Abuela made me change my clothes and Mamá dried Yanet and changed her clothes, too."

"You're such a brave girl!"

"I know, but I couldn't find her wig. She wears it all the time." She slides off the rocker and takes Yanet's other hand. "This is her favorite bata." She straightens the collar on Yanet's housedress. "I gave it to her last Christmas. She loves daisies. I think she peed herself."

"I'll clean her up—don't worry."

"Will she be okay?"

Marysol's vocal cords stiffen. "I have to check her," she says once she can speak. "Can you bring me a couple of bottles of drinking water? And a straw, if there is one. The gas stove works, right?" Lisi nods. "Great! Please ask your mom or your abuela to bring me a basin with hot water. Can you remember all that?"

"Claro que sí. Bottled water, straw, hot water."

"Good girl!"

Lisi runs off.

After Lisi goes, Marysol assesses her patient. Lisi is right—Yanet has peed herself, but no one has changed her clothes or the bedsheet.

"I'm Marysol." She strokes Yanet's arm.

As she examines her, Marysol keeps talking to Yanet in a low, soothing voice. Yanet's skin is a light mahogany. Her feet and earlobes are mottled and cool to the touch. She's nearly bald and has new and old bruises along her temporal and parietal bones, scabs on her scalp, and dried blood by her left ear. She has numerous black-and-blue patches on her arms, her legs, her torso. Some are more recent than others. Her right ulna is possibly fractured. Her left ankle has swollen to twice its normal size, as has her knee. Marysol has to control her emotions as she imagines Yanet's terror during the storm.

Lisi returns with the bottled water. "Mamá is looking for a straw."

"Thank you, Lisi. Can you find me a clean hand towel?"

The one she brings smells of mildew. Everything made from fibers smells like that since the hurricane. Marysol pours water on the corner of the towel and pats it on Yanet's lips. No response.

While Minaxi led Marysol to the patient's room, Graciela studied the kitchen. It was like a stage set for a cooking show, featuring three sinks, expensive-looking stainless-steel appliances, two dishwashers, and enough china to supply a diner. Every surface was littered with items from the collapse, including the shoe that matched the red-soled stiletto the woman outside was hugging when Graciela and Marysol first arrived.

"I know it's a mess," Minaxi said when she returned from guiding Marysol to where Yanet was. "Let's sit there." She led Graciela to the dining room, also crammed with salvage. "A week ago, this house looked completely different."

"Could you please turn off the generator while the patient is being examined?"

Minaxi made a sound between a hum and a grunt and went to the back door. "Nadiya," she called like a fishmonger, "apaga ese aparato." She sashayed back. "It keeps running for a while before it goes off entirely." She pointed Graciela to a chair and found her own spot at the head of the table.

"I have some questions . . ." Graciela checked her list.

Minaxi interrupted her. "You live afuera, don't you?"

"Uhum. In Maine."

"Not New York?"

"I was born there, but we moved to Maine when I was little." Graciela rustled her pages. "I do need the patient's medical history. You said she's seventy?"

Again Minaxi made her hot-and-bothered sound. It was hard to read her expressions. Other than expanding or contracting her eyelids, her face was rigid. Her smile was lopsided, higher on one side than the other, and when speaking, she talked out of the right side of her mouth. Graciela wondered whether she'd had a stroke or perhaps it was cosmetic surgery gone wrong.

"Why Maine?"

"My mother grew up there."

"That's right—I forgot Shirley's from there."

"Do you know her?"

"I knew Luz, Ada, and Shirley." She fluttered her lashes. "La negrita y las lesbianas."

"We don't call them that."

"But that's what they are, aren't they? And Luz is Black, right? Like the one in there?"

"Her name is Marysol." Graciela's hair was stuck to the back of her neck. She fluffed it away and felt tension building between her shoulder blades. She remembered Ada saying, "Puerto Ricans never meet as strangers. We're all long-lost relatives." Minaxi seemed to be an exception. She lacked the Puerto Rican curious-but-respectful manner.

"Esas dos son carbon copies. But you . . ." Minaxi shook her head as if she did and simultaneously didn't quite believe it. "You're a Worthy through and through."

"A what?"

"A Worthy, one of the sons from a prominent family. El Vikingo was a couple of years ahead of me in school."

"El Vikingo? I don't know who that is."

Lisi came running from down the hall. "La doctora needs bot-tled water, hot water, and a straw."

"Ask your mother. I have no idea where anything is."

The girl ran outside.

Until this moment, Minaxi had seemed listless, but as soon as Lisi went, she launched into a breathless monologue. "Your father. It threw me off when I first saw you. Your physique is so different, and of course, you pass for white. El Vikingo and Luz were skinny and taller than the average Puerto Rican and from the neck down, you don't look like either. But, ¡Dios mío! Los Worthy no te pueden negar. You're definitely El Vikingo's daughter. You have his face, and the rest of you is like all the other Worthy women, who are petite and curvy."

Lisi ran in, grabbed a couple of bottles of water, and ran down the hallway.

"Oh, this is my daughter, Nadiya," Minaxi said when the woman with the stiletto came inside. She was average height but her bust and buttocks were out of proportion to her body, as if she'd been constructed rather than naturally grown.

"Mucho gusto. I have to heat some water for the nurse." She rattled around in the kitchen.

When she's nervous, Graciela's chest turns pink and the color creeps and blooms up her throat as her anxiety increases until she's red-faced and her freckles are darker brown. By the time the blush reaches her hairline, her scalp is unbearably itchy.

She scratched. "Who is El Vikingo?"

Minaxi smirked. "That was our nickname for Claudio Worthy Villalobos. His father was a banker and owned television and radio stations. His mother was a newswoman."

"I've never heard of them."

"No?" Minaxi peered at Graciela as if she were a specimen. "That's interesting."

"Is it?" She was certain Minaxi had noticed her flaming skin.

⌒

Lisi's mother, Nadiya, brings a steaming basin into Yanet's room. "Is this enough? I've been taking care of her. I couldn't find a straw." She turns to her daughter. "Wait outside, Lisi."

"But—"

"Outside. Now." Lisi hangs her head and drags her feet all the way to the door. "Close it." Lisi does. Nadiya waits until Lisi is out of hearing. "She's dying, isn't she?"

Marysol is startled by this direct question. She gestures for Nadiya to follow her into the bathroom.

"Yanet can hear you," she says.

"Oh! I didn't realize. She's been so out of it . . ."

"Why do you think she's dying?"

"The ceiling fell on her. We couldn't get to her right away. When we did, she said she was okay, she just wanted her alcoholado and Vicks. That's why it smells like it does in here."

"So she was conscious when you got her out?"

"Oh, yes. She kept thanking us for saving her life." Nadiya leaves the bathroom and cranks open the louvers all the way to bring in more light. She lights another candle on an altar in the corner. She opens and shuts drawers on a dresser as if searching for something she can't find. "She said María beat her up." She chuckles mirthlessly. "I would have taken her to the ER, but did you see our car?"

"How long has she been asleep?"

"Well, after we rescued her, she was sore but she could move, no problem. She helped us with what we could bring in from the collapse. I gave her aspirin, but I don't think she took it. Then she fell in the bathroom."

"When?"

"Yesterday. She had coffee with us in the afternoon. She came back here to use her bathroom. She called me to pour the water from the tub into the toilet because she couldn't lift the bucket. I heard her fall. She might have slipped on the tiles."

"Did she hit her head?"

"I don't know. She vomited and wet herself and . . ." She scrunches her nose. "She had diarrhea. My mother helped me clean her up and put her to bed. It looks like she did it again. Peed herself, I mean."

"I'd like to change her housedress and sheets. Can you find some fresh ones, please?"

"Sure." Nadiya rummages around the drawers and passes the items over as if they're infectious.

"She needs a hospital," Marysol says. "Can a neighbor drive you?"

Nadiya twists her features. "This neighborhood has changed a lot. No one helps anybody."

"My experience here has been exactly the opposite."

Nadiya doesn't respond. As Marysol cleans Yanet, Nadiya doesn't offer to help, doesn't even look in their direction. Marysol invites her into the bathroom again.

"To answer your question earlier," she says, "yes, Yanet is near death. I'm not a doctor, but she obviously suffered serious trauma during the hurricane and probably again soon after. She has fractures and possibly a concussion. If she doesn't get medical care, she'll die on her bed out there."

"Can't you give her something?"

"No."

Marysol tends to be circumspect and compassionate with her patients and their families, but Nadiya and her mother give her hives. She can't ascribe their behavior solely to the anxiety caused by the hurricane or the loss of their possessions. There's something ungenerous about them that Marysol resists.

"Well, can you take her in your car?"

"I don't have a car." Marysol returns to the bedroom. It takes all her self-control to finish cleaning Yanet and change her bata and underwear without spewing some words she'll regret later. She tugs the bedsheets under the dying woman, still unresponsive, her breath a shallow wheeze. "I can't do much more for her than what I've done. You must get her to the hospital. Pronto."

"I'll see what I can do." Nadiya's eyes dart to all corners of the room, as if a solution will jump from the shadows.

"I'll wait here," Marysol says. "She shouldn't be alone."

Nadiya consults with her mother in the kitchen. Marysol can't hear their words, but Minaxi seems to be giving her daughter an address.

⸏

When Nadiya interrupts Minaxi and Graciela to ask whom she can call to take Yanet to the emergency room, Minaxi says, "Kelvin will help. He always does." Minaxi says this as if that were his most salient character flaw. She scribbles the address on a scrap of paper. When Nadiya leaves, Minaxi enlarges her lids at Graciela. "Kelvin is El Vikingo's best friend."

"He lives next door to where we're staying."

"He told me. He was shocked by the resemblance."

"Why are you telling me all this? We don't even know each other. And . . ." Graciela stammers. "Lots of people look alike . . ."

Minaxi pretends she didn't hear her. "He had a major crush on Luz, but El Vikingo claimed her."

"What do you mean he 'claimed' her?"

"Claudio was the leader among the boys, a couple of years older than us, and a bully. His family is important here, and no one dared challenge him." According to Minaxi, he left Puerto Rico in early summer, 1976. "We heard he was going to basketball camp, but the truth was his family was covering up a scandal."

"What did he do?"

The right corner of Minaxi's lips curl toward her cheek, while the left side remains in place. "Ada caught them."

"Caught who?"

Minaxi's huge eyes study Graciela, as if determining whether she's smart enough for subtlety, deciding brutal honesty will get through to her quicker. "El Vikingo and Luz. Ada taught us how to tell when Luz went into her fits. Once he saw one coming, he . . . well, today we'd call it rape."

Her words are like a punch into Graciela's throat. She's been told Luz can never be alone because she's defenseless during her achaques. Neither Shirley nor Ada have specified the most obvious danger for a vulnerable female. "Oh, my God!"

"Lisi!" The girl is in the hallway. Minaxi raises her hand toward her and the child scurries into a room at the end of the corridor.

"Always skulking in the shadows." Minaxi hands Graciela a paper towel. "Here. Wipe your face."

Minaxi continues as if there's been no interruption. "We thought it was funny that when Luz was mental, anything could happen and she wouldn't remember."

"That's awful."

"We were kids, drunk or high half the time. We didn't give her drugs. Ada told us she was on medications, and we didn't want her to die in front of us."

Minaxi's cruelty is unbearable. Graciela wants to say something, but from the moment she entered Minaxi's kitchen, she's felt as if she's thigh-high in quicksand, slowly sinking, and about to drown in it. She's so upset about El Vikingo assaulting Luz, she's having trouble thinking beyond that. When her mind clears a bit, she considers Minaxi. The woman is so callous, Graciela wonders whether she's making up her stories. But why? She's bursting with questions but doesn't trust Minaxi.

"Can I have another paper towel?" she asks.

Minaxi hands it to her and makes a face as Graciela honks into it. Minaxi hears Lisi talking to Marysol, and she calls the girl to the kitchen.

"¡Condená!" Minaxi scowls at Lisi. "Go to your room. Stay there until I call you." The girl doesn't move. "Don't make me say it twice." There's such menace in her voice that Graciela is about to interfere, but Lisi returns down the hall, and in a moment, a door closes.

Minaxi leans back to take a long drink from her water bottle. Graciela has a few seconds to gather her thinking into a list. She covers her writing hand as she takes notes on her sketch pad. Minaxi watches her, smugly.

"What happened to Luz after El Vikingo left Puerto Rico?" Graciela asks.

"Ada and don Alonso took her to New York. We thought they were chasing after Claudio." She chuckles. "But we knew El Vikingo's father and Pastor Josué would clean up his mess. We'd heard Luz's grandfather had cancer. I guess he died there. Shirley came and went to and from New York, and after he died, she put his house on the market. It was a beautiful place. Our friend Perla's father snapped it up, tore it down, and built a monstrosity on the site. Have you seen it?"

"We walked over there."

"That neighborhood was very exclusive, gated, private, well maintained, the homes owned by professional people. It was really nice. Now it's all basura."

"Where's El Vikingo now?"

"He's around. His father died in the early eighties and Claudio squandered his inheritance en un dos por tres. Same old story: drugs, girls, rock and roll. Last I heard, he was driving trucks for a living. You can find him if you want to. He can't stay away from social media."

Graciela has Minaxi repeat El Vikingo's full name as she writes it down. Without the Internet, she'll have to wait to find out more about him.

She's always been told she was the product of a one-night stand. Given the times and her mothers' liberal outlook, she's accepted that explanation and has done her best not to judge Ada. Now she learns Ada might not be her biological mother. A hole opens inside her, a pit of anguish, horror, and rage. If Minaxi is telling the truth, her mothers have been lying to her for forty years, Luz is her mother, and her father was a rapist. Probably still is. She can't bear the thought that he was a heartless predator who violated Luz while she was inside achaques, unable to defend herself. It's outrageous that he and his friends thought it was funny. Graciela is so angry, she's shaking.

"This is all new to you, isn't it?" Minaxi says quietly, almost as if she pities Graciela.

"Why do you tell me all this? Why now? I'm on social media, too. Why did you never think to reach out?"

Minaxi becomes defensive. "I didn't know you even existed until Kelvin recognized Ada, Shirley, and Luz in the house next door. We thought Ada was cool, with her hippie van and how she never wore a bra. She tutored a bunch of us on Puerto Rican history, independentista, of course, even though our parents were estadistas. She always said that even the staunchest pro-statehooders wish Puerto Rico were an independent nation, but don't have the guts to vote for it."

"That sounds like my mother," Graciela says.

"She tried to get us to march in protests in Río Piedras and San Juan but our parents wouldn't allow it."

Graciela's ears are ringing. She needs silence, to be alone, to unravel everything she's heard from this woman, who continues talking as if she's been waiting for this opportunity.

"For a couple of years after Ada left, every time Los Macheteros robbed a bank or blew up a busload of soldiers, we wondered whether she was involved because she left here in such a hurry. Josué put a stop to those rumors by telling everyone she was a high school teacher in New England. We'd admired Ada because we thought she was a guerrillera, but it turned out she was as boring and bourgeois as our parents. She and Luz left here without so much as a goodbye but we knew the truth. Ada is not your mother." Minaxi waited for her words to sink in further before continuing. "I'm sure you hate hearing this from me, and I'm sorry you didn't know. It's awful that Ada and Shirley have been lying to you all these years."

A smug Minaxi smiles, and Graciela has the urge to rearrange her Cubist face.

❧

Once Nadiya left to find someone to take Yanet to the hospital, Lisi slipped into Yanet's room again. "Your friend is crying."

"She is? Why?"

"Abuela said something mean." Lisi took her place on the rocking chair. "She's like that. Mamá says Abuela's tongue is made from thorns." She chewed the inside of her cheek.

"Lisi, get over here," Minaxi called from the kitchen.

The girl flinched.

"I'll come with you."

"You said Yanet shouldn't be alone."

"Now!" Minaxi's voice was like sandpaper.

Lisi went but Marysol couldn't hear what they were saying. A few moments later, a door closed down the hall.

Minaxi and Graciela then resumed their conversation, too softly for Marysol to pick up.

Marysol breathes through her tension so she won't convey it to Yanet. She keeps her hand on hers, partly to soothe Yanet, partly to keep track of her pulse. Yanet gasps and gurgles, short inhales, long exhales, as if vacating her body. Marysol recognizes the absence of volition as Yanet submits to the inevitable.

The glass surface of photos on the wall reflects the candle flame. It appears Yanet is part of a large family. In one of the pictures taken at a wedding, she's seated in the middle of a row of six elderly women with similar features, possibly her sisters. At their feet, eight cross-legged boys and girls grin in response to the photographer's command to say cheese. Standing behind the women, the bride and groom smile for posterity. Marysol won-ders where all those people are. If they're in the United States, they'll be wondering about Yanet, thinking the worst yet unable or unwilling to envision her dying in this stuffy room.

Marysol regrets she isn't traditionally religious. She knows the Lord's Prayer, the Ave Maria, and a few of the Psalms, remnants of her Catholic-school education. As a teenager she rejected the misogyny and intolerance in the Bible. The church-sanctioned genocide during the European conquest of the Western Hemi-sphere and the wealth it extracted from the slave trade are inde-fensible. In her opinion, religion has a lot to answer for when it comes to human rights. Hours of meditation haven't made her less judgmental about the atrocities committed under the crosses and banners of their well-organized dogma.

Many of her patients in New York are devout, and derive com-fort from their faith. Sometimes, Marysol envies the solace reli-gion brings, the sense of community in the rites and spectacles in places of worship, the joyous singing spilling from storefront churches in the Bronx. Every year she and Warren accompany Luz to Christmas Eve, Palm Sunday, and Easter Sunday Masses. She loves the grotto at St. Lucy's. A priest blesses tap water, and his gestures and prayers transform it into holy water. People believe it cures illnesses, brings buena fortuna, and even performs miracles.

In one of those trips to St. Lucy's, Marysol and Warren noticed Luz was praying in Latin. When they asked, Luz couldn't tell them where she learned the prayers, and Marysol wonders what meaning she's ascribed to them. It's another of the mysteries of Luz.

Marysol's eye now catches the rosary dangling from a nail within easy reach. She grabs it and nestles it in her free hand, caressing the faceted surfaces of the beads and fingering the metal loops between them, thanking each for bringing Yanet comfort. She focuses on the figurines of saints and virgins, among pebbles, seashells, and feathers, on a shelf. A saucer holds a cigar among ashes. A shot glass has a dark liquid, probably rum. Marysol has seen this, too, in her patients' homes, a syncretism of Catholic, Indigenous, and African practices. Each object means something to Yanet, and Marysol appreciates and thanks them for having accompanied the dying woman in life.

In her years as a home-care nurse, Marysol has marveled at her patients' altars, some as elaborate as cathedrals while others, like her own, spare, honoring her mother's parents and her father, the only blood relative other than Luz she's known in life. Danilo was a gregarious, social man, beloved on their Bronx block, where most of the residents were Puerto Ricans and their descendants. A practicing Catholic, he believed in sharing with his neighbors, and gave credit at the bodega to those whose paychecks didn't stretch far enough for baby formula or a bag of dried habichuelas. Marysol was too young to discuss religion with him. She now understands his faith was untarnished by church history.

She breathes into the rosary beads and winds them around Yanet's wrist and fingers.

Down the hall, the conversation between Graciela and Minaxi changes rhythm. They're sharing secrets. Marysol wonders how it's possible for Graciela to so easily go from being strangers, to crying because of something Minaxi's barbed tongue said, to the rushed whispers that sound like teenagers sharing gossip.

A male voice breaks into their confidences, and soon Kelvin and Nadiya enter Yanet's room.

"He can bring her to the hospital," Nadiya says.

"We can lay her down on the back seat of my van," he says, "but we have to go now. We have to be off the streets before the curfew goes into effect."

Marysol wraps Yanet in the sheet. Kelvin picks her up tenderly and carries her from the house, followed by the four women, who point out where he should step to avoid stumbling over the broken cinder blocks and upended, splintered furniture. A few steps behind them, Lisi hugs a stuffed pink unicorn with an off-kilter golden horn.

"Can I go?"

"No," her mother and grandmother snap simultaneously.

"Can Nini go with her?"

Minaxi and Nadiya frown. Kelvin, having settled Yanet, takes the stuffed animal from the girl's hands.

"I'm sure she'd love your fluffy friend for company." He tucks the unicorn next to Yanet.

"We'll drop her off," Nadiya says, "and come right back."

The others watch the van drive away.

"I left my notebook inside," Graciela says, and returns to the house.

Marysol slaps a mosquito and realizes she hasn't been bitten since the hurricane started.

"Que jodienda," Minaxi says. "I have to find another housekeeper."

Marysol stares at her. "Is this what you're worried about now? Another housekeeper?"

"It's not a problem for you, obviously. It is a big one for me." She appears dumbfounded by the wreckage around her, and for a moment Marysol feels sorry for her until Minaxi turns to her. "Do you happen to know any domestics looking for work?"

"You're asking me?"

"Well, you know . . ." She scans Marysol, head to toe, with a disdainful gaze.

Marysol knows that look. The woman is hateful and a racist. "When they go low," she remembers Michelle Obama saying, "we go high." But she's not feeling magnanimous right now.

"I don't, and even if I did, I wouldn't tell you."

Minaxi squeezes her lids, steps toward the house, stops halfway. "By the way, what do I owe you?"

She's the first person to ask, and it hasn't occurred to Marysol to expect payment for her services in the aftermath of the hurricane. People have volunteered to make things easier for her, like Felicita and her husband, Otto, and Kelvin and his sons. Unlike them, Minaxi means to offend her, wielding money like a weapon to elevate her own self-importance and keep the rabble in their place below her, Marysol among them.

Minaxi hasn't said a kind word about Yanet, who's cleaned her messes and has now become inconvenient, who'll be abandoned at an emergency room and left to die among strangers. Yanet is as disposable as a used tissue. Marysol recognizes that Minaxi's offer isn't meant to respect or recognize her skill and knowledge. She means to let Marysol know she's as expendable as Yanet.

She refuses to be baited. "Since you insist, one of those boxes of bottled water next to your refrigerator will do."

Minaxi can't raise her eyebrows. Too much Botox. While Minaxi isn't generous, she doesn't want to appear miserly. "I don't think you can carry so many."

"I assure you, I can."

Minaxi says nothing, steps over the rubble between the sidewalk and the house. Marysol follows her until she hears a little voice. She didn't notice Lisi nearby.

"Is Yanet going to die?"

Las Madres

"Oh, sweetie, I hope she doesn't," Marysol says. She crouches to be at eye level with the girl. "You have such compassion, Lisi. Don't ever forget that in a crisis, you, una niñita, were brave and daring. You saved Yanet's life and did everything you could to help her." She hugs the child, who wraps her arms around Marysol's neck and holds tight until Minaxi orders her inside.

A Shower

Thick clouds have ushered in an early dusk. Marysol has forgotten the way back to their house and Graciela seems confused whether they go left, right, or straight ahead. Marysol carries the box of bottled water on her head. They stop at the corner as the sun sets and murky shadows envelop them.

"It can't be too far," Marysol says.

"This way." Graciela steps into the middle of the street to avoid the detritus mounded along the sidewalks. Stagnating puddles on roads, roofs, and abandoned receptacles, birds that fled or were killed by María, bats and insect-eating reptiles windswept, drowned, or crushed by falling debris all provide the perfect conditions for mosquitoes to thrive, with no predators to check their growth. They're beginning to hatch, hungry and unimpeded. Marysol can't slap them away because one hand holds the heavy box on her head, while with the other she clicks her dead flashlight's button as if it will spark enough to power it. They stop at the next corner to get used to the gloom. It's been raining on and off all day without relieving the oppressive heat. People are on their porches and marquesinas. As Marysol and Graciela pass, they call out, "Buenas noches!" and remind them of the curfew.

The light from oil lamps and candles dissolves into the darkness, framing living dioramas. In one marquesina, four men sit around a domino table. One slaps his tile in triumph as the rest groan or laugh, depending on how many of theirs are left in their hands. In another, three girls jump rope, calling a rhyme Marysol can't make out. On a balcony, a woman coos at and tickles a giggling baby. It would be romantic were it not for the intrusive whir of generators in the near distance.

Graciela walks a few steps ahead of Marysol.

"Are you okay, Graciela?"

"I'm fine."

"You don't look or sound fine."

"Let's just get home."

Lightning flashes, quickly followed by a boom. In the momentary brightness, they recognize where they are. Graciela increases her pace. Marysol can catch up with her easily, can pass her and leave her behind, even with the bottles on her head. But she won't abandon Graciela alone in the dark, although her sullen attitude is irritating. Marysol allows her privacy and hopes they can make it home before the imminent downpour. Lightning strikes again, and bowling balls roll across the heavens as the squall intensifies. Graciela tucks her sketchbook under her shirt and they hurry toward las madres, who are sitting on the porch, oblivious to the weather, their ghostly faces illuminated by the eerie light from their screens.

"Kelvin fixed their generator," Ada says. "Jason and Felipe charged our computers, phones, and tablets."

"Can you get a cell signal?" Graciela asks.

"No such luck," Shirley says. "All the cell towers are down. We're incomunicada."

"Warren estará panickeando," Marysol says as she sets the bottles on the kitchen counter. "We've never gone this long without at least a phone call."

Ada flings her arms around Marysol and presses her close. "I'm sure his will be the first message you get when we get connected again."

Across the counter, Shirley opens a bottle of water and dispenses some for everyone. "I never imagined water would be such a luxury. Where'd you get it?"

"My wages," Marysol scoffs, with a side glance at Graciela, who is pouting over her phone.

"Put it aside," Ada says. "It's only making you tense."

Graciela frowns and slips her phone into her pocket.

Marysol raises the oil lamp on the kitchen counter, and peeks under the lids of the pots and pans on the useless electric stove. "Smells good."

With the diminishing supplies, las madres made rice with sliced Vienna sausages and a side of kidney beans. Loreta's sofrito was consumed days earlier, but they made good use of half a can of tomato paste and plenty of salt, pepper, and dried spices, which approximate familiar flavors.

"Les voisins aimaient ça," Luz says.

"The neighbors loved it," Graciela translates automatically.

"The boys will look for propane for the grill before we run out," Shirley says. "Everything's in short supply. Kelvin could get only a couple of gallons of gasoline for their generator."

"That won't go far," Marysol says.

A thunderclap startles them, and wind and rain pummel the walls.

"I'm taking a shower." Marysol runs to the backyard, dropping clothes as she goes.

"You'll get hit by lightning," Ada says, chasing after her. The others follow, keeping one hand on the wall and the other on the familiar shoulder of the woman ahead in the unlit hallway.

Marysol offers her face to the sky. Rain pelts her skin and forms rivers over her body. The water is cold but it feels good to get rid of days' worth of sweat, salt air, grime, and the sadness bubbling beneath the surface she won't allow to boil over.

"Come on!"

Luz readily joins Marysol, followed by Ada and Shirley. As if afraid she'll melt, Graciela tiptoes into the spongy backyard. Once the lightning stops, they can barely see one another. Like Marysol, the others shed their clothes. They cup their hands as if in supplication to the ancestral goddess of the natural world. They splash their faces with her tears, rub them under their arms, their breasts, between their legs and buttocks. For the second time that day, they laugh like delighted children.

Almost as suddenly as it began, the storm drifts out to sea, and las madres and las nenas scamper indoors, shivering and rubbing goose bumps. They follow the wall toward the glimmering oil lamp in the kitchen. Ada reaches the handrail leading upstairs. Like the tile floors, the steps are slippery.

"Oops! Be careful, everyone."

"Wait, wait." Graciela grabs and distributes their phones from the dining table.

"Thanks, I forgot about our thousand-dollar flashlights," Ada says.

"Stop shining your light on my butt," Shirley jokes to Graciela behind her.

"That's the last thing I want to see up close," she retorts.

The dancing beams guide them to clean but stained towels on the bathroom racks, and dank clothes in dressers and closets. Even with the louvers open, the bedrooms are steamy, the concrete walls holding moisture the daytime heat didn't dispel.

Las madres have waited to have dinner with las nenas. They reheat the food on the grill, and in the stillness following the storm, mosquitoes swarm. The women take their food indoors, where the window screens keep most of the insects outside. Ada finds bug repellent in one of the cabinets, and sprays their bodies, under the tables, and around the furnishings. Luz discovers a box of coils with enough for each of their bedrooms. Graciela refuses hers.

"That's poison," she says.

The joyous moments in the rain have been forgotten. Graciela is in such a foul mood again, neither Marysol nor las madres want to set her off or trigger another cry-fest like the previous night's.

Earlier that afternoon, after Graciela and Marysol left, las madres walked to the avenue in search of supplies. They returned empty-handed but with stories and news.

"It's possible to get cell signals in the hills," Ada says. "One neighbor connected to his mother in Pittsburgh. She said Hurricane María opens all the news reports. The Red Cross and other organizations are doing what they can, but it's obvious they weren't prepared."

"The mayor of San Juan has become a television star on the continent," Shirley adds.

"But here, people are angry and frustrated by the inadequate response from the government," Ada continues, "including from la alcaldesa. I imagine she's doing her best under these circumstances, but like the rest of us, she's overwhelmed."

"The good news . . ." Shirley raises her index finger to emphasize her point. "Diasporicans are organizing and collecting supplies to bring or send. They're figuring out other ways to help, including opening their homes to those who've lost everything. If we were there, that's what we'd be doing."

"Et aujourd'hui, d'autres avions sont arrivés," Luz says.

"More planes landed and took off," Marysol says. Luz nods.

"They brought supplies and volunteers," Ada says.

"On the other hand, desperate people are making their way to the airports with no reservations or tickets," Shirley adds. "The terminals have no power, no air-conditioning, no food, no water. It's bedlam."

Ada shakes her head. "It doesn't occur to them the airlines have to deal with travelers stranded here since Tuesday."

"Ich hoffe, dass Leute mit Tickets Priorität bekommen," Luz muses.

"Something about ticket priority," Marysol says. Luz nods again.

"If we don't show up with tickets on Wednesday," Shirley says, "they'll probably give the seats to someone from the waiting lists."

"Maybe Kelvin can bring us to the airport," Marysol suggests. "His car works."

"Oliver will have made his way here before then," Ada says.

Neither she nor Shirley mention the floods where Oliver and Miriam live. None want to imagine they could be among the drowned.

Graciela and Marysol collect the dishes. They skirt each other in the kitchen. Marysol is disturbed by Graciela's surly behavior. She senses she's been affected by something Minaxi said, something that made her cry, according to Lisi. What could have happened between Graciela and Minaxi, who were strangers to each other until a few hours ago? On the other hand, Minaxi has a cruel streak and might have pushed one of Graciela's emotional buttons, like her weight or the stigmatization by ignorant people who say she doesn't "look Puerto Rican" because she's pale-skinned, blue-eyed, and lives in Maine. That same person will challenge Marysol for not being Puerto Rican enough and for being too Bronx.

Las madres settle into their electronic games.

"Don't exhaust your batteries," Graciela calls. Las madres look up, but ignore the warning.

"Do you want to talk?" Marysol asks in a low voice.

"What?"

It's as if Marysol has startled Graciela from a dream. Over the past few evenings, lamp and candlelight have softened their features and brightened their eyes. Graciela now looks like the mask of tragedy, her eyelids and mouth downturned, her forehead etched with lines. The folds from her nostrils to the edges of her lips are deeper. Marysol follows her first instinct and wraps her arms around Graciela, who resists the embrace.

"Stop that!"

Las madres look up from their screens.

"What's going on?" Ada comes over as if to separate pugilists.

"I'm tired." Graciela leans into the kitchen counter and covers her face. "Really, really tired."

"It's been a long day, mamita. Why don't you go to bed? I'll come up with you."

"I don't need your help." She rubs her cheeks and temples, as if rearranging her features, pulls her phone from her pocket, turns on its flashlight, and stalks up the stairs. "Hasta mañana."

Ada gets up to follow her.

Shirley stops her. "Let her go. When she's in one of her moods, she needs to be alone." Upstairs, Graciela's door slams. "We're all stressed, but she feels responsible for our predicament."

"Why?"

"She planned every detail of this trip so we could have a good time," Marysol says. "She didn't count on a hurricane."

"How could she?"

Marysol joins las madres at the table. "Graciela isn't used to sick people. Maybe helping me is too distressing."

Ada sighs. "We've been through a lot the last few days, but María has hit her hard."

"Graciela wants to fix things," Shirley says. "Right now, there's more to do than she can handle."

Sleepless

SEPTEMBER 25, 2017

The smoke coils keep mosquitoes away for a couple of hours. As soon as the repellent drops into ashes, the insects return and find Marysol. She awakens to intense itching on her bare arms.

She knows she shouldn't scratch, but it's unbearable otherwise. When she turns on her side, she notices Graciela's door across the hall, still closed, but a blue light along the threshold means she's on her laptop. Marysol raises her wrist to her face, momentarily forgetting she stopped wearing her smart watch when it lost its charge. *Oh, well,* she thinks, *time doesn't matter.* Days and hours have melted into one another after María. She stares into the dark. Why care about time? But not knowing stresses her. She scrabbles for her phone on the night table: 1:37 a.m. Such precision has become irrelevant. When it's necessary to tell time, las madres and las nenas talk about "earlier," "today," "later," "mañana." Since María, they've been suspended in the present. *Be here now,* she reminds herself.

To encourage cross-breezes, the window louvers and bedroom doors are kept open. The din of generators obliterates other sounds beyond their walls. Neighbors use them to power fans or room air conditioners at night. The air smells of fuel and rot.

She hears Luz moan in her room on the opposite side of their shared bathroom. She tiptoes in to check on her. Luz is a heavy sleeper, who groans and talks without awakening, who holds conversations and arguments with her ghosts in French and German.

Marysol has recorded some of her mother's dream-induced vocalizations but hasn't shared them with her. It worries her that, like the videos of the achaques, they might cause an adverse reaction. Still, she's curious about the mysterious yet specific ways her mother's condition manifests. In over a decade as a nurse, she's never encountered a patient with a similar array of outcomes from her traumas. As a child, Marysol sought to fix her mother. As an adolescent, she was ashamed of her idiosyncrasies. As an adult, she's accepted Luz for who she is and doesn't love her any less for her imperfections.

She now peeks across the hall from Luz. Ada and Shirley sleep peacefully together, neither one stirring despite the other's snorts and snuffles.

A breeze whispers through, and soon rain patters on the roof and terrace tiles. Marysol returns to her bed, eyes fixed on the eerie light under Graciela's door. She wills her to open it, and is disappointed that telepathy is beyond her powers. The door is six paces from her. She can easily traverse the distance in seconds, but she can't force herself to do it. Graciela was clear she wanted privacy, but Marysol senses a wound has opened. Isn't she a healer? She tiptoes to Graciela's door, scratches on it, and is about to open it when Graciela does.

"Oh, it's you."

"Were you expecting somebody else?"

"I'm too tired for banter. How come you're up?"

"Mosquitoes woke me up. Saw the light under your door. Thought we could be awake together. If I'm not interrupting your work . . ."

"I was doing some digital housekeeping."

"What's that?"

"Reorganizing files on my computer, archiving, trashing old documents, stuff like that. That's what I do when I can't sleep. It's very satisfying." She shuts the laptop, and they can no longer see each other.

"Someone told me if you have trouble sleeping, you should turn your devices off at least an hour before bed. Blue light disrupts the sleep cycle."

"You're repeating advice I gave you years ago."

"Am I?"

Graciela lies back on her bed and Marysol stretches alongside her.

"At home," Graciela says, "when I can't sleep, I take a walk in the middle of the night. Even in winter. You'd be surprised how many people I run into. Fishermen coming in from a trip, or about to go on one, or those who depend on the tides. I meet shift workers coming or going. Teenagers hooking up after their parents go to bed. It's a hamlet, not New York City, still, people wander around at all hours. Here, if I go out, I'll get arrested for breaking curfew."

Marysol slaps her arm. "Not to mention you'll be eaten alive by insects." She doesn't want to be specific about the potential for mosquito-borne illnesses. Graciela must have seen the news. A year ago, more than thirty-five thousand Zika infections were recorded in Puerto Rico and the media pounced on the heartbreaking images of babies born with congenital disorders. The year before that, they covered stories about chikungunya, another virus carried by mosquitoes. "If you don't want the repellent, at least try Agua de Florida. I've heard the citrus keeps mosquitoes away. Ada has some."

"Thanks," Graciela says listlessly.

They're silent for a while, then a sob.

"Are you okay, Graciela?"

"No. I'm not. Not at all."

"Let me help you. What can I do?"

"I don't think you can help, but thank you."

"Lisi told me Minaxi made you cry."

Graciela sniffles and Marysol feels her grab the corner of the top sheet to wipe her face. "That woman is evil. I feel sorry for that kid."

"Me, too, but right now I'm more worried about you. What did she say?"

"A lot of things, lies, probably, but some made sense. Like why my mothers didn't want to be in this neighborhood." Graciela takes a moment to catch her breath. "People remember them and Madrina before we were born, and they know things my mothers don't want us to hear."

"Like what?"

"Like how I was conceived." Graciela turns as if to search Marysol's face, but it's too dark to see. "Not the mechanics," she continues. "We've heard about Mami's one-night stand, but it's likely that's a lie. I can't say more until I talk to las madres. Well, not Madrina, you know . . ."

Another long silence.

"Graciela, before you get yourself and your mothers into a state, think. Minaxi is, as you said, evil. I'm sure Ada and Shirley will answer questions about your dad, but don't accuse them of lying. If they've kept something from you all these years, they don't think they've lied, they think they're protecting you or themselves. Either way, I'm sure they thought . . . think . . . they're doing right by concocting a story."

"We'll see whether you'll defend them after I tell you how they react to Minaxi's stories. I can't say more now." Graciela turns faceup again. "Can you do me a favor? Actually two."

"Sure. Anything."

"Number one, can you take Madrina on a long walk or something tomorrow so I can be alone with my mothers?"

"Of course. I'll bring her to the beach to sketch or draw. She can spend hours doing that."

"That's great. Thanks." Graciela yawns.

"And number two?"

"I can sleep now."

Tamarindo

When Shirley opens the front door in the morning, four people are waiting to see Marysol. She rustles las nenas, and within minutes, the porch becomes Patient Intake and the living area a Treatment Room again. While Graciela and Marysol do their best with the injuries and medical issues, las madres collect the dirty towels and their clothes to hand-wash using captured rain. With no rope for a clothesline, they drag the porch chairs into the yard and drape everything over them to dry in the sun. By the time they've finished with the laundry, the patients have scattered, most feeling better.

Graciela does an inventory. "We're almost out of alcohol and bandages."

"We'll have to ask people to boil their cotton sheets to make dressings," Marysol says. "I don't know what else to do."

"Tu peux leur dire d'aller à l'hôpital," Luz says.

"She says you should tell them to go to a hospital," Graciela translates.

Luz smiles.

"Buena idea," Ada says. "You can't keep doing this, Marysol. You're not Mother Teresa."

"I'm no saint, but the thing is, as a nurse, I vowed," Marysol says, curling her fingers to indicate quotes, " 'to consecrate my life to the service of humanity.' I meant that oath, Ada, and will do my best to help my patients get better, or to respect their dignity upon death."

"That's very inspiring, but you, too, went through this experience. You're still going through it, actually. You need a break. People expect miracles."

"Most want to tell their stories, Shirley. They're physically and psychologically wounded. I guess we are, too. Talking about the experience helps us get through it. I see it all the time with my patients in the Bronx."

"You're a psychologist, then, not a nurse."

"Healing their physical wounds doesn't mean I ignore the effects of invisible trauma. I don't have the medical supplies to treat all their injuries, but I can listen to them. There's healing power in a compassionate ear."

"All her patients leave happier than when they come in," Graciela says. "Even when she can do no more than clean their cuts and scrapes."

"I worry if they don't get better or get worse or get an infection, or a relative dies, they'll blame you."

"Ada, I can't worry about whether they might sue me."

"The really sick are taken to the hospital," Graciela says. "Marysol is right. People need to talk about what they went through."

"Ein feierliches Pfand ist eine lebenslange Verpflichtung," Luz says.

"Translation, please, Mom."

"Un engagement solennel est une obligation permanente," Luz says.

They turn to Graciela. "I think it means a vow is a lifelong obligation."

"You're right, Mom. I made a vow," Marysol repeats, "and mean to fulfill my commitment and its duties."

"Yo cumplo," Luz says, and looks at Marysol as if seeing someone else.

"Así es, Mom." She brushes her lips across her mother's forehead, grateful she seems to be emerging into one of her daylight languages.

◦——

After afternoon coffee, Marysol helps Luz gather her sketchbooks and colored pencils. "We're off to the beach," she announces to the others.

"We'll go with you," Shirley calls.

"They want some time alone, Mommy," Graciela says.

Shirley frowns at Graciela's tone, but doesn't pursue it.

◦——

Marysol hasn't been to the beach since the afternoon María began its assault. Wind-driven sand is piled into dunes on the roads and sidewalks, against fences and walls. Volunteers have shoveled sand from the grates, drains, and gutters to keep squalls from flooding the streets. Even with daily sweeping, the floors are gritty indoors and out, as no amount of brushing cement walks and pathways disperses the sand completely.

"I never expected it to be so slippery," Marysol says as she skids off a driveway curb and nearly falls to the ground. "Watch your step, Mom."

At the end of the street, María's wind and surf have created a berm with debris, seaweed, and fine sand. They sink into it as they climb over it. Down the beach, a few houses list half-in, half-out of the water. Marysol can't tell whether high tide or erosion has reclaimed them. The long, flat, pristine beach they walked on six days earlier is narrower and littered with a shocking number of unlikely objects. An air conditioner is partly buried near a solar panel and several trees seem to have been uprooted from a forest and replanted in the sand. People of all ages pick up the detritus, mounding what can be carried into a pile that presumably will be picked up by trash collectors.

"Doña Tamarindo nunca vio la mar," Luz says.

"Who never saw the sea?"

"Doña Tamarindo."

"Who was that?"

"Who?"

"Doña Tamarindo?"

"Je ne sais pas."

Marysol can't push her. Luz might have had a fleeting memory of a character she read about, or a place, or someone called Tamarindo. Puerto Ricans are fond of nicknames and wordplay. Among her own friends, Marysol knows a Pepita as petite as a seed (an exaggeration), and Oso, big as a bear (an apt description), and Cocaína for obvious reasons (and never in front of his mother). Doña Tamarindo could have been a friend, a joke, a tall tale, a song lyric in a vortex of experience Luz is unable to grasp or hook into a narrative.

"Lassen Sie uns helfen, den Müll am Strand abholen."

"Translation, please."

"Aidez-les à récupérer les poubelles sur la plage."

"¿La playa?"

Luz nods. She digs a plastic bottle from the sand.

"Oh! Let's help clean up the beach?"

Luz grabs a half-submerged plastic bag. "Oui."

Instead of spending the afternoon with Luz sketching and Marysol reading a novel, they join the cleanup, working side by side until their shadows lengthen and their backs ache. It's dark by the time they reach home, lit from within by a single candle on the kitchen counter.

Secrets

After Luz and Marysol leave, and before talking to Ada and Shirley, Graciela needs to settle her nerves. She meditates for ten minutes, intending to ward off paranoia, to honor and respect her mothers, to avoid accusing or judging them, as Marysol so wisely counseled without even knowing why Graciela was upset.

Her phone vibrates when ten minutes are up and she resets it for another fifteen. She can't let go of her anger and can't define what she's angry about. Is it because Shirley and Ada have lied to her for forty years? They have friends with adopted children, and not once have they said she was among them. She wonders whether her grandfather Winslow knew she was not Ada's biological daughter. It pains her that if he did, he wouldn't tell her. On the other hand, it fills her heart to think he loved her as much as his other grandchildren. Actually, he loved her more. He left her his house in his will, even though he knew she wasn't biologically connected to him because Winslow's daughter was Shirley, not Ada. She wishes he were alive to help her cope. He'd know how to ease her turmoil over Minaxi's disclosures or to help her unravel Minaxi's lies.

She opens the password-protected folder of personal documents on her laptop with pdfs of her passport, bank accounts, credit cards, marriage license, divorce papers, and birth certificate. NAME: GRACIELA GIL-TEMPLETON. She's never used the hyphen. In Puerto Rico, it's assumed everyone has two last names, with no dash required to indicate the child has two parents. She now wonders why her mothers used the estadounidense convention of hyphenating children's surnames.

She reads: MOTHER: ADA GIL MÉNDEZ. FATHER:_____. Graciela has always interpreted the blank line where the father's name should be as Ada's folly. Unnamed in life, officially unnamed. The certificate indicates she was born on February 2, 1977.

The next thought forces Graciela to put the laptop away. If she's Luz's daughter, does Luz know? She walks to the back terrace, where she gulps air like a dying fish. It's inconceivable Luz would forget something like that, even with amnesia. On the other hand, she's forgotten so much! Another checkbox to add to her list.

Shirley and Ada are in the backyard, collecting the dry clothes. A plane rumbles overhead, meaning more flights have resumed, although only in daylight. Down the street, children are playing.

It's late afternoon and she's spent hours processing information and listing questions, delaying talking to her mothers but wanting nothing more than to do so. They're giggling, and Graciela's innards churn. She takes a few more breaths and whispers a mantra she depends on for stressful moments: "Be brave, be calm, be clear."

⌒

Shirley and Ada carry the sun-dried clothes into the house over their arms and shoulders. They heap the garments on the dining table and then sit side by side to fold and sort it into piles. As Graciela comes downstairs, Ada is sniffing a blouse.

"Cotton dried in the sun smells so good."

Back in Maine, their drying lines are in use even in winter.

"Did you get some rest?" Shirley asks as she folds shorts into an almost perfect rectangle.

"I had some work to do." Graciela places her computer on the table. "I need to ask you something."

"This sounds serious." Ada laughs uncomfortably.

Graciela opens the laptop, creating a barrier between las madres and la nena. She reads the first item on her list several times to herself, reconsiders whether this should be the first question she should ask, takes a breath, and, looking at Ada, begins.

"Who is El Vikingo?"

"Who?" Ada's features tighten.

"Claudio Worthy Villalobos, but his friends called him El Vikingo because he was so jincho."

"Why do you ask, if you know who he is?"

"Because someone said he's my father and Madrina is my mother."

Shirley winces. "Where did you hear such rubbish?"

"Is that all it is? ¿Chisme?" Graciela checks her list, but those questions aren't in it.

"Who have you been talking to?"

"Minaxi Otero Polanco."

"Una bochinchera." Shirley pretends to spit.

"Of all people," Ada says as if to herself. She seeks something other than Graciela or Shirley to look at and settles on one of Oliver's paintings, once all color and glare, now faded. Another plane rises into the sky, a dog barks, a car drives past. A pall of hot air drops over them. Shirley lowers her gaze. Ada closes her eyes.

Graciela reaches her hands toward her madres. "You're my mothers and that won't ever change. But yesterday I heard things I'd never imagined. I don't know why Minaxi said what she said.

With an Internet connection, I'd do some research before talking to you, but I can't do that now and I'm confused and bursting with questions." Her eyes water. She has trouble speaking. "The last thing I want to do is challenge or hurt you. I love you so much! I hope you deny her stories but if I find out later that Minaxi wasn't lying . . ." She catches her breath. "I've always trusted you, Mami, Mommy. I don't want to lose confianza in you. Please tell me the truth . . . Lies and secrets are like wedges between people who love each other. I don't want that to happen to us. Never. Jamás. Nunca."

Shirley and Ada lower their heads. They squeeze their hands inside Graciela's, release them to reach for each other's, and interlace their fingers.

"We understand," Shirley says.

Ada sends a venomous look toward the laptop. "What else is on your list in there?"

⌒

Until yesterday, it was inconceivable to Graciela that her mothers could keep a secret for hours, let alone more than forty years. Sitting in front of sun-dried clothes, they explain themselves.

"The day you started working with the genealogist," Shirley says, "we knew this day would come. The first thing Ada said was, 'Just wait. She'll be expecting us to spit into a test tube soon.'"

Ada agrees.

"We never intended to keep it from you," Shirley continues. "We just never got around to telling you."

"It didn't occur to you I'd wonder about it?"

"It did," Ada agrees. "But you never brought it up until now. Where did you see Minaxi Otero Polanco? How did this happen?"

"It doesn't matter, Mami. More crucially, why do strangers know more about me than I do? That information should have come from you, not her."

"Our friends who have adopted, talked about the kids feeling different from other members of their families," Ada says. "You never felt that way, or at least, you never expressed it. We would have told you if you'd been curious."

"I was curious! I asked! You made up a story!"

"Don't raise your voice, Graciela. We're right here."

They all take a moment.

"The reality was so complex, we wanted to wait until you were old enough to understand what happened and why," Shirley says. "The more time passed, the harder it was to bring it up out of the blue."

"Who or when or how isn't important," Ada says. "All these years, you've had three mothers who love you. You didn't know, and until now, it didn't matter. You even call us las madres."

Graciela wants to scream, but instead, grabs a bottled water from the kitchen. She drinks as if she's been trekking across a desert. She brings water for Ada and Shirley. She faces her laptop again. "I do have a list of questions, Mami. Can we get back to that?"

"Of course."

"Just to confirm . . ." Graciela studies her checklist. "Claudio, El Vikingo, is my father?"

"Yes," Shirley and Ada say.

Graciela adds a checkmark. "And Luz is my birth mother?"

"Yes."

"Sí."

Another check on the list. "So, even though I look like this"—Graciela presses her index finger on her arm—"I'm actually a Black woman."

"Or biracial, if you want to label yourself," Ada says.

Graciela scratches her scalp.

"Let us help you, hija." Shirley says. "We made a mess, but our decisions were made with good intentions."

None could speak, each woman lost in her own thoughts,

revisiting, redrawing, revising the past. Graciela is speechless, not because she doesn't have more to say, but because it's hard to articulate the most difficult question on her list. She takes another swig from the water bottle, sets it down like a cowboy who's just drained a bottle of whiskey, swipes the back of her hand across her lips, scratches the back of her neck, takes a breath. "Does Madrina know she's my mother?"

Ada and Shirley silently consult. Graciela has seen that exchange between her mothers, as if they have an extrasensory connection triggered by a gaze.

Graciela's hands go to her belly, protecting herself from the punch she expects her mothers are about to deliver.

"We don't know," Ada says.

"How's that even possible?" Graciela wails.

Las madres come around the table to sit on either side of her so they can touch her, lean into her, wrap their arms around her, hold her hand, and console her as they tear her apart.

"She was recovering from serious injuries and a coma," Ada says, once Graciela is able to control herself.

Shirley hands Graciela a clean T-shirt from the pile.

"She was on drugs that might have been helping her brain function but were probably making her memory issues worse," Ada continues. "We'll never know."

"Forty years ago doctors tried their best but medicine we take for granted today was still in the distant future," Shirley adds.

"Also, think . . . Luz looked like a young woman but, emotionally, she was a child grieving her dead parents. In seconds, everything in her life went upside down and sideways."

"A few months before the accident"—Shirley picks up from Ada—"her grandfather Alonso learned he had cancer. Maybe her parents, Federico and Salvadora, knew, maybe not. We have no idea. We never met them, or the grandmother she lived with for a few months, who might have known, but again . . ."

"Alonso asked us not to tell Luz as he sought treatment. When he had procedures or hospitalizations in Puerto Rico, we told her a client needed him in one of the towns for a few days. Oliver took him there and back," Ada says. "It was harder to keep it from her in the Bronx. The treatments made him sick. We don't know how much she took in, but obviously, it crushed her when he died. She went into labor a week earlier than expected."

"Luz . . . she couldn't deal, hija," Shirley says. "A pregnancy on top of everything else going on was too much for her. At least, that's what we think. No one knows. But she loves you, Graciela. You know she does, as much as Ada and I do."

"And I love her. It breaks my heart how much she's endured."

"In many ways, her memory issues have saved her. She's still the innocent she was before the car wreck. Innocent by 1975 standards, anyway."

"Minaxi and El Vikingo weren't innocent back then."

"They were entitled kids who could do no wrong in their parents' eyes. And all of us, including Alonso, wanted to avoid a scandal that might cause Luz to relapse. She'd made so much progress."

They're silent. Graciela sniffles.

"Did anyone consider an abortion?"

"No," las madres say at the same time.

"Why not?"

"Alonso wouldn't. The idea was that the baby, er, you, would be put up for adoption."

"To you."

Again, las madres confer with a gaze.

"Well, not at first," Ada says. "We wanted to, but we weren't sure we'd be able to, as a—"

"Nontraditional couple," Shirley finishes the sentence. "That's when we came up with the idea that if you had the same last name as Ada . . ."

"Gil," Graciela says, "instead of Peña, and you added Templeton."

"Exactly. One of Josué's disciples worked for the agency that issues birth certificates and she arranged it. We didn't want the details. There was no adoption process. Officially, I delivered you in the Bronx. No one questioned it. Thousands of single women have babies every day. At the time, those sorts of documents were easier to fix if you knew the right people."

Graciela drops her head on her forearms on the dining table. Her mothers knead her back as if to release forty years of history from her shoulders. "Esto está brutal," she says.

"Which part?"

"All of it, Mami!"

"It's a lot to take in."

"It's intense. I'm sure of only one thing—I'm mad as hell at you both."

"We get that," Ada says.

"But can you forgive us?" Shirley pleads.

Graciela wipes her face. "Let's leave that until I figure out what I'm forgiving you for."

Ada starts to talk, but Shirley shakes her head to shush her.

"What those kids did to Madrina was sadistic," Graciela continues. "I'm afraid when I tell Marysol she'll track down El Vikingo and beat the shit out of him. She was this close to doing that to that awful Minaxi, and Marysol doesn't know half of it."

"Marysol is a pacifist—you know that," Ada says. "Don't buy into the stereotype of people from the Bronx."

"Always the teacher." Graciela is unable to keep sarcasm from her tone.

"Why does Marysol need to know?"

Ada and Graciela turn to Shirley.

"There's nothing to gain by it," she says calmly. "Your first thought was that it would upset and enrage her."

"But . . ."

"At least, don't tell her now. Do it once you've processed it yourself." Ada firmly closes Graciela's laptop. "You didn't even get to number four on your checklist."

"It's not right to keep it from her. It's part of her history, too."

"We can't change the past, Graciela, we can only try to get over it. She doesn't need to know any of this now. She doesn't talk about it, but Luz is not doing well. Marysol has enough to deal with."

"She's my sister. I can't lie to her."

Again, Shirley and Ada speak with their gazes.

"Hija mía," Shirley says. "You don't have to lie, but you can dance around it."

"Oh, like you two have been doing for decades?"

Ada sighs. "We deserve your scorn and sarcasm," she says. "We'll continue to apologize until you forgive us. But putting Marysol in the middle of this now is too much. Let's tell her everything once we're home. We've had enough drama."

~

Marysol and Luz follow the light toward the rear of the house, where Shirley, Ada, and Graciela are preparing dinner. Marysol feels the tension when she comes in, greets them, but continues toward the yard, leading Luz to a covered bucket for washing up.

"Brr!" Luz rubs her arms as Marysol pours rainwater over them.

"I know it's cold, but we're covered in sand," Marysol says. "Might as well take off your dress."

Luz stands naked on the patio as Marysol bathes her. Graciela appears with a towel and fresh clothes for them.

"I'll help her, you bathe." Graciela takes over, slowly dribbling water over Luz's long limbs and back, offering her handfuls for Luz to splash on her face, behind her ears.

"Food is ready," Ada calls out.

Their meals are getting increasingly creative, bits of this and scraps of that, salted, peppered, seasoned. None of them like canned corned beef or Spam, the only tins they haven't opened until today.

"We've reached the darkest corners of the pantry," Shirley sighs as she serves corned beef over the last of the rice.

Ada and Shirley are uncharacteristically silent throughout the meal. Graciela keeps the conversation moving by asking questions about Luz and Marysol's adventures on the beach.

"We collected trash," Marysol says. "We dumped it and scavenged for more."

"Un homme a utilisé un seau pour jouer de la musique."

"At the end of the day, a man started banging on a bucket," Marysol says, "and a woman got two stones to hit together, and other people found cans or bottles to strike and rattle. It was an impromptu party. They played plenas and we sang and danced."

"You did?" Ada asks, but her mind is elsewhere.

"On a chanté! J'ai dansé." Luz is proud of herself. "Oui, j'ai chanté, j'ai dansé."

Neither Graciela nor Marysol translates. Shirley and Ada stare into space.

Dry lightning flashes over the sea.

"Mom, you're nodding off," Marysol says. "Time for bed."

It's earlier than her usual bedtime, but Marysol knows the conversation she expects won't happen with Luz around them. It's been a physically active day and Luz doesn't protest. Marysol brings her upstairs, makes sure she takes her medications, and puts her to bed.

"Sie sind alle traurig."

"What does that mean, Mom?"

"Ils sont tous tristes."

"Triste? Sad? They're sad?"

"Ja, das sind Sie."

"We're all sad. Maybe tomorrow you can draw something cheerful for us to look at."

"Gute Idee."

"Sweet dreams, Mom."

"Toi aussi. Je t'aime, ma chère."

Marysol's breath catches. She kisses her mother's cheek, turns off her phone/flashlight, goes into the bathroom, and leans over the counter. She can't remember the last time her mother has said, "I love you," to her. It's rarely spoken in any of the languages Luz knows. She behaves as if she loves Marysol, but it has just struck Marysol how rare it is for Luz to say those simple words.

She stays in the dark bathroom until she hears her mother's breath sounds, deep and even. She steps into her bedroom, but again, stops for a moment, her eyes closed, listening to the metallic sounds of pots, the tinkling of glass, the muted conversation downstairs, passing rain showers, and the first trilling of the coquí she's heard since María.

⌒

"Did you hear the coquí?" Marysol joins Shirley, Ada, and Graciela on the back porch.

"Luz will be happy to know they survived," Shirley says. "She was worried about them."

Ada hands Marysol the insect repellent. "There are coquís in other places, but ours are the only ones that sing."

"I didn't know that," Marysol says.

The candle flame dies. Graciela turns on her phone.

"No," Shirley says. "It's nice in the dark."

No one speaks. Once in a while, a breeze stirs the air without cooling it. Their silence enhances nearby voices, motors, and the distant surf hitting the shore. Marysol is aware how hard it is for them not to speak. When together, they chatter, cackle, and tease one another in an endless conversation.

"I feel your anxiety," she says. "¿Qué pasó?"

More silence.

"Who wants to start?" Graciela finally says. Ada and Shirley scrape their chairs on the tiles. "You want me to tell her?"

The coquí sings, a generator is switched on.

"Tell me what?" In the dark, it's impossible to see their features and read their body language.

Deep exhales from las madres.

Graciela clears her throat. "You wondered what Minaxi said yesterday that upset me so much, I had to talk to Mami and Mommy."

"Yes?"

Graciela resettles herself on her chair. "She knew my father."

"Aw, come on, you believe her?"

Shirley or Ada harrumph.

Graciela coughs delicately. "Mis madres have known who he is but never told me."

"Really?" Marysol addresses the silhouettes of las madres. "Why not?"

"I was ashamed," Ada says in a near-whisper.

"Hmm." Marysol has never thought Ada could be so conventional. It seems out of character. On the other hand, a culture's conscience can stifle even its freest spirit. "Ada, you had a one-night stand. Haven't we all done that at some point?" Marysol feels the mood shift. Her ears ring, meaning her blood pressure is rising. Theirs, too. The air smells of collusion. "There's more you're not telling me."

Three sets of lungs inhale discordant rhythms.

"Well," Graciela starts. "The thing is . . ." Her voice is reedy. "You see . . ." Again, she coughs to relax her larynx. "Uhm . . . he was Mami's cousin."

"Distant," Ada says. "Distant cousin."

A short silence, then Marysol guffaws. "Are you kidding me?"

Shirley, Ada, and Graciela try to figure out what that reaction from Marysol means.

"I'm sorry . . . I'm so sorry." Marysol is laugh-crying.

"What's so funny?" Graciela is offended.

"It's just . . . I'm sorry . . . It's not funny . . . but it is . . ." Marysol catches her breath. "Every time something happens to us in Puerto Rico, another cousin crawls out of the woodwork."

One by one, as they reprise the events of the past couple of weeks, Shirley, Ada, and Graciela review their vacation through Marysol's perspective. It's true—in the time they've been here, almost every man and woman they've met has seemed tenuously connected to their family. They giggle, they belly-laugh.

Clouds clear the sky and they can make out one another's figures on white plastic chairs. A plane lifts into the sky.

"Night flights!" Ada and Shirley clap.

"Maybe we'll be able to get on ours day after tomorrow," Graciela says.

They watch the airplane disappear into the sparkling sky. The waxing crescent moon hangs in the purple void like a lustrous closed parenthesis.

El lamento de los ausentes

SEPTEMBER 26–27, 2017

Three patients are waiting in the driveway the next morning, their injuries caused by flaming candles, oil lamps, and open-fire cooking. Marysol treats them with the last of her supplies.

"We'll have to close this impromptu clinic," she says to Graciela.

"Let's deal with it later. We haven't had breakfast."

"Coffee—that's all I want right now."

Graciela grunts. Marysol stops. "Don't tell me we've run out . . ."

A vehicle turns into their driveway. Graciela gasps and then screeches at the sight of what was once Oliver's pristine van, now mud-encrusted, scratched, dented, and storm-battered.

⌒

"We've lost everything," Miriam cries. "We barely got out with our lives."

"That's all that matters," Ada says. "You can replace things."

"We keep saying that," Oliver says, "but it's hard to believe it or accept it."

They slump around the glass table on the porch, drinking strong tea and wishing it were coffee.

"The river flooded," an overwrought Miriam continues. "Water, mud, leaves, branches, and rocks tumbled through our doors and windows. We almost drowned."

"Our neighbors rescued us—"

"But my sister and her baby grandson were taken by the currents." Miriam collapses into sobs.

"We've been searching for them every day."

"We went to the morgue," Miriam whimpers. "I never want to smell anything like that again."

"They had too many bodies and no air-conditioning."

"Men, women, children . . . just rotting."

"Yesterday they brought a refrigerated truck."

Neither las madres nor las nenas can break through Miriam and Oliver's anguish. She heaves and trembles, wails, groans, and whimpers. He frowns, twitches, and fidgets. Every effort to distract them is insufficient, but Shirley, Ada, Graciela, Luz, and Marysol do their best to console them. They pat their backs and shoulders, embrace them, let them cry uncontrollably, then wipe their faces with their own tear-stained fingers. Oliver and Miriam relive the ordeal even as they moan that they don't want to think about it anymore.

"Our house caved in around us. It's still underwater," Miriam says. "The whole neighborhood is under filthy, slippery mud contaminated by sewage and dead animals. Helicopters flew over the area a few times every day, but no one came to help us."

"Lucho came to check on us yesterday," Oliver says, "and at first, he thought we were dead under the rubble. He'd borrowed my van the day before the storm, and left me his car. It ended up on top of the limousine."

"After we were rescued in the middle of the storm, we made our way to a school shelter."

"Someone told Lucho where to find us," Oliver says. "We spent last night in his house."

"On the way there, we saw mile-long lines for gas and water." Miriam rubs her eyes as if erasing the image. "People had run out of food."

"The Red Cross was handing out supplies, but there wasn't enough for everyone. People pushed and shoved each other to get to a gallon of water and a box of crackers," Oliver adds.

"I never expected to see so many desperate Puerto Ricans," Miriam jumps in. "This isn't a Third World country, but that's what it looks like now. In el campo, the hurricane might have come yesterday, not a week ago." She grits her teeth. "We're a proud people. We take pride in bouncing back from every challenge, but María stripped us of all dignity."

"Cálmate, mujer," Oliver says quietly.

"Don't tell me what to do!"

Neither las madres nor las nenas wants to get in the middle of a spousal spat.

"Have some more tea," Shirley offers. No one takes her up on it.

Oliver resumes. "On the way here we saw people walking around like the Statue of Liberty, with their phones in the air, like this. It was on a hill near a broken cell tower but people could connect for short periods. I called Warren to let him know we were on our way to see you."

"Oh, thank you, thank you," Marysol cries.

"Danke. Merci beaucoup."

"He saw you on TV," Miriam says.

"He'll be waiting for you at JFK tomorrow."

"Do you really think we'll get on our flight?" Graciela asks. "We've heard it's pandemonium at the airport."

"It is, but . . ." Miriam looks at Oliver, checking to see who will say more.

"Lucho's mother-in-law is a supervisor at the airport," he says. "She'll make sure we all get on the same flight."

"Mother-in-law?" Graciela's chest turns pink.

"All of us?" Ada and Shirley ask.

"*All* of us," Miriam says.

Shirley points to Oliver and Miriam. "You're leaving, too?"

"We don't want to." Oliver drops his chin to his chest. "It feels like a defeat. Puerto Rico will recover, eventually, but we've lost our home, our business, everything we owned. We have to file documents we can't get to because our computer is in the mud, and anyway, there's no power or Internet."

"You stay with us as long as you need to," Ada says, and Shirley agrees.

"I told you they'd say yes," Oliver says to Miriam.

"It's a lot to ask," she says.

"We're family," Shirley says. "We take care of each other."

"But it's not just us," Miriam says. "It's us, and Violeta, Lucho's wife, and their baby."

"Their baby?" Graciela's skin has turned crimson.

Marysol covers her face. Graciela is still disgruntled over Marysol's expression when Graciela walked down the aisle preceded by six bridesmaids dressed in what looked like seaweed and her own bridal gown like a *Project Runway* reject. *This isn't funny,* Marysol tells herself, *not by a mile,* but like on that long-ago day, she is on the verge of the giggles. She can imagine Warren saying, "Hashtag Uh-oh."

"You have no idea how much this means to us." Miriam is overcome again.

Oliver, also, wants to make sure Shirley and Ada understand what they're committing themselves to. "Do you mean you can take us all? Me, Miriam, Lucho, Violeta, and Junior?"

"We have plenty of room, Oliver," Ada assures him.

Graciela is horrified. "In Maine?"

"Ou vous pouvez rester avec nous dans le Bronx."

"You can stay with us in the Bronx," Marysol translates.

"You don't have to decide now," Ada says. "You're all welcome for as long as you wish in whatever configuration works best. Nuestras casas son tus casas."

"Thank you, cousin. Thank you, Shirley, thank you, Graciela, Luz, Marysol." Oliver stands and looks into each one's eyes so they can see he's moved and sincerely grateful, offering his hand for a shake, as if concluding a business deal. "We can't thank you enough."

"Come on, Oliver," Ada says. "No es pa' tanto. We've all been through a lot together. This is the least we can do."

A helicopter disrupts the afternoon.

"They're still assessing the damage," Oliver says. "So they can report to Washington. Nothing will happen here until they decide up there."

"And people still deny we're a colony," Ada says.

"Let's not talk politics now," Shirley says.

"We should go," Miriam says, "before the curfew."

"You can spend the night," Shirley says.

"I'll double up with Mom," Marysol says, "and you can take my room."

"We'll stay tomorrow night," Oliver says. "We have to let Lucho and Violeta know that we all have a place." As they head for their van, he hears the generator running next door and gets an idea.

"Wait here," he says, and knocks on Kelvin's door. Someone

invites him in, and a few minutes later, Oliver comes back with Felipe. "If you saved your travel reservations on a computer, he can print them. It will make things easier at the airport tomorrow."

Graciela sprints inside, returns with her laptop. "I have them all," she says, and follows Felipe to his house.

Oliver turns to the others. "Kelvin and his younger son went to check on his in-laws in Utuado." He's gloomy again. "Those towns in the Cordillera Central were hard-hit. Bridges disappeared and neighborhoods are cut off. He might not even make it to their barrio."

"I hope he finds them," Miriam says.

Oliver sighs, opens the van's door for his wife. "Bueno, vieja. Vámonos."

Las madres and Marysol wait in the driveway until long after Oliver and Miriam have gone. A few minutes later, Graciela emerges from Kelvin's house, waving paper copies of their flight reservations as if she's won the first prize in a contest.

◠

Violeta's mother meets them in the parking lot at five in the morning. She leads them past throngs of weary people sleeping on the damp tile floors, in the dark, their heads on their suitcases or bundles. Most of the airport workers have been on the job for days, taking short naps between shifts in the employee lounges. The Department of Agriculture and TSA staffers inspect every suitcase and package by hand, using flashlights when the generators that power the X-ray machines aren't working. They're skeptical about the rocks in Luz's suitcase but Marysol explains they're for her artwork and they allow her to take them.

Marysol gets the window seat, Luz the middle, Graciela the aisle. Luz has been in and out of achaques since they arrived at the terminal. She jabbers incomprehensibly, as if her four languages have coalesced and she's unable to distinguish one from the other. The plane is full and the flight attendants are frazzled but tender with the anxious passengers. Most are elderly, sick, or both. Children cling to their parents and other adults, who do their best to soothe the little ones' agitation. The grown-ups' fears are etched in wrinkled brows, puffy eyes, set jaws, and tight lips. No one believes the plane will actually take off until it's in the air.

As it rises, everyone seeks a view through the closest window. Below them, a once fecund land seems to have been swept by a giant rake. The emerald forests are now brown pincushions studded with gray, spindly skewers. Seeing the island from above, the horror of what they've experienced seems to hit, all at once. Even the most stoic are weeping, including Marysol.

"Adiós, adiós, adiós, Borinquen querida," Luz sings quietly, still in an achaque but somehow aware they're saying goodbye.

From the seat behind them, Oliver sings the next phrase. Miriam raises her voice, followed by Ada's, Shirley's, Graciela's, Marysol's, Lucho's, and Violeta's. Others add theirs, reaching their hands across the aisle to grasp those of friends, loved ones, and strangers. Before long, a plane full of bereft Puerto Ricans are singing and crying for the island they love, goddess of the sea, queen of the palm groves. The uncertainty of what lies ahead is tempered by the song's promise that someday they will return. To love again. To dream again.

Too soon, Puerto Rico is behind them. Clouds envelop the plane as it rises until there's nothing to see for a brokenhearted people now suspended in an opaque, cottony sky between here and there.

Coda and Acknowledgments

OCTOBER 2022

As I write these words, Puerto Ricans are reeling from another hurricane. Like Irma, Fiona was expected to veer off course. The electrical blackouts, wind, and rain would be less powerful than those produced by Hurricane María five years ago.

In *Las Madres,* the protagonists—Shirley, Ada, Luz, Graciela, and Marysol—were disconnected from anyone other than their neighbors once the hurricane went out to sea. They had no idea that the United States president refused to believe María had been the disaster people said it was. He scoffed at reports that thousands had died and dismissed its effects as minor compared to other storms that had affected the U.S. continent. He was surprised to learn that Puerto Rico is an island and made sure estadounidenses knew that meant it was surrounded by water. His advisors highly recommended he travel there to assess the damage. Ten days after María, he spent a few hours in San Juan, where he dismissed the bad news cycling through media outlets back in the States, where there was electric power and functioning cell towers. He glad-handed his way through a neighborhood that had been cleaned up and made visually appealing. At a reception after his walk-through, he lobbed paper towels at a politically connected roomful of people, gente con pala eager to make him look good so they would look good. It was a farce that wasn't funny.

The Puerto Rican governor following POTUS around was ousted by el pueblo twenty-two months after the hurricane. Following jockeying among top functionaries in his pro-U.S. party, he was replaced by a woman who had initially publicly stated she did not want to become the next governor but was constitutionally next in the line of succession. Accepting her destiny, she promised transparency, political stability, and a close look into the expenditures of millions of dollars meant for recovery efforts following María that had not made it to those who most needed essential services and goods.

Four and a half months after she took office, Puerto Rico was rocked by a series of earthquakes that flattened homes, businesses, and schools, created sinkholes, broke water and sewer pipes, and cracked paved roads, making them impassable. Tens of thousands of residents were displaced, forced to sleep outdoors for weeks as the earth shook and buildings around them collapsed. The governor declared a state of emergency and designated millions of dollars for recovery. The White House also approved money to help those left unsheltered and reluctantly but temporarily loosened the stranglehold of the Jones Act that makes it difficult for Puerto Ricans to receive necessary goods unless they arrive on U.S.-owned and -staffed merchant ships.

In that summer's primary election, the governor lost to the then resident commissioner to the U.S. Congress, a position that carries no power and no vote but is a stepping-stone toward the top office on the island. It turns out the majority of Puerto Ricans had little confidence in him. He won the gubernatorial race with less than one-third of the votes cast in the general election. In August 2022, his predecessor was arrested by the FBI, then indicted by a grand jury investigating corruption during her tenure. As of this writing, she insists she did nothing wrong.

A few weeks later, on September 18, 2022, Fiona blew through Puerto Rico's southern shore as a Category 1 hurricane, causing an island-wide electrical blackout, floods, extensive structural damage to already unstable buildings, and the deaths of at least twenty-five people.

Like my other fictional characters—Oliver, Miriam, Lucho, Violeta, and their baby—more than two hundred thousand real Puerto Ricans left soon after Hurricane María dissipated. Many have settled permanently in the United States and other countries. As the exodus continues, an uncounted number of estadounidenses have moved in, taking advantage of tax breaks unavailable to its residents or local businesses. The newcomers are buying houses and land from desperate homeowners unable to fix and/or maintain their properties following the disasters. The beaches are being privatized as deep-pocketed corporations and individuals from afuera create gated compounds where Puerto Ricans are unwelcome and are violently ejected if they manage to reach their island's shores.

As a Puerto Rican who lives in the United States, I ache for the place where I was born and its people, here and there. I rage at the laws that force us to live as subjects of a government that refuses to acknowledge Puerto Rico is a colony and treats its people with disdain as second-class citizens even though it was their idea, not ours, that we be born, live, fight for, and die with the U.S. flag over our heads.

It's difficult for me to write about Puerto Rico and its people without sentimientos even as I resist sentimentality. Controlling my emotions is a survival mechanism built over decades of wrestling with being a Puerto Rican, fulfilling my responsibilities and obligations as a citizen while simultaneously chafing at the yoke forced upon me by a history made by men across an ocean.

There are times when I dread the news from the Puerto Rican archipelago, overwhelmed by the challenges my people must endure just to live in the place we call home. Even if we've never visited our islands, it is nuestra patria we love and long for.

To be a Puerto Rican wherever we are is to fret over the uncertainty of often violent weather, natural forces, and repressive political directives that have shaped us for more than five hundred years of colonization by Spain and the United States. Resistance has been constant and consistent, but unlike the other islands in the Greater Antilles, we've been unsuccessful in our revolutionary efforts. But one thing that's true about Puerto Ricans, we do not give up. Nosotros no nos rendimos.

For that, I am grateful. It is the struggle for self-determination that has shaped me as a woman, and as a writer.

I bow to those who have survived their history to give testimony to what they have witnessed. They inspire all my work. In preparation for *Las Madres,* I watched and heard countless accounts, scrolled for hours through social media posts, read books, newspaper reports, and blogs, and listened to anyone willing to share their experiences with me as I built this story.

But a storyteller without an audience is an unheard song. I thank every man, woman, and child who's read my work and reached out to let me know they've found a connection between our experiences, preoccupations, aspirations, and ambitions even when they're not Puerto Rican themselves.

I'm grateful for my friends and loved ones who make my work possible.

My beloved husband, Frank Cantor, has designed and built tranquil and beautiful spaces where I can be free to listen to the voices whispering each word I transcribe on their behalf. As an artist himself, he respects my need for focus, silence, and long stretches of solitude.

My children, Lucas Cantor Santiago, Ila Cantor Santiago, their spouses, Allison Cantor and River Rudl, have created their own lives surrounded by music and art. Their love and support have lifted me when I'm low and made me a grandmother who can now pass on stories to another generation, just as my abuelas did for me.

My agent, Molly Friedrich, has encouraged and supported my efforts, read endless rough drafts, and always asked the right questions to keep me going even when she was initially skeptical. She's my comadre and my comrade, whose advice, friendship, and shared history I treasure.

The team at the Friedrich Agency: the fearless Lucy Carson, and Heather Carr, Hannah Brattesani, and Marin Takikawa keep me and all their authors inspired and motivated. Special thanks to Mercedes Navarro, who as an intern at the Friedrich Agency read an early draft and provided queries and insights that enriched the narrative.

My writers group read drafts and/or listened to portions of *Las Madres* in several iterations under different titles: Joie Davidow, Judith Dupree, Marilyn Johnson, and Cathleen Medwick. Their comments and suggestions gave me courage to say what I meant without frills or apology.

Several trusted readers gave me notes at different stages of the writing. Sandra Guzmán reminded me that how we speak should be reflected in what we write. Rossana Rosado read a draft while traveling all over New York State in the middle of a fraught political brouhaha and still managed to give me notes and one of the best compliments I've ever received about my books. Anjanette Delgado set aside precious hours while she was on a writing retreat to read and comment on this novel.

Pamela Putney and Louise Katzin, both medical professionals, paid attention to Luz's issues and Marysol's actions as a nurse. Luz's mysterious condition is based on research but owes most of its expression to my imagination.

Friends have provided home, nourishment, advice, entertainment, and laughter when I've most needed them. I've written entire chapters in Peter Jason's lush garden, later to enjoy his home-cooked dinners featuring the harvest steps from the casita. Eileen Rosaly has patiently listened to my doubts and worries without judgment or flattery. Virginia Mileva opened her home, fed me exquisite meals, and allowed me to ask endless questions about the daily obligations, responsibilities, joys, and sorrows of nursing.

Nina Torres Vidal arranged for me to stay on the campus of Universidad del Sagrado Corazón, down the street from the house where I lived as a child. The university president and his staff made me feel welcome and valued. The students and faculty asked fantastic questions during my visits to their classrooms that still resonate. Mercedes Rodríguez López's commitment to human rights continues to inspire and move me. Her brother Miguel Rodríguez López is a consummate teacher and scholar of Puerto Rican history. The three make my visits to the island educational and fun.

I'm blessed with a large family who knows how to celebrate and who know the importance of staying positive: Delsa Santiago, Héctor Santiago, Alicia Santiago Funes, Edna Luz Santiago, Raymond Santiago, Francisco Cortéz, Carlos Manuel Martínez, Carmen Beatriz Martínez, Rafael Alejandro Martínez, their spouses, children, and grandchildren.

I'm lucky to have a fantastic team at Knopf. Thank you, Reagan Arthur, for championing my work. It's been a pleasure to work with my thoughtful editor, Jennifer Jackson, who has guided me through several drafts, querying intentions, motives, and entire scenes, suggesting alternatives but respecting my choices, especially when we disagree. Maris Dyer, Tiara Sharma, Amy Edelman, Kathleen Cook, and Jenny Carrow have helped me navigate the production process with little friction and great care.

And finally, thank you, reader, for having come this far with me. You're the reason I do this work.

A NOTE ABOUT THE AUTHOR

Esmeralda Santiago is the author of the novel *Conquistadora* and the memoirs *When I Was Puerto Rican* and *Almost a Woman,* which was adapted into a Peabody Award–winning movie for PBS's Masterpiece Theatre. Born in Santurce, Puerto Rico, she lives with her husband, documentary filmmaker Frank Cantor, in Westchester County, New York.

A NOTE ON THE TYPE

This book was set in a version of the well-known Monotype
face Bembo. This letter was cut for the celebrated Venetian
printer Aldus Manutius by Francesco Griffo, and first used in
Pietro Cardinal Bembo's *De Aetna* of 1495. The companion
italic is an adaptation of the chancery script type designed by
the calligrapher and printer Ludovico degli Arrighi.

Composed by North Market Street Graphics
Lancaster, Pennsylvania

Printed and bound by Lakeside Book Company
Harrisonburg, Virginia

Book design by Pei Loi Koay